i

YESTERMORROW

2055 – 2099

A FAMILY ECO SAGA

NOEL HARROWER

The Orcombe Press - Edition 3
August 2018

Some assistance from author's royalties goes to the Tse Ataa Mensah Foundation, which helps fund education for poor children in Ghana.

Retail price £12.99

Dedication

This book is dedicated to
my great-niece, Beatrice Dees,
with her steadfast vegan principles.
Also to the Ghanaian artist,
Naa Ahinee Mensah,
whose personality and outstanding
mural paintings
provided inspiration for the characters
of Amina and Isabella.
The book is also dedicated to the ongoing
Transition Town Movement.

Contents

PART THREE - Voices from Yesterday

PART FOUR - Moments in Time

Introduction

Welcome - the story you are about to read is not a prophecy of things to come. It is a fictional tale set forty years ahead, in Parts One and Two, and spanning the rest of this century later. I dare go no further. In order to help you find your way to the start, I am suggesting that the interval between now and 2055 goes something like this:

2020 The past few years have continued to be chaotic both at home and internationally. The planet is still deeply troubled by an excess of CO_2 emissions, which are increasing global warming, despite the promises made by states as long ago as the Paris Conference in December 2015. The world experiences hurricanes and continual melting of icecaps. Meanwhile, fighting continues in the Middle East, northern Africa and many parts of Asia and Africa, often around areas that are rich in natural resources that other countries envy. The world economy is suffering badly, and there is a loss of faith in political parties, experts, and even in the whole concept of democracy, because promises have not been kept, and there is growing evidence of rival state sponsored interference in national elections. These mounting troubles force the United Nations to recognise that a third world war is being fought despite the fact that there has never been any official declaration. So many countries are now secretly engaged in each other's affairs, with soldiers, spies and political reporters embedded in international war zones and hundreds of drones being despatched, that it is difficult to keep track of who is fighting whom. What originally started as a battle against disparate militant extremists has led to total mayhem. The UN is unable to act because it is crippled by competing vetoes in the Security Council. In the light of the fact that nuclear weapons might be used, the Secretary-General calls for a new form of global authority with far greater powers, but recommends that the General Assembly and the UN Specialised Agencies stay intact.

2021-2024 Now that a new American President is in power there is more hope. He restores the USA commitment to reduce carbon emissions, but despite the Secretary-General's call, many wars continue. Vast areas are devastated, and refugees are desperately trying to escape to safer places, with little hope of being accepted anywhere. Worn down by the conflicts, and alarmed at the consequential damage to the world climate, global leaders finally agree on a new world authority. The five former permanent members of the Security Council reluctantly agree to this surrender of their powers in the face of the ultimate dangers facing life on Earth.

The new authority is established and sworn in under the name of the Global Organisation for Sustainability (GOS). All international wars are declared illegal and all fighting is ordered to cease. A GOS Peacekeeping Force, with regiments drawn from member countries, is sent into all war-torn areas with the responsibility to keep the peace and help establish law and order, in collaboration with local police forces, where they exist.

Instead of the Security Council, a new GOS Elders Council is elected by the General Assembly from a list of distinguished diplomats, retired statesmen, scientists, academics, lawyers and others who have been nominated as candidates by their governments. The General Assembly elects four Elders for each of the nine regions of the world. These Elders have to work towards achieving five-year targets in the quality of the Environment, Social Development and Economy of their region.

The regions are:-

1. China, Japan, S. E. Asia, and North West Pacific. (CAP)
2. Australia, New Zealand, Indonesia, Philippines and South Pacific islands (SAP)
3. North America and Caribbean (NAC)
4. South America, Antarctic (SAA)
5. Europe and neighbouring states (EUK)
6. Greater Russia incorporating the Independent Central Asian Republics (GR)
7. The Indian sub-continent (INPAK)
8. Iran, Afghanistan and Middle East. (IMEA)
9. Africa and surrounding islands (AFI)

The main responsibility held by GOS is to care for Planet Earth and its living creatures, especially the care of humankind across the globe. There are to be no prosecutions for those involved in WW3. Instead, a Court of Truth and Reconciliation is established in each region, where cases are heard and guilty parties are required to meet some of their victims. Officers of The Nuclear Weapons Control Agency collect all known stocks of nuclear and chemical weapons for mass destruction or de-commissioning. A new GOS army, with regiments drawn from many countries, is established, under the command of the Secretary General. State armies are discouraged, but some countries insist on retaining them on a smaller scale than before, but they are forced to be subsidiary to the UN forces. No wars are allowed between recognised nations. All these disputes have to be settled by arbitration, but unfortunately this action does not stop all terrorist acts or fighting between illegal forces, although every attempt is made to scale these down.

2025 Scotland becomes an independent country within the European Union, and a new state of United Ireland is also established. Disruption in U.K. makes the government decide on a new form of devolution. England is divided into five provinces: **Northumbria**(North of England), **Mercia**(The West Midlands), **Anglia** (Norfolk, Suffolk, Cambridge, and Essex), **Sussex**(Kent, East and West Sussex and Hampshire) and **Wessex** (West Country including Wiltshire and Dorset).

The English provinces and London are all given their own assemblies, and **Wales** retains its parliament. The assemblies have full powers in all areas, except for the exchequer, international affairs and defence. These remain with the central parliament in London, although there is discussion about a more central location. Votes are invited from the people of England and Wales about their new designation, and the name **Britannia** is adopted.

2026 Devolution in Britannia is finally agreed. This has been the subject of much debate over the last three years. Each Province receives an annual payment from the exchequer, reflecting the size of the population.

2028 The general election in Britannia is very confusing. There is no overall winner. There are now many different political parties, following the splits between the right and left wings of both the Conservative and Labour Parties, the establishment of the new Responsible Party, and the surge in support of the Green Party. A Unity Government is formed, which includes members drawn from the six major parties. This has become a real possibility following substantial devolution to the provinces. The Prime Minister is not a party leader, but an elder stateswoman who commands universal respect and holds moderate views. She is an enthusiastic supporter of the new devolution.

2029 – 2032 During the last ten years, great changes occur in the human psyche. The old concept of globalisation is replaced by one of regional awareness. A new sense of belonging is inculcated, not so much to a state as to a local community within an international region. There is less concern about individual identity. Instead, interest in discovering the contribution each person can make to the local community is engendered. Many multi-national companies break up. Worldwide media advertising and the cult of celebrity become things of the past. In Britannia people find that loyalty to their province means more to them than loyalty to their country.

An international outburst of radioactive diseases is traced to the over use of computers, mobile phones and long periods of cyber viewing. This results in new health legislation, reducing the amount of broadcasting, and setting limits to the hours that can be spent using computers in schools. Internet expansion had led to the closure of many newspapers, but the international shifts towards regionalism and localism have encouraged newspaper revivals, in a rather different form. The Wessex Sphere and the Wessex Times compete with each other for political and social news, while the Woodleigh Journal has its own niche, casting a chatty glance at happenings in the coastal communities.

An international plague of radiation sickness is also traced to overuse of mobile phones. Usage of them becomes much more restricted.

Football and cricket become games played for fun rather than watched on TV. The idea of hosting international professional players and rewarding them with huge wages is thought of as stupid. Instead local amateur teams compete with each other, and the most popular sporting competitions are at provincial level, sometimes finishing up with a national winner who can play at international regional level.

Although multinational corporations are now discouraged, because they lead to extremes in poverty and wealth, some rebels still continue to crave the old idea of global dominance. Some of these people secretly band together in underground groups. GOS prefers to let the regional economies find their own humane levels, improve the quality of life for the vast majority and maintain international peace. A new awareness of the planet as a living body evolves in the GOS Elders Council, recognising that every creature has a contribution to make to the whole. There is much debate about what the human task should be and public discussions are held between people of religious persuasion and humanists. These become popular at all levels -i.e. in schools, universities, on TV, in community halls and pubs.

Robotics has vastly reduced employment opportunities, so part-time work becomes the norm in many developed countries, and many people spend the rest of their time on community activities. Some ultra-rich people, however, reject community responsibilities and become increasingly unhappy and troublesome to their neighbours. New illnesses start to kill people off at relatively young ages. These ailments all resist antibiotics and conventional medicine. Some theorists ask "Is the planet starting to reject the human species?"

2033 In the autumn of this year an Atlantic tsunami causes massive damage in Britannia and north-west France. There is devastation in several coastal towns in the Province of Wessex and several other parts of Britannia. Some towns and villages have to be largely rebuilt, and a real interest is established in creating sustainable housing and resolute, self-sufficient communities. Portugal and Spain are severely storm damaged.

2034-36 There is sudden alarm, as melting glaciers in Arctic regions and some on tropical mountains begin to create havoc. As the Himalayan lakes supply water to over a billion people, a migration starts into the surrounding lands and beyond. Additionally, rising sea levels require all the people of the Maldives and some other island groups to abandon their homes. Evacuation and rehabilitation schemes are put in place by GOS. Countries around the world are called upon to take their fair share of refugees. Some are reluctant to do this, and GOS is forced to set up a network of large camps in its six regions, to house all the remaining climate change refugees, temporarily at least.

2037-39 A series of enormous cyber-crashes, due to the over-use of electronic technology, alerts GOS and climate scientists to the realisation that we are damaging the atmosphere which sustains the planet. Damage is discovered to the quality of both the air and the sea. Medical scientists and psychologists also report physical damage to human beings and unborn children through radiation, and psychologists discover damage to the psyche. GOS imposes major restriction on the use of cyber space. Personal computers and televisions become a thing of the past in many homes, for both financial and security reasons. Thinking people across the globe decide that there must be an urgent change in the culture of modern life. People are living in a world of social media, becoming self-interested and consequently losing the essential need to build family lives and wholesome communities. Governments are urged to make to special efforts to turn things round. Most see the dangers and respond accordingly. Internet addiction is recognised as a hazard, and the rising gap between rich and poor is destabilising societies.

Massive increases in renewable energy storage facilities across the world encourage big international investment companies to switch their portfolios from oil and gas industries to renewable ones. Following this trend, there is a marked international move towards community cooperatives, and the introduction of standardised wages policies.

2039-2042 As global disasters lessen in these years, some optimists hope that the worst might be over. Rich people who yearn for the former times of economic growth become more vocal. China has successfully developed huge new energy pools through its Great Sun-power Revolution and clearly emerged as the world's greatest superpower. The old communist concepts are long forgotten. The new leader, Mr Lee Chong, encourages some Chinese companies to go global, and this angers equally vocal western entrepreneurs and causes considerable disquiet to many of the GOS Elders. The climate becomes hotter in the area between the tropic of Cancer and Capricorn. It is now impossible for people to continue living in central Africa and a huge programme of relocation has to be undertaken by GOS, with many more refugee camps. An International Peace Corps is established which enables young people to help the refugee programmes, acting as assistants to professionals. The Peace Corps is under the command of GOS. A series of hurricanes and tornadoes break out, and, at last, everyone accepts that climate change is a very serious problem for the whole of mankind. World leaders agree to restrictions on the use of refrigerators and heating and cooling systems in moderate zones, and an international licensing system is imposed. It is recognised that massive use of popular electrical equipment like home computers, smart phones, and I-pads are requiring too much power, and restrictions are put on them. Some wealthy people resent this, and a black market is created. Immigration becomes a bigger issue in richer countries due to the vast numbers of climate refugees.

2043-2045 Much of central Africa, Asia and Central America is becoming uninhabitable. Desertification, a diminished groundwater table, erosion and the build-up of salt in the remaining rivers and lakes is speeding up the tide of refugees. Illnesses such as malaria and dengue fever plague many refugee camps. Many young women in richer countries find they cease to have their normal periods of fertility, and the world population starts to fall back to earlier levels. Ocean acidity causes coral depletion, robbing the seas of shoals of fish, and numerous woodland fires break out across the globe. There is increased tension between the super-rich, living in gated communities who wish to ignore the new regulations, and the majority who accept them as necessary in these times of international emergency.

In Britannia, an attempt by the British Legion to commemorate major World War 2 battles, as was done with World War 1 battles, proves unsuccessful, due to growing anger on the part of national veterans. Many served with the GOS peace keeping forces, and feel that much more emphasis needs to be given to international peace-building. It is realised that arms manufacturers and secret private armies are fermenting much of the violence in failed states, and undermining peace building attempts by GOS. National Freedom parties in numerous different countries are hampering essential progress.

2046–55 In the UK, the Unity Government breaks down and two main parties become the centre-left Responsible Party and the hard-right Freedom Party, which opposes many aspects of international control, and supports the power of nation states. The Responsible Party gains control at the election in 2045, and stabilizes the situation, but in the next election in 2051 the Freedom Party win the election. The new government is tight on immigration and restrictive towards refugees and asylum-seekers. Some of the environmental restrictions are lifted and people are now allowed to decide for themselves again whether they wish to enjoy rich lifestyles or commit to sustainable living. This means that new divisions begin to emerge in all the six Britannic Provinces.

PART ONE - Voices from Tomorrow

(Woodleigh in Wessex, Britannia)

2055

...

"The child is father of the man"

William Wordsworth

CHAPTER 1 - The Assignment

2055

The pupils had their heads down as they gazed at their holographic tables; half of them were boys and half were girls, and they sat in sixes around ten screens. At the press of a button the circular white-board surfaces were instantly transformed into magical three D computers, with a depth and scope of their own. Animals seemingly rushed out of one table and danced round each other; one minute they were wolves, the next they were ostriches. In another part of the room a stately camel train walked across a desert to the sound of eastern music and, by the window, a flight of geese flocked up towards the ceiling.

 They were so absorbed that they had not noticed the teacher came into their learning space. He smiled and watched all the excitement, as he sat down at the control desk. Things were so different now from the school he had attended fifteen years ago. The teaching methods were freed from a rigid examination system, and Matthew Farnfield was also learning from and with his students. In his time each pupil had a personal computer, which was kept at home. Now that so much more had been discovered about radiation dangers, the computers were built into the learning tables, and the time spent on them was monitored.

This was lunchtime and instead of rushing out from the dining room into leisure field, here they were playing with the holographic computers in their learning area.

"Games ended," he cried, as he pressed his control button, and the animals vanished, along with the music. A new challenge was being set.

"Yesterday: that's the theme of your special project this year. I challenge you all to uncover the mysteries about what happened here twenty two years ago. Over the next few weeks, you'll become detectives and journalists, taking and recording evidence about Aceton, the place that disappeared. We all know about the great disaster, but few people are aware of what really lay behind it. Can you discover the truth?" Mr. Farnfield's eyes were sparkling and everyone in the class was listening intently.

"I'm giving you an assignment. The neighbouring village of Aceton was swept off the map twenty-two years ago. I'm sure you've all heard different stories about it, possibly from your parents or grandparents, if they were living here around that time, but the truth is, a lot of people don't talk about it. They bottle it up inside them. I think we need to know the whole story, so that we can ensure it will never happen again – not in your lifetime anyway."

"My family weren't living here at the time," said a voice from someone.

"That doesn't matter, you can still ask around. There are thirty-six of you in this class. I want you all to talk to the oldest people you know who were here at the time. Ask them to tell you about it. You must take notes. Some of you might like to record their voices. We will bring all the evidence together here and build up as big a picture as possible. Then we can decide how we're going to present the story. It could be a continuous narrative. It might be a newspaper or a collection of different tales, but whatever form it takes, you will need to verify the stories. You'll have to look for evidence to corroborate the facts. That's where the detective work begins. There could be clues lying in the fields, or among the rocks on the cliffs or the beach below. Perhaps we will be able to draw a map of the village that disappeared under the waves, and mark on it the places where particular things happened. I hope that we will be able to answer the questions on your tables.

Mr Farnfield pressed a button on his wristband, and the list was suddenly seen on each white table surface.

1. Why did Aceton disappear?

2. Might it have been saved if people had heeded warning signs and changed behavioural patterns?

3. If so, why did so many people ignore the warnings?

4. Could something similar happen today?

5. Which lifestyle would you prefer to be born into - our present one or the one in 2033?"

It was the first day of the autumn term, and this was the second of the three tasks that the enthusiastic young form master had set for his class. The first one was to design posters about their home area, as it was twenty-two years ago. Everybody had to prepare one and they were told that the posters would be displayed in the school hall for everyone to see.

This second task, to seek out the causes of the Great Storm, excited them more though. The assignment would have to be completed for the last day of the Spring term. The third task, given to them in the following term, was the most difficult of all; to create posters about what the area might be like in 100 years' time - 2155. This one had to be ready for the end of the school year. They seemed to like these special projects.

He studied them as they sat in groups at their round tables. A stranger would have to look carefully to make sure which were girls and boys. They all had shoulder-length hair these days and wore their own colourful self-selected tunics and leggings, with the regulation calf-high boots.

* * *

Later that day, a gaggle of youngsters, all wearing their school uniform of green ponchos, walked back together, talking enthusiastically about the new assignment.

"I'll ask my Gran about what she remembers," said Adam. "She's often talking about Aceton, but I've not been that interested before. I couldn't see the point when there's nothing left to see."

"Gramps is the one to talk to," said Beatrice. "It's a funny thing. Sometimes he doesn't know where he was yesterday, but when he meets one of his old mates they seem to know everything that happened before and during the Great Storm that swallowed it all up. They yatter on about things that I've never seen and can't imagine, like those old television sets and giant fridge freezers that all people used to have in their own homes, instead of just in the community buildings."

"They may not be or our homes, but many people do have more modern versions," said Carry. "We're living in a time warp here in the clusters, aren't we? I don't mind though, because I'm used to it. We can go over to the community building whenever we want to see a TV programme."

"That's not the same as living with the thing every day and every night." Beatrice was adamant.

"But some of the cluster people yearn for the way it used to be when they were young, like that old Mrs Broomhill across the cabbage patch. She prattles on for hours, about those strange programmes called 'soaps' they used to watch every day, and about all the marvellous fruits they could buy in those prehistoric shops they called supermarkets, things like pineapples and bananas and coconuts and avocados. Exotic food from around the world."

"Yuk," said Brook. "What I don't understand is how they could possibly bear to eat all those things when they were out of season. It couldn't have been healthy. The food had to be frozen and unfrozen again like some magic water pond."

"They ate loads of foreign stuff in the bad old days," said Adam, "and they never seemed to care about their health or people who worked like slaves to fill their groaning dining tables. It's not as if they didn't know the hypocrisy of it all. They watched people slaving and starving on those huge TV screens that they sat idolising every night. They must have been a stony-hearted lot before the Great Storm hit them."

They had almost reached the old white roundhouse now, the point where their separate paths diverged. From the hilltop here, they looked out across the placid sea, which lazily lapped the pebbles on the beach below the cliffs.

"It's very calm, today," said Carry. "You can't imagine how fierce the sea is sometimes. Just think of all those houses that must lie there under the tide."

"Aceton, swallowed whole," said Beatrice. "Tell you what, let's meet here again on Saturday morning and see what we've managed to find out from the old folk. If we all swap our stories, we'll be able to present a united front in the classroom when old Farnfield asks us what we've found out." There was a determined glint in her green eyes.

"If we're going to do a newspaper, someone will have to be the editor," said Adam.

"That'll be old Farnfield," said Brook.

"Not if we sweep the board," said Beatrice, excitedly. "If we're organised, like a team, and the others are all over the place, we'll be in a strong position to be joint editors – and run it like a cooperative. Farnfield will buy that. He told us that he likes original thinking." She leaned forward enthusiastically and grinned. Brook noticed that the excitement made her bob of fair hair bounce.

"That's a good idea," said Carry, and they all agreed. The Cornfield Cooperative had been born.

Adam and Beatrice turned left and walked down the path that led past the area wind turbine to their family clusters behind a clump of trees, while Carry and Brook walked straight on. "See you at ten on Saturday morning, then," Carry called after them.

Max was waiting for Beatrice under his favourite watering tree. He jumped up, barked, wagged his tail, and bounded forwards to sniff them both.

"Good dog, Max," said Beatrice. He trotted after them, tail wagging.

The trees enfolded the youngsters in a welcoming way. A bridge over the brook marked the boundary of the two housing clusters, where they lived. Beatrice and Max approached a circle of homes facing each other across a plot of common land. This was Coppice Cluster. The houses were two storied, with large windows angled to catch the mid-day sun and every roof was covered with solar panels.

"Cheers," Adam waved, as he continued along the lane to Sylvan Cluster.

The people of the clusters grew most of their daily food on the common plot that faced them and reared their sheep and goats in their wicker-worked pens. A pig was tied with a loose rope round his neck but the hens and chickens were roaming at will, across their own fenced off area.

Beatrice was welcomed by the cockerel that sounded a very loud "doodle-doo" when he saw her coming. She waved to him, and he pranced across the green to see if she had something special in her pocket for him today. She hadn't, so he retreated with a disgusted fluff of feathers thrown backwards in her direction. "Sorry, cockie, not today," she said. He flew off to perch on a neighbouring rooftop and doodle-dooed his disgust.

Beatrice paused at the drone zone to see if any airborne letters had arrived for her home. No: there seldom were. The drones were not carrying as many letters as they had done when they were first set up, after the old custom of chatting on visual phone lines had been ruined by all the cyber attacks and air pollution that scientists had discovered.

She walked past the play area, with the swings, slide and round-around, where several of the little ones were enjoying themselves. She and Dorrie, today's child-minder, waved to her. Tommy ran up to show off his new red jumper, knitted by Dorrie while she did her stint of child-minding last week. Max bounced around Tommy.

"That's a nice jumper you've got. Who knitted that?" asked Beatrice.

"Dorrie. She asked me what colour I wanted and I said red because it's my favourite colour. What's your favourite colour, Beetroot?" Beatrice didn't mind. She knew Tommy got his words mixed up and called his beetroots 'Beatrice'.

"I'm not sure what my favourite colour is. When I was your age I think I would have said blue?"

"Why was blue your favourite colour, Beetroot?"

"It was the colour of my first school satchel."

"Why aren't you sure which is your favourite colour now, Beetroot?"

"Because I've started painting, and there are so many different colours. I keep on discovering more by mixing up the paints. Have you ever noticed how many different shades there are of red, green or blue?"

"No, how many shades are there?"

"I've lost count," said Beatrice.

"So 'ave I," said Tommy, and mercifully he ran back to the swings. Max followed him and then became so excited when Tommy climbed on the round-around that he started to run along too, trying to keep up with his little friend.

"Hi Mum, just going to have a word with Gramps." Beatrice waved to her mother.

Everyone knew Beatrice's Mum. She was Elsa Whiteoak, the red headed American woman who ran the community shop with so much enthusiasm that she had become the most popular woman in the clusters. Elsa yelled, "He's on the bean plot, honey," and carried on pegging her washing to the second communal line that stretched right across the common land. She had to duck beneath a shirt, blowing in the breeze, and walk around the humming wind-turbine generator, which was busy supplying all the electricity needed for the coppice houses.

16

Elsa had two voices, one strident and the other gentle. Sometimes she hollered and sometimes she cooed, and Beatrice had grown up knowing that the gentler voice was the real one. The bravado was acquired when needed and today she was busy washing.

Gramps was picking beans off his section of the garden: a long strip divided by coloured bean poles.

"How are they doing, Gramps?" asked Beatrice.

"Fine," said old Mr. Whiteoak. "Try one. What do you think?"

"Thanks, Gramps... lovely and juicy... just right."

"So, young lady, what have you been doing in school today?"

 "Funny you should ask. That's why I've come to speak to you. Mr Farnfield has asked us all to talk to some of the older people in our area about what things were like in the old days; before the Great Storm, I mean."

"What was it like? Oh, it was very different then."

"In what ways?"

"Well, we all had so many things for a start. It was like that in my home anyway. We had what we called furniture in every room. We had dining tables, and sideboards and cupboards full of china, and book cases and shelves stuck on the wall, and ornaments on the mantle-piece and the window sills, and curtains there, and several radios and televisions and sound equipment and mirrors and carpets and video films, and the children were deluged with more and more things every time it was a birthday and Christmas. We never knew where to keep it all. I remember when your dad was a little boy, your Gran and I used to scratch our heads and think what can we give him for Christmas? He's got so much stuff already, but we had to keep buying new things, and we didn't know where he'd put it all."

17

"I don't know why you had to go on buying more things and keeping what you didn't need. Surely Dad could understand that, even if it was Christmas."

"We did it because everybody else did it. We'd have looked mean if we didn't do like the neighbours did. There were all those advertisements for new things every night on television, encouraging young people to pester their parents. There were these big shopping malls filled with goodies and somehow we all got dragged in, and the government encouraged people to spend. They said it would boost the economy, create more jobs and make us all wealthier. It was a sort of merry-go-round and, much as you wanted to get off, you couldn't because the damn thing never stayed still and gave you a chance."

"This is just the sort of thing I want to ask you about. Can we go inside, Gramps, so I can record what you're saying on my machine?"

Gramps picked up his bucket of beans. "Yes, I reckon I've picked enough for today. Come in, me dear, and we'll have a drink of apple juice. It's fresh crushed from our trees in the orchard. I made it last night."

Gramp's bungalow was next to Beatrice's home. It was compact with a living room, bedroom and shower to the right, a kitchen to the left and a compost loo just outside. On the wall hung his wedding day photograph, and on the window sill were three photographs of Beatrice, at different stages: baby, toddler with her older brother, Rory, and a recent one of her with her mum and dad, all holding spades and digging on the common plot.

It was a cosy room and Gramps took his favourite position in his rocking chair made by his son, Mark, in the Coppice carpentry shop.

Beatrice took her wristband off, plugged it into the local electrical generator socket on the wall and switched on the recorder.

"Mr. Farnfield, our citizenship teacher, is asking us to do a project on Aceton. We've got to find out as much about it as possible. Do you mind being recorded? Could you repeat what you just said outside about there being so much clutter?"

Gramps happily obliged, and then went on to elaborate. "It wasn't just clutter in the houses, it was clutter everywhere you turned.   There were dozens and dozens of TV companies, hundreds of channels to view, enormous daily newspapers with scores of pages carrying advertising, and people pestering you all the time on the telephone and knocking on doors inviting you to change your energy supplier or take out a new insurance policy. There was constant noise and light pollution, people wearing earphones listening to loud music and going deaf as a consequence. The whole world was in overdrive. What's worse the government was encouraging a 24/7 lifestyle, with shops open all the time and loads of people having to do night-work, which spoiled family life and was very bad for our health."

"How did all this affect people?"

"Differently - a lot had nervous problems. They hid themselves away and tried to switch off. Others led frantic lives. Families often became dis-functional with mothers and fathers separating and children being hurt in consequence. There was a growing gulf between the rich and the poor. A lot of old people were very lonely, because of family breakdown, and the grown-up children often went to live in other places – sometimes even other countries. People found it very difficult to adjust to all the changes. Towns got bigger and bigger and when people retired they often wanted to move away into the countryside. House prices went through the roof in the nicest places, and it became difficult for young people to stay in their home villages, because of property speculators."

"You're raising so many issues, Gramps, I think we'll leave it there for this afternoon."

Beatrice thought he would never stop. It was like pulling the cork out of a bottle of fizz. What would she do with all these facts? Gramps had enjoyed it, though. and said that he'd lots more to say, and he hoped she could come back tomorrow so that they could carry on recording.

"I don't know about tomorrow but yes, we really need several sessions, and perhaps we can go into more depth with one or two topics then. It's nearly time for our evening meal at home. Mum will wonder where I am. See you tomorrow, Gramps."

I'll start making a few notes myself to keep the memory green, he thought. Moving over to his desk, Donald Whiteoak switched on his computer. There was a buzzing noise and then three pips, before the screen illuminated. "Good," he mumbled to himself. There was still some spare electricity in the c.g.p. (cluster generation pool). He smiled and started to type on the keyboard.

The Sylvan Cluster, where Adam lived had a very different appearance to that of the Coppice. Although it was entered in the same way, by crossing a wooden bridge over a brook boundary, the setting was more formal because this was an adapted cluster, not an original one. The homes had been built around fifty years ago, facing each other in straight lines. The suburban front gardens, two pavements and wide road in the centre, intended for traffic, had all by replaced by a large common plot. Solar panels covered every roof.

Knowing that Dad was doing his shift today in the car pool, Adam looked in at the community garage at the other end of the row of houses, and found him servicing one of the four cars available for hire by anyone in the cluster with enough credit on his household score card. (Credits were earned thorough performing several hours of community service, such as the task now in hand.)

"I've just popped in to let you know that I'm going over to see Gran in the community home. I'll be back to help with dinner in about an hour."

Peter was dressed in overalls and lying on his back underneath a modern Electric Serena on a raised platform. "OK. See you at 5.30 then," said Dad, "and ask Gran to join us on Saturday for the family lunch. It's her birthday, don't forget."

Adam walked along to the end of the common patch and opened one of the big wooden gates. The Sylvan Community Home was a large double-fronted house set in a wild-flower garden. A notice board by the door displayed its name "Oak Gates," in memory of a local tree that had been struck by lightning shortly before the present house was built.

Adam rang the bell and the girl on the duty desk opened it. He explained that he'd come to see his gran. She nodded a welcome, so he crossed the hallway towards the residents' lounge: a comfortable room with a French window opening on to a brick patio and sunny garden beyond.

Four white haired elderly ladies were chatting and sipping tea on the patio. One of them looked up and smiled.

"Adam, " she said "We don't usually see you at this time of day."

"I want a word, if it's convenient," he explained eagerly, "We're doing a special project at school and I thought you might be able to help me." This was really addressed to Gran, but suddenly he felt it might be a good idea to extend it to the other old ladies too, so he glanced round at them all. "It's about Aceton and the Great Storm. At school, we've been asked to talk to people who can remember it all, and how it used to be, twenty two years ago."

There was a moment's silence. The ladies all looked at him, expressionless, and then at one another with uncertainty.

"Why do they want us to tell you about it?" Gran was precise and guarded in her reply. Everyone watched in silent interest. Adam was a little embarrassed.

"Well," he said awkwardly, "there were a few questions." He fumbled in his pocket and pulled out a piece of paper, and then realised that they were all watching his every movement.

"What sort of questions?" a wizened old lady demanded.

"Well," looking deliberately at Gran. "There's this one. Do you know anything about what might have caused it?"

"I'm no expert on the weather. Perhaps you'd be better to send a question like that to the MET Office," said Gran, rather sharply.

Adam realised he was handling this rather badly, and put the paper away.

He glanced at the wizened lady and smiled. "I'm sorry to barge in like this." He turned back to Gran. "There were several questions, so perhaps we could have a word about them at some other time, when it's more convenient. Oh, and Dad said don't forget to join us for the family meal at lunchtime on Saturday. Perhaps afterwards…"

But Gran intervened. "I'm not sure that I can be of any help. My memory is not so clear these days. It was all so tragic… so many people died…friends, whole families.. so we don't talk about it."

"I'm sorry," said Adam. "I didn't realise."

One of the other ladies intervened. "Can't the teachers think of better things to do in school today? Why should they ask children to pry into such private affairs?"

Gran stood up. "Come with me, Adam," she commanded. "Come to my room."

Gran reached for her walking frame and left the room. Adam followed her, blushing.

They went up in the lift together in silence, and across the landing to her door. Gran ushered Adam in first, and indicated that he should sit down on the settee. She sat in her favourite armchair, and looked at him for a moment in a strange way.

"I'm sorry," he stammered. "I shouldn't have burst in like that."

Gran smiled. "It's all right, dear," she said slowly. "You don't understand. How could you? It's not your fault, but it was all so painful, and some of the ladies here don't ever want to speak of it. Not in public that is. Privately, to a close friend, they occasionally unburden themselves, but not in the lounge, and not to visitors, like you. I'm surprised that your teacher didn't realise what he was asking his students to do."

He didn't ask us to come here. That was my fault. I won't mention it again, not to you, I mean. Forget I ever asked about it. I understand, if you don't want to speak about it."

"Oh but I do, Adam. I would love to tell you about those things, but privately, just you and me. Give me time, Adam, that's all."

"How long Gran?" Adam was puzzled at a sudden change of tone.

"Come back tomorrow, darling. Come here to my room around this time."

"Is that all right? Are you sure?"

"Yes, darling. I'm absolutely sure. After school tomorrow and I'll be ready for you. Oh and thank your father for inviting me on Saturday. I've got two things to look forward to now, tomorrow and Saturday. Goodbye, dear."

"Goodbye Gran." Adam could not understand at all. Old people were a mystery.

CHAPTER 2 - The Cornfield Cooperative

Carry and Brook lived in the next ward, half a mile up the miry hill, in other cluster of sustainable houses. Carry's home was in the Lapwing Cluster and Brook's in Redshanks. Neither of them managed to discuss the project until sometime later. Carry had to prepare a meal for her two little sisters, as her mother had died two years ago and her father was a Woodleigh police officer, on duty today. Carry didn't have any grandparents, but she knew who she wanted to speak to, and made a telephone call after the meal.

"Hello, Mrs. Broomhill. I want to have a word with you when it's convenient. We're doing a project at school about Aceton and the Great Storm, and I wondered if I could ask you about your memories. Well, how about tomorrow evening. I could call round after school. O.K. See you then."

Brook was cycling along the road that crossed the heath. The old woodcutter lived in a wooden caravan, near the ancient earthwork on the hilltop. Brook thought that Reuben was probably the oldest man in Woodleigh. Over the last few years, Brook had learned a lot from him about the birds on the common and the estuary. He reckoned that Reuben would know more about the Great Storm than anyone else, being such an observant old man, with a memory that was still as clear as it must ever have been.

Reuben's horse was grazing in the little paddock beside the caravan, which was painted in gypsy style, with two shafts so that the horse could pull the caravan whenever required. The shafts were tied neatly to the post that usually held them.

Brook knocked on the door. "Who's that?" said a voice from inside. The old man was suspicious of visitors in the evening. "It's Brook." The door was cautiously opened   and then the lined old face broke into a smile.

"Come in, boy, Come in. What brings you 'ere this evenin' time?"

"It's a project. One of our teachers has asked us to find out all we can about Aceton and the Great Storm. We were told to talk to the oldest and wisest people we know and collect all the information we can, and so you're the first person I thought of."

The old man rubbed the stubble on his chin. "Aceton. The storm! Now what do you reckon I'd know about that?"

"Why you know just about everything round here, Reuben. I thought you were the obvious man to come to."

"Did you now? What do I remember? My, I could never forget it, if I live to be an 'undred. Sit down mi' lad, and let me brew you one of my 'ome grown 'erb teas. Not often I has a visitor in the evenin'. Not seen you about birdwatchin' recently on the estuary. This is a good time of year to catch a glimpse of the avocets at neap tide."

"I've been busy with other things. I've started doing a voluntary job at the library."

"'Ave ye now? That'll keep ye out o' mischief." Reuben bustled about preparing the herb tea as he was talking.

"So what exactly was it ye wanted to know about that storm?"

"Well to start with - was there a proper warning? Did people have time to prepare?"

"Well, there was signs all right. Signs for those wi' eyes in their 'eads and sounds to listen for, but most folks 'as their eyes shut, and their ears attuned to different things. I knew somethin' was brewing for sure, but I never expected the devastation. The birds left suddenly three weeks before it 'appened. There was no songsters in the trees, and the skies over the estuary was clear of 'em. The usual migrants never came in the autumn. They changed their flight paths and went elsewhere, so I knew for sure that somethin' was up - somethin' big. The seas had been risin' for four years or more, an' the sea front had been swept by waves every 'igh tide. Most of the 'otels there had closed down that summer, 'cos they'd been flooded two years runnin'.

The weathermen told us an 'urricane was coming in a few days, and they delivered sandbags and advised everyone to leave the 'ouses on the sea front, but when it came it was like no 'urricane known to man nor beast. T'was a wind that swept the world, that ripped up trees and played with 'em like toys. Threw 'em in the air, and tossed 'em 'ither and thither all over the moor. Some of 'em crashed into 'ouses – and the sea – why she came in like a ragin' torrent, and smashed those big 'otels like matchwood. There was a clock tower on the promenade that was 'urled into the big 'otel behind it. The ole' village was swallowed up in two long days, together with all the families that lived there. It was like the judgement of Satan. Thank the Lord, I never seen the like afore nor since."

"And have you any theories about why it happened?"

"Theories? I'm no man for theories, but I knew in my bones that it was comin'.

*   *   *

"I'm very glad you've come again, Adam." Gran was a changed woman when he called to see her the next day. "You see, I've always wanted to tell you some things about your grandfather, but somehow I've not had the courage before, and that's stupid really, because he was a lovely man. "

Adam sat down to listen. "If only he could be here now to see you. He'd be so proud. Do you know, you actually look like him, when he was your age. Not that I knew him then of course, but I've seen the photographs. We didn't meet each other until we were in our twenties. He was a very smart looking man. He worked in the post office in a managerial job. He'd done very well for a young chap. We'd only been married for fifteen years when he was killed in the Great Storm, like so many of our friends.

We were living in Aceton at the time. Your mother was 10 years old and little Edward was 8. We were a very happy family. We had wonderful times together on the beach. He taught your mum to swim, and we all used to go for drives in his sports car. We went out a lot when he was free. We loved climbing the cliff paths too. You could follow the trail for miles.

We'd heard about the hurricane that was expected from the BBC weather forecasts, and we thought about going away somewhere inland that weekend, but we decided it would be better to see it through. We thought it would be terrible if the house was damaged whilst we were away. We'd absolutely no idea what it would be like. We knew the tides would come over the promenade, but we never thought they would come so far inland. We were half a mile from the sea, but then we were in a low lying part of the village.

The wind came first. It terrified us. We'd never heard anything like it, and then there was the rain – torrential. We all stayed indoors, away from the windows, in case they were blown in. We went into the pantry under the stairs and huddled together. People said that was the strongest bit of the house – but suddenly there was this terrible crash.

It sounded as if the house had been struck by lightning. Everything shook. We tried to open the door, but we couldn't. It wouldn't budge. Something was fast against it. Then the roof caved in – our staircase and the four of us were struggling in water and we saw the dining room table sweep past us and smash to splinters on a great tree.

Your granddad tried to protect us. He put him arms round us all somehow, or tried to, but then he was suddenly swept away in a great flood - I never saw him again."

Gran paused. She could not say any more. Adam held her hand, very gently. "But somehow, you managed to get to safety," he suggested.

"I don't know what happened. I woke up in hospital. They told us afterwards that your mother and I were rescued by soldiers. They sent them in from the marine camp nearby. They came in boats when the storm was subsiding and picked people out of the rubbish. I woke up a week later. We'd lost everything. The house had been smashed to smithereens, but the worst thing was, I'd lost little Edward, and I'd lost Colin, your granddad."

They sat together holding hands in silence. "So, now you understand why it hurts to talk of these things – but I'm glad you asked those questions, Adam. Otherwise, I might never have got round to telling you all this. It's right... you should know. Some other time, I'll tell you more about your grandfather and Edward, your little uncle. We'll keep that for another day. You must come round and look at the photo album with me. I'm glad about that project you're doing at school. Just talking to you like this has helped lift a load off my mind."

*   *   *

Four cyclists met at 10 am on Saturday morning by the roundhouse on the sea front.

It was a convenient place to meet on this sunny day, but not a suitable one for discussing something important. The promenade was busy with walkers enjoying the wonderful views over the bay. Yachts and surfers rode the waves below and the sky was alive with multi-coloured kites.

"Let's cycle down the estuary path and discuss our plans under the old beech by the cornfield." Beatrice took the lead and the others followed. The golden corn, ripe for harvesting, was rippling in the breeze as they cycled alongside it. By the hedge at the top end of the field a convenient bench offered a quiet spot where they could gather under the shade of a beech tree.

"Well, what have we discovered so far?" Beatrice and Brook stayed seated on their bikes, as Carry and Adam dismounted to sit on the bench.

28

"I got lots of info from old Reuben, the woodcutter," said Brook. "He's an amazing old man. He can feel things before they happen. He watched the birds leave the area and he knew that the storm was coming."

"That's awesome." Beatrice was impressed. "My grandad's a great talker too, but in a different way. He's more of a people's person and when he got going he talked non-stop about the way folk behaved differently in those days. He thought there was going to be a crash of some sort too. He said people brought it on themselves because they were all in overdrive."

"Old Mrs Broomhill's a big gossip, so I knew she'd say something interesting. She'd like to see the big shops come back again selling exotic fruits," said Carry. "She really enjoyed shopping in the old days. It was the place where she met her friends. They'd have a cup of coffee together in the café at one of the big supermarkets and then go round with those old fashioned shopping trolleys seeing what was on offer and comparing prices. The shops had a huge range of things that we never see today."

"How about you, Adam?" Beatrice prompted, and everyone looked at him.

He was a little shamefaced. "A lot of the old people don't want to talk about the Great Storm," he said. "It was really terrible and it took them a long time to get over it. I don't think some of them ever will. We've got to be aware of that, and not pester them, if they don't want to talk."

"Didn't you find anything out?" asked Brook.

"I talked to my gran, but I made a mistake at first. She lives in the community home, Oak Gates, and when I arrived there she was in the garden with three other old ladies. I thought it would be a good idea to involve them all. "

He stopped. The others nodded him to continue.

"It wasn't a good idea at all. They said I was intruding into personal things and I felt awful. But afterwards, I spoke to Gran in her room. She told me about my grandfather and how he'd died trying to protect the family in the storm. She'd never told me about my grandfather before, but afterwards she said that telling me about it had helped her somehow." They were quiet for a moment.

"I think that's awesome too," said Brook.

"What are we learning through all this?" asked Beatrice.

"We really must be aware of how other people feel." said Adam.

"And we must listen to other people's points of view," said Carry.

"So how are we going to tackle this project?" asked Beatrice. "Are we just going to tell Mr Farnfield what we've done?"

"I guess that's what he wants," said Brook.

"But is it what we want? Can we take the lead?"

"What do you mean?" asked Carry.

"I think we four have all learnt something about ourselves. Perhaps the other members of the class need to wake up as well. Of course we can all just respond to Mr Farnfield's questions and leave it at that. We can put our hands up first and feel proud about it, but perhaps we can do something more. If we want to, we can take charge of this whole project and make it ours. He told us last week, that the best way to learn something is to do it yourself. You can be helped when you're learning to ride a bike or swim in the sea, but when you take control yourself, you learn much more quickly. O.K. How about getting the whole class really involved, not just the four of us. Why should he rule the show? He wants us to learn by doing? Let's do that. We can run this process ourselves. That's the principle behind the house clusters, isn't it? They generate most of their own electric power. Every house owner is responsible for the power that's used. That's the basic rule and people keep the records and each year they are on display in the library to show that nobody's used too much. Let's show Mr Farnfield that we've learned this lesson. He can sit and listen to us."

There was silence.

"I'm not sure what you're on about?" said Adam.

"Let's run this as an Open Space event, like the group discussions we have in the clusters. We can elect a facilitator and then listen to all the contributions without any interruptions. The facilitator will put key points on the board. Then we can group them under topics and everyone can join the group discussing the topic that they are most interested in. Then we share thoughts and decide how we move ahead."

"How do you think he'll react?" asked Brook.

"That doesn't matter, as long as we show him we mean business. He'll probably be taken aback, but when he's got over that, he might well fall in line. If he doesn't we haven't lost anything. We've just made our point."

"Doing things like this…where do you think it will lead us?" asked Carry.

"I don't know. It's a process. If you start with a destination, there's no journey, and the learning bit is on the journey."

"OK," said Carry. "I'll buy that. Let's do it."

"All right by me," said Adam.

"We'll see what happens," said Brook.

"How about forming a co-operative." Beatrice was thinking ahead, and there was a determined gleam in her eyes. "We can all have equal shares – the whole class, I mean, and we'll all have equal rights and responsibilities."

"Sounds a good idea," said Brook. "And as we've come up with all this here, we can call it 'The Cornfield Cooperative.' "

And they all mounted their bikes and spun off along the estuary cycle path, leaving the waving cornfield behind them.

CHAPTER 3 - Ripples in the Corn

"What are your memories of the Great Storm, Mom?" It was the next Saturday morning, and Beatrice was walking to the community shop with her mother. Elsa's red hair was done up in a bun today. She let it down to relax, when she was with friends. It made her look younger, but there was usually a bun in the mornings when she was brisk and busy.

"I wasn't here when it happened honey, I was in California."

"How come? You told me that you first met Dad when you were teaching here, and that was before the storm, wasn't it?"

"Sure, but I was on a short assignment. I came over on a one-year teacher exchange from the States. I was back in San Diego when I heard about that great storm, and I was devastated because I'd made so many buddies over here. As soon as I heard the name of Aceton mentioned I rang Fran, fast as I could. She was my special buddy. She was the librarian in the school I'd been workin' in. We'd been exchangin' text messages quite often. She phoned me back and I was so relieved to hear her voice. She was shaken o' course because she knew so many o' the victims, but most of our crowd were safe she said. We had several talk and view sessions on skype, as they used to call that ole' system, and Fran sent me film of the damaged areas. Huh, it was terrible. My heart went out to everyone over here, and I had this huge urge to come back. I'd fallen in love with Aceton and all the folks around."

"But you'd just settled back there with your family and had your old job and everything."

"It wasn't like that, sweetheart, but now we're here at the store, so I'll explain it all on the way home." Elsa was a shopper herself today, not the store manager.

The community shop was a very friendly place and when Elsa was buying anything it was a slow process. Everyone loved to chat to Elsa, who had helped set the shop up in the early days. Beatrice did not know why so many people wanted to tell her things. Perhaps, it was her quaint American accent, or just her very friendly interest in everyone she saw. Elsa always remembered things that people had told her and enquired after children or visiting relatives or pets that had been hurt. They usually ended up with a group chat in the coffee room and a pile of purchases, much of which was surplus local produce from the common plot. Beatrice sometimes pushed the laden trolley back home by herself because she knew that Mom would be talking in the coffee shop for another hour. Today she waited though, so that they could finish their own conversation over the short walk home.

"So what was the situation like in San Diego, Mom?" Beatrice reminded Elsa about the earlier discussion. There was a pause before her mother answered, and then it all came out in a rush.

"I suppose I may as well tell you now. It's not something I usually tell folk."

Beatrice was more keen than ever.

"Oh dear - it wasn't good at all. In fact it was dire. I've not told you about these things before because it still upsets me to talk about it, but during the year I was over here, my Dad left my Mom. They'd always had rows, but they tried coverin' things over. My Mom found out he was having an affair with another woman, and she thought while I was away she'd have an affair too, to show him up and bring things to a head. When I got back I hadn't really got a home at all. There was this man living with Mom and another woman I couldn't stand at all living with my Dad. It was awful - such a shock. I was so happy with them as a kid, but things got difficult as I went through teenage years. Anyway, after I got home again in the USA, I stayed with my Mom and this man for a week and then went to stay with one of my girlfriends for a while, and then I got a rented room somewhere, but I just felt San Diego was not the place for me anymore."

"Hadn't you got lots of friends there?"

.ost of them had moved on. After uni, most folk liked to get jobs away from their home. I'd had a boy friend called Andy, but he'd got a partner living with him when I came back, so I decided to break free too. I'd enjoyed it here so much. This was the obvious place to come."

"Even after the storm which had destroyed Aceton!"

"Yes, I'd always liked this whole coastline, and I'd got real friends here in Woodleigh to meet up with again. Fran was engaged to marry Peter, and she asked me to be her bridesmaid. They were deeply involved with this transition town thing, an' the storm seemed to highlight the importance of not just talkin' about it, but also creatin' a new way of livin'. Fran told me how enthusiastic Peter and your Dad were about the plans for buildin' these cluster homes and livin' in a sort of community, and it was just what I felt I needed then."

"Had you and Dad been special friends when you were here on the exchange?"

"Nope. We were friends, but nothing special, but when he noo' I was coming back he sent me a lovin' letter saying how delighted he was. I guess he was a bit shy, but he found it easier to write about his feelin's rather than talkin' direct, and when we met up again, I jus' sort o' fell for him. I was interested in his organic food too, an' rather than get stuck in another teaching job, I helped him set up the farm shop in the community store. Although the store had a big buzz to it, Mark was a quiet man, unlike Pete, who's always so much to say for himself."

"Like you have."

"I guess so, I like folk and I like talkin', but Mark's a deeper sort of guy. He thinks things through and I felt I wanted a man like that - a steady, reliable guy who I noo I could depend on. Things moved quickly after I came back, I can tell ye."

Beatrice had learned quite a lot of important things through this project. If it carried on like this, it could be really worthwhile. She decided that she would certainly push it as far as she could. It wasn't only the fair complexion she'd inherited.

*　*　*

Beatrice's learning room was set out in the modern style, with white board circular tables instead of desks with six pupils sitting on their own labelled, stacking chair. Great efforts were made by most of them to personalise those chairs with ornate coloured labels. Beatrice's label had different coloured letters in the shape of a rainbow.

Matthew Farnfield watched the class file into the room after the morning break. They lived in three different housing areas. Those who came from the cluster groups were the liveliest, chatting freely to anyone. The "newies" hung together in the playground and often sat together in a bunch, except for Ahab and Sorrinda, who chose to move around. Ahab was chatting to Brook today, so he collected his chair from the pile and joined him at his table. Sitting at different tables was allowed, but not swapping chairs, Sorrinda, neat and quiet, as usual, sat down beside her friend, Carry.

Alfred and Ernie were obviously "selfies". He could see that at a glance because they both had both just decided to have their hair cropped in the latest hairstyle and marched in with the confidence of military officers. The "selfies" occupied the right hand side of the room. Most of them, like Alphie, lived in expensive gated areas and had developed a rather superior attitude, which the cluster crowd resented. Their chair labels were unadorned by drawings and their names were written boldly in black lettering and underlined three times.

"Well, how did you all get on with the Aceton Project that I set you last week?" asked Matthew, at the start of their double-time session.

To his surprise, no one responded. None of the usual hands shot up.

"Come on. Don't tell me that no one bothered to talk to any older people. Did you, Adam? "

"Yes, sir. I talked to my gran' but it was hard going at first. She was a bit upset…"

The teacher sighed and moved on before Adam had an opportunity to expand.

"What do you think, Martin?"

"I was ill in bed last week, sir. So I wasn't here for the project setting."

"Oh, so you've some catching up to do. Yes, Adam."

"But my gran' did open up later and told me a lot about the family. She'd never talked to me about my grandfather before, because he was killed in the storm along with other family members and it upset her to talk about it. But she told me later that she was glad you'd set this exercise. It helped her to start talking about it."

"Good. And did you learn something more about your grandfather?"

"Yes, he was the postmaster, and he died trying to save his family."

"Brave man." Mr. Farnfield turned to an exchange student who was studying with the school this year. "Lina, I know you have had many floods in the Netherlands. I think there were some around 2033. Did this affect the area you live in?"

"Yes," Lina replied. "The dam walls broke down about five miles from where we were living, and our town was flooded. My mother was a girl at the time and she told me she had to help sweep the water out of the kitchen, and they needed dozens of sandbags to help soak up the mess."

"The clusters have teams of volunteers who are trained and ready to deal with those situations," Adam offered. "And they have a stock of sandbags stored in readiness at the community shop."

"We don't all live in clusters, though, and we don't all have a community shop," Alfie called out. "We have a drive in mega-store instead, and my Dad owns it."

Beatrice intervened with a suggestion. "Sir, can I make a suggestion? Some of us have been giving this project quite a lot of thought..."

"I'm glad someone has."

"We thought, as you want us to be pro-active, perhaps we could run this session on Open Space lines, like we do in home cluster meetings, where everyone is given an opportunity to speak for three minutes, and no one can interrupt them."

"Right then. You come up here and show us what you mean."

Beatrice walked to the front, stood by the teacher's control point, an started speaking. "Those of us who live in house clusters all know about the weekly meetings when any subject can be put on the table and the household representatives can share thoughts on that topic in turn. Each person can speak for three minutes without interruption. Those are the rules in Open Space. Who wants to tell us about their findings now?"

Brook shot his hand up, and he was invited to talk. Beatrice looked at her watch.

"I learned a lot from old Reuben, the woodcutter. He's lived in these parts all his life, and he's eighty now. He knew that the Great Storm was coming because he always watches the wildlife – especially the birds. Most of them disappeared a few weeks before it started. The migrant birds didn't come to the estuary at the usual time. On the day before the storm his old dog wouldn't stir from its kennel. The animals know what's coming, and he told me that humans used to have that sort of instinctive knowledge hundreds of years ago. We need to ask ourselves – why are we not tuned into the environment like the animals are? What are we missing?"

"Thank you, Brook." Beatrice smiled at him. " Carry, you've got your hand up. Come up now and say your piece, and then I'll take questions for you and Brook, while things are fresh in our minds."

"I spoke to Mrs Broomfield. She's an old resident and she says that when she looks back she often feels sad because she lost a lot of good friends around her own age, in the Aceton disaster. She was a member of a group of young mothers at the time of the storm, and they liked to go shopping together and use those old-fashioned trolleys. They'd have a drink in the cafe first and they popped the little kids on the trolley seats, when they went round the aisles looking at the displays and comparing prices. There used to be a huge spread of food from around the world – bananas, melons, coconuts, mangoes and oranges – all the things that are very rare and expensive now. We can't buy these things at the country stores. It's all local food, and, if people want these luxuries, they have to pay steep prices. Those young women were like a happy family. They'd seen each other's children being born, but in those days there were a lot of nasty illnesses like measles and chicken pox that have been eliminated now, so they used to help each other when the kids were sick. They actually had some measles parties, where the kids got a mild form of measles at the same time, and they could get over those quite easily then. Mrs Broomfield lost several of those friends and their children in the Great Storm."

"Thank you, Carry. Now are there any questions you want to ask Brook or Carry, or any further thoughts you have about what they've said?" Beatrice looked round the room.

"Yes, Adam."

"The reason those oranges and things were cheap was because the native workers weren't paid proper wages. Now we have an international fair trade system, and that makes it better for the field workers. It's worth paying a bit more for that."

"We don't all live in clusters, though," Alphie called out.

39

"That's true," said Clancy. "And I think that woman Carry was talking to was just missing old friends. Young mothers still watch all the babies growing up and help each other. They don't have to wait till shopping day to meet up now. They're living closer together in the clusters, and they have play parks alongside the houses."

"Watching the birds and the animals is a good idea. They've got instincts and it can be a guide to us," said Ivy.

"We've got a cat and we moved into another house two miles away," said Tim. "But the next day it disappeared and later on the people that had bought our old house brought it round, so it's instincts must have shown it which way to go."

"Thank you everyone. I think that Beatrice, Brook and Carry have pointed out some important things in the last few minutes." Mr Farnfield had taken over again. "Let's show them our appreciation." He led the clapping as they returned to their desks.

"Well now, I'm sure a lot of you others have something to tell us, but before we invite anyone else to come forward, let's get a few key issues recorded." He pressed the button on his wristband, and the words KEY POINTS appeared on every table top. "What lessons have we learned through those reports?"

"No interruptions when anyone is speaking," called out Beatrice, with a glint in her eye.

"Good point, Beatrice." This list was soon compiled.

1. No interruptions   (Beatrice)
2. Watch animal and bird life in your area   (Brook)
3. Get to know the whole local environment   (Brook)
4. Get to know your neighbours   (Carry)
5. Help people whenever you can   (Carry)

"What else comes out of those two reports?" asked Mr. Farnfield. "Is there something really important about eating locally grown produce?" The answers were swift.

"It tastes better when it fresher".

"It doesn't have to be frozen and unfrozen and that saves our local energy quota."

"It's better for your health to eat local food."

"Why do you think it's better for your health, Jessie?"

"Because it's part of our environment, and the Great Spirit provides everything we need in each locality, and it works well as long as the balance of nature is not disturbed."

Alphie groaned. "She's on her soapbox again."

"We'll ignore that rude remark," said the teacher. "I think Jessie's got a really important point there. Would you like to elaborate, Jessie?"

"Well, everyone knows that I believe in the Great Spirit, and go to the open air Sunday picnics, where we learn about nature, the wild flowers and the herbal remedies. We have a saying in the Movement: "There's enough in the environment for everyone's need, but not enough for everyone's greed.""

"I agree with that," affirmed Mr Farnfield. "The environment around us is rich in biodiversity. The migrating birds come to the estuary here because instinct tells them where they can find the particular worms they feed on at low tide. Nature supplies our needs, and if we are sufficiently aware of the environment around us, we can enjoy a much fuller life. How many of you have been on the Sunday walks and talks."

About half the pupils raised a hand.

"Well, I'll tell those of you that haven't that you're missing something special. I've been on some of them, and they have specialists explaining

41

about the birds and the wild flowers. Now, come on, you others, what have you to tell us about your discussions?"

"Well, it's not only the cluster kids that have been thinking about the old times," said Alphie. "I've asked my Dad and he told me that the world changed after those storms. The trouble wasn't just in Britannia, you know. There were hurricanes across America, where my Uncle Wilbur lives and Dad told me that a two-speed system started there too. Some people started to go backward thinking, just like our cluster folk did. A few country places started to live like there'd never been an industrial revolution, and went back to using horses and carts, but my Uncle Wilbur had more sense. He moved into the fracking business and he made a pile. Last summer I went over there. It's a real eye opener. Now, he's got his own private security business with dogs yapping everywhere. They've made a bomb. They're raking in millions."

"What's that got to do with the natural environment?" asked Mr Farnfield.

"Everything: he runs a big game park with buffaloes there, so people go in trucks to see the wildlife. They have shooting trips and run an annual championship."

"Fat lot of good that'll be for the wildlife." Brook was scornful.

"No. That's where you're wrong. He's helping to preserve the buffaloes. They only release the old ones for the shoot, and keep the younger ones alive for breeding purposes. He runs a zoo full of them, and they have wild dogs and coyotes too. I went to a performance where they did tricks. If it wasn't for people like my uncle W those animals would all be dead."

"P'raps they'd prefer to be dead than in your Uncle Wilbur's menagerie," said Jessie.

"Maybe, and you're straying way off the subject, Alphie," said Mr Farnfield. "I asked you all to find out about happened here in Woodleigh, and to talk to old people about their memories and ask

42

them how life has changed since the Great Storm. What did you find out, Alan?"

Alan said that he had talked to a woman who helped to set up the car-pool scheme. She was on the first car-pool committee and it was this body that had set up the network of car servicing schemes in Woodleigh and organised the system whereby people with the necessary skills volunteered to do regular checks on all the vehicles to make sure that they were in good working order. This servicing was done in one of the bigger car parks at first, but later they established a network of service stations, where cars were checked for safety free of charge. There were now service stations all around the town, running the hire car pools in each district.

"What are the advantages of the car pool system?" asked Mr. Farnfield.

Several hands shot up, and he was able to add.

"It's cheaper to hire a car than own and run one."

"They are always checked for safety."

"It's led to less road congestion."

"It has freed up a lot more space, by enabling the council to close some side roads, and just have pavements to the houses. The road space is sometimes turned into common plots, more people could grow their own food."

"Some people have got bigger shared gardens, and it helps the neighbours to know one another better."

Dorrie shot up her hand and said it wasn't only allotments on that spare road space, it was children's play areas too, and she was a volunteer play helper like lots of others in the class.

Gradually the screen filled with more ideas. Julie spoke of her conversation with a retired policeman, who had to face rioters when the old gas and electricity supplies collapsed and people had no power in the homes.

Alice's grandfather had been a soldier in the bad old days, and, some years ago, he was asked to help establish the local security training schemes for eighteen-year-olds.

This had now become very popular and when they left school in addition to getting a paid job for two and a half days a week, many people had become community volunteers as well. They could usually train to do something they enjoyed.

Beatrice told them all about her grandfather's fears of life becoming a mad rat-race, before the Great Storm. There was more free time now, because robots did a lot of the jobs people used to do, like street cleaning, rubbish disposal and recycling, and a lot of the clerical jobs were now done electronically. In the old days all the mail, now delivered by drones, had to be handled by postmen and women who had to walk along the streets with heavy bags.

Adam spoke about some of the old lady's reticence to talk about the great storm, and the class all agreed that no one should be forced to speak about things they didn't want to, but sometimes it was good when people shared bad stories that worried them.

At the end of the lesson, it was decided that a core team of seven would be elected to carry the Great Storm Project forward. The four members of the Cornfield Cooperative all volunteered, along with six others. Mr. Farnfield announced that they would have a ballot, and asked everyone to write down the names of the ten candidates and then put a tick by the ones they favoured. He asked two other pupils to collect all the papers and then read out the names of winners. All the members of the Cornfield Cooperative were elected. The other winners were Sorrinder, Alphie and Ernie.

What began in the classroom spilled out across the community. In Sylvan Cluster the old ladies at Oak Gates did not forget Adam's visit.

Although they had not welcomed his questions at the time, they were inspired by the change in his grandmother. Grace Forester had become more enlivened, and started organising new activities at the retirement home. She began with music appreciation sessions, where they met in the lounge, shared their favourite recordings, and discussed them afterwards.

Alice found a long lost flute amongst her belongings, and played tunes that they all remembered from the days before the Great Storm. Then Maureen told them how she used to go circle dancing and demonstrated a few steps, and one by one they joined in.

They started devising dances to fit the music, beginning and ending them by holding hands in a circle. They didn't need partners and there was no embarrassment.

Soon there was a regular pattern of events at Oak Gates: dancing evenings, a weekly art session and storytelling afternoons. Barbara produced her paints, shared them, and everyone tried their hand at sketching or painting in oils or watercolours.

In Coppice Cluster, Gramps had started writing his life story. Family and friends were entertained with new extracts every week about his exploits as a young lad. The idea caught on with several of his older friends, who were forgetting how to use the computers, so Gramps gave them a helping hand. Eventually a small booklet emerged called "Tales of Aceton" in which ten very different life experiences were shared.

These innovations were admired in the weekly cluster discussions, and a ripple of interest and amusement ran right across the whole of Woodleigh.

*   *   *

"It's my turn to chair our cluster meeting tonight. Would you like to come along, this time?"

"Sure." Adam was not usually invited, but was glad his father had suggested this.

He felt it important to keep in touch with local developments.

Cluster meetings were held each week in the community hall. Each of the four cluster groups gathered on a different night to share information and resolve issues affecting the families. Tonight was a special night because it was a quarterly meeting when all four clusters were meeting together.

The community hall was an essential part of the cluster development, providing the community shop, workrooms and a comfortable lounge, equipped with television and facilities for phoning and viewing. Most cluster families elected not to have these facilities in their own homes as they were considered to be such time wasters. Sharing them was also a good way to cut down on carbon emissions.

The community hall was a long building, which had been constructed with its back wall dug into a hill to take full advantage of the warmth of the earth. It also enjoyed the heat of the sun, as the front of the building was built of re-enforced glass. The community shop and workrooms were on the ground floor, but the entrance to the community hall was via a sloping ramp built beside it, that led to a high walkway along the length of the building on the upper level. They passed the entrance to the coffee shop, which was closed in the evening, and entered the main hall through the glass door in the centre of the building. The hall had long curtains, which could be drawn over the windows in the evening, but to offset any extravagant use of electricity, eco-superior glass had been fitted to these large windows, which stored solar energy in the daytime. This energy was used for community purposes.

There was a buzz of conversation, and the noise level increased when Elsa Whiteoak came in the room, with Mark and Beatrice. Elsa's charismatic personality was conveyed wherever she went. It was certainly not contrived. At heart, she was modest and gentle woman, but this was mixed with a clumsiness caused by her desire to do the right thing in an English culture, to which she had never totally adapted.

Instead of opening the event in the usual way with a welcome to everyone in the circle, Peter asked Brenda to start by playing some quiet music. She unwrapped a small harp, held it under her left arm and gently plucked the strings. A gentle old melody kept them spellbound. After five minutes there was a shared silence. Then Peter looked slowly round the ring of neighbours, and asked who would like to speak first. This was the opportunity to agree the topics for tonight's discussion.

Gramps started by thanking Brenda for setting such a serene atmosphere. "While I was sitting still with you all, Brenda's playing helped me realise how rich life is in Coppice Cluster. There are twenty-five families living here in each cluster, one hundred in total, growing most of our food and sharing transport. I love the way that aim we get up early soon after sunrise and in the summer we take our rest soon after sunset. It sets a natural rhythm to our lives. Sometimes we have disputes, but we can sort them out in the circle, and it's the same in every cluster. What a contrast to what it was like in the bad old days, when we scarcely knew the family next door; then people used to each charge off in different directions in their own cars to work miles away. We were always in a hurry because we had to collect children from school in our cars, for fear of them being run over because there was so much traffic on the road. I'm glad we've all slowed down. Thank you, Brenda, for enhancing the quiet atmosphere."

"You're right there," said Martin. "But there aren't many places like this. Most of the country still hasn't wakened up. That's why we have all these people coming here from all over Britannia to see how we manage to do things in Woodleigh."

Two minor issues were raised and after some discussion resolved. Then Peter observed, "Well, as it happens, it's convenient that no one's brought other matters to discuss. My agenda can be postponed until next week, because tonight I want to introduce Councillor Heathershaw." He turned to the lady sitting next to him, who was unknown to many of those present. "She's recently come to live in Skylarks Cluster and is keen to meet representatives from all the cluster meetings to tell them about the visitors who are coming to Woodleigh in the next few months. Over to you, Jill."

"Thank you for inviting me. I have some news for you." The visitor smiled at the ring of faces in the circle - parents, grandparents, partners and singles, and a sprinkling of older schoolchildren. Councillor Heathershaw was a woman in her thirties with long blonde hair, and a winning presence.

"As you know the Woodleigh clusters have became quite famous across the country. Between us all, we are pointing to a new way of living and a lot of other areas are expressing interest in exchange visits. Borough counsellors are meeting their groups to discuss this to see how many visits we can organise. Last year you were twinned with Hastings. How did you feel that went?"

"Very well," a lady on the front row said. "We were happy to host the Bramwell family and we enjoyed the return visit to their farm. I think they picked up quite a lot of useful tips, and so did Philip and I."

"Meeting the grockles round there was quite an experience," joked Frick, her twelve- year-old son, who got a scowl from his mother.

There was an awed hush.

"What are grockles?" asked eight-year-old Jamie.

"Oh, it's a term loosely used round here for people who don't understand our ways.

No hopers," said Frick.

"Well, there must be some who do, or they wouldn't have opted in." Councillor Heathershaw was firm. "That's why I voted to include them this year."

"Good for you," said Peter. "Perhaps we'll have one of the families to stay in our house. What do you say, Fran?"

"Err - perhaps, but we'll have to study their profiles carefully." His wife did not look pleased.

"Well actually, you need not worry," the councillor continued. They are going to stay in the East Clusters, not the West Clusters. I've brought the profiles of your families with me. But the big news is that this year we are being twinned with an inland town, Tamcaster in Mercia Province. It's the capital of Mercia actually, so it's a big city. We are quite privileged. Usually we are twinned with towns of a similar size, but apparently the people of Tamcaster were very interested to learn more about the cluster system, and that's why we've been selected. These are the profiles of the two families who are coming to West Clusters." She handed some typed sheets of paper over to Peter.

"How many cluster towns are there now?" asked Frick.

"Around a hundred at the latest count," Peter told him. "It's growing all the time. The largest clusters are on the east coast from the Humber right down to the outskirts of London. That's where the sea is doing the most encroachment, but there are several in London boroughs, others up north and here in the south-west. We had a head-start around here with Totnes Transition Town being the first in the country."

"The real grockle territory is in the north," said Frick.

"I don't think we should talk like that, Frick," said Peter. "You can't make such sweeping statements. It's neither kind nor true."

"There are some very good cluster towns in Yorkshire," said Caroline.

"I don't like the term 'grockles' at all," said Mrs Heathershaw. "It's slang really, but it's widely used and I don't think there's an alternative."

"Perhaps we should call them 'beginners'," observed Peter. "We all have to begin sometime." Turning to the councillor, he asked "How many families wanted to visit Woodleigh this year?"

"Twenty. It was only ten last year, so it's catching on. We've twelve wards in Woodleigh, and eight cluster groups, four here and four on the east. We know that the west groups are always happy to arrange a link, and our visitors always ask about the cluster groups, so it should not be difficult to organise. Take your time. I won't hurry you in making your decision. Sometimes I wonder if we should organise visits to the clusters from some of the other wards in Woodleigh because some of our own residents still have so much to learn."

Most people smiled or laughed at this.

"No I'm serious. I wouldn't ask you to take these people as boarders. They could come on a day basis, but you could teach them so much."

"Yes, we could. We know all about that at school." Frick had interrupted again. His mother frowned at him, but he carried on talking. "Those from the posh, gated communities have no idea about real life. They've got T.V's and play stations in their bedrooms and all the latest clothes to wear. We call them the 'selfies' and they call us 'cluster kids' and say we live in a bygone age."

"That's one thing I'm very concerned about. We don't want to develop two different cultures in one town," Councillor Heathershaw affirmed. "Anyway, that's something for the future. Today, I'll leave these profiles with you, Peter, and you can return them to the Town Hall with your offers. When we have all the bids in, we'll do an allocation, and be as fair as possible. We want everyone to have a good experience, and it helps if the families coming and their hosts have interests in common. If you need to ask any more questions, call in to see me at No. 7, Skylark Cluster."

After she had left, the discussion continued for another hour. Four families asked to see the profiles, and three of them said that they would be willing to host. A coin was tossed, and it was announced that those doing the hosting this year would be Mark and Elsa Whiteoak and Peter and Frances Samphire.

As they walked back home, Adam asked his Dad where most of the clusters were in Britannia and Peter promised to show him on a map.

Peter's map of Britannia was in the filing cabinet in his study and Adam looked at it with interest. His father had marked the cluster towns in red, and they were widely scattered, but many were on the coast. Large tracts of land were shaded black and Peter explained that these were fracking areas, where drilling had taken place to unleash shale gas supplies. Around a hundred towns had a large T beside them.

"They are the transition towns," Peter said. "It means that they are aiming to be sustainable. They hope to be carbon neutral within the next twenty years."

Adam looked with interest at Tamcaster. It was situated right in the middle of England, just below the Peak District, and the great curve of the river Lent ran through it, working its way north east towards the Humber estuary.

"Are there cluster groups like ours in many other countries?" asked Adam.

"Yes, many of them," Peter told him. "I've got a list of around fifty overseas groups. This is an international thing, and there are some exchanges with them too."

When they were in the bedroom that evening, Frances took the opportunity to speak her mind.

"What on earth were you thinking about telling everyone that we might host a grockle family here?"

Peter took off his glasses and put them by the bedside. He smiled in his jocular way.

"I was just trying to be helpful," he said. "After all, they're the ones who most need assistance."

"Don't you think you should consult me before you come out with things like that in front of all the cluster groups?"

"Well we aren't going to have one, are we? They're go to East Clusters."

"What if they don't want the grockles. Now Jill Heathershaw will assume they can come here."

"No. She won't do anything of the sort. We've agreed to have that Langland couple. She knows it has to be a joint decision, and you made your feelings clear."

"I had to, didn't I? You put me in a embarrassing situation. Sometimes, Peter, You can be very thoughtless. You're so keen on being the cluster organiser that you confer with everyone except me."

Frances reached out for her bedside book, and Peter thought it best to say no more, tonight.

She's in her neat and tidy librarian frame of mind. It'll be over this in the morning, he told himself. *But I must watch my step. I suppose I did speak too quickly. Sometimes I get a bit carried away. Perhaps I should be more slow and steady like Mark Whiteoak.*

*   *   *

In early December the school pupils presented their posters about Woodleigh and Aceton in former times. Beatrice had gone to the library and sought out an old map of Aceton, and neatly redrawn this. It showed a long promenade enclosing Mussel Bay towards the cliffs at the point by Benbow Bay. Behind the promenade were several streets of houses, a square, near which an old community hall stood, with a park beside it. Gardens were also on the seafront near to a clock tower. These features created a great deal of interest amongst the pupils.

Mr Farnfield looked through all the posters, and suggested one or two changes, after which they were displayed around the classroom. Adam had produced a montage of photographs, loaned by his grandmother, featuring her home and the family. Carry had found photographs of the big supermarket, which had been swept way in the Big Storm.

Brook had painted a scene from an old postcard, which showed the clock tower and some of the gardens. Other drawings showed children playing on the beach, a fairground on the recreation park, an ice-cream stall on the promenade, and drawings of people climbing steps beside the cliffs at the east end.

The display provided a lot of interest for the school pupils, who were all invited to look at it.

"I think you've done a first class job," Mr Farnfield told them. "At the end of next term, I'll want to see the evidence about what might have caused the Great Storm, and its effects on the town. It will take some time to sift through all the material and decide about the best way to present it to the whole school, so the headmistress has suggested we do those presentations at the end of the summer term. This will allow time for you to polish them, and also for you to tackle the third project on your visions about what things may be like forty years ahead. What sort of world will there be in 2095?"

CHAPTER 4 - Questions and Answers

Matthew Farnfield was a little apprehensive as he cycled to the secondary school this morning. He did not normally feel like this, as he enjoyed teaching and was usually comfortable with all his pupils. His thoughts were running on as he turned a bend and checked ahead.

Those two odd lads, Alfred and Ernest, don't put me at ease. It's so much simpler to deal with the cluster kids. Beatrice is a really promising student. That remark she made about not interrupting and letting everyone have their say for example. She was right. Enthusiasm sometimes gets the better of me. I sometimes do the very thing that I dislike in others. I must be on my toes. But, not to worry, it's only the small steering group that I'm dealing with this afternoon – not the whole form, and I have plans all ready.

They met at the cycle shed, as arranged. "I'm glad you all remembered to come on your bikes," he said. "I didn't tell you where we were going, but as you're the elected leaders for the project group, I thought we might go to have a look at some interesting evidence. Have you any ideas where we might be heading?"

No one volunteered an answer.

"Well," he said. "You all got quite a lot of interesting information from the old folk, but you haven't really probed into the heart of the matter. Why was that storm so devastating? We're going to find some answers to that question today in the Woodleigh public library. They have some interesting old records there that I want you to see. You've all brought notebooks and pencils, haven't you? Good, I'm glad you remembered. I said pencils because library staff don't like pens and biros. They can leave ugly marks. Follow me." With that he spun off towards the school gate, and the others were quick to follow.

They took the cycle track along the road towards Woodleigh town centre. A driver-less bus rumbled past them on its way to Exeter, and they passed several other cyclists with shopping bags on their bikes and three older people on trikes. As they went by one of the housing estates they passed a horse-drawn delivery cart. *Good to see horse-power being made use of again*, thought Matthew, as they turned left into the town centre. The pavement was busy with pedestrians here.

Five civic buildings dominated the heart of Woodleigh: the town hall, which contained the community theatre as well as the administrative offices, the higher education academy, the hospital, the sports centre and the library. All these buildings faced a green sward and behind them were glimpses of a grove of silver birch trees. This was both a busy place and a quiet ordered one.

Leaving their bikes in the cycle park, they went through a revolving door into the library, where a spectacled member of staff was waiting for them. She smiled as they approached and led them upstairs to the reference library. Pausing on the landing, she introduced herself as Frances Samphire, the Information Librarian.

Adam said nothing to indicate that it was his mother, and neither did she. Beatrice was the only other person who knew and, as they seemed to prefer to be quiet about it, she was too, although it seemed a bit odd to her.

"Mr Farnfield tells me that you are doing a project on the Aceton Disaster.

We have a lot of resources here that you might want to look at and I have arranged some of them on the central table," she explained, "There are old copies of the Aceton Journal, which date back as far as the year 2,000. If you want to see earlier papers, you'll need to go to the Central Library in Exeter. I've sorted out some of the Woodleigh Town Hall documents for you – the council minutes around the time of the storm, some official reports, and also some articles published by scientists who believed that human behaviour could have affected weather patterns at the time. Some of these are rather long and quite heavy reading, so I've highlighted references to Aceton by putting some cardboard arrows on the relevant lines. I'll be sitting at the desk by the door, and if you have any questions please come over to have a word. It's possible to photocopy some of the material. See me, if you want to do that."

Matthew Farnfield thanked her, and held the door as they filed into the reference room. They gathered round the central table, which was broad and circular.

"There are three sorts of documents here." He spoke quietly. "There are seven of you, so I suggest you split up, one group looking at newspapers, another one reading some of the town hall reports and the others at the articles with the arrows on. We've got an hour, so there should be time to swap over, later."

Alfie, who had already decided to be the editor of the newspaper project, told everyone, "We'll deal with the papers." He seized Ernie and steered him in that direction.

Beatrice looked with interest at the arrows on the long articles and Brook was caught by one of the titles there, "Why have all the birds flown?" So they both sat down to study them.

Carry, Adam and Sorinder took their time to look around and then turned to the town council records. The minutes of the council meetings did not seem very interesting, although they found the subject index helpful. There were also some official reports. Carry started to read "Recommendations for Coastal Protection." Adam found himself studying a later document "The Report of Enquiry into the Great Storm Disaster." Sorinder settled for "Comments by Residents on the survey carried out, one year later."

Matthew Farnfield watched them with interest from the other side of the room.

Notebooks and pencils had been pulled out of pockets and they seemed absorbed in the information. His plan was working.

Alfie was a bit disappointed with the trivia in the newspapers, but then Ernie found an index of topics for the main news items. Each story was given a reference number. Alfie marched over with it to the information desk and soon he and Mrs Samphire were getting big files of old newspapers down from the shelves and thumbing through them for news about the Big Storm. Ernie started taking notes about a protest meeting held about the building of a supermarket beside the river estuary on land that was thought to be a floodplain.

Beatrice found herself reading about how the environment was damaged by the loss of trees and grassland when big construction projects were undertaken. At that time there had been many local campaigns against such development schemes, and heated arguments about the merits and demerits of fracking.

Brook was deeply absorbed in a wildlife article, which explained how whole species of birds and insects were disappearing from the ecosystem. In the early years of the 21st century, a call to stop this drift had been made on television by leading thinkers of the day including Prince Charles and David Attenborough. Both of them had expressed concern that the Arctic icecap was melting. This was clearly shown in photographs. Obviously, the sea levels would rise and islands would be imperilled. Why hadn't people listened?

Carry and Adam were concerned to read that there had been many early warnings about coastal erosion in the area. The National Trust had published a proposal about the protection crumbling cliffs, with maps indicating some danger areas, where the sea was likely to encroach, but still the warnings were not heeded. Why was this?

Sorinder was moved by accounts of personal tragedies revealed in the survey carried out in the following year. These would make interesting reading for the newspaper. She took notes of names, facts and reference numbers, so that these items could be easily found later and written up by the school reporters.

* * *

When Beatrice arrived back home later that afternoon, her mother greeted her joyfully.

"Hey, kid, we've got a wonderful letter from Rory. He's coming home soon!"

When Elsa was excited her eyes sparkled and her American language and accent became more pronounced. "Just you just read this. It will knock you for six."

Rory was Beatrice's elder brother, doing voluntary service with the European Peace Corps and now stationed in Italy. His letters were always written at great speed with huge enthusiasm.

"*Hi, Mom Dad, Beatrice and Max,*" it began, "*I have great news for you all. I'll be with you in two months!! Will have completed my two-year tour.*

I told you I had another three months to do. I thought I had, but when I saw my commander last week, he said that the month I spent on the refugee project in Africa counted. I didn't think it did. It was my own choice to go. I volunteered to spend my leave-time there, because of the urgent need for helpers after those terrible floods. What an experience! I was whacked, I tell you. The big man said it must have been gruelling for me. No holiday and it was my leave time. Anyway, they counted that in because I was given a good report, and brought credit to the Peace Corps, so he said. Tra la tra la. Shouldn't blow my own trumpet. Have to. No one else will!! That's not true. He did! My boss. Anyway, I'll be home four weeks earlier than you thought, or I thought, or anyone thought! Can't wait.
I've got so much to tell you all. Great News! Honest, big surprise but I'll save it till I can see your faces, all of you – Dad, Mom, Max, - oh and Bea too of course. I'll be exhausted – coming by train from Pisa, through Germany and Belgium - sailing from Ostend to Dover - trains to London and Exeter and then a bus from Exeter to Woodleigh. Should make it for the evening meal one of these fine days. If I'm late put it in the oven and keep it warm, Mom! Whatever it is. I'll be hungry as an elephant - watch me. No, perhaps you'd better not. Never was a dainty eater. Love to

everyone, including all those neighbours in Coppice Cluster who keep asking after me.

Your doting son,   Rory

P. S. Thanks for darning those socks, Mom. It'll be a long walk from Pisa, if there's a train strike, or if landslides in the Dolomites block the track, like they did last week.

"Home in June. Great News, isn't it Max? Rory's coming home."

Max cocked his ear at the name and ran out to scratch at the front door, tail wagging wildly.

"Not today, in two months, Max. He's got two months to do and then he's got be here not in Italy."

Max looked disgruntled.

"Sorry, later Max."

Max went back to his basket grumpily, tail drooping. He shut one eye and pretended to sleep, but kept the other eye open, just in case.

* * *

Mark Whiteoak was a loving father, but unlike his energetic and voluble wife, he had a quiet disposition. Beatrice had to choose the right moment to sound him out.

Sometimes they both went for long walks together with Max, and this was always a good opportunity, but, as manager of the community store, he was extra busy doing the annual report, so Beatrice had to take Max out on his own this Sunday morning. Elsa was visiting a friend in hospital, so she had to dash off immediately after lunch to catch a bus. This left the two of them together.

"I'd like your opinion on one or two things, it's connected with a project we're doing at school."

They were clearing the dining room table and taking things through to the kitchen.

Mark took off his glasses, rolled up his sleeves, and said, "Fire away."

"Well first, I know you and Mom set up the community farm shop. How did that get started?"

"Through Gramps' farm. I loved helping him there as a boy. I was very fond of the animals, and of the open-air life. I used to think I'd take it over when he retired, but there was one thing that troubled me. I got very fond of the animals and I hated seeing them sent for slaughter. We had an old-fashioned mixed farm and it was becoming uneconomic because supermarkets were dominating everything, and encouraging bigger specialisation. They wanted crops sprayed with chemical fertilisers and pesticides, and we used the old organic system. My parents were both very upset by these changes but they carried on with what they believed in. When I left school I started up a farm shop in one of the old barns. I developed some organic milk. It was made from oats, mixed with water and sea salt. It became very popular, especially with people who are allergic to cow's milk. Your mother was one of my best customers. When the clusters were built, a few years later, we had just got married and we opened up the community store together."

"Why is it that some people in Woodleigh live in cluster groups and others don't?"

It was a very simple question. Beatrice was not sure how the decision had been made.

"Did they have a choice?"

Mark was washing up after the Saturday lunch. "Yes, of course they did." He put a plate on the drying rack, and Beatrice started to wipe it dry.

"There was a lot of discussion about these things after the Big Storm. There had to be a big building programme, because those who'd lost their homes were all in temporary accommodation - caravans mainly. Most people blamed the council for not preparing and warning them better. A man came here from the Environment Department and held a Town Consultation - that's what they called it. The government was very worried because similar things were happening in other coastal areas. They had a sustainable housing fund, based on a circular economy, and Woodleigh applied for a slice of the money."

"What's a circular economy?"

"One that cuts down on waste. The aim is to get everything recycled. Some of us like your mother and me were very keen to have a sustainable home and asked to be put on the list. We saw it as a good way to start our married lives together, in a friendly community with people that had similar ideas. We were so keen that we were prepared to wait, but a lot of others wanted to be housed quickly so they opted for the ordinary homes."

"Why did it take longer to build the cluster housing?"

"Because there was a lot to sort out. The conventional houses were done to a standard pattern, but the cluster housing was done in consultation with the local teams that were formed. A lot of time was spent discussing things. Some of the clusters, like this one, were completely new-build, but others like Sylvan, were adapted from existing streets. Several people, like Peter Samphire, were members of Transition Woodleigh. He wanted the road to be closed to traffic and converted into a common plot. The difficulty was that two or three people wanted to keep their cars and didn't agree with car-pooling. As the majority did, they were outvoted and they had to move into traditional homes nearby. You can imagine the delays all that caused."

"Didn't they realise there's no future in traditional homes? They're very expensive to run and are a huge drain on natural energy sources."

"They didn't see it like that. People had always owned their cars. Big ones were a status symbol. That's the way they were marketed."

"But surely people could see through all that, with all the congestion, and deaths and injuries on the roads."

"They didn't. In the bad old days, there was such a thing as subliminal advertising, which manipulated people's thinking."

"But it's so much more efficient to have a fleet of pool cars, kept in a garage, just off the motorway, that you all have a share in."

"It's another way of living, and people didn't like change. We had to fight to get things done properly. The clusters aim to be carbon neutral. Generating enough energy through the solar panels, wind turbines and biomass heating for the whole group, and the rain harvesting, means that we only need a small water supply. Community work helps too, because under the old system there weren't enough jobs to go round. In the bad old days, there was a very high rate of unemployment. Some families got used to this and never gained the skills needed. They became a sort of underclass. This simply doesn't happen under the cluster system, and the community work is so localised that we all get to know one another in the neighbourhood. There's so much less crime in areas like this."

"It all seems so obvious to me that this is a better way of living. How could so many people be so unaware. They must have known about the crime rate, the road accidents and the damage that they were doing to the climate and the natural world."

"They never thought it through. They grew up in a cocoon of television soaps and commercial advertising. In those days, most people were following fashion and admiring the lives of popular celebrities. It was just a minority who recognised that lives were being shaped by the big multinationals. These organisations were so powerful fifty years ago that people were losing the capacity to think for themselves. Every time people switched on their TV's and computers they were bombarded with subliminal advertising. It still goes on in some places like the gated areas, but we turned our backs on it all. That's why we don't have TV in our homes, we don't all carry mobile phones and we ration computer time in the cluster groups. It was our choice. We opted to do this and we were prepared to wait for the housing we wanted."

"Was that very frustrating when you saw other people getting housed before you?"

"We weren't homeless or stuck in a caravan. I was living with my parents over on Blackberry Hill, as you know. When I met your mother, who came here on a teaching job, we fell for each other because we had the same ideas. Your grandmother had died so, after we married, Elsa and I carried on living with Gramps. We were given the big bedroom and your grandpa moved into my old room. It wasn't ideal for any of us, but it worked until the cluster house was available."

"Thanks, Dad. That's helpful for my project. It explains a lot. Most of the folks in school still live in conventional homes. We call them 'selfies' because they think so much of themselves with all their fashionable hairstyles and modern gadgets, but I'm glad I'm a 'cluster kid'. It makes life so worthwhile." Beatrice hung the tea towel on the rail on the oven door, and belted back to her room to make notes about what she had just heard.

Mark watched her running upstairs with all the energy of a fifteen-year-old.

He pulled out the plug, and watched the water in the sink go down into the storage tank below the draining boards. He found himself thinking that it was rainwater really piped into the kitchen from the water buts in the garden, and it hadn't finished its use because now it was being piped into the toilet tank. "That's the circular economy in a net-shell". He realised he'd said those words aloud.

Suddenly, unexpectedly as always, he was eclipsed in one of his unaccountable dark moods. He never knew when or why they hit him so hard. They usually lasted for about an hour or two, but there was no telling when they would lift.

Mark walked into the lounge, where the afternoon sun was flooding the room, but this did not help because some bright jagged waves of light nearly blinded him. He sat down on the sofa, and closed his eyes. He could still see the jagged lines, but they were not so overpowering. Why were these depressive attacks hitting him like this? He had enjoyed his chat with Beatrice. She was such a bright, loving child. Why had the dark cloud hit him now?

Why do I get these attacks? Am I afraid for the future? Most other people I know share these fears, but they don't suffer like this. How does Peter Samphire manage to keep that ebullient smile? And Elsa...she doesn't give way. She's so lively... always has been. That's what I love in her. She does most of the talking when we're in company. It's her endless American energy. Her Dad was like that too. He could be overpowering. But it was her carefree spirit that first attracted me... It still does, thank God... What did she see in me?...tongue-tied on the first date. But she quietly came to the rescue... simply took my hand and held it tightly. I hope I don't get any of these attacks when we're on the exchange visit this summer.

Gradually, the mood lifted and later in the afternoon, Mark went to work on the common plot, alongside Elsa.

It's being in the open air and doing practical tasks that keep me grounded. It's a healing experience, Mark told himself. *And, of course, the other reason that many people don't want to live in a cluster is that they don't want to job-share, go on half salary and spend the rest the week doing community tasks. That's the big shift that many people can't or won't make, but it suits me...I love it."*

CHAPTER 5 - Tamcaster

Bruce Langland sat on the terrace behind his house and looked down at the Breckfield Cooperative, laid out before him, with great satisfaction.

Twenty gardens have now been added to my scheme; only two still have their own hedge and fence. Everyone else has now joined in. It makes things feel good at last. It's was a battle over the last ten years, but now, the whole plan is virtually complete. All the householders on this side of the Crescent and those in Cowper Road have now enrolled. So have the people at the bottom of the hill, and the only access, except through the private driveways by the properties, is through the little lane that leads to the padlocked gate.

All the shareholders have their own keys, and this allotment is now feeding every family with vegetables and fruit. If the other two don't want to cooperate, that's their loss. It's quite an achievement to have pulled this off. When I moved to the top Breck Hill, this was one of my dreams. The other one was to marry Gwen. That was much easier than persuading Trevor next door to take down his fence and share an enlarged garden. That took four years of gentle hints. Then, one by one, several other neighbours joined, and eventually we set up our small business.

It was hard going leafleting all the neighbours. Only two showed any interest at first but, slowly they came round as they realised how this would reduce the cost of their food. There was no more work in growing vegetables than there had been in planting and maintaining a garden, and the flowering shrubs and trees give it a similar visual attraction. All the children have a large grassed area to play in, and most families have kept a patio near their house. The fruit orchard makes a central feature, with the vegetable beds surrounding it. The greenhouse is filled with thriving tomatoes, the hen house, with its fenced run and the pig-sty, add constant activity, and the small wild flower meadow and poly-tunnel give colour. At last, we now have a registered cooperative, and Gwen and I have just been registered as company secretaries!

Bruce was wakened from his contented reverie when Gwen called him through the kitchen hatch.

"Bruce, a drone letter's arrived for you from Wessex."

He got up, walked through the French windows and collected the letter through the serving hatch. He looked at the postmark. Yes, and it was from Woodleigh.

"Just what I've been waiting for" He'd always been interested in those cluster groups he'd read about it Woodleigh. His letter was from the town hall there, and signed by the town clerk. It said that his application for an exchange visit this summer by four families from Woodleigh, had been accepted. There were two sets of dates, the first for the Woodleigh families to come to Tamcaster and the second for the Tamcaster families to go to Woodleigh. He was asked to confirm the dates with a Mr. Peter Samphire, at 14, Sylvan Cluster, Woodleigh, Devon, Province of Wessex DEX 3DT. Tel: 01395 851732.

"Hi, read this Gwen," he called, and when he heard no reply, but just the clatter of crockery, he put his head through the serving hatch.

"It's on, Gwen, the exchange," he said. "The dates we suggested as well. There are three people coming here called Samphire, funny name. Married couple and a lad, and we're invited to stay with them afterwards in one of those cluster houses. I think I'll ring them. I've got the phone number."

"Fine," said Gwen, "but leave it till after breakfast. I've just done the toast."

Bruce carried a tray out on to the patio. It was a lovely, bright day. Gwen followed him.

"Best to speak on the 'phone. There are four families down there of course. Two in the clusters and two elsewhere in the town, but I've only got the details of the local organiser at this stage, and I'll have to liaise with the other three families here."

"I'm glad we're going to the seaside," said Gwen. "We must take the swimming things. I've never been to Wessex. They've some wonderful beaches, cliffs and coves down there."

"And some famous storms," added Bruce, tucking into his cereals. Half an hour later, he was on the phone.

"Hi there, is that Peter? My name's Bruce Langland. I'm in Tamcaster, and I've just got a letter to say that you and your family are coming to stay with us in July, and we're coming to you in August. It's a twinning arrangement with four families, isn't it?"

"Yes," said the voice at the other end. "That's right. I've got a copy of the letter here too. The local councillor brought it round last night. I believe your wife Genevieve is coming with you isn't she?"

"That's right. She likes to be called Gwen, and she's bringing her swimming costume. She loves swimming. How's the sea behaving these days at Woodleigh?"

"Oh, pretty well really. We're getting long hot summers now...what we used to call a Mediterranean climate. We can get quite short of water, but we make up for that in the winter. It sometimes pours down for days on end, so we have quite a big water catchment scheme. It's one of the things you'll want to look at."

"Yes and we're looking forward to seeing your allotment scheme."

"What about the other family involved in the hosting?"

"We've quite a mixed bag. There's a gorgeous family of Afro-Caribbean descent who are good friends of ours. They're going to host the Whiteoak family. They have two lovely young daughters, and then there are two families on a big learning curve. They live in one of our rougher neighbourhoods, but they're making huge strides to help improve things there, so we thought that this was an opportunity they shouldn't miss. They're hosting the team from the other side of Woodleigh though."

"Councillor Heathershaw showed us some profiles, so we understand the situation, and I think the council have placed them carefully with good people. They're on the east side of Woodleigh, in a neighbourhood that has overcome difficulties with some problem families. There's a first class mentoring programme there, and some experimental youth counselling going on. I'm not really the person you need to talk to about that though, I'm a climate change fanatic and I'm not into social engineering."

"Neither am I, but Tamcaster is into all sorts of things. We're a canny lot up here."

"Good for you. The other host family in the Clusters, is Mark and Elsa Whiteoak. They're good friends of ours and they've two youngsters – a schoolgirl called Beatrice, and a 22-year-old called Rory. He's abroad somewhere with the Peace Corps now, but he's expected home in time to join them."

" Well, we're looking forward to meeting you all. Hope the lad in the Peace Corps can come to. He'll add a useful dimension."

"I agree. He's a great guy. Full of bounce and energy, or he was last time I saw him, just before this overseas assignment."

"We can talk in more detail later. Gwen and I are due at a community centre in about half an hour. We'll be in touch again soon."

"Sure. Thanks for ringing. Bye then."

Bruce turned to Gwen, "He sounds a decent sort."

"Just as well, since we're moving in together," said Gwen. "I'll speak to the other half later."

Ten minutes afterwards, Bruce and Gwen were making their way towards the centre of the city. They both wore blue safety helmets, as they jostled alongside double-decker electric trams, cars and delivery vehicles. Bruce was on a bike and Gwen on her electric scooter. They were both in their mid-thirties, of lean, athletic build and cheerful countenance. They went down a long shopping street, over a hill, and past some tall Victorian homes. They turned right by the traffic lights before a roundabout, into a leafy lane with brick terraced houses on one side and playing fields on the other. This was an area that had once belonged to affluent people, but now the properties looked shabby, and were clearly divided into small flats and bed-sits.

Bruce and Gwen got off the road outside a rather dismal church hall, where they parked their vehicles, but once through the doors, there was a hive of vibrant activity. A large room was filled with young mothers and excited toddlers; big bouncing Caribbean kids jumping on trampolines, brown Asian girls with sleek black hair, identifying animals in picture books, and a tangle of white and yellow arms and legs scrambling with toys on a red carpet in a fenced area entered through a neat little gate.

Gwen went over to speak to the big-breasted Caribbean lady who was in charge today. After signing her name in the attendance register, walked through the gate and squatted on the floor with the toddlers, all of whom she knew by name. One of the mums was on the floor too, with several kids, who were working at a big jig-saw puzzle. Others were watching, as they perched on stools by the coffee bar and chatted over drinks.

Bruce signed in too, and took over from the Thai girl who had been helping behind the bar. His task this morning was to serve the drinks and answer the telephone enquiries. The two jobs were ill matched, but this could not be helped because they were short-handed today. Usually he was based in the office, where phone calls could be confidential. People rang about a whole range of situations, and it was not good practice to have to use the phone in the noisy hall. If some one phoned about a really tricky issue, he would have to switch the call to the office phone, move over there and ask Gwen to do the drinks, but although they were both busy all morning, that did not prove necessary.

As they were tidying up at 12.30, the telephone rang again.

"Hi, Bruce," said a cheery voice, "Thought I'd catch you there. Ranjit Singh here. You're a wanted man. Mrs. Paynter asked me to call you."

"Do you mean the Deputy Mayor?"

"No less. She asks if you could look in the City Hall this afternoon."

"I'm teaching an adult group this afternoon at Shakespeare St. It finishes at 3.30. Would 4 o'clock suit her. Do you know what it's about, Ranjit?"

"Four o'clock it is. I think I know, but it's best for her to explain."

Odd, thought Bruce, as he replaced the phone.

The City Hall was an imposing building built in the classical style, with two bored looking stone lions squatting on either side of five stone steps. Bruce up-ended his bicycle and carried it up the steps, and struggled through the revolving doors with some difficulty, because his bike projected and hindered the rotation.

"Careful with that one, man," called a voice from inside.

Bruce negotiated the doors, to find the dark skinned cloakroom attendant laughing at him on the other side.

"Thanks. Can you mind this, please? "Bruce asked. "I've got an appointment with one of the councillors."
"I'm not equipped to stack cycles. Why don't you ride your bike along the corridors?" laughed Les.

Bruce looked at the blue carpeted curving stairway. "I can't ride up that, can I, mate? Mrs. Paynter wants to see me."

"We have a lift."

"I prefer to leave it your safe custody," Bruce laughed. "I don't want to dirty the mayoral carpets."

"O.K, I'll issue you with a cloakroom ticket and hang it by the spokes on the peg," said the porter, with a wink.

Good humouredly, he wheeled the bike behind the counter and hung a cloakroom ticket round the handlebars.

Bruce climbed the imposing stairway towards the first floor, walked along the corridor towards the mayoral suite, and knocked on the deputy mayor's door.

Councillor Paynter was a sturdy woman with a matronly air. She broke into a bright smile when she saw who it was.

"Ah, Bruce, thank you; just the man to help me. At least, I hope so."

"Well, I trust I can be of service. It depends on the request, Mrs. Paynter?"

"Now, that's not a good start, Bruce. I'm still Jenny, even if I am deputy mayor now. Do I usually ask for the impossible, Councillor Langland? Oh, sit down please. I need your help. Well now, I'm going to be lord mayor here in two month's time, and, as you know, the tradition is to have a lord mayor's chaplain and a civic service in the cathedral. Well, I'm not an Anglican, and I don't think I can be described as a Christian, since I don't attend any church. I find it very difficult to believe in a loving God with the world in so much turmoil. This is a multi-racial city, as you well know, and we have many different faiths here, all with their own places of worship, so what I would like to do, if it's possible, is to have a multi-faith chaplaincy, and I think you are the most suitable person to consult on this."

"Why think of me? Why not the bishop?"

"The bishop's a Christian, you dolt! He'd probably say yes, but he'd dominate the whole thing and keep the other spiritual leaders in the background."

"Not necessarily…"

"Of course, he would. I know him. I can't go straight to the imam. I'm not a Muslim, either. So where do I start? You're the secretary of the inter faith group, aren't you?"

"Yes, I am, so I'll see what's possible. But first, there's a question I need to ask, Jenny. If you can't believe in a god in this wicked world, how can you believe in the power of all the faiths together? Interfaith isn't a marriage of non-believers, it's a union of believers who strive to find a central core running through the wisdom of the ages."

"That'll suit me, Bruce, I didn't say I could not believe in anything. I said I found it difficult to believe in a loving God when the world's in such turmoil. I want to believe, but I don't find it easy."

"If that's the case, we can go on a journey together," Bruce smiled. "It will be good for us both, and it'll be good for the city. This isn't going to be easy though. There are very strong memories of prayers in the cathedral for the Lord Mayor's service. It's steeped in tradition, and some people won't be comfortable."

"I'll deal with them."

"But if not the cathedral, where will the service be?"

"I've thought of that. I wondered about a community centre, but then, which one? Eventually, I decided it should be here in the City Hall, and we'll invite representatives from all our cultural community centres, but the service has got to be inclusive and intelligible to everyone. That's where I need your thoughts."

"It's a challenge I relish. But it would give offence if we invited the community centres and not the ethnic places of worship. We could have readings and prayers from many different traditions. The core could be symbolic of a community reaching out to divine love. I knew you'd find the words. But then there's the chaplaincy. It's not just a one-off service. I need spiritual support."

"You could have a small team of chaplains from different faiths, but I'll need to talk this through with the inter-faith council and get their approval."

"Of course. And then, there's the opening of full council meetings. We usually have prayers. I'd thought of a minute's silent reflection. The alternative would be to use different chaplains in rotation."

"I think I prefer the silence, but that's another thing for us to discuss. And during the year, do you plan to visit to different faith headquarters? That would be appreciated and it's never been done by mayors in Tamcaster."

"Great idea – a civic pilgrimage."

"We've a lot to teach you. And then there's the mayor's charity. It's often been Christian Aid?"

"Not this year. It will be Save the Children."

"Good. And then there are occasions when you might need spiritual counselling; times of national emergency, for example."

"I was hoping you'd be my spiritual counsellor."

"If you think I'm up to it. I do happen to be a Christian, you know – United Reformed Church."

"As long as you're not an Anglican or a Catholic, that's all right by me. I've not got anything against those churches. It's just the dogma – it doesn't suit me."

"I'll put all that to our council and come back to you. Is that O.K?"

"Of course. And if there are problems in the next few months, there's someone else who will carry the can – not just me." Jenny Paynter winked at him.

"You always were a quick thinker, Jenny. Do you have any faith at all? I know you have a big heart. I think, as your spiritual adviser, I'm entitled to ask."

"If you mean do I think that Jesus Christ was the creator of the universe, No. But I do believe that he lived, was a good man and an inspiration to us all. Does that answer your question?"

"No, not really. It'll have to do for a start. I can live with that for today, but during the year, we'll go on a journey, you and I."

"A spiritual pilgrimage, around the faiths. I mean to enjoy it."

There was a tap on the door. Ranjit Singh put his head round; "Excuse me, but just to let you know that your next interviewee has arrived, Councillor Paynter."

"Good. We've just sorted everything out, haven't we Bruce?"

"I don't think so, but we've made a good start." They shook hands with a firm grasp.

"I knew I could depend on you, Bruce."

"I'll do my best. I suppose I have twelve months to complete my mission."

"I won't end up as a member of the URC, but I might join the Inter Faith Movement, if you'll accept agnostics like me."

"I'll put that one to the inter-faith council too ...when you're ready."

As Bruce went out, he saw the bulky figure of Councillor Seagrave, slumped in the waiting chair. *You've a tough one there, Mrs. Paynter,* he thought.

CHAPTER 6 - Rory

Preparing their presentation was no easy task. Beatrice and Brook had each made copious notes from the records they had read and key issues they had heard about in videos viewed on the school computers. Matthew Farnfield had read their reports and commended them both.

"You've both learned a lot and set it out clearly here," he said. "Now you need to list all the key points in logical order and then write them into a continuous narrative, and it's most important to give credit to your sources, each time you quote them or choose to show a piece of film. Remember that your focus is on Aceton. Several of these articles are about the whole region. Only include the ones that affected the town here, Otherwise, you'll find you're trying to write a complete book and your presentation would take all night."

They did as they were advised and produced quite a long narrative. The next question was how were they going to put it over. Should they have two separate presentations, each focussing on what they had contributed to the whole.

"I don't think that's a good idea," said Brook. "It's more important to follow the ideas through logically. I suggest we have one long script and one of us read the first half, and the other the second. We could toss a coin to decide that."

"I think it would be better, if we alternated," Beatrice suggested. "We could use both the lecterns in the school hall for our papers, and we could both be there throughout, speaking for about five minutes each, and then handing over to the other one."

This was what they agreed to do, and Beatrice won the coin spin, and chose to open the event. They had a rehearsal in the school hall, which was well equipped with microphones and film projectors.

Beatrice started to read her script, but after two sentences, Brook stopped her.

"I can't hear you properly. You're speaking across the mike, not into it...Yes, that's much better. Yes, remember to glance up frequently from your notes and look at the audience. Lovely, yes. I like that," Brook advised.

They encouraged each other and slowly gained confidence. "Speak a bit more slowly...take a deep breath each time before you speak. I was given that advice in the school play." Beatrice called.

Mr. Farnfield came in to their second rehearsal, sitting at the back of the hall.

"It's really coming over well. Congratulations to you both. I'll be there to help with the equipment on the day, so you needn't have a last minute panic," he assured them. "Oh – another thing. I'm glad that you both look up quite regularly when you're speaking. That holds the interest. It might help if you looked at the hall clock at the back there though, over the heads of the audience. You'll know how you are doing for time, and it's not so distracting as catching someone's eye."

After that last rehearsal, they had both gained confidence, and felt a special warmth about working on the same project together.

* * *

One week later, Beatrice was doing some work in the kitchen when she heard a familiar cry from the garden "Cocker-doodle-doo".

Rory was pounding up the path, with his kit bag on his shoulder, his familiar red mop of hair, and sporting a new ginger beard.

Everyone ran to greet him, including Max who kept taking huge leaps up, trying to lick his face.

"Steady, Max," he cried. "You'll have me over. Mom, Dad, Bea, my you've grown. Hey you're a young woman, not a scruffy kid."

He gave everyone huge bear hugs and then collapsed into an easy chair.

Rory had grown too. He was three inches taller, had put on weight, but his eyes still sparkled with their usual glee.

"Did you have a good, journey?" asked his Dad.

"I've been travelling non stop for forty-eight hours and feel whacked, but it's magic to be here. I've got so much to tell you all – I just can't wait. I've some stunning news, but I'll save it till I'm fed. I'll tell you everything after dinner. This place is so peaceful, isn't it? I've flown across the world: Belgium, Germany, Italy and Africa but it's cool to be here, the gentlest town on the globe, I should think. You don't know how lucky you are to live here, honestly. I never appreciated it as much as I do now, because I can make comparisons."

"Do you want a drink, son?" Elsa asked. Her American voice returned with her excitement.

"Have you one of your home-pressed apple juices. I've dreamt about them."

Beatrice fetched the apple juice and Rory quaffed it down in four huge gulps. "I was parched. That's so refreshing. So clean, so good."

"It should be. It's straight from the community orchard."

"Am I in my old room?"

"Of course you are."

He stood up and shouldered the kit bag. "I'll dump this and have a shower. Civilisation - isn't it wonderful?"

Rory's poundings shook the stairs. Max bounded after him.

Both parents looked at each other. Elsa reached out and suddenly they were in each other's arms. "Hey, it's great to have him home again, But what are we going to do with that great hulk in the house?" asked Elsa.

"I've no idea," said Mark. "But he'll find something to absorb his energy. He always did."

"What's this stunning news? Can you guess?" asked Beatrice.

"I won't try," said Elsa.

Rory was plagued with questions over the meal that evening. He answered with vigour, in-between bites, talking about his duties with the Peace Corps and the wonderful experience of living with people from so many different countries.

It was only when the plates had been cleared away, and they were drinking some home-made elderberry wine that he dropped his bombshell.

"Well folks," he said "I've answered lots of questions about what I've been doing

and seeing while I've been away. Now, I've got something awesome to tell you."

He ran a hand through his tousled hair and grinned at them. He looked first at his Mom and then at his Dad, and broke into a huge grin. "I'm going to be married."

"Married?" His parents spoke in unison.

"Who to?" demanded Beatrice.

"No one anyone here knows," he smiled, "But she's the most wonderful girl in the world, and her name is Amina Adong."

"That's an odd name," said Elsa. "Where's she from?"

"The name's unique, like my fiancé. She comes from West Africa - Gambia - teaches art and music in a Peace School for Disabled Children in Hungary. I'm mad about her and you'll all love her too when you meet her. I know you will."

"Are we likely to see her soon?" Mom's voice trembled ever so slightly.

"Next week. She's coming over here to meet you. I fixed it. Well, perhaps it was a bit presumptuous on my part to do this before I told you, but wow, you can't put these things in letters. It's best to tell you straight. You'd never believe my luck, but she's got an aunt who lives in Exeter, and she's due for some leave, so we fixed it that she will stay there for three weeks. We'll probably have the wedding here too. She flying to Heathrow next Monday, and I'll be there to meet her. Do you think I can get a share of the cluster car, Dad, or is it best we use the train?"

"We'll see, Rory. I'm not sure - but how long have you known her?"

"A year, and we know one another very well now. We've been sharing a pad for the last three months. I should have told you both, I know, but well - these things happen."

"What things?" asked Elsa urgently.

"Falling in love. It changed the world for both of us."

"It usually does," said Mark. "I wish you well of course, but have you really thought things through. Look, I want you to be happy, both of you I mean, but you need to be sure about these things before you talk about marriage. It's a big undertaking. Yes, we want to meet her. Of course we do, but don't rush things."

"I'm not. We're engaged, but we've got no date for a wedding, so it won't be next week?" Rory laughed. "First thing is for Amina to find out how she likes living in Britannia. She's never been here. The climate will be a bit of a shock for a start."

"Does she speak English?" asked Beatrice.

"Of course, she does. Gambia was a crown colony before it gained independence."

"What kind of schooling did she have?" asked Elsa.

79

"She went to a good school and trained as a teacher, but life is very tough there now. Climate change is making it unbearable and people are trying to get away."

"Are her parents living there?"

"Her father's dead, and her mother's in Italy. This is Amina." He produced a photograph out of his wallet, and passed it round the family.

Amina was a bold-looking African woman with woolly black hair, a big smile, shining white teeth, high cheekbones and broad lips. She was dressed in a colourful gown, and sported a feathery headband.

"She makes all her own clothes. That gown has a batik design of her own making."

"Well, we hope you'll be very happy. Do you have interests in common?" asked Mark.

"Everything. We're like two peas in a pod."

"She's beautiful," said Beatrice. "And she looks good fun."

"You bet she is," said Rory.

"But why didn't you tell us about her in your letters?" asked Elsa.

"It was just a friendship at first. Then it sort of caught fire, but I only asked her to marry me just before I left there. It was after that last letter I sent you."

"When did you make the arrangement with her aunt?"

"The next day. Everything happened so quickly."

"That's why you mustn't rush things. Have a long engagement. So you're really sure about each other. It's especially important when there are two cultures involved."

"Oh Mum, you're such a fusspot," said Beatrice.

"Your mother knows from experience. When we married we had to make adjustments, and Americans are closer to Brits than Africans." said Mark.

But Rory ignored this and ploughed on. "She's coming on a solar flight from France, and I'm going to London to meet her in ten days time, We're staying in London for three days with friends who were in the Peace Corps with me. They'll help her acclimatise and she can see some of the sights. Then I'll fly back with her to Exeter, where I'll see the aunt, and then bring her to meet you all. Saturday, 15th July." He opened his arms expressively.

"You've got it all arranged, haven't you?" said Elsa.

"I can't wait to see her," said Beatrice.

* * *

Next Saturday was one of those energising days when a brisk wind ripples the cornfields and invites everyone outside. Rory wanted to have a walk on the beach, and the moment he suggested the idea, Max ran excitedly to the front door determined not to be left behind.

Beatrice decided to join them. It afforded her the first real opportunity to have a long talk on their own, and they set off cheerily down the lane that led to the style in the hedge.

"It must seem strange to be here again after all that time abroad," Beatrice suggested.

"It's wonderful to be home again with you all, even if Mom does go over the top sometimes. She can't help it. It's in her American blood. You know, sis, I used to find that gadding when I was a kid like you. I got so embarrassed when I brought friends home from school. I never knew what she might come out with next in some of her Yankee talk. I'll never forget that Saturday when two of my mates looked in and asked me to join them in a football game. It was just a friendly knock about, but Mom got the wrong idea, and when we were half way down the lane,

81

she hollered out, 'Hey Rory, you've forgotten your pants.' I pretended I hadn't heard her and carried on walking, but she came running after me shouting and holding out the white shorts she'd just finished ironing. I was mortified. The lads couldn't stop laughing, and the story went round the whole form. My shorts became 'Rory's panties'. I became so conscious of their gleaming whiteness that I used to deliberately smear them with mud, as soon as I was on the pitch, just so that they looked normal. Then the laugh became 'Rory's dirtied his panties again.'"

"I can just imagine that, poor Mom, after all that washing, but I know how you must have felt. She's so different from all the other mothers. When I was in primary, I told her once that I'd rather she didn't come to the open days. I said something awful before one parents' evening. I told her she could come as long as she didn't speak. She exploded, and later I overheard her telling Dad about it. He laughed out loud when she said 'I don't know what's got into that girl of ours! Can you imagine me going to a parents' evening and staying dumb all night!' "Dad said "No, darling not really, but you might give it a try, just for a change!"

"Oh, yeah, that's Mom and Dad all over. He never has a problem just sitting and listening, but Mom has to get her oar in. But, gee, isn't she wonderful. With all her hollerin' and her ham fisted way of fixing things, she's still the greatest Mom in the world, and I wouldn't swap her for anyone else's."

"Neither would I. But it's great to have a brother back to share these things with, and there's so much I want to ask you about. Tell me more about Amina. How old is she?"

"She's 21. Just a year younger than me."

"And how good is her English?"

"Pretty well as good as ours. She can speak a native tongue too, but she did all her schooling in English. She learnt some Italian too because she came over when she was quite young. I was taught Italian too in the Peace Corps."

"And after you first met her, in that school; how long was it before you took her out?"

"I asked her, then and there. The first time I saw her. I wasn't going to fool around, There's too many hot blooded guys in Italy, and I didn't want to lose her to some Romeo character. We used to go dancing in a little bar on a Friday night, a group of us from the Peace Corps, so I asked her if she would like to come along. It was a Friday when I went to the school, so when she jumped at it, I said I'd collect her from the school at seven thirty that evening."

"And how did it go?"

"Zip ho. There were six of us: three other guys and a girl from the Peace Corps, so she wasn't intimidated, and then we all agreed to meet there again next Friday. After that we started going out. Oh, she's a pearl, is Mina."

"It must have been a dazzle for you, getting paid to go to those exciting countries. I've never had the chance to go abroad in my whole life and neither has anyone in my class at school, except Lina, and she's Dutch... oh, and that awful Alfie lad, whose a big 'Selfie.' He brags about his rich American uncle, who owns a game park. I only know about Devon. I've been no further than Cornwall and Dorset, but you seem to have whizzed everywhere in the last two years. In the old days, people used to have holidays in the Mediterranean. They used to fly to Spain or Rome or Greek Islands: everyone did, even Mom and Dad. When they were still at school, they went all over the place."

"Yes, I know how you feel. I was frustrated too, when I was your age, but those air flights abroad didn't do much good. Nobody thought about the damage that was being done to the environment by all those aeroplanes sending out carbon emissions when mom and dad were young. Besides, people used to earn big money then. They had full-time employment contracts with big companies or corporations, and people lived in a get-rich-quick society that was blind to the cruelties of employment conditions in the poorer countries that provided their high standard of living. A lot of the factories here in Britannia, and elsewhere in the western world, degraded the planet, poisoning the air with gases and wasting precious water, which is the life blood of creation."

"Yes, I'm beginning to find this out through a project we're doing at school."

"Mom told me about that. I want to know what you're doing, 'cos that sounds good. I got very screwed up when I was at that school."

"I'll tell you about it later, I want to pick your brains, but not now. I need to know first about the world beyond. I want to know about those other countries that you've been living in. What are they really like? I've looked them up in the atlas, Germany, France, Italy, I've read a bit in books and seen the odd film, but I still don't know what it must be like to live in any place outside Wessex."

"Yes, going abroad was a big shock. So was going to London. People who grow up in Woodleigh here have no idea what a paradise this is compared with places beyond. Outside this bubble, and a few more besides, the whole world is in turmoil with yawning gaps between the super-rich and the underdogs. There are loads of places that people won't go to because they're afraid of being robbed and left in the gutter in a pool of blood."

"Where do you mean. Here, in Britannia?"

"Yes, there are plenty of no-go areas even in this country. I first realised this on the train to London. There were four coaches – one for the super wealthy with a restaurant car and cushy seating, one for people like us which was adequate, and two separate compartments for the poor – one was crammed full of angry rough men and policed by security guards and one was for poor women and children with a female warden."

"But that's terrible."

"That's life today! It's like that right across Europe and much worse in the southern world. The poor are desperate there, because there's not enough food to go round and the air's poisoned, and people are falling sick. Europe's part of the rich world; like China and North America. The only tranquil zones elsewhere are a few super-rich islands, Japan, and some gated parts of India, Australia and New Zealand.

Britannia's a great mix, too. Half a century ago, we were a United Kingdom - England, Scotland, Wales and Northern Ireland. The first one to go was Scotland, which voted for independence, then Northern Ireland, which joined the Irish Republic, and now we just have England and Wales, and we've changed the name to Britannia. My eyes were opened to all this when I went to Strasbourg. It's the same in France and Germany. There are mixtures of seething violent towns, empty rural areas, ugly districts designated as fracking zones and areas that are pools of tranquillity like this place, because people live in small communities sharing resources equitably and enjoying life. Woodleigh isn't typical, Beatrice, it's a show place. That's why people come here every year to learn how we've done it."

"But how have we, Rory?"

"It was mainly because of the Great Storm. It was a wake-up call. The elders saw the damage and knew that things had to change. Life had to slow down. We had to live more simply and only take our fair share of everything. That understanding's built into the cluster housing systems."

"I'm beginning to understand this. We're working on a project at school, and I'm doing a power-point talk about the Big Storm and the lessons we had to learn, but it's difficult to understand how people could ever have been so stupid."

"They still are – in most rich parts of the world. "

"Perhaps you can join us, and tell everyone about the world beyond."

"I can't do that, Beatrice. This is your project, and that gives it strength because tomorrow belongs to you and all the other school kids."

"And to you - you're not all that old."

"True. I'd like to help shape the future. That's why I joined the Peace Corps, but we must each go at our own pace, you and I. We can help each other but I can't become part of your project, or you part of mine."

This avid conversation had carried Rory and Beatrice right along the promenade, and down the steps that led to the beach. Max was straining at his lead now, and knew that he had come to the part open for dogs. A few seconds later, they were on the sand and Beatrice released him. Max ran round and round in excited circles and then made a dash for the sea as she threw his ball in that direction. He bolted back with it and barked for another throw.

They began to walk alongside the red Triassic cliff-face that jutted forwards towards the sea. The tide was out, but they had to pick their way over rocks slippery with seaweed, and glistening with the sparkle of tidal water.

"Look here." Rory had stooped to point to a limpet stuck to a rock. "Did you know that there's life in many of these creatures? They all look like discarded shells, and some of them are, but there are still living sea creatures inside many of them. They keep alive by scooping algae off the rocks, and occasionally they move towards little pools like that one over there: and see over there. That's a starfish, with its sprawling legs. It looks dead, but if I probe it with this bit of stick, it may respond. Would you believe it? There's often competition between these two creatures. Battles like that have been fought between these sea creatures for millions of years. And look at this slimy bit of seaweed. There's rich nutrient in there for creatures such as these. Explore any deep rock pool at low tide and you might see a battle going on between the living creatures in it. What's amazing is that 9,000 types of seaweed that have been identified by marine biologists."

"How do you know all this?" Beatrice gazed at in him.

"I had an inspiring schoolteacher, who used to bring us here, when we were kids. We explored rock-pools together: he and a group of us."

"I wish I had a teacher like that."

"See this barnacle here. There aren't as many around as there used to be. They're becoming scarcer but, would you believe it, some of them could outlive us. Some things like this are older than human beings. They date back to ancient times."

He stood up and looked around.

"I've dreamed of this place, sister," he said quietly. "As a kid, I always loved these timeless rocks, dating back, as some of them do, before there were any human beings on earth. Those red cliffs belong to the world of dinosaurs and flying monsters, and round that bend over there lies Benbow Bay. I came here with a group of school kids and that inspired teacher who made us understand that time was carved in the face of these cliffs. On one occasion, he produced a big pebble out of his pocket and showed us how a claw had been embedded in mud in ancient times and then had solidified into the rock. He told us how these rocks had once been in a desert here before the sea rolled in, and how a great river had forged its way north in the days when England was joined to France. I was awed as a child, and now, I'm awed as a man. There was a tropical forest here once, and then a scorching red desert, and all this before the ice-age, which heralded a new beginning for life on earth. Can there be a new beginning again, if we wreck the wonderful world we have now? That's the question I ask myself a thousand times over."

"Are we wrecking the world?" asked Beatrice, looking out at the widening sea and back at the cliffs, with their thin layer of green fertility at the top.

"I fear we are, sister, and people don't want to believe it. Those that have the power to change things skulk in their rich mansions in gated communities, watching trash television shows made to distract them from any real thinking. They eat and drink like gluttons and they'll probably die young because they do no exercise and ruin their bodies; meanwhile, the great majority of people on earth die hungry and in poverty, unable to afford medical care."

"But Britannia is a democracy isn't it? Why don't the politicians change things?"

"The politicians know that if they told the people the harsh truth they would never be elected, because people don't want a government that delivers salvation in the form of shared austerity. So people go on living in their little bubbles of contentment or squalor, as the case may be. Most people live in cultural cocoons, and have stopped looking beyond. It's only a few young people, like those in the Peace Corps or the armed forces who can travel abroad these days and face the awful truth. The bodies of Africans trying to get to Europe are washed up daily in the beaches in Italy. It's become so common that the locals aren't shocked by it any longer. It's just another task for the garbage man." Rory threw the ball again, and twizzled his beard thoughtfully as he watched the dog find it and come running back.

"So," said Rory, retrieving the ball and throwing it again, "it's up to us few who do see beyond to keep on trying, whatever the odds. No one else will. And it's up to those of us who have found a shared contentment to welcome exiles into our community. If there are enough of them around to tell their tales, perhaps, people will wake up."

"What about Amina? She's African isn't she? Does she understand?"

"Oh yes, she understands it better than I do. She came to Europe when she was young. Her mother was a refugee and, as she was a Commonwealth citizen, she wanted to come to Britannia, but wasn't allowed to because of our immigration rules. She was told the quota for asylum seekers had been filled, so she had to stay in a GOS Refugee camp in Italy. She went to school and trained as a teacher, and I met her when I gave a talk to the kids about the work of the Peace Corps, and as soon as I saw her - Wow, she knocked me out!"

"I must meet her. I can't wait. Mom and Dad are a bit uncertain as to whether you're doing the right thing, but I want you to know that I'm on your side."

"Thanks, sister. It's great to have you along again."

They high fived each other, and Max barked excitedly as they turned the bend in the cliffs and saw the great sweep of Benbow Bay, with its glistening rocks and waiting sands.

CHAPTER 7 - The Aceton Chronicle

A week after his visit to the library, Matthew Farnfield called another meeting of the project team. He had received and evaluated seven reports, one from each of them and was quite pleased with the quality.

"I can tell from the way you've written these articles that you were all interested in the subject," he said, "but you've tackled the task in different ways. It's clear that you have read different things. Two of you have written accounts that have the style of a newspaper story, quite snappy and to the point, with a flavour of local interest for the readers. Others have given a summary of what happened here in Aceton, with a good assessment of how human activity might have encouraged the storm, and a list of suggestions about desirable behaviour changes to avoid similar tragedies in the future. Lina has done a comparison of the disaster with one in Holland that occurred in the following year. Have you seen each other's contributions yet?"

Most of them shook their heads.

"Well, pass them around. You didn't have time to study all the papers in the library, so if you read through this lot, you'll all learn something new. Now, how do you think we could present this sort of information to the school and the parents?"

"We need to produce a newspaper," said Alfie decisively.

"I think that it would be better to do a power-point presentation," said Beatrice.

"Why do you think that would be better?"

"You could assemble all the facts, and emphasise the important ones. In a newspaper the facts are all jumbled up," Bea responded.

"But they have editorial articles in good papers, where the editor says what's most important, " Alfie announced.

"So, we have two different ideas to consider. If it's to be a newspaper, when would it be published?"

"The first week after the storm. It could be a weekly paper, and there'd have been seven days to collect the news."

"Probably only five, Alfie," Ernie pointed out thoughtfully. "The first day, people would be stunned. No one could start writing anything, and you can't still be writing up stories on the day it's being printed."

"When you were in the library, you were looking at a weekly paper produced shortly after the event," Mr. Farnfield reminded Alfie. "You can't just copy the stories out and present it as your work. Lina has made a very interesting comparison with a disaster in Holland the following year. How could that information be presented?

"If the paper was published one year on from the Aceton disaster the comparison could be made because the one in the Netherlands was nine months later," said Lina.

"Good point. There are some interesting differences. The sea defences were much stronger in your country, Lina, and so there were fewer lives lost."

"If the paper is a year after the event we can take the long view," Adam observed.

"Give it a different perspective," added Bea.

"Such as?"

"We can make comparisons with other disasters, both at home and abroad."

"You could but, if you take another place and another time, there are too many different factors to consider, so I don't recommend that you go down that route. What do you think about Alfie's idea of publishing a school newspaper a week after the event?"

"It's something that could involve the whole class," said Ernie with enthusiasm. "If everyone had to talk to someone who remembered it and wrote it up properly."

Alfie glowered at him. Ernie did not usually have much to say. He followed Alfie. That was his role.

"It wouldn't be good enough. It has to tell the whole story and it couldn't, just one week after the event," said Brook.

"Well, we could have them both," said Bea. "A local paper account and a power-point presentation taking the long view."

"Are you prepared for that?" asked Mr. Farnfield, with a slight smile. "Its much more work if we have two projects."

"I'm up for it," said Bea.

"Well now, if it's two assignments, it means two teams. We need a newspaper editor and a chief reporter, and we also need…."

"That's me and Ernie. The editor and the other one."

"Wait a minute. You can't pick jobs and I'm not making appointments. We're going to have an election. This is a civics project, remember, and we live in a democracy, so it's up to the class. We'll have a secret ballot. Anyone interested in applying for a post will have to study the job description and then give a short address telling the class why they could do the job well."

"I'm quite happy to make the speech, but why has the ballot got to be secret?" asked Alfie, indignantly.

Everyone looked at him and for a moment nobody said anything. Alfie's face went red.

"Wessex is a democratic region in a democratic country called Britannia. Did you forget, Alfie?"

Everyone laughed, except Alfie.

The posts were advertised and applied for, and the election was organised by Mr. Farnfield. A week later he announced that Beatrice and Brook were the joint winners of the election for presenters of the power-point talk, Ernie had been elected as editor of the class newspaper, and Lina was the Foreign Correspondent.

The senior students' den was turned into a newsroom, where Alfie, a rather cross chief reporter, wearing an eyeshade on his forehead, went through all the contributions brought in by the team. He rejected about half of them and altered others, as they dribbled in each day. Sallie and Deb, the newsroom typists, sat at two computers, and converted the edited stories into columns of newsprint.

Ernie, as editor, had taken possession of the stationery cupboard and enjoyed the task of cutting out the stories, attaching suitable photographs and approving the overall layout. Some stories were discarded. Others were returned for a rewrite with pencilled comments. He kept the Oxford dictionary on his desk, and when he spotted spelling mistakes missed by his chief reporter, they were corrected. Grammar remained somewhat problematic, but the final scrutineer, Matthew Farnfield, wielded the authority of a strict newspaper proprietor, whenever he deemed it appropriate.

Lina produced her own news-sheet outlining the tidal precautions in her own home-town, the impact of the flood, and compared it to that in Aceton.

The newspaper project was relatively straightforward. Most of the incidents that the old folks relayed were rewritten as if they had happened last week. They were edited, trimmed and fitted into place on the pages. Ernie aimed to have at least one photograph on every page, and sent Tom and Clancy back to the library to search old newspapers for suitable ones. There were few that were relevant and they did not copy well, so everyone was asked to look at old family albums and bring photos of anyone who had told them about their memories. What had been local history was fast becoming a live event for all the class and their families. The newspaper had been sorted by the time of the Easter break, but it was ruled that the printing could not be done until the summer term was ending.

Beatrice and Brook had a much harder task, and their script was only in early draft form by April. There were clearly many reasons for the tragedy. The early years of the twenty first century had been troubled by similar disasters elsewhere, as the world climate changed rapidly. They read how melting ice caps in the Arctic were causing a dramatic rise in the ocean levels. Scientists said that there had always been climate changes, but the speed of this one surpassed all previous records, and most experts agreed that this was because of human behaviour. There were magazine articles and videos of old BBC documentaries explaining this in the Woodleigh Library. Adam viewed several of them and picked out key points relevant to Aceton.

What shocked all three young people was that the dangers had been widely understood in the western world. There had been public protests calling for a low carbon lifestyle, and well known naturalists had drawn attention to declining species of animals, birds and plants. Prince Charles had spoken about the same thing in an international broadcast and an American presidential candidate had made a film called "An Inconvenient Truth", about the perils of global warming. None of these significant interventions by very prominent people had seemed to prompt any changes to western lifestyles. Why?

In 2015, there had been a UN international conference held in Paris, where all nations had pledged to reduce their carbon emissions, but the election of a climate-denying president in the United States one year later had set things back considerably. Several European countries had a good record on carbon reduction, however, including the Netherlands, whose vulnerability to the rise of sea levels was obvious. Support for the UN proposals was restored when a new President was installed in the White House, four years later.

Mr Farnfield acted as guide and consultant and helped when it came to selecting the appropriate extracts from films, applying for permission to use them and copying them. Appropriate credit was given to the originator and the town library.

Eventually a script emerged, which showed that there had been substantial building by developers on reclaimed mudflats over a long period of time, and a failure on the part of local authorities to heed warnings about further development on the floodplain. No single cause could be proved to have brought about the disaster but numerous warnings had obviously had little effect locally.

Beatrice and Brook decided that they would alternate as presenters and they invited Ahab and Sorrinder to work alongside them. This added variety to the talk and gave them useful breaks. They rehearsed their readings and criticised each other positively.

"It would be better to pause on that word, and look up to see the effect on the audience."

"That might throw me."

"Try it. Risk it. Otherwise you'll never know."

"Yes, that's much more powerful."

They challenged each other and responded. A bond of respect began to grow between Bea and Brook as they rehearsed. The experience encouraged them to continue researching and Adam and Sorrinder found additional facts from books in the library and identified specific clips from films. These ideas were shared and slipped into either Beatrice's script or Brooks. There was no jealousy. Neither said, "I found that one." Ideas were used or fed to each other according to their appropriateness.

The presentation was becoming a very serious one, so it was decided to lighten it with a little humour by using some film sequences of children and animals at play. Rabbits were shown frisking on the common and a short sequence of a homemade film about Max, when he had been the new family puppy, was included. He was seen romping in circles on the beach, and then trying to challenge approaching waves by barking at them and dashing off when they cascaded. The point made in the dialogue was that rising tides could not be ignored or underestimated.

It was just as that the headmistress had ruled that the newspaper and the power-point presentation would both be delivered around the end of the summer term. The teams needed maximum time for the work to be completed on both projects and also for the necessary publicity to be organised.

The final version of the school newspaper was agreed after many disputes. Alphie contended in his obstinate way that the publication date should be the week after the event. Ernie pointed out that, if this was done, most of the articles would have to be discarded as they were about subsequent events.

"But the Big Storm was the cause of all them and we've got brilliant photos of it all."

"All right then, we'll be democratic and have a vote on it." Ernie knew he would win because no one wanted their articles discarded.

The vote supported his view.

Ernie put all the stories in date order and then had a brainwave and made his big announcement. "We'll publish four news sheets. The first will be dated the week after the storm. The others will be on the first, second and third annual anniversaries. Alphie can edit the first one and choose the pictures he wants of the damage. I'll edit the other three."

This suited everyone, and was a good way of getting Alphie out of the way. Each paper was to be a four-page spread. The first one was to cover the storm in graphic detail: the second would focus on stories of the families in their temporary housing, the third would feature the day King Charles came to unveil the memorial stone and the fourth would describe the new homes being built. Lina's news sheet was included in the third and fourth editions.

The class was divided into four groups, each working on one edition. Beatrice, Adam and Brook, who were not involved in this, were now free to work on their power-point presentation.

Alphie's team had difficulties choosing which photograph to feature on their front page. There were several dramatic photographs of gigantic waves pounding the sea front, of a bus on a shopping street stranded in water, and of the collapse of the new supermarket on the estuary.

Eventually, it was agreed to use a photograph of the sea surging forward against a row of white fronted hotels on the promenade. The big headline and main story was as follows:-

"Devastation of Sea Front Hotels

The raging sea in Aceton was so strong on January 10th that it destroyed the sea wall and the marine slipway, together with all our expensive sea defences. Paving on the promenade was smashed. Stone-sets and other debris were dragged back in the tidal surge, and then flung forward again to hit the front walls of the hotels, which have graced our promenade since Victorian times. Some of these walls caved in immediately, others withstood the attack for a while and collapsed later. All remaining walls have huge cracks in them. All windows have been smashed and none of these buildings are now habitable. The handsome row of white hotels, which was part of our heritage, has disappeared.

John Whitstable, our District Councillor, issued this statement next day offering the condolences of the whole council. 'We are all devastated by this tragedy and offer our profound sympathy to all victims and their loved ones. We congratulate the emergency services and the numerous members of the public who rushed to help those in need, often risking their own lives in these attempts. This bravery is in character with the true spirit of Aceton. I assure everyone that the District Council will do everything in its power to help the survivors.'

The raging sea returned with the next high tide and continued its destruction. This second deluge came in the night and carried away our famous clock tower. Waves penetrated every building on the seafront and large blocks of masonry swept along streets, which had now become raging rivers. Some of the debris crashed into buildings: huge lumps were deposited on roads and pavements. The emergency services evacuated most people from these roads, but some of those who insisted on staying there were trapped behind their front doors. Boats were despatched to rescue them, as soon as possible.

Gigantic waves ploughed through the gardens of the Palladian Conference Centre, rendering our largest hotel uninhabitable. In destroying these buildings, this incursion by the sea has restored the original coastline. It has reopened what used to be called Mussel Bay, an area of mudflats, which was built over in Victorian times. The promenade and sea wall had protected it for over a hundred years.

On the third night, the Coronation Housing estate, also built on mudflats north of the harbour, was devastated. Several of the houses have completely disappeared and none are now habitable. Bill Johnson, our town historian, declared 'the sea has a mind of its own and is completely ruthless. What is left of Aceton has been returned to it's original shoreline.' "

 A photograph showing a couple of Royal Marines rescuing an eighty-year-old woman by boat from the upper window of her home, was followed by the this article:-

"Marines to the Rescue" By Carry Thompson

May Armitage, aged 80, of Sea Lane, proved herself to be a very strong-minded woman. In spite of the dreadful flooding at her home, May refused to leave, when the police advised her to do so. All her neighbours went to shelter overnight in a local church hall, but she would not go. 'All my memories are in this house,' she declared, 'and I can't leave it to be destroyed. I've lived here all my life and I'll stay here, with my two cats, until the water carries us out.'

But it was not the waters that carried May Armitage out; it was the Royal Marines, who came in a dingy the next day. 'Hold it steady for me, so I don't lose the cats,' May said, when the dinghy appeared at her bedroom window. They took her to a temporary refuge, with the cats, Blackie and Amber.

Other residents reported the sea cascading like a waterfall down the grassy bank opposite their homes. 'There was no holding it back,' said Mollie Edwards, aged 79. 'Minutes later, great waves shattered against my front door, and I were terrified that the windows would be smashed. I had to escape by the back door and rush down the alley. There was no time to collect anything.'"

A montage of photographs of the flooding was printed on pages 2 and 3, with some explanatory notes and a sketch plan showing the lost areas.

An article written by Adam, described his grandmother's memories of his lost grandfather, Colin Forester, who had worked at the lost Post Office. There were photographs of Colin, Grace and two year old, Eddie, who had also been killed, in the storm. Alongside was a photograph of a box of shells collected by the little boy from the beach. Amazingly, the shells were preserved, and were now one of his mother's treasures.

Brook had taken a picture of old Reuben and quoted his memories about watching the wildlife, under the heading "The birds had flown." Beatrice had written an article about her grandfather, together with a photograph of him in his twenties.

The third edition was to have pictures of people living in the newly built houses, and an article about the sustainable homes in the cluster groups, which were then under construction.

Although all the class read these proofs, they were advised not to say much about the paper before it was printed next term. It was agreed to mount an exhibition in the school and have it on sale to the public, in the last week of the summer term.

* * *

The last Wednesday in school year Matthew Farnfield praised the newspaper, and said he was looking forward to the power-point presentation that afternoon.

"I've every reason to think that will be every bit as good, or even better, than the newspaper. You've all worked very hard on this, and I'm proud of you," he told them.

"So, what have we learned from the disaster?"

A forest of hands shot up.

"The big storm may have happened anyway, but if we had been properly prepared there wouldn't have been so many lives lost."

"What could we have done differently?" Matthew asked.

"They shouldn't have built on the floodplain."

"They should have had people trained, so that much more help was immediate."

"Built stronger houses."

"If people had listened to all the warnings, years earlier and changed lifestyles, the tragedy might never have happened," volunteered Brook.

"O.K. What could we have done, years earlier? Not just in Aceton, but everywhere: right across Europe, in the Americas, in Africa and Asia."

"We could have developed a circular economy."

"What's that, brain box?" This came from Wills, the class clown, and brought a laugh.

"I read an article about it in the library," Brook was enthusiastic. "It was in an international magazine that was published around 1980. It recommended that people develop lifestyles where there's no waste. Everything could be recycled, even our own dung."

This caused a big laugh, but Brook ploughed on.

"It could be collected and used as fertilizer. That's what happens in many poor countries."

"And who's going to do that job? Are you volunteering Brook?" asked the class clown.

"What would be the advantages and the disadvantages of a circular economy? Discuss this round your tables, key your ideas on your table computer. Then, we'll have the best answers on the screen. You have five minutes. Start with the advantages, and I'll call half time."

At the end of the lesson there were two long lists on large class whiteboard. Matthew noticed that those from Cluster Groups were much quicker to spot the advantages. They identified creating a healthy environment and aiming to reduce carbon emissions. Those who lived in ordinary housing, however, were quicker still with the disadvantages: we wouldn't be able to run our family car, we'd have to ration time on the computer, we might not be able to have TV in the home.

Matthew decided against holding a vote on which style of life they preferred. He noted with interest that the cluster students were much more self aware, and did not appear resentful of their simpler lifestyles. He was pleased that there was no hostility between the two groups of pupils. This was quite remarkable. The cluster residents were much more open and friendly, and had qualities which the others admired.

So he ended by asking everyone to clean their table whiteboards, and called for a show of hands for those who had enjoyed the exercise. Every arm was raised.

"In view of your hard work on this, I'll let you all chose whatever project you like to do during this year's summer holiday. When we come back in the autumn, everyone will be asked to put something from their holiday work on display in the library."

That unusual idea even earned him a clap.

CHAPTER 8 - The Presentation

There was a great flurry of activity to finish the third part of the school project in the last fortnight of the summer term. The classroom had to be decorated with posters about the area in fifty years time.

Several of the pupils took the easy route, and drew pictures of robots and space machines. Some envisaged an attack on the planet by little green men from outer space. Alphie drew a scene showing people flying through the air on newly invented electronic wings. Ernie had robots doing all the cleaning up, whilst the people sat back and read copies of his newspaper. Others like Carry and Jane took a more considered approach, concentrating on the devastation caused through climate change, with trains running into snowdrifts, and town streets being swamped by flooding. One pupil prepared a poster which simply read "World closed today through over development." Someone else drew pictures of people living below ground, while hurricanes above them uprooted trees and blew roofs off houses.

Beatrice, Adam and Brook and some other helpers were excused this task as they put their last minute touches to the power-point presentation, which they were told would be given twice: first to the assembled school, and secondly to the invited parents and members of the public. The school performance provided a rehearsal for the evening event, but it still looked formidable to the speakers, when they stood on the platform that afternoon. The headmistress sat on the front row, with the other teachers, and all the pupils were in tiered ranks behind them.

Beatrice's hands were shaking as she stood up, and the clarity of her voice surprised her as she spoke into the microphone.

"Thank you, Headmistress, for inviting the Cornfield Cooperative Group in Year Ten to present our findings into the matter of the great storm at Aceton." Beatrice began tremulously. She looked down at her notes and read. "We'd like to thank Mr Farnfield, our Civics teacher for his guidance, and the staff at Woodleigh Library, who have given us permission to use quotations and show images from their records."

Beatrice looked up and fixed her gaze at the clock that was on the wall just above the back row of pupils. She had identified and underlined key words in the script, and memorised phrases, so that she could speak with authority and keep everyone engaged.

"The Aceton disaster was one of the most notable tragedies of its kind in the last forty years, but it's not unique. Similar things have happened in many places of Britannia and other parts of the world. On this first slide, (can someone dim the lights please?) Thank you, that's better. This map shows all the encroachments by the sea in Lincolnshire and along the coast of East Anglia and in other places marked in red along the south and west shoreline. Notice the dates when these things occurred throughout a period stretching from 2020, when the great storm hit us, through to the most recent one in 2055.

The destruction at Aceton took most local people by surprise. (Next slide please) Here, you can see how the lower part of the town was submerged. What happened was that this area, which had once been called Mussel Bay, re-emerged when the marine wall protecting the promenade suddenly collapsed under the pressure of wave power and all the hotels and houses were engulfed. The sea pressed on, rushing across gardens and right into the old town centre, the square and shopping streets.

Another great wave crashed into the new superstore on the riverside embankment to the north, swallowing up streets of houses, built on old mudflats in Victorian times. If you compare this map with an earlier one, dated 1850, you can see how the sea reverted to its original shoreline of two hundred years ago. Because this all happened so quickly, on three wild days and nights, the people living there were stunned. Help came quickly from emergency services, and fortunately there was a big Royal Marine Camp here up river. The soldiers came to the rescue. You can see this in an old photograph from a newspaper of the time caravans were quickly provided, and later, the survivors were rehoused on the hill behind the old town."

Beatrice sat down and Brook stepped up to the podium. They had each rehearsed their lines, but kept the flow natural by varying it a little from the official script. Brook talked easily too.

"The story of the rescue and the new beginning has been brought to you this morning by our newspaper, 'The Aceton Chronicle.' The presentation we are doing now tells a different tale. Why did this disaster happen, and how can we stop this type of thing in the future? There had been warning signs, which a few people had noticed. Old Reuben here in this photo was living there at the time and told me that he knew something was afoot weeks before the disaster struck. He was a birdwatcher and noticed that most of the traditional migrating birds did not come that year and many of the resident ones had flown away, even the seagulls. They knew something was going to happen, and so did Reuben. I asked him about it and this is a recording of what he said."

Reuben's rural voice crackled as he spoke. "Anyone 'oo wants to know about the weather, should watch the birds. They sense it in their bones, and so do most wild creatures. Per'aps early man did too, back in the days when they lived in that great earth mound at the moor top. We calls it intuition, but it's somethin' we've lost down the years, with all our learnin' and our books and computers. We no longer live in tune with the rhythms of the planet. People seem to think everything is 'ere for them to take for our own, but they're wrong. We plunder at our peril. If we don't live in 'armony with it, the planet will shrug us off, as it did with the great mammoths with their 'uge tusks and the dinosaurs who roamed this land in bygone times. To live in 'armony, you must rise at dawn and sleep at dusk, and eat the local produce that the Good Lord provides, not frozen food from fridges, out of season. You must listen to the wind and 'ark to birdsong, and learn from the trees and woodland creatures, as our forefathers did in times gone by."

"That's poetry, Reuben, and I love to hear you speak so," said Brook's recorded voice. "But how did you know there were going to be such wild happenings in Aceton?"

"Why else would the birds fly away from the feedin' grounds? Why else should the moles and voles dig so deep in the soil that they could ne'er be found? Why else should the creatures who normally wake stay deep in 'ibernation? I didn't know what form the destruction would take, o' course I din't, but somethin' was clearly goin' to threaten their territory, an' stands to reason that what threatens them, will trouble us too."

"Reuben is a wise old man, and so was Beatrice's grandfather and she'll tell you now how he saw changes in human behaviour."

Beatrice had made a recording too, and she switched on Gramp's voice. He told how people were getting more and more frantic in their behaviour before the Great Storm. "The roads was churning with motor cars, in those old days, nose to tail they was going into towns, and the smell of the oil got into the air and into your clothes and the noise was something terrible." A recording of street noises followed with honking horns, running engines and police sirens.

"Gramps is happier with things as they are in Woodleigh today. We live a more natural way now. We monitor the way we use our energy for example, we share our cars and discuss all this at cluster group meetings," Beatrice told them. "In the bad old days, there were dozens of different power providers competing for custom and all trying to make a profit. The market competition was supposed to bring down prices, but the big firms got together in what was called a cartel and kept prices high to suit their shareholders."

Ahab took over the presentation at this point. He had assisted in the research and come across some interesting facts.

"The Nature Conservancy published a report in 2014 saying that Climate Change could mean that one-fourth of the earth's wild animals could be heading for extinction by 2050, if the trends continued at the same rate.

We now know that this actually happened, and the cause of the speed in climate change was largely due to human activity." He went on to illustrate this by showing a number of graphic images taken from a selection of BBC films.

Beatrice took over again. "Now let's get back to the question of what went wrong in Aceton, all those years ago. In the official report of the disaster, which we found in the public library, it was said that warnings had been given about building on the reclaimed land. A coastal survey had warned about the rising tides and the danger of flooding, but little notice was taken of these things. The report said, 'Contrary to the official warnings, developers continued with their plans, and approval was given for new buildings on reclaimed land, and areas where the shoreline could not be effectively defined.' These reports concerned this area here."

She then indicated an area on the map by shining a small red light that pinpointed Aceton.

"But mistakes like this were not just made locally. They happened in many areas, despite the fact that warnings had been given nationally on popular television shows, and in those days almost everyone had a television set in their own home. There was no concern then about the damage being done environmentally by using so much power right across the whole world. It wasn't until the terrific electrical explosions in China and India that people wakened up. TV is rationed today in the cluster groups and similar places. There was no excuse for the lack of preparation for climate change. Popular presenters had filmed the ice-caps melting in the Arctic." As she mentioned this, an image came on screen of a lonely, white polar bear prowling gingerly on an icy surface and the picture widened to show that it was imprisoned on a floating iceberg. A gasp rippled through the audience."

Beatrice was on her feet again, "One naturalist, called David Attenborough, who was a well loved TV person in his day, had filmed graphic images like that one, and he explained that many species of wild animals were being lost to the planet. This, he told his audience of millions, was endangering our fragile world, because living things were part of the diversity that holds life together. All this should have been common knowledge but urgent action was not taken quickly enough."

Brook took over again here. "Films had been made to warn people. This is a short sequence from "An Inconvenient Truth", made by Al Gore, who was a presidential candidate in a United States election. Al Gore was not elected, and the American people voted instead for a President from Texas, who let them carry on driving huge oil-guzzling automobiles." As Brook said this, a massive Mercedes Benz rushed across the screen.

"In Britannia, even the Royal Family got involved. Despite some inevitable political controversy, Prince Charles set up his Rainforest Appeal." An aerial view of the Amazon jungle was followed by film of huge acres of desolation caused by tree logging. Then came a close-up shot of the troubled, elderly prince appealing for people to fight for an end to this wilful destruction of the very lungs of the earth. Juxtaposed was film of huge newspapers and bulging magazines full of lurid advertisements and piles of packaging being dumped at a refuge collection centre.

Sorrinda then spoke of pollution at sea, saying how thousands of creatures died there because of plastic waste. Several snatches from Attenborough films followed and then a shot showing a trail of waste being discarded from a luxury cruise ship.

Brook illustrated damage to the air quality with chemicals, and pollution of rivers by industrial waste, reduction of habitats for birds and piles of elephant tusks on sale in an Asian luxury shop. "These things didn't happen locally, but we only have one planet, and what happens hundreds of miles away affects the whole world."

Beatrice was on her feet again. "How could people have been so blind only thirty years ago? There was a report published by the European Commission back in 1982 recommending a circular economy, but most people in this country seemed not to be bothered." She looked angrily at the audience. "How could most of our own parents generation care so little about the future, that they allowed these things to happen? How could the builders and the planners have ignored the warnings in Aceton? It seems as if they preferred to live in comfort and hope, and write off the risks, but fortunately, in Woodleigh, our parents learnt the lesson and now, at last, we and they are planning for a better tomorrow."

There was complete silence in the hall, as Beatrice sat down. She realised that she was trembling but, underneath her nervousness, she felt a deep satisfaction. She had said what she wanted to and now she must await the response. Some girls towards the back began to clap, and suddenly everyone in the hall followed suit. Someone cheered. Then everyone started cheering, and the headmistress climbed the platform steps to thank Beatrice and Brook for their excellent delivery. and Adam and Carry for their technical help.

"We teachers lived through three years of anguish while the debates raged," she said.

"The truth was often difficult to face, and those in power preferred to believe that our scientists would find a solution. Now we are all facing this truth together. So I am glad that Mr Farnfield was brave enough to give his pupils this painful challenge. Thank you, Matthew, for putting these things on the school agenda. We must now do everything we can to deal with the consequences."

She touched Beatrice gently on the arm, smiled, and then turned to reach out to Brook.

That evening there was a repeat performance, but the atmosphere was even more daunting because the audience was one of parents and interested townspeople. The mayor was there with some of the councillors and a local newspaper reporter, who took photographs.

This gave a different feel to the evening event because no one knew what to expect or how the adult audience would take it. There were likely to be some who would be challenged by things the young people were bringing back into the public arena. A few elderly people might be there who had been directly involved, but the main culprits were all dead by now. Others who had been bereaved might be cross that the subject had been raised again after so much had been laid to rest.

Beatrice had won the right to open the school presentation by the toss of a coin, so tonight it was Brook's turn to start and finish the event. He had told Beatrice and Mr Farnfield that he had prepared a different ending, which introduced a sharper criticism.

As his parents were separated, Brook and his mother shared an evening meal, but he was excused from the usual task of drying the crockery, because Mrs Graham knew that he had to check the equipment with Adam, before others arrived in the school hall.

He found everything in order and by the time that Mrs Graham arrived, parents and friends were filling the seats in the hall. Adam was sitting by the projector, and Brook and Beatrice hovered in the wings.

The Headmistress welcomed everyone, and then introduced Brook and Beatrice, before taking her own place beside the mayor, on the front row.

"Mr Mayor, ladies and gentlemen," Brook commenced. "The events that our presentation covers tonight will be familiar to you all. Although Beatrice and I have grown up in Woodleigh and have always been aware of the Great Storm, it had not featured in our lives directly until Mr Farnfield, our Civics Teacher, gave us this challenge. We were introduced to a mass of information in the Woodleigh Library and the county archive office. Most of this presentation is based on these materials, but we have also got permission to use extracts from various films made around the time."

Beatrice took her place on the podium and the familiar ground was covered once more. The audience was attentive and responsive. The young presenters both gained confidence as the talks continued. Brook closed the session with his own thoughts.

"Of course, what we need to recognise is that the worst effects of climate change are not being felt here in Britannia. We all know about the tsunamis, tornadoes and devastation wrought by floods and growing deserts in the tropics. Vast stretches of land are being made uninhabitable by human activity. Africa, which was once the cradle of life, is now the most plagued continent on earth. All those who can are trying to escape and find a life in more temperate zones, like Europe. Can we blame them? Thousands die on their journey. Those that get here we usually call illegal immigrants and they are either sent back or imprisoned. This has been happening for years in Europe. There used to be an International Charter of Human Rights, but now that's been forgotten. Countries started to introduce their own Bills of Rights, and thousands of refugees were excluded. But it's not just Europe. Similar things are happening today right across Asia and Central America. The South Sea Islands, once called the most beautiful part of the world, are slipping under the waves of the Pacific and the luxurious coral reefs are dying. It is we, in the north, with our extravagant life styles, who are helping make this happen. The world does not belong to human beings. Our fathers and grandfathers presided over this developing chaos, and it is the student generation who are being left to face the whirlwind. Many adults seem to prefer to believe the fantasy that new developments in science will probably solve everything, rather than face the truth. How irresponsible this is!"

He sat down shaking in rage. Beatrice reached out and held his arm.

As in the afternoon, a stunned silence followed, and then came some lively clapping, which others quickly took up. They glanced up and saw that some of the audience were standing to applaud, whilst the majority stayed seated. The smiles on their faces showed that most, but not all, appreciated the presentation.

"You were great. Where do we go from here?" whispered Beatrice.

"I don't know. I think I got too emotional and blew it," said Brook, blinking back a tear.

"No, your passion was needed. Look, they're still clapping."

A few were, but others were beginning to move away. Then the mayor approached them. "Wonderful performance by both of you, Congratulations, " he said. "How long did it take you to assemble all this material?"

"Oh, a few weeks, said Beatrice. "We had a lot of help from our Civics Teacher, and from others like Ahab and Sorrinder."

Matthew Farnfield joined them with the headmistress. It was clear that the mayor was pleased with the evening, despite the fact that some other councillors had been taken aback.

"What's the matter, Brook?" They were walking back towards the bike shed. "I'm thrilled it went so well, and I loved the way you ended the meeting."

"I don't know. I feel a bit down actually. I got too wound up. I was angry and it showed. I lost control at the end and made too many accusations, not just about Aceton, but about the whole world."

"Nonsense, you were marvellous. You always are," suddenly Beatrice kissed him.

He stiffened slightly, and then responded.

"Do you really mean that? Do you think what I said was O.K?"

"Yes, I do, and we must meet each other tomorrow and talk about where we go from here. The Cornfield Cooperative, I mean. It's the holidays now, and we'll have bags of time. Now we've finished this project, we need to start a new one."

"A new one! What sort of project?"

"I don't know, but now we've started, we can't stop, can we? I mean we've got to sort things out. Put the world to rights, somehow. Well, some of it, here in Woodleigh anyway"

She looked up at him, and suddenly Brook was very conscious of her shining green eyes. "I'm going back in there to hear what people are saying. They'll be having cups of tea now."

Brook watched her rounding the corner, her fair hair bouncing in the summer air. Suddenly he slapped his thigh.

"Well, what do I make of that?" he said aloud. He mounted his bike and set off for home, with the beginnings of a smile on his face.

CHAPTER 9 - The Next Day

The following day Brook awakened with a glow in his heart. He had one thought in his head, which dominated everything else. *That wonderful girl, Beatrice, seized the moment and showed me her affection.*

I really enjoyed the times we spent together working on our project. It was the task that we were engaged in that absorbed me so fully. Seeking out those facts and then piecing them together was fascinating. We worked so well together as a team - all of us, including Adam, Carry, and Sorrinder. We worked as equal partners.

But Adam's been my friend for years and somehow I'd always thought of Beatrice as his girl. I'm not sure why. Well I suppose it's because they live in twin clusters, and so often come to school and go home together, but Adam's a quiet guy who doesn't mess around with girls. Adam's never bragged about Beatrice like some of the others do about their girls. That's not his Adam's way. If she really is Adam's girl, I don't want to barge in. It would be awkward. He's my best friend and I want that to continue. I'll watch out and pick up any signals. But that girl – she blows my mind.

Beatrice isn't like Carry, though they're friends with each other, of course. Carry's a real young woman with family responsibilities. She's cared for the little ones ever since her Mum died. She's a great girl. Actually I think she's more mature than Beatrice, but probably that side of her developed because of the circumstances: with her dad being the local policeman who has to be all over the place. Without Carry's help, I can't see how her dad could do his job properly. What really comes first, the job or the family? It's difficult to answer that one. It's essential to have solid, mature people like Carry around.

Suppose it had been Beatrice's dad who'd died, and she'd had to look after some little kids. I know she would have done, but it would have changed her. I like Beatrice as she is – spontaneous, excitable, and enthusiastic – with that marvellous glint in her eyes. How does she feel about me? Well, she showed that last night, didn't she? Or was she just being kind because I was upset? Last night I was overcome by emotions. I nearly broke down in tears – in front of everyone: the mayor, the headmistress, mum, and all those people. I nearly lost it completely. It was Beatrice who saved the situation. I couldn't do that with her there. I couldn't allow myself to.

Why was I so emotional? I've been through all this before. I rehearsed the script with Beatrice. No I didn't – not that last bit. I wrote those words out and rehearsed them in front of a mirror yesterday. I've not gone over that ending with anyone else. Yes, that's the problem. It was the first time I'd had faced the cold truth in front of anyone at all. And the truth's so terrible, so frightening, and I and my generation are going to have to live with it. Not the adults: they and their parents have created this mess, and they're leaving this dreadful world to their children.

Such terrible decisions have to be made. Do we help all those thousands of refugees or do we let them die? Do we destroy our own family lives by helping them - or do we leave them to rot? What about those millions of endangered species too? He went cold at these thoughts. And then he remembered Beatrice. *At least I'm not alone. I must see her again and learn more about how she sees things. I'll give her a call this morning and arrange to meet her. Yes, I'll do that now.*

Beatrice's mobile was ringing. *Wow, it's Brook. Can we meet this morning?* Yes, Of course we can. When, where? On that seat beneath the old beech tree, the one by the cornfield. Yes, of course, we can... in two hours time...Yes.

It was all arranged. *What does it mean - this sudden call? What will I wear? What's he so anxious about? I'm not sure, but I'll be there.*

"You did very well last night. I was proud of you, Brook." Freda Graham was unusually talkative over breakfast today. Mornings started slowly for Freda. She was much more alive in the evenings. She had not seen Brook when he came back from the school last night. He had gone straight to bed, and left her a note saying he was very tired and please don't wake him. It was the first time he'd ever done that and she was puzzled by it.

Brook was not at all tired this morning. He seemed very excited, so she said. "You did very well last night."

"I'm glad you thought so, Mum, I wasn't sure."

"Why not? You got a huge clap and were personally congratulated by the mayor and your headmistress."

"I know, but those sort of people are always polite on public occasions. What did you think of the things we were saying?"

"It was all very well done. You spoke up clearly. The film shots were excellent, and I thought it was a great credit to the whole team and especially to you."

"Why especially me?"

"Because you and that Beatrice girl came over as the team leaders."

"I'm glad you liked it. What did you think about the message?" Brook looked up from his bowl of muesli and added more sheep's milk.

"It's an important one, and you clearly take it to heart."

"Was I a bit too emotional at the end?"

"No, the way you ended was terrific."

"It wasn't just done to impress, you know. I really meant it all."

"I'm sure you did. Full marks!"

Mum obviously enjoyed the performance, but did not seem to have got the message.

"Is your headache, better now, dear?"

"I didn't have a headache. It just made me very tired. What sort of things were people in the audience saying when you went into the refectory for tea afterwards?"

"They were expecting to see you there, and wanted to congratulate you. Mrs Hargreaves was very keen to do that. Beatrice came and joined us, and a lot of people congratulated her. I think she seems a very nice girl."

"Yes, she's all right. But what were they talking about?"

"About your performance and the films, of course. That was a funny one of the little dog on the beach barking at the waves. Who took that?"

"Oh, Beatrice's Dad, I suppose. It's their dog."

"Well it was a pity you didn't join us. I was a bit disappointed about that."

"Look. I've got to go out this morning. I'm meeting someone."

"Oh, all right, but don't you want some toast first?"

"Not now. See you at lunch time."

Brook escaped through the back door, and collected his bike from the shed.

Beatrice and Max were waiting for him by the beech tree. Brook leant the bicycle against the tree trunk, which Max had watered to claim as part of his territory. Beatrice jumped up to greet him.

"Hi," she said. "I've been giving things a lot of thought, since last night. We need a new project: something local, which we can achieve ourselves. We could start it now, during the holidays, and then when school starts in the autumn we can bring the others in. It can be a sort of youth cooperative that runs alongside the adult cluster groups, don't you see? We made an impact last night. I was talking to the mayor after we'd finished. He said that if we'd got a really good idea, we might get some support from the council, not necessarily money, but practical help. He thinks that it would be good to have more youth involvement in the cluster projects."

"I don't know," Brook said. "The problems are so huge, I don't see that we can change the general situation. There are times when I'm really frightened about the future."

Beatrice was disappointed. "I thought you'd agree with me. We made a big impact last night. Now, we must follow it through."

"What sort of project? What can we do to change the whole world."

"Every big change starts will a small step. Don't you believe that?"

"But you have to know what you are aiming at."

"We're aiming at helping to create a sustainable world, but we start where we are here in Woodleigh, and everything we do successfully makes a little ripple which reaches out and touches others. There are going to be some exchange visits this holiday. I'm going with Mom and Dad to Tamcaster for two weeks, and those folk are coming down here, If we've got a great idea, We can share it with the kids over there. Don't you see the possibilities?"

This was the first Brook had heard about Beatrice disappearing to Tamcaster for two weeks. His heart sank.

"When's all this. Who else is going there?"

"Adam's coming with his parents and some others from the East clusters."

"Well I'm not going anywhere."

"No, but if you're still here, you can be the anchor man for our project throughout the summer."

"Oh thanks, that's great. You go off swanning around the country with Adam and I keep things warm for you when you come back. Is that it?"

"No. It's not like that at all. I thought you'd be excited about this."

"But what's the project?"

"I don't know yet. We'll have to work that out between us."

Max realised that they were both quite angry and became concerned. He jumped up on the seat and bounced around them.

"Oh dear, you've upset Max now."

She picked the dog up and sat down again on the bench with him in her arms.

"I'm sorry. I didn't mean to. Oh dear, this is no good, I think I'd better go."

"No, don't go. I need to talk to you – to get your ideas. I'm thinking that we could really develop the Cornfield Cooperative. We could form a team of young people who do a practical project in each of the cluster groups, something linked with sustainable living which is really needed in that cluster. It might be planting new trees, or collecting things for recycling, or organising a sponsored activity. It could be a fun thing. Don't you see? I think the mayor would be very pleased. He'd really like to see more youth engagement. He said so to me last night after you'd gone home. What's more, he said the council might help us, if we came up with a good idea."

"Did he? Perhaps I should have gone back like you did. But, quite honestly, I didn't feel up to it, then."

 "What's the matter, Brook? Something troubling you, like it did last night. What is it?"

"Of course, it is. Last night was a very troubling experience for me. Wasn't it for you?"

"I thought it was a big success."

"Yes, we successfully told our elders that they had created a hell on earth, and they're leaving us to sort everything out."

"But Woodleigh isn't a hell on earth. It's a symbol of hope."

"In a well of darkness!"

"Britannia isn't a well of darkness."

"No, it's chequered, but most of the world is. That's the way I see it."

"You sound a bit like Rory."

"Who's Rory?"

"My elder brother. He's just come home from being with the Peace Corps in Italy."

"That sounds great, I'd like to meet him."

"You must. He's in London now, but he's coming home with an African fiancé on Saturday."

"An African fiancé. Good heavens. I'd like to meet them both."

"You will, I'll introduce you. Rory's inspiring. I bet he'll be able to help change your attitude."

"I thought you said I reminded you of him."

"You do, He knows about the dark side too and it troubles him, but there's something which helps him look beyond. I'm not sure what it is, but he's a star. He gives me hope that we can start changing things. Between us all, I think we're going to find a way forward. I must go now, but we'll fix another time in the next few days for us all to talk together." She jumped on her bike, blew him a kiss and rode off, with Max trotting and bouncing after her wheels.

CHAPTER 10 - Amina

The following Saturday morning Rory took the train to Exeter and caught an airbus to London.

Late in the afternoon, three days later, Mark keyed in an order for one of the e cars in the cluster pool to come to Coppice Cluster. When he saw it arrive, he pressed the keys on his wrist pad to disengage the door lock, got in, set it to take him to St. David's rail-station in Exeter and off he went in the car.

Elsa and Beatrice were busy in the kitchen, anticipating his return with Rory and Amina. Beatrice was setting the table, when she heard Rory's loud "Cock-a-doodle-doo."

Dropping knives and forks in surprise, she ran to the door. Rory was pounding up the path with his arm round the shoulders of a tall, young woman with striking, African features. A colourful sarong, flapped round her ankles. Mark was following, carrying a bulky bag.

"Welcome to my birthplace," Rory was ecstatic, "and here come Mom and sister, Beatrice, to welcome you!"

Elsa overtook Bea, embraced the girl, and kissed her on both cheeks. Beatrice flung out her arms, with an excited shriek.

"Come in, and sit down in the lounge. How was your journey?" Elsa was flustered and unsure of herself.

"The train was crowded but we managed to get seats." It was Rory who replied.

Bea and Amina hugged each other on the doorstep. There was a whiff of exotic perfume, but Elsa had rushed into the lounge and pointed to the sofa.

"Sit down, Amina. Are you tired after all that travelling?"

Amina sat down, looked round at them all, and then suddenly broke into a huge laugh, exposing a flash of great white teeth.

"I guess I'm too delighted to be tired." She laughed. "Gee, I've dreamt of this place and you guys. Rory showed me photos, but now I'm really here, an' I just can't take it in!"

Beatrice was surprised by a slight American tone. *Probably a teacher's influence.* she thought. Amina laughed again and wiggled on the sofa.

"Would you like something to drink?"

Rory answered for both of them. "Yes, Mom, we'll have some of your home-made apple juice. I've been telling Mina about it and she's keen to taste the flavour."

Beatrice ran to get it and brought back two filled glasses. Rory and Amina were now sitting side by side, on the sofa. Rory was doing the talking.

"Good thing Dad could get the cluster car, because Mina's aunt was waiting for her at Exeter Station, so we were able to take most of her bags there before we came on."

"Well, I guess the first thing is, what do we call you? Are you Amina or just Mina?"

Elsa was keen to get this right.

"Oh, I don't mind really. My name is Amina, but friends usually just call me Mina."

"Well we're friends, so it's Mina then. No formalities here. And you're a schoolteacher, Rory tells me. I think he said that you taught disabled children in Italy. That sounds like quite a challenge, Are they local kids or ones from different parts?"

"They're from all over. It's a very special school, and it's based on the principles of Rudolf Steiner? Do you know about Steiner schools?"

"No, I don't, but I have heard of them."

"Steiner believed that every child has a gift, and that it's the job of the teacher to discover the nature of the gift and make it flower." Mina was serious now, and spoke with real enthusiasm, opening her arms to illustrate the points she was making. "There are children of varied abilities in the school. Some are disabled, but most aren't. They live together in a community and learn from each other. Two of my special subjects are Art and Music, but I teach all subjects to the younger ones. We find that children can do amazing things, given the right stimulus, and they learn to help each other. That's important. Education should not be competitive. It should be a wonderful growing experience," she added with conviction.

"Mina is a great teacher," said Rory. "She's a natural gift is relating to young children and bringing out their skills. I just sat in her class gob-smacked at their friendly banter with each other."

"That's so important," Elsa affirmed. "Establishing the right relationship with kids, and I guess they love you. And what a stunning dress you're wearing. Did you make it yourself?"

"Yes, it's my favourite one. It features the native colours of Gambia: red, blue, white and green."

Mina stood up and twizzled round, displaying the swirling colours and a discrete slit on the left side, which revealed a glimpse of shapely dark brown calf.

"Oh my, that's beautiful. And it's your own batik design. That must have taken some time."

"Yeah, it did. My mom helped me with the fitting."

"Your mom. I'm interested to hear more about her. How long have you two been in Italy?"

"We came when I was ten. That's eleven years,"

"That's quite a time, and you settled there happily, I hope?"

"Yes, we were refugees, and I grew up with her in the camp, and went to the school there, and then I trained as a teacher at a college in Italy."

"Good for you. It must have been tough in the refugee school."

"Yeah, it was, because new pupils keep arriving all the time, and they're from all over and speak different languages, and they're all ages too, so the school has to be very well run. It was a GOS Camp and a GOS school."

"They had arranged it in Florence because the locals were more welcoming there than at the port areas," Rory explained. "Now that GOS is doing so much work to improve living conditions in Africa, the stream of refugees has lessened, and things are under control in Europe, with a fair allocation for each country."

"It was good because we had teachers from lots of different countries."

"And you had some from America. I can tell that from your voice." Elsa was delighted to find that this made her feel comfortable with Amina.

"Yeah, I did. I got on well with them. We had two American girls teaching in the Steiner School too. They were good friends of mine."

"And what are your impressions of Britannia?"

"Oh, everyone seems very friendly to me. That's good. But many things seem strange. There's so many people in London, and everyone's in a great hurry. I found it a bit overwhelmin' – so many places to go to and people to meet."

Rory came to the rescue, "There were a lot of big street protests in London, so we couldn't get to see all the sights. I meant to take Mina round, but it was so difficult. There were barricades up at lots of corners, and police and soldiers all over."

"What were the protests about?" asked Beatrice.

"Oh different things, and there were people protesting at the protests. It was chaotic. Barricades and police directing the crowds into roads they didn't want to go down. I'd meant to show Mina the Houses of Parliament, but we couldn't get anywhere near, though we did manage Buckingham Palace and the changing of the guard."

"We didn't see King William there, though. He was out of town, we were told, but we went to some of the big London Parks," added Amina. "And we met some friends of Rory's and had dinner with them one evening. I enjoyed looking at the waxworks, all those famous faces, and we went for a sail up the River Thames."

"We visited Richmond and Kew Gardens, " said Rory. "It was a bit quieter there."

"Well you won't find it noisy here in Woodleigh," said Beatrice. "Do you have any brothers or sisters?" she added.

Amina's bright smile disappeared immediately. She looked at the floor and said is a hushed voice. "Not now. They are dead."

"Oh, I'm so sorry," Beatrice apologised. "I didn't think!" She was embarrassed and bit her tongue.

 After an awkward pause, Rory spoke.

"We've got some photos to show you. Here I am with Mina and her mother."

"My, what a handsome woman," exclaimed Elsa. "What's your mother's name?"

"Her African name is Ahinee, but some people use her baptismal name, Elizabeth."

Ahinee Elizabeth was smiling. She was a big strong woman. Her colouring and high cheekbones were similar to Mina's. As the photograph was passed round, Elsa thought she could be looking at Amina in twenty years time. It gave her quite a jolt.

125

Why doest it? She asked herself. *This is the face of a competent, honest and strong woman. Isn't that what I want for Rory?*

The next photograph was a simple gravestone with flowers on it, and three names, carved boldly: "Benjamin, Luke and Toby", and beneath were the words "Father, and sons, Rest with the Saviour."

"Where is this grave?" asked Mark.

"Deep in the woodland ... in Tuscany," said Mina. "We couldn't bury them in Gambia, so we buried some trinkets and clothes of theirs in a quiet, safe place, thousands of miles away ... that was all we could do. We had to get away... My father was the chief in our village. He was killed because he became a Christian. Our home was attacked by rebels. He died defending us - my mother, my brothers and me."

"Holy Smoke! That's terrible!" Elsa took Mina's right hand and enclosed it in both of hers. No one spoke for a minute.

"Those rebels wanted an Islamic state... madmen, not true Muslims," explained Rory. "Ahinee escaped with Mina. She bought a passage on a ship, which was supposed to be going to Italy. She didn't realise that the captain and crew were crooks. A crowded boat, full of Africans, set sail from Senegal. They were supposed to be going to Rome, but the ship was abandoned one night somewhere in the Med. The refugees managed to raise a distress flag. They were drifting dangerously, and eventually the old tub started leaking. Fortunately, fishing vessels rescued them and took them to Naples. There was a row when they arrived there, though, because Italy already had her full quota of refugees. They were kept in a warehouse at the dockside while enquiries were made. They feared that they might be sent back to Gambia, but fortunately, a GOS Refugee Commander intervened, and they were taken to a UN camp in Pisa.

When they had recovered, Ahinee was employed as an interpreter and welfare worker for African women refugees, and Mina went to school and then trained as a teacher. As you know, when we met she was teaching children in a Steiner School. I was going to explain all this later, of course, but it's better that you know everything now. It's all so emotional. I thought it was best to let you meet Mina, rather than read about it second hand in a letter from me."

"Of course." Mark spoke first. "We understand and want you to know, Mina, that you are very welcome here."

"I know when I am in a good house," said Mina.

*　*　*

Elsa heard the front door close and the murmur of voices. Then footsteps, as they both came up the stairs.

Mark entered their bedroom quietly and shut the door. Elsa was sitting up in bed, trying to read a book, but unable to concentrate on it, her head in a whirl of thoughts and emotions. She looked up at him.

"What do you reckon?" he said.

He looks tired, Elsa thought. It was the first opportunity they'd had to speak to one another privately since Mark had come home with Rory and Mina. Later, Mark, had taken them both back to the aunt's home in Exeter, brought Rory back with him, and returned the car to the compound.

There was a slight pause. Mark studied her face. Suddenly, she smiled. "Well, I like her – gee – I like that girl, such spirit! But it's all so sudden."

"Quite. She's so open and direct. I think I'd have fallen for her, if I were his age, but they shouldn't be talking about marriage – not yet."

"Well, we've only just met her, honey. They've been together for about a year, by my reckoning."

"I know but … why didn't he tell us?"

"I dunno, he should have. I sure hope it wasn't because he thought we might not want him to marry a black girl, and feared we might rock his boat."

"Perhaps we might have said something tactful in a letter. Delicate words of advice etc. that he didn't want to hear. But it's difficult now because of this Tamcaster business. She's here in Exeter for a month, and we're due in Tamcaster in two weeks time. He's expected to come with us as part of the delegation."

"Well. He can't, can he? Not now. He has to stick by Mina, that's clear."

"Just so. But there's a problem. He wants to go, and he wants her to go with him too, and she's looking forward to it."

"She can't come. We haven't booked a place, and she isn't from Woodleigh, so she couldn't be part of a Wessex delegation."

"Of course, we haven't booked a place." Mark sat down on the bed. "We didn't know she existed, did we? But as he pointed out to me, coming back in the car today, this means we'll lose the opportunity to see anything of her for two out of the four weeks of her visit. I agree they must be together. He can't leave her at a loose end in Exeter."

"She'll be with her aunt, and there are a lot of things to see in Exeter and around this area, but I suppose that not what she came for. She really wants to get to know his folks."

"And we really want to get to know her, don't we?"

"Yes, I sure do, for one," said Elsa. "Gee, I can't go walking around a strange town for two weeks when I should be gettin' to know my future daughter-in-law."

"Nor can I and Mina needs him, of course. She hasn't come here to explore the cathedral, the city walls and the underground caves."

"I think he must pull out of the Tamcaster trip."

"But he wants to go. He's very keen indeed. He's been reading up about the place, and he knows more about Tamcaster than you or I. What's more those people we are staying with are interested in his experience with the Peace Corps. It adds a new dimension to our delegation, so I've just told him that I'm going to ring that chap Milton who we're staying with and explain. I promised to see if it's possible for her to come too. They should be able to find a bed for her there. It's a big city."

"Oh well, if you've promised, go ahead, honey. It's a bit of a cheek really. It'll put up their costs."

"Yes, but I think they'll get value for their money. She's a real character. You should have heard the things she had to say on the drive over there. She brings a touch of Africa and Italy to the delegation, and she's a teacher, painter and musician."

Mark started to undress. "Kid's honestly," he said as he hung his jacket and trousers in the wardrobe. "Rory's grown into a great big bear of a chap, and he's clueless as a child when it comes to tact."

He padded to the door in his socks and disappeared into the bathroom.

When he came back, Mark was more resigned to the situation.

"I think it's for the best really. I've been turning if over. It gives us the chance to see her in a very different situation. When she's here, she's under pressure to give a good impression – so much depends on it. It will be quite different if we can have her with us in Tamcaster. She'll have to cope with a wide range of people and situations. We will see how strong she is. We'll soon know it if she's brittle or has a temper. Tamcaster's one hell of a place, you know. Some people call it a jungle."

"Why do they say that?"

"It's not very polite, but there are so many different nationalities there, Afro-Caribbean, Indian, Pakistani, Vietnamese, Poles. Most of them are quite well behaved, I'm told, but then there are the English grockles."

"I thought you didn't like that word."

"I don't, but I can't think of another word to use without foul language."

"We'll see how she copes with that lot, then. She's a very strong young woman."

"Rory says she's marvellous with dumb kids."

"I heard him say it, but Rory's in love, remember, and you know the saying 'love is blind.' "

"Well we aren't, yet. We shall see for ourselves."

"Speak for yourself. I'm not sure."

"Not sure about what?"

"About whether I've fallen in love with her in the last few hours."

"Come to think of it. Neither am I."

"Oh dear! Put out your bed-light, darling. I need to sleep now."

Mark obliged.

"Now we might as well be blind. Good night, love. Happy dreams."

But it was a long time before they got any sleep. Thoughts of Rory and Amina kept them awake and, when they did eventually drop off, Mark and Elsa both dreamed of the young lovers. There really was no escaping.

* * *

The next day, Beatrice wakened up and lay in bed thinking. *If Rory's going to marry an African, and I'm going to have an African sister-in-law, I'd better start getting to know her. I don't know anyone, who's got an African sister-in- law. It's quite exciting. I must have a talk to her, and find out as much as I can.*

"Would you like me to take you round the area and show you how things are arranged in the cluster groups?" Beatrice volunteered after breakfast.

Mina was delighted, so the two girls left the house, with Max trotting at their heels.

"There are eight housing clusters in Woodleigh," Beatrice explained. "Four here on the west of the town centre and four others on the east side. The one we live in was the first to be built, and it's called Coppice Cluster because of the trees around it. They're older than the houses. Sylvan Cluster is our nearest one; most of the others are called after the names of birds that are found in the area. Would you like to come to the Community Hall, and see our big shop there?"

Mina agreed, and they talked as they walked along.

"The idea is that we aim to be carbon zero," Beatrice explained. "That's important because carbon emissions do a lot of damage in the world. There was a big conference in Paris, France, a long time ago, I think it was around 2015, and the countries represented there all pledged to keep the rise in emissions below 1.5 degrees. The only way countries can do that is if families keep their carbon footprint small, so several towns decided to set the pace. Woodleigh entered the challenge, and we're leading the way through the cluster monitoring scheme. We create enough energy in each cluster to meet our needs in heating, lighting, transport, and food preparation. You saw last night that we lit candles around the table for our meal. We do have electric lights in the home, but we use them as little as possible."

"I love candle-light," said Mina. "It's cosy, and it reminds me of my first home in Gambia. We didn't have electricity in our village."

"Yes, I like candles too. We've got electricity all right, but it tots up our carbon emissions, so we use it a little as possible. We usually get up early in the morning, soon after sunrise, and then we get drowsy in the evening, so we don't use much electric power in the summer. It's

131

different in the winter, of course, but candles help a lot. Cluster people restrict the use of electric machines in the home too. We do a lot of our washing by hand and we've brought back the kitchen range idea. You saw mom's range this morning over breakfast, with a fire in the middle and the ovens on either side. There's a workshop up the road that makes those stoves. Most of our food is home grown or bought from the community shop which is the place we are going to now."

"Again, this is like we did in the village where I was brought up in Gambia, but, despite the great river which is polluted, we were short of clean drinking water there. I had to walk to a well to fill a bucket each morning and carry it back on my head. I didn't dare spill any because it was so precious."

"I couldn't possibly do that. How do you learn to balance a bucket on your head?"

"Everyone learns that. You practice as a little child. It's necessary."

"We have plenty of water in Britannia, because we have a lot of rain, so we catch the rain from the roof and store it in a big tank. It's used for washing and flushing the toilet. There's a separate supply of drinking water. See – that's our community hall over there. Mom and Dad's shop's on the ground floor, and there are several workshops there too. Above them are two lounges with TVs in them and a big meeting hall for our discussions, parties and special occasions."

Outside the village store there were displays of vegetables and fruit. People were helping themselves and putting things they wished to buy into wire baskets and taking them inside for checking. The coins being used were mainly Woodleigh pennies and pounds, a local currency, which as Beatrice explained, kept the money in the area, because the coins were only of value in the town. On the counter there was a charity collecting box, and on the wall beside were posters about local activities and fund raising opportunities for good causes.

The community shop served the four west clusters, and many of the other Woodleigh residents used it as well, because the food on sale was locally grown, much of it organically. It was clear of preservatives, and most of it looked fresh and appetising, although the shop had an ugly section for good food, which was misshapen or otherwise unattractive. These items sold well too, because they were cheaper.

Mina enjoyed looking round the shop, which also had a handicraft counter. Ladies and men's clothing were sold at the back of the shop, and Beatrice explained that many of the items had been made on the premises. To prove the point, she open a door and they were able to step into a workshop, equipped with several sewing machines and a retro treadle-spinning machine, which was being operated by a man. Mina laughed to see him. "I don't think you'd see many African men working one of those," she said. "They'd say that's women's work."

"Plenty of men would talk like that in Woodleigh too, but we don't hold with stereo-typing in the clusters," said Beatrice.

In a woodwork room next door, as if to prove the point, a young woman was sawing a plank of wood. "I'm making home furniture," she told them. "It's local timber from trees that have had their day. For every tree that's felled, we've planted ten saplings in Sylvan Cluster. I'm furnishing my own flat there."

Mina was surprised that so many people were finding the time to do these jobs, but Beatrice explained, it was all part of the cluster contract.

"When they sign up for one of the houses," she explained, "they sign a contract to say that at least one member of each household will do half-time community work in the cluster. It's all logged down in the community register, and has to be verified by the Task Co-ordinator. What you have to remember is that most people in the clusters have volunteered to do half-time paid work and also some community work. Without this the cluster system could not be run properly. Apart from all the jobs here in the community hall, we have a garage, where the pool cars have to be regularly maintained and then there's the essential work on the community plot. All families have their own section, but some elderly people can't maintain their plots, so volunteers do it for them. There are other jobs too: technical ones like running our vital system for electricity storage or erecting and inspecting wind turbines and social tasks like looking after the elderly, and running the child day nursery. All this is volunteer labour. Motherhood is recognised as an important job for the first five years, and a standard wage is paid by the government. Some young mothers have a half-time task looking after children in the playgroups, or tending their own parents if they're ailing. This time is all registered and people get credits for it. Even when it's something in their own extended family."

"It was like this in the African village," said Mina. "We didn't have any rules and regulations though and there were no log books or wages paid, it happened naturally, and then we had the wise women who helped with child-birth, and knew a lot about herbal cures."

"My mom's a wise woman that way. She keeps a cupboard full of herbal medicines, and she works on the health counter some days in the store and gives out loads of advice. Dad's the store manager, so he has to do all the stocktaking and organises the shop assistant timetable. You remember last night we had a vegetarian meal. Most of the people who live in cluster houses are vegetarians. That's because we realise that we can't feed the hungry world otherwise, because so much land is taken up with growing crops for farm animals. Farming has become inhumane too. Animals are just bred to grow fatter, and often aren't allowed a natural lifestyle. "

Beatrice and Mina continued their conversation over glasses of local mulled wine in the community coffee shop.

"I can't imagine what it would be like to live in a refugee camp. How did you feel when you arrived there?" Beatrice asked cautiously.

"It was a great relief. We knew we were safe at last, but it was also very strange for us. My father had been the headman in our village in Gambia, and, of course, we knew all our neighbours. Our family had been leaders in Nkobo for generations. In the camp, there were hundreds of refugees from many different countries, speaking languages we didn't understand, and we'd no status there. I started going to school again. That was a big relief and I made new friends with people from different African countries and elsewhere. We had good teachers and I did well there. When I had really settled in, they invited me to help some of the new arrivals, and I liked doing that. My mother became a main interpreter for new African refugees in the camp too, so we did similar tasks and became valued again. When I left that school, the head teacher introduced me to the Steiner school staff, and I started helping new arrivals there. In the evenings and at weekends, I studied part-time for a local teaching certificate, organised through an Italian college."

"That must have been difficult."

"It was. I had to do a correspondence course, and attend some lessons on Saturdays.

I also learned to play the guitar." She smiled, "That made me popular. I was asked to entertain at birthday parties in the camp and at both schools. That's why I have so many bangles on my arm. Some of them are 'thank-you' presents and remind me of these people. They're only cheap ones really, but they mean a lot to me."

Beatrice gazed at the multi-coloured bangles: red, gold, blue and green tints glinting against Mina's strong, black arm. Beatrice counted ten of them.

"I think they're lovely, and so is that big engagement ring on your finger." Beatrice looked at it admiringly and, for a moment, she held Mina's hand in her own, and was surprised to note the contrast between the black of Mina's arm and her lighter palms.

"If I'm going to marry your brother, we might as well give each other a love token. Choose one you fancy," Mina invited.

"Oh, that's very kind, but if they have memories for you, it wouldn't be fair." After a twinge of disappointment she added, "But, if there's one that's not so special, perhaps we could swap it for one of mine." There were three on her wrist.

"It's not easy for me to choose, because you only have three and I have ten. Which one can you spare?" asked Mina.

"Tell you what," said Beatrice. "Instead of exchanging them permanently. Let's have a daily exchange, while you are staying here. Then neither of us loses any."

"That's a good idea," Mina replied, with a big grin and a glint in her eyes.

So that's what they did - each day for the next few weeks.

"Here's to Amina, my future sister-in-law," said Beatrice, as the first exchange took place.

"And here's to Beatrice," said Mina. "My new white sister-in-law."

"And to Mina, my new black one."

They clinked glasses, laughed, and a little spark of delight warmed both hearts.

PART TWO - Wessex and Mercia

"Never before have we had so much awareness about the damage we are doing to the planet, and never before have we had the power to do so much about it."

(David Attenborough)

CHAPTER 11 - Discovering Mercia

The journey to Mercia was a great learning experience. None of the party from Woodleigh had travelled far north before. There was little need for this nowadays, as each province of Britannia was organised sustainably according to the GOS regulations. Members of the cluster groups had a moral reason too. They had all pledged to keep their ecological footprints as low as possible and travelling far by rail had meant off-setting in other ways. Now however, solar air travel had taken over.

They boarded the first air-bus at Exeter, and found that the seating arrangements were similar to those on the old trains, with seats facing each other rather than in rows. Instructions were given over loudspeakers for everyone to strap themselves in safely before take-off. The engine noise was subdued as they rose vertically, watching the land moving away beneath them.

Approaching Bristol, they passed over several massive wind-farms. They looked down on two miles of winding turbines and, when they lowered at the airport, they saw a vast sea of solar panels covering the city. Most roofs was encased in them, but here and there, they caught glimpses of green, red and yellow, where rooftop gardens intervened.

The solar bus station was alive with passengers and all empty seats were soon occupied. Some of them appeared to be fairly new arrivals in Britannia, as they spoke to one another in foreign languages. There were several Africans, some Asians and groups of Europeans amongst the travellers. Bristol, it seemed, had become a truly cosmopolitan city.

The flight continued north. Soon they were passing over another vast forest of wind turbines. Little else could be seen through the windows, and the rapidly turning blades made dizzy viewing. Beyond this were some green fields and villages, and a glimpse of rolling hills. But then came a formidable sight: barbed wire fences, interspersed with observation towers, which clearly must signal the boundary between Wessex and the mile long strip of no-man's-land.

When the plane landed the airport was bristling with security staff and waiting dogs. As they emerged, loudspeakers announced the Wessex boundary: "All change here for Mercia and Cymru."

Everyone had to collect their baggage and leave the air-bus at this checkpoint. They saw armed police on duty and barriers to pass through, where grey uniformed staff were waiting to check the luggage, with the help of electronic controls, robots and sniffer dogs.

"What's all this fuss for?" asked Beatrice.

"It must be checks for illegal immigrants. We met this right across Europe," said Rory.

After they had all disembarked and gone through these barriers, where robots electronically checked their tickets and security staff examined their identity cards and bags, they saw four entrance points labelled Mercia (British), Mercia (Aliens), Cymru (British) and Cymru (Alien). Clearly, Mina had to join a different queue. Rory took her arm and went with her as far as the barrier. The security officer reached out for Rory's papers, and after a quick glance, handed them back and pointed him towards the other queue.

"This lady and I are engaged to be married," Rory said, as Mina handed over her documents.

"You go through different corridors." There was no hint of a smile.

Mina's eyes were downcast. "Look at me," snapped the guard. He compared her face with the photograph on her card. "You are a refugee with permission to enter Wessex," he announced. "Have you clearance to enter Mercia?"

Mina did not reply. She was clearly terrified, and could not look the man in the face.

"She is a member of our visiting party…" Rory began.

"You go through the other gate," shouted the man. An armed policeman intervened. He put his hand on Rory's sleeve and another on Mina's. "Detained for questioning," he said. "Come this way please, both of you."

Beatrice was the only one who saw this happening. She cried out to tell the others, as she passed through the barriers with Mark and Elsa. They turned to see an angry Rory and a sobbing Mina talking to an armed policeman.

"Please, board the Mercian air-bus." An attendant was standing by the queue.

"There seems to be a problem for my son and his fiancé," Mark said.

The attendant shrugged his shoulders and turned to others in the queue, urging them to board the flight. Peter urged Frances and Adam to go and claim the seats booked for the whole party. Then he and Mark walked back towards the barrier and spoke to one of the policemen nearby.

"Two people in my party are being held up over there. I've got documentation for the whole group," Peter said. "We are an official delegation from Wessex to Mercia - Tamcaster in fact." The policeman led them back through the barrier to join the others.

Peter explained everything again, and showed the authorisation papers to the officer, who looked at them carefully. "I see that the name of Miss Adong has been added at a recent date. Who authorised that?"

"I did this with the approval of the Tamcaster local authorities," Peter explained.

"Do you have the contact details?"

"Yes, it was arranged through Councillor Langland. That's the telephone number there, on the paper you are holding."

"Good. I'll ring him."

The policeman pressed the number into his wrist-pad and fortunately Bruce answered the telephone quickly, and was able to confirm the arrangements.

"We were delighted to hear that Miss Adong has been added to the group. Accommodation has been arranged for her through another councillor and the lord mayor is expecting to meet them all on Monday."

This assurance seemed to satisfy the policeman, who then said that they needed to pay £50 for an extra visa. They found the money and filled in the documentation and eventually Mina was waved through the barrier.

When they looked back, however, they saw several of the other foreign passengers being bundled into police vans.

"See those are people over there. They must be more illegal immigrants," said someone nearby.

"I don't know how they all get here", another voice said. "The province is swarming with them."

Once on the air-bus, Rory held Mina's trembling hand for the next hour. They both knew she had had a narrow escape. Mina did not a say word. Her eyes were downcast, with her hands on her lap.

When all the approved passengers had boarded the flight, it airbus rose slowly and moved towards a control tower bearing the name "Mercia." It did not proceed, until a green light flashed. It moved slowly forwards and then landed again on the opposite side of the barbed fence, where a team of Mercian security staff boarded. A policeman kept watch while another ticket check took place. Mina kept her eyes downcast throughout. Eventually the airbus was allowed to proceed. It rose again and the flight continued at a steady pace. They all heaved a sigh of relief.

"It's disgusting," said Beatrice. "I'd no idea that there was all this fuss about borders. What difference does it make? Britannia is one country isn't it?"

"Doesn't seem like it," said Rory. "It wasn't like this on trains before I joined the Peace Corps."

"It's this stupid government we've got now," grumbled Peter. "They're so terrified of people smugglers and illegal immigrants that they make life impossible for ordinary people."

"It was like this when we crossed Europe," Rory told them. "It upsets Mina because of what she's been through. When I first left Britannia there was only a simple border check at Dover and then by the French at Calais, but when I came home there were checks in Austria, Germany and France as well as Dover."

"They've tightened up on security again all over," Peter replied. "But this is completely over the top. The stupid thing is that this government of ours calls itself the Freedom Party. Freedom for the rich and powerful they mean."

Beatrice tried to catch Mina's eye with a re-assuring smile, but she stayed clutching Rory's hand and did not look at any of the others for most of the journey.

The air-bus flew over rolling green hills and quiet farms, while cattle browsed timelessly in large open fields. They caught glimpses of villages and church spires mixed with woods and winding lanes, followed by parades of wind farms and fields covered in solar panels, reminding them of the age they were in. The journey also crossed over a succession of desolate areas, where the landscape looked ravaged. Huge hills of earth were piled beside deep pits, many of them filled with stagnant black water.

"What's happened in these places?" Beatrice was shocked.

Peter answered with a single word: "Fracking."

"What's that?"

"The plague of the north: drilling for shale gas. They promised these sites would be restored once they'd finished their exploration, but just look at the mess left behind."

Adam remembered the map in his father's study. It made him wonder what sort of place Tamcaster would be.

The airbus landed twice en route, at Gloucester and Worcester. Soon after leaving, they crossed a huge area of farmland entirely manned by robots. Machines shaped like humans, with metal arms and legs, were gathering crops. Other robotic implements shaped like heavy vehicles were scattering manure or showering seeds. A robot dressed in shirt and trousers was plodding beside this machine.

"Look!" Mina cried in surprise. Elsa laughed and Mark looked at the machine with interest.

"That's the first task I was given on my Dad's farm, when I was a nipper," he observed. "I played the part of a scarecrow when the seed was scattered."

"That was a huge co-operative farm," Peter added. "I saw a sign saying that it belongs to the county council."

Several more farms of this kind were passed before the air-bus landed at the provincial capital, Tamcaster: a great tangle of buildings, seemingly presided over by a notable old castle, which stood high above the rooftops on its ancient rocky platform.

*　*　*

Bruce Langland was waiting with Milton and Christine Lamb at the barrier in the airport forecourt. They all wore labels on which their names were printed in bold letters.

It was not so easy for them to identify the Woodleigh visitors, as so many people were streaming through. *The airbuses must have been packed,* they thought.

"Bruce." A shout came from Peter. They shook hands, and he introduced Frances and Adam.

"Hi there." It was easier for Mark to recognise the large Afro-Caribbean couple, with their welcoming smiles. Greetings followed from Elsa, Beatrice, Rory and Mina.

"Good to meet you all. We have two of the pool cars waiting, so Bruce and I will run you to our homes in a few minutes. My, you got a lot of luggage there. We try to cramp it all in mi' car," said Milton, with a cheery smile. "We'll get you all in, but some may have to carry bags on laps."

After handshakes, they moved towards the cars.

"Your train was on time. Did you have a good journey?" Gwen asked Frances.

"Yes, but there was there a scare at the border! It was a struggle finding our seats, but once we all sat down again together, everything was plain sailing."

Bruce's car was the first to leave the forecourt, carrying Peter, Frances and Adam.

Milton's car could carry all his passengers but not all the luggage.

"Is it far? I can walk if you show me the way," said Rory.

 "No, no, tell you what. I take all the ladies and the luggage," suggested Milton. "If you and your dad, set off walkin' down that road over there, I be back to meet you on the corner of the street. Just keep on till you come to the T-junction, and I'll collect you from there. It's not far to my place, so I'll drop the bags off and come back for you quick."

The second car turned out of the airport approach, threaded it's way into busy traffic, and set off in an opposite direction from Bruce's car.

Mark and Rory strolled along the pavement together. Fortunately, it was a fine, sunny day. The road they were walking down was lined with warehouses and office buildings.

"Not a very interesting part of the town this," Mark looked around. "I've never been here before."

"Did you notice the castle, standing high on the rock, as we came into the station?" asked Rory. "I'd like to have a look around there while we're here."

"Yes, this is an interesting old city, I'm told," said Mark. "It's got a long history. It used to be a big industrial base but, of course, but that's all gone now. Although, for all we know, factories might be coming back again now that it's so difficult to ship commodities from overseas. Not that it would do much to decrease unemployment. The factories would quickly fill up with robots."

"It wouldn't surprise me," Rory responded. "So many of the factories didn't last long in the hot countries. If the floods and the storms haven't driven them out of the tropics, the endless wars soon will. It seems as if all Africa and most of Asia is fleeing now and trying to get into Europe or Australia and everyone in South America is trying to escape north. Can you blame them, when they compare their living conditions to ours?"

"Yes, it's a terrible thing. It's been happening off and on for a very long time. It started around 2012 I believe, when there were terrible wars in the Middle East and Northern Africa. Then it stopped with the settlement made to prevent World War Three, when GOS was formed, and they set up refugee camps all over Europe, like the one you helped with in Italy. They were in America and Australia as well. After the tragedies occurred, governments at last saw sense and began to take an equal share of the poor souls. Now it's all starting up again. I never thought it would, but these new nationalist governments have started quarrelling again. It's seems as if the clock has turned back to the terrible twenty-teens when you had idiots like Trump and Putin in power, threatening each other with nuclear weapons. Thank God there were wiser people around who managed to save the world. I was a child at that time, but Gramps told me all about it."

A beggar was squatting on the pavement, with an empty cap placed strategically in front of his tattered trousers. Rory tossed a coin into the cap as he went by.

"I never quite know what to do about guys like him," said Mark. "I feel I want to help, but don't want to feed drug habits. That's another sign of the times. I remember there were people like him around when I was your age, but they disappeared after the Responsible Party got into power, and started reforming our welfare provision."

A honk from a horn made them turn to see Milton waving to them from his car on the opposite side of a busy road, signing that he would find a place to turn round. Minutes later he drew up alongside.

Milton's delightful daughters, Bonnie and Trish, opened the door when Mark and Rory arrived. Bonnie was a sturdy young lady with a big Afro-Caribbean smile.

Trish was a quieter girl with a lighter complexion and a gift for putting everyone at their ease. They both wore brightly coloured ribbons in their frizzy hair, carrying the word 'Welcome'. There was a buffet meal. Everyone was invited to select a plate and fill it with samosas and sandwiches, and to dip celery sticks into a range of delicacies.

"I think you all know that we've a full house here, so you'll be sleeping next door. After we've all had enough to eat, I'll introduce you to our neighbours, Merfin and Glynis, a lovely Welsh couple. You can take your bags over and settle in then."

Christine explained. "We'll all meet here again in the dining room at around 7.30, and Peter's family will join us to discuss the programme for next week."

Peter, Frances and Adam arrived with their hosts, Bruce and Gwen, while the others were still next-door. They waited until everyone had crowded into the room, and then Bruce gave them all a copy of the programme for the visit. At first glance, it looked a bit formidable.

Programme for Visitors from Wessex

Monday	2pm.	Civic Reception at the Town Hall
Tuesday	10am.	Visit to Forest Community Centre
Wednesday	10am.	Visit to Eco-House and community housing
Thursday	10am.	Visit to St. Luke's allotment scheme
Friday	2.0 pm.	Visit to Afro-Caribbean Community Centre
Saturday		Free Day
Sunday	10.30am.	Forest Community Church Service
	3pm.	Interfaith Activities
Monday	Bank Holiday.	Multi-racial Carnival activities
Tuesday	10am.	Visit to Tamcaster Eco House & Co-operative
Wednesday	10.30am	Visit to Mercian Power Generating and storage
Thursday	11.am.	Visit to Mercian Provincial Offices
Friday	10.am.	Visit to Mosque and Asian Community Centre
Saturday	10.am.	Visit to Synagogue and Hebrew Congregation
Sunday	2.pm.	Visit to Hindu Temple and Farewell Party

"I don't want you to feel that this programme is too crowded," Bruce told them. "There's a lot to see in Tamcaster, and we've included as much as possible, but we have only planned one activity for each day. This leaves you space to do other things too. I'm sure that there will be

147

many more places you want to visit. Feel free to make your own arrangements. I hope you will find the programme allows this and that you all enjoy your time with us. You know of course, that there are five more guests from Woodleigh arriving later tonight. Councillor Simpson, who is their main host, is arranging that programme. You'll be seeing them at the council meeting tomorrow afternoon and at the farewell party. They're going to some of the same places as you but at different times. We didn't want the groups to be too big, but you may want to meet them socially."

"Yes. They come from the other side of Woodleigh," explained Peter. "I've been in touch with Angela Belfield, the leader of that group. When we go home, we'll do a combined presentation on this visit to the Woodleigh Town Council."

"Do we all have to stay together the whole time?" asked Rory.

"Not at all," said Bruce. "I hope you'll all be present for the opening session at the City Hall and the closing one on the last day. Apart from that, the only thing we require is some of the delegates attend each occasion. You can pick and choose which events you go to, but for courtesy's sake, we hope that there will a reasonable number of people at each of these events. I think you'll find all of these places well worth visiting."

"That sounds fair to me," said Peter. "We are planning that you will have similar opportunities when you come to Woodleigh."

"On Wednesday," Bruce continued, "I've arranged a viewing of one of our three cluster housing areas. These are all based on your model, but of course they were not purpose built. People who have opted for cluster houses rent them, and agree to the behaviour model, but the properties are scattered around the housing estate concerned.

On Thursday morning, Milton will show you round the community allotment in the St. Luke's District. This is one of our biggest council housing areas. The allotments cover Hunger Hill, belying its old name.

148

What used to be a lean, scraggy slope is now bursting with fertility. On Friday, we'll escort some of you round the Afro-Caribbean Community Centre. I think the young people will be interested in the youth activity programme there."

"There's different things to see at each place you are invited to," explained Milton. "At Forest Community Centre, there is a pre-school play-group which is run by Chris. There's also a women's group, and a very active youth club. I guess some of you might want to go into different rooms to meet all the people."

"And beside what's on the programme, there are also other things you might like to see," said Christine. " I run a reading class at the women's' prison on Friday mornings. We organise it like a book club, with discussions, but a lot of the women need extra help. It's not on the programme, but some of you ladies might like to join me there."

"Sure, I'll join you!" said Elsa with enthusiasm.

"Please count me in too," Mina raised her hand.

"We can pencil that in then for next Friday morning. I need to get clearance.

You have to complete forms, and you'll be given printed name badges. It won't interfere with the visit to the Afro-Caribbean Centre visit because that's in the afternoon."

"Thank you for organising such a good programme, " said Mark. "We hear a lot about Tamcaster in the news, but unfortunately, the press seems to make more of bad news than good. I'm very impressed at the multi-cultural tone of this programme you've arranged."

"We've learned quite a bit in the last few years," Bruce replied. "There were some race riots here about four years ago and it served as a wake up call. More people became involved in developing good community programmes and we got some financial help from the Mercian Provincial Offices. We were able to set up some of the projects that you'll be seeing. There are still serious problems. We have a very high rate of youth unemployment and that's very bad for morale. There's little worse than completing your schooling and then finding little at the end of it, so the council have developed a number of area work clubs and associated training schemes. This isn't on your programme at present, but it's something you may like to add in."

Beatrice and Adam said that they would be interested in seeing these.

"Some of the work clubs are in the community centres you're going to," commented Christine, "and training schemes are close by, so this can easily be arranged. Several of the women in the prison go on training courses to learn skills needed in the employment field, after they're released. A lot of those who were involved in the rioting are helped to learn more about different cultures and, if they show interest, they're invited to meet a trained mentor, who will take them to different racial groups and let them sit in at certain sessions and participate if appropriate."

"We've had interfaith football matches, sometimes against each other and sometimes with mixed teams and we've boxing and judo and martial arts; all under careful instruction, you understand," added Milton.

"What about the girls?" asked Beatrice.

"Oh, there's a girls' football team. I'm in that," said Bonnie, with an eager smile.

"An' there's all sorts of music groups," said Trish. "Gospel, soul and folk. Then there's jazz an' steel bands an' marching bands. You must see our Caribbean Festival."

"I can't wait. I love that sort of thing," said Mina.

"There's so much to learn," said Elsa. "Two weeks is never gonna' be long enough, but we promise to do our best. I don't think we'll ever forget this visit to Tamcaster."

CHAPTER 12 - The Official Welcome

A blackbird perched on an ash tree by their bedroom window woke Peter and Frances. They lay there for a few minutes watching the shadowy patterns on the white ceiling above their bed. The sunlight on the pale curtains gave promise of a pleasant summer day.

When Peter opened the curtains he marvelled at the rural view, despite the fact that they were in a big city. Immediately under the window was stone patio, set with wooden chairs and a table. From the patio, curving stone steps led down to a lower one, where a range of herbs were growing in long pots. Yellow and pink wild flowers grew in the borders. Beyond, the land fell away into a gentle dale, with an orchard of apple and pear trees, and a broad stretch of communal allotment, which had clearly been formed by merging the gardens of around twenty houses. The house walls, on either side enclosed the whole area protectively.

Frances came to join him. They had been told about the allotment and glimpsed it last night in the dusk, but to appreciate it all, they needed this high bedroom view. A central path ran between trees and bushes, leading to a chicken run at the far end, by a jumble of sheds.

"Come and join us. No hurry." Bruce was hailing him.

Peter looked down and saw that the patio table was set for breakfast.

He opened the window and called, "My – what a wonderful view from up here."

Bruce nodded. "Glad you appreciate it, that's why we put you there. It's our room really. Join us, when you're ready. No hurry."

When he was dressed and shaved, Peter found Adam sitting on a patio chair next to Gwen, tucking into honey and toast.

"It looks as if we're going to have a lovely day," Bruce observed, "We like to eat outside whenever we can. Help yourself to cereals on the sideboard and bring your bowl down here. We've got yoghurt and goat's milk here on the table. Tea or coffee?"

Peter gave himself a selection of rice, nuts, corn and oat flakes and carried his bowl as he stepped outside through the French window.

"Tea please — milk but no sugar." Gwen poured this out and passed it over.

"You're giving us a feast this morning. When is it that we're due at the City Hall?"

"Not till two this afternoon, so the morning's yours."

"Fran will be here in a few minutes. What a marvellous job you two have made of this community allotment."

"Glad you think so, but you haven't explored it yet. There's a wonderful view of it from that bedroom up there because the land falls away, as you can see." Gwen was enthusiastic. "When we first came here it was a patchwork of little gardens, divided up by garden fences and hedges. Bruce was the one with the idea, but those neighbours of ours took a lot of persuading."

"They were concerned over so many issues, leaseholds and land rights for example," said Bruce. "There are still boundaries. We set stones in the ground mark them. You'll have to look to find them though, but they're there alongside the allotments. People were worried that they'd never sell their houses at first, but the reverse is true. Now we have a waiting list of people who want to move here. Some of them would almost buy any house in the crescent, or the road at the far end, to be part of the scheme."

After breakfast, the visitors all went on a stroll round the allotment with Bruce, who pointed out the way the produce was managed. Gwen went with them.

"Although these pebbles mark the boundaries of the old gardens, everyone works on our share-system which crosses the whole area." Bruce explained. "Most people who live here are in half-time employment in the city. They sign a contract agreeing to donate several hours every week to the allotment. The number of hours varies according to the seasons, of course. Each shareholder agrees to carry out certain tasks, and others are crop supervisors: potatoes, beans, peas, etc. Rob's responsible for the orchard and Adrian for the beehives, - you'll see those at the end of this central lane. Eleanor does the hen run and Andy's our pig and goat man. These people have a target crop that they set and aim for. They also keep an eye on the volunteer workers and deal with any crop surplus. Everyone has an equal take and the crop supervisor monitors this, though we find people are very open and honest actually, because it's a happy family and it's in our common interest to keep it so."

There were ten hives at the end of the dell and bees were buzzing all around the area. "One of the things we're quite proud of," said Gwen, "is that we've persuaded the neighbours around here to grow buddleia in their gardens to encourage them.

We were worried about the loss of bees, and the damage being done through lack of pollination, so we wrote some articles for the local paper explaining how our native bees were becoming endangered through air pollution, We advertised the Breckhill Honey we were producing, and had such a good response that we've now got a series of buddleia trails right across the city, and also a network of customers all over Tamcaster."

"So, if we get stung by bees in the Town Square, we know who to complain to," joked Elsa.

The others arrived later in the morning, and so they discussed what they wanted to do.

Fran, Elsa and Mina decided to explore the town shops with Gwen. "We must all be sure to meet up together at the City Hall at two o'clock," she advised them. She took them into the city in the car.

The others went with Bruce to have a good view of the city from the top of Breck Hill.

At the far side of the playing fields, they looked down on a huge stretch of urban development, dotted with green patches here and there. There were still some old factory chimneys standing, and a few church spires, but most of the tall buildings were concrete towers: blocks of housing, offices or warehouses. Most buildings had flat roofs, which were covered with solar panels, but some of them had been turned into green fertility. An electric tram-line ran through the city, and a railway track curved round the edge. Castle walls and a high tower stood on a rock at the opposite end of this urban vale. A line of turning wind turbines dominated the skyline to the east.

"This is a patchwork town, as you can see. We have new housing estates at the fringes, older properties next and then the city centre in the middle. That grey tower is part of the city university building and those blocks over there are the U.E.E. powerhouse."

"What's U.E.E?" queried Beatrice.

"United Engineering Enterprises. It's an amalgamation of several engineering companies – Baxter and Bowker, Hawthorne Engineering and Sellers Electrical.

We're glad it's still running because we've lost so many factories. Some of the clothing work, which was sent overseas in the 1970's, has come back now. Transport costs are too heavy, but it's all so mechanised that it doesn't provide many jobs. We're mainly an administrative and trading town now. Most of the larger buildings, like the university, UEE and the City Hall are generating enough electricity to power themselves and they send their surplus to the Tamcaster grid."

"How old is the city?" asked Mark.

"Now, you've got me on my hobby horse. I take classes in local history at the University Adult Education Centre. That's where it all started," said Bruce, pointing to the castle. "Long before the castle was built, people lived in the caves below that cliff. That was in early Saxon times, and even before then too, they had a fortification of some rough sort on the cliff top where people could go in times of danger.

The Danes came in the longboats up the river and made a great assault, but they were beaten back and had to retreat. There was a strong woman called Elfleda, who held the fortress. She was a daughter of the great King Alfred, and was known as the Lady of Mercia because she was bravest woman in this Saxon Kingdom. She created the town here with its walls and gates, and had the first castle built, not because she was a warrior but because she wanted to protect the people from all around here.

She built other fortified towns round here too, but Tamcaster became the most important defence town in Mercia because it lay in this vale, with the wild hills to the north and the dense forests on either side. It was cut off from the south by the wide river, so it helped make it defensible. You can't see the river from here. It's behind the hill that we're standing on, so this place had to be fortified too. Years later, the Normans came, seized the old fort and built their own castle on the rock. For a couple of centuries there were two towns here, the Norman one on castle hill and the Saxon one below. The Saxons held the hill we're standing on too. The two communities traded with each other in the vale, and this was the start of our big market square. You can see it over there in front of the City Hall: the building with the big dome.

There were weavers and tanners here in medieval times, but the industrial revolution brought power looms and then lace factories and bicycles, cars and machines of all types. The lace market was over there and the jewellery quarter nestled beside it. People poured in from the countryside to work in the mills so back-to-back houses got crammed in yards and alleys all over the town. It sank into a shameful slum, but when we had reformers conditions were improved. Some factory owners built decent housing. You can see an example there in Arkwright Court where the houses are set round a green, and there was a church, school and a library provided by Arkwright."

 The men moved on, but the youngsters lingered looking at the view. Beatrice thought she could recognise the defensive position that Bruce had spoken about between the castle and the clock tower. The woodlands had disappeared under the urban sprawl. Below them was a churning city built for traffic with flyovers, underpasses and trams. Mixed up in the middle were concrete towers, office blocks and warehouses - a noisy, dirty and exciting jungle of activity.

"Elfleda, Lady of the Mercians. He said she was King Alfred's daughter." She looked curiously at Adam. "I wonder what she was doing here, so far from Wessex."

Adam shrugged his shoulders.

"I've never heard of her," Beatrice observed "She must have been a powerful woman to hold out against those Viking marauders. I'd like to go over there and look around that castle, wouldn't you? Perhaps there'll be some more information about Elfleda. I could make her the subject of my school project."

Meanwhile the men had walked on towards the rose gardens.

"I'm glad you've arranged for us to attend a council meeting this afternoon," Peter said to Bruce. "Do you get much support there for your community schemes?"

"That's a tough one. I used to be a member of the Green Party, you know. I didn't get much help in those days. There were only four Green Councillors, and control of the council was always swinging between the two main parties. Some years ago, the Greens held the balance of power, but not in my time. I lost my seat and became disillusioned, but then I saw so much going wrong that I wanted to be able to do something about it, so I bit my tongue and joined the Responsible Party.

I stayed firm for all my principles, and suddenly I found that there were ways of changing things after all. I'm the Councillor for Arkright Ward, one of the toughest in the city. No one else wanted it but I find it stimulating, and we're doing things."

"Such as?"

"Neighbourhood Co-operatives. We've set up a network of small groups where people support each other. They've done some amazing things in the last three years - credit unions for example, and children's play schemes, adopt-a-granny and community choirs. There's a kid's steel band called Pandemonium and a Feel-Good Factory in an empty warehouse. I didn't invent any of these things. They were all there waiting to be developed. It was a question of listening to what people were saying in the shops and pubs. I asked what was going wrong and, what bright ideas people had?

All I had to do was listen and then lend a hand by drawing up a proper business proposal where it was needed, then discuss it with the appropriate councillors and suddenly we had lift-off. If a critical mass of local people got behind the schemes, they thrived. If we didn't get that level of interest the projects were terminated, but around half of them are still running well, ten years later."

"You sound optimistic."

"I am, on the good days, but we're fighting against a rising tide. There are powerful forces pulling in the opposite direction."

"Tell me more," said Rory.

"Well, I must be careful. Please don't quote me. There are underground forces. Have you ever heard of G.F.?"

"No. What's that?"

"The Goodwill Foundation. Sounds wonderful, doesn't it? What could be more benign? Well, it's quite strong here. Several members of the local Freedom Party are big supporters. They're in opposition now but next year they might well control the City Hall.

The Foundation has strong links with some big multinationals, and the far right in the U.S.A, who are now driving the fracking industry round here. They are in close liaison with big financiers in London, the Gulf and China. Quite frankly, some of these people frighten me. They are so suave. You'll meet one or two of them this afternoon. They'll give you a hearty handshake and say how pleased they are to welcome you here, but you should see where these people live. They're all in gated communities, patrolled by security guards with fierce dogs, and some of them rub shoulders with very unpleasant elements in our inner cities.

You must have heard of the race riots we had here four years ago. We learned a lot from those. The city council has spent big money building up our community relations, but there were some shadowy customers who moved between the yobs, threw bricks and shouted obscenities. I've said enough, but keep your eyes skinned in the city hall this afternoon."

"Where are these gated communities?" asked Rory. "Are they in the city or the countryside around it?"

"Both. There's one of them rubbing shoulders with the historic castle on the rock. There's another a mile west of where we are now, and there's a big one south of the river. Don't get me wrong. I'm not saying that that all the Freedom Party members are mixed up in this – of course they're not. Some of them would be horrified if they knew, but the tentacles reach out in different directions, and it's difficult to know how far they will stretch if they get into power again."

"What about racial harmony? How do all these folk rub along together?" asked Peter.

"We're making a big effort. The Lord Mayor is a good woman. She's the first one ever to set up an Inter-faith Chaplaincy, instead of the usual Christian one, headed up by our dear Bishop. I've nothing against him

159

mind, but he's steeped in Anglican rites, and finds it difficult to think laterally. The Inter-faith Group includes the Muslim leaders, of course, and we've issued a joint statement on the need for tolerance and understanding. This has been backed up with a small grant, which enables us to have some paid workers, who organise the programmes, so that Muslim schoolchildren visit church youth clubs and vice versa. There are also some twinning arrangements in the offing for children in faith schools. We're trying to prepare our young people for what is likely to be a rocky ride, when the time comes for them to take over."

* * *

They travelled into the city on one of the frequent shoppers' trams, terminating by a large park-and-ride station.

"No vehicles are allowed in the city centre between the hours of nine and six. It's all pedestrianised within a quarter of a mile of the City Hall," Bruce explained. They walked briskly along busy shopping streets, which led towards the Market Square.

Gwen, Elsa and Mina were waiting by the stone lions outside the City Hall. The great clock in the dome above was booming 2pm, as they climbed the steps to the revolving door.

On the first floor they were warmly received by the Lord Mayor, who led them into her parlour. Councillor Jenny Paynter was a tall, chubby lady, with rosy cheeks and a slight Tamcaster accent.

"I'm delighted to meet you all, and particularly interested to see we have some young people here in the delegation. I've never been to Woodleigh, but I've read about your famous cluster groups and, as you may have heard, we're trying to do something along those lines here, I'm proud to say. It's not easy to replicate on a big housing estate, but we've invited volunteers to opt in to our sustainable life programmes and we've had some success. I hope, while you're here, you can make a point of visiting the Burnage cluster. That's in my ward, so I'd value your impressions."

"We're going to one of the housing groups, tomorrow," said Peter.

"Yes," said Milton, "But that's in my ward. We can easily add a visit to Burnage, if the Lord Mayor requests it."

"Only if they really want to come," added Mrs Paynter briskly. "Discuss it later, please. I don't want to upset your programme before you've started."

"I'd like to be able to see the experiment on a big estate," said Elsa.

"So would I," said Mark.

"No problem," said Milton. "It's easy to arrange an extra visit."

Mrs. Paynter beamed at him, "We are proud of the fact that all our new housing is kitted out with solar panels and water harvesting systems. We have a wide selection of properties including some community housing, where several families can share a large residence. These are usually well built older properties which were owned by wealthy people in Victorian times. Rather than knock them down, several of these have been specially adapted to make good community living accommodation."

"How are the families chosen?" asked Elsa.

"They aren't. The properties are advertised and families that have decided that they would like community living, band together to buy them. It's one of our innovations.

Talking of these new developments, you really must see our eco-superior glass windows in the reception suite here. Bruce will explain them to you. It's too technical for me, but we are very proud of them and also our solar panel display on the roof of this building. There's a wonderful view over the city centre rooftops from there. We ran a campaign to encourage the roofs to be properly used and the result is that most buildings have solar panels, and a few of them have gardens too. I'll ask Ranjit to show you the roof areas. Now, have you any questions?"

"I'm glad to see Tamcaster has a lady Lord Mayor," said Francis. "How many women are there on the council?"

"Good question. We have a fairly even balance. There are twenty-three out of forty councillors, so we are the majority. There are ten of us in the Responsible Party and seven in the Freedom Party, and one Asian Independent. It should be 50:50."

"That's a big improvement on how it is in Devon," said Elsa.

"We've made a big push in the last few years. Now that we're focussing on more family issues, women are much more ready to get involved, and with so many people working half-time, it gives women the freedom. Men used to dominate local councils in the bad old days, when women were thought of as housewives, child-minders and decorative entertainers. Those days are long gone."

"Yes, now that household tasks are shared equally, we've noticed that in Woodleigh," said Frances. "Unfortunately, though a lot of people are apathetic about politics, and some of the younger ones don't bother to vote, which I think is very sad when you remember the great struggle all those years ago, when all adults got the right to vote."

"A lot of people are disillusioned with party politics" said Rory. "What do you think is the biggest problem in politics today?"

Mrs Paynter hesitated. "Lack of courage," she responded thoughtfully. "There are a host of problems out there, and there are no easy answers. The big parties' pretend that they have the answers because they want to be elected. I think the most important issues today are climate change, peace with justice and racial harmony. There are no simple answers to any of those, but we've got to keep chipping away at them. I could spend all day talking to you, but I've got a full council meeting starting in fifteen minutes, so thanks for coming and enjoy your time here. We'll keep on meeting each other over the next fortnight I'm sure and, on your last day, I expect to learn something worthwhile from you. Perhaps, we're missing something, and you can put us right. I hope so!"

With a wave of her hand and a broad smile, Mrs Paynter disappeared through the door to her inner sanctum for a quick briefing before she emerged in her robes of office in the Council Chamber.

"An honest woman" Peter breathed the words.

"Yea, I like her style. She won't stand any nonsense," Elsa affirmed.

Bruce smiled. "Glad you think so," he said. "She's a tough cookie, but her heart's in the right place: retired headmistress."

Bruce ushered his visitors out of the parlour and Ranjit, who was waiting outside, took them up in a lift to the roof garden. There was a grassed area and several flower- beds with wooden benches alongside.

It was a sunny afternoon and the view of the city was quite spectacular from this vantage point. Ranjit pointed out other rooftop gardens on the university building, a bank and a large department store.

"Some of the staff bring sandwiches and have their lunch up here," Ranjit explained.

Peter and Rory started counting the number of solar panels they could see, and eventually agreed on at least forty.

"What did the Lord Mayor say about eco-superior glass windows?" asked Peter.

"You'll see those when we go into the reception hall for tea," answered Bruce. "They look slightly tinted, but they're strengthened to capture the warmth of the sun like solar panels do. The strips surrounding them act like batteries and store the energy, which is reused later to warm the rooms on winter days. They were very costly to install, but over the years those windows have greatly reduced our heating bills in that big room."

"We've used that system in our community hall in the cluster group," Peter said proudly.

They lingered in the sunshine for around ten minutes, identifying features, the castle, the cathedral tower, the railway station and Beatrice sought out the parkland hilltop from which several of them had surveyed the city earlier that morning. Then, conscious of the time, they returned in the lift to the floor below, where Ranjit escorted them to the Council Chamber. It was a large circular room with two rows of desks and seats for councillors, and a visitor's galley running round the walls. Thirteen seats on the visitor's gallery had white cards with the word 'Woodleigh' printed on them. Seats had been reserved by the walkway for the hosts, Gwen and Christine.

Five other people came into the visitor's area a few minutes later. Elsa and Frances recognised Councillor Angela Belfield, the leader of the other Woodleigh group, and had a few words with her before the party filed into the remaining marked seats.

Bruce and Milton had disappeared, but entered shortly later, amidst the forty robed councillors. They quietly filled the circle of green seats. When everyone was seated, a slim man in elaborate livery appeared with a staff in his hand, which he banged on the floor three times before he made an announcement in a high, vibrant voice: "Please rise for the Lord Mayor of Tamcaster, Councillor Jenny Paynter."

They hardly recognised the dignified lady in her red robes and black hat with red feather. All the councillors, except two, rose and so did those in the visitor's gallery.

One of the councillors who did not rise was in a wheelchair; the other one was a young man with a bald shaven head, which appeared to have something placed on top.

It's not a hat. Is it a small skullcap? And then Beatrice realised - it was a tattoo, but she could not make out what it represented. The man did not look up to recognise the entrance of the Lord Mayor. Instead, he studied the paperwork on his desk.

"Who's that fellow?" whispered Rory to Gwen, who was sitting next to him.

"Councillor Fabian – People's Revolutionary Party," she mouthed.

"Please be seated." The Lord Mayor looked round the whole chamber, with a friendly smile, and then looked directly at the visitors.

"We are very happy to welcome our thirteen guests from Woodleigh in Wessex, who are on a two-week exchange visit. As you know, everyone is invited to join them for afternoon tea at the termination of this meeting. On behalf of Tamcaster City Council, I bid you all welcome. I was able to have a few words with the first group, and will make a point of seeking out the second delegation over the tea. " She smiled at the newcomers and then looked down at her papers.

"The first item on our agenda is a minute's silence for reflection on our responsibility as councillors in this ancient city. Instead of Christian prayers previously read at the opening of each full council meeting, we have resolved to make space for a silent prayer or meditation from any tradition at the start of these meetings."

The Lord Mayor sat down and the room fell silent. Several people shut their eyes. Others stared at a point straight ahead and a few, including Councillor Fabian, looked down at their papers. After the silence, Councillor Paynter rose again. "Thank you," she said. "The second item is to approve the minutes of our last meeting. These have been circulated. Is everyone in agreement with them?"

"No, Madam Chair," Councillor Fabian was on his feet. "Can I draw your attention to Minute 4 on Page 2. Would the Council please note that I did not vote in favour of the resolution to hold another artificial seaside event by the fountains in the town square next year. I consider this a costly waste of valuable money, and an insult to the natural coastline of this country. The record says that this motion was passed unanimously."

"I do not remember you voting against it, Councillor Fabian."

"I did not, because I was escorting a party of poor children to the real seaside at Skegness, on the occasion of that meeting, but I emailed my vote to the Town Clerk's Office, together with my apologies for absence."

"I'm sorry if there was an oversight made in the office. Will the clerk please note that correction? I hope the children enjoyed their trip to the real seaside."

"They did, Lord Mayor, and we sent you a stick of Skegness Rock to commemorate the occasion."

"Ah, yes. I seem to remember that. It came with a handwritten note on a piece of paper from a group of children in my ward. I hadn't realised that you had instigated the gift."

"It was their own idea, Lord Mayor. They are members of the Pandemonium Steel Band and they were pleased that you came to their concert in the low dive Kids Club, wearing your glad rags."

"If there are no other amendments, we will pass on. The Report from the Transport Committee: can that be approved?"

"I'm afraid not, Lord Mayor," another councillor was on his feet. "Several of us in the Freedom Party are concerned about the cost of the City Car Pooling Scheme, so the matter has been referred back for further consideration." Another councillor was on his feet, but was told to sit down by the mayor.

"There's no need to discuss this again now, if it has been referred back."

The next item was a proposal that an option of housing should be provided for people who were moving to Tamcaster to take up posts in some essential services such as health workers, teachers, or local authority staff."

A red faced and angry councillor stood up to denounce "this despicable proposal to favour the chosen ones. Why can't council officers, doctors, nurses and teachers join the queue for housing like other mortals, instead of being molly coddled by the mayor and her extravagant followers?"

This received groans and angry shouts from members of the Responsible Party and cheers from the Freedom Party councillors.

The Lord Mayor replied in icy tones. "There is no reason for such an uncalled for remark, Councillor Seagrave. The motion has been agreed by the Finance and General Purposes Committee, and I heartily recommend it to Full Council for the very good reason that our services desperately need people with these special skills. If they can't find somewhere to live in a suitable price range for their pockets, we will loose these excellent people to another part of this province, or even some distant place. We simply can't afford this. We need more nurses, more social workers, and more teachers in Tamcaster, and we have devised an excellent scheme to welcome them, so that our services can continue to improve. I call for a show of hands. All those in favour - all those against. This proposal is carried. Thank you."

As the really important work had been carried out at the committee stage, Full Council was mainly a ratifying body and an opportunity for point scoring points between rival politicians. It lasted just under an hour.

The ballroom on the floor below provided an excellent setting for the reception. It was a spacious room whose long windows overlooked the big City Square. The opposite wall contained a larger than life painting of King William, done soon after his coronation in 2030 when a trace of lost youth was still evident in his eyes.

Long tables were set out with delicacies to choose from. Red and white wine was on offer, as well as coffee or tea.

Beatrice and Adam felt a little ill at ease, in the midst of councillors and invited dignitaries. The Lord Lieutenant was there in his uniform, and Beatrice saw him shaking hands with her father, who tried to introduce her, but she disappeared behind a bulky woman who was stooping to fill her plate with small pork pies and sausages on sticks.

She saw a blond young woman wearing a badge saying 'Cathy, Community Youth Officer' and made a beeline for her.

"Hi there. We're from Woodleigh", Beatrice started. "I'm glad to see a younger face here. What's your job all about?"

Cathy smiled. "I know how you feel," she replied. "It's the first time I've been sent to a big do like this. I started the job six months ago and I'm still learning. I work for the City Council, and liaise with the youth leaders and community workers all over Tamcaster. There are sixteen youth projects that get grants from the City Council, and I have to make sure that they use the money well. They have to meet agreed targets for funding to continue, so I drop in and chat to the young people, as well as the leaders, and see what they think about the activities. I ask them about any difficulties or disappointments they have and whether there are other things they'd like to be doing?"

"Sixteen youth projects. I wish we had that sort of choice in Woodleigh. Are these all set up by the Council?"

"No, most of them are run alongside area community groups, ethnic organisations and church-run projects."

"What do you mean by ethnic organisations?" asked Adam.

"Afro-Caribbean, Asian, Vietnamese, African: these groups all have their own centres, and the Council is keen to encourage them to carry on and develop their own traditions, provided that there are common values, about respect for others and an interest in the neighbourhood they live in. Sometimes there are no problems, but there are times when we can suggest a new approach to a project. We have exchange visits too,

168

sometimes from other countries. We had a group of youth workers from Germany a few weeks ago and we like to see groups learning from each other."

Meanwhile, Rory and Mina had been approached by a portly councillor who shook hands and invited them to tuck in to the food, but prevented them from doing so by his quick firing questions about the cluster schemes in Woodleigh. Rory looked round desperately for Mark, but could not see him.

"Hi, this is the man you need to speak to," Rory said, catching hold of Peter's arm. "He is a world expert on the Woodleigh Cluster Groups." He and Mina then resumed their foraging exercise and scanned the room for someone more interesting to talk to.

"The youngest person I can see here is that man with the tattoo on his head," said Mina.

"He'll do for a start," Rory went over to him.

"Councillor Fabian, isn't it? Tell me, how many members are there in the People's Revolutionary Party?"

"Well, there's me. I'm the Chairman, and there's my partner, Beppo, he's the secretary, and there are eight others in our community squat. The population comes and goes, you know, because of the shortage of affordable housing. We're campaigning for empty houses to be occupied because there are so many homeless people in Tamcaster."

"How many would you estimate?" asked Rory.

"I don't estimate. I get the figures from the night shelters and the Sally Army. I do a weekly check and report it to the newspaper and the housing department. It was a hundred and fifteen last week."

"How many refuges are there?" asked Mina.

"Four."

"Is there a women's refuge?"

"Two."

"I must try to visit them while I'm here."

"You must. You should contact Charlie Blain. She's the community worker from Refugee Action."

"Where's she to be found?"

"Under the big railway arch next to the Central Station."

"Is that a squat?" asked Mina.

"No, it's just a waste of space, because as the road that ran through it hasn't gone anywhere else since they built the ring road: so it's a tunnel to nowhere and we've adapted it, and organises things for lost refugees there. If you want to meet the squatters, go to the tower block opposite the fire station. Liz runs that, and does a great job for the mums and babies. Where are you from? I don't mean Woodleigh. I mean in the world, if you don't mind the question?"

"I was born in Gambia."

"Do you have a Certificate of British Residency? Forgive the question. I don't mean to probe, but I'm worried about the great tide of asylum seekers who are destitute and on our streets. We try to get them into safe squats, if we can."

Mina smiled. "Good for you, but I won't be needing a squat – not for the next two weeks anyway. I haven't got residency status, so you never know."

"No, you really don't. That's the tragic world we live in. Half the people on the streets are stateless people, you know, so they can't start to make an application for asylum. Many of them have been smuggled here, and some have been held in slavery."

"Is Tamcaster one of the worst places for this sort of thing?" asked Rory.

"Not at all, we are more aware of it here, that's all. At least there's a network of organisations trying to do something, and we have a Lord Mayor and one or two councillors who really care. That's more that you can say for most other places in Mercia. I can't speak for anywhere else."

"And how widespread is the P.R.P?"

"There are two other cells, one in West Bromwich and one in Nottingham, and we exchange information with a few similar groups in London. We've got a website - 'www.prp.com.' He ducked his head to reveal that the website address was tattooed on his head.

"Just in case I forget it," he joked.

"But you can't read it up there, can you? ", laughed Mina.

CHAPTER 13 - Exploring the City

The plans for the visit went well throughout the first week. On Tuesday, the Forest Community Centre Junior Youth Club greeted them with a song of welcome and gave hand-made greeting cards to all the visitors. The children then led them through the rooms to show the range of activities going on: art, music and drama, computing, and some exploratory scientific work in a laboratory. They saw reading lessons, a book club discussion and indoor physical exercises for all ages and were shown a programme of outdoor games and discovery walks.

Bruce explained that the community centre building had been a school before it was given to the Forest Community Association. It was now managed by a Voluntary Trust, of which he was Chairman. The Forest area was a run-down part of the town, without much evidence left of trees, except for the grove to be seen on a rising bank beside the playing fields.

"Years ago this area was prosperous," Bruce explained. "It was on the edge of the countryside, and there were woods to the north, so this was where rich Victorians chose to live. The houses are quite large round here, but now that it's become part of the inner city most of them have been converted into flats. Many of the families living here today have either come from abroad themselves, or their parents have. A second generation are brings a big cultural mix, with many stories to share and lessons to learn from each other."

In order to make most of the time available, the visitors split into pairs and went into different rooms to watch the activities. Mark and Peter went into the science rooms where a group of ten and eleven year old children had just returned from a foraging task identifying wild flowers and insects in the woodland grove behind the playing field. They had brought specimens to name and study and they used illustrated books to help them. Then a youth leader showed them a short computer film, made by another group of youngsters when they visited a nearby farm the previous week.

Elsa and Frances chose to stay in the playroom with the pre-school children, and help some of them identify animals in the big picture books. Rory and Mina went into the art and music rooms to listen to eight and nine year olds preparing a song for the forthcoming Afro-Caribbean Carnival and saw some of the exotic costumes that the children were going to wear in the big street parade. Beatrice and Adam played table tennis with a teenage group.

The afternoon being free, the visitors went on a sail along the River Lent in the direction of Bridgeford. Bonnie came with them and Elsa took the opportunity to chat to her, and learn more about the family background.

"My Mum was born in Tamcaster," Bonnie explained. "Her parents came over from Jamaica last century, but my Dad was born in Clarendon, that's a district in Jamaica. He came to Britannia when he was in his twenties and used to work in Hawthorne's electrical, but then he went to Bible College and became a pastor. He married Mom in the year he left college and I was born when he was running this church. When I was four, my parents took me to Jamaica to meet my grandparents. Trish was a baby then, and all the local families wanted to see us. We stayed with Dad's parents. I loved the bright sunshine there and everyone was so friendly that I didn't want to come home. My grandmother was very ill when we were there though. I can remember saying goodbye to her. She was in bed, and they laid me on the pillow beside her. I can just remember that. She died the next year. After that, my granddad was very lonely, and he decided to come to join us in Britannia. If you haven't met him yet you soon will. Old Joshua still has his strong Jamaican accent and I love to hear the way he talks."

They were sailing on a large motorboat, where good views of the industrial city soon gave ways to quiet suburban areas. These in turn melted into green fields where cattle browsed and willow trees welcomed them in August sunshine. Mina, who had brought her guitar, sat in the bows entertaining them all with folk songs from around the world. She explained that she had a big collection because she used to teach them to the children at the Steiner school.

"I made a point of trying to find a special tune for each new refugee child. There was an international songbook in the school library, but what was even better, some of the pupils taught me songs themselves. If they did that, I got the whole class singing them. If the refugees didn't know a national song and there wasn't one in the book, I talked to the child about the area they came from and we made up a song especially for them. When they'd finished singing, the children liked me to look round the class, and choose another child, and then they all started singing that song. I had my guitar on my lap and soon picked up the rhythm. This was so popular that it could go on all day, so I had to make a rule of no more than five songs each day. Otherwise we'd never have got down to the serious stuff like maths. Each evening I noted the names of those who'd had their turn, and chose five different children next day. It was always a secret who was going to be celebrated, and I had to make sure that no one was forgotten."

"Did you have a lot of children from the same country?" asked Elsa.

"Yes, if that happened, I had to compose more special songs. It kept me very busy. I usually put words to a suitable well known tune."

That evening, Rory told his parents that Mina and he would not be joining them on the visit to the Housing Association the next morning.

"We met a refugee worker at the community centre, today," he explained "and she's on duty tomorrow morning at the Tamcaster Refugee Centre, so that's the best time for us to go and see what they do there. They don't usually allow visitors but, Laura telephoned the centre and, as Mina's a refugee, they agreed that we could go tomorrow morning."

Beatrice overheard this conversation. Visiting a refugee centre sounded much more interesting to her than going to a housing office, and she remembered that Adam had told her that he had chosen to make refugees the subject for his school research project. Perhaps they could both go too? She mentioned this to Rory later in the day.

"I doubt if it's possible," he responded. "We are invited because of Mina. Laura had to ask the hostel manager, and she agreed that we could, because of our circumstances."

"What's the problem? We won't say anything. We'll just listen."

"But there may be a restriction on children going there," Elsa cautioned. "I guess it's all very confidential work they do, so they'll have to be careful about who's around."

"But I'm not a child, and we're not going to tell everyone about it. We can be discreet."

"I hope you can, but people go to refugee centres for help and privacy. They don't want to be on display to visitors."

Despite the warning, Beatrice borrowed the group's mobile phone from Mark, telling her father that she needed to ask Adam something, and took it up to the privacy of her bedroom.

Peter answered the call and as Beatrice requested, handed the phone to Adam.

"Hi. About that project thing we've got to do for school. You told me that you were doing a write up about refugees. Well, Rory and Mina are going to the Tamcaster Refugee Centre tomorrow instead of that boring housing thing. I'd like to go with them too, and I thought it would be helpful for your project if you could come as well. Bring your notebook."

Adam jumped at the idea, but Beatrice did not explain that there could be problems, thinking that she could overcome any difficulties.

"We're car sharing, aren't we? So, I expect Bruce is bringing you over here, like he did this morning. The simplest thing would be for one car to go to the housing office, and the other to the Refugee Centre with the four of us in it, but we can sort that out tomorrow."

The next day Bruce brought Peter, Fran and Adam in a large pool car ready to take them all to the housing project. Rory and Mina explained to him that they would like to be dropped off at the refugee centre, which was on the route, and that Laura had telephoned last evening to confirm it was OK. Then Beatrice suggested they changed cars because she and Adam would prefer to go there too.

"Adam's writing a special project on refugees and I'm helping him," Beatrice explained.

This change of plan was news to everyone else. Rory expressed some concern, which was echoed by others, so no one changed. Both cars set off in the same direction. Despite this, when Rory and Mina got out, Beatrice and Adam joined them on the pavement outside the tall building.

"I'll ring the bell and give our names but you two will have to explain and get permission to come in," Rory advised them rather abruptly.

Laura opened the door, and smiled at Mina and Rory, but then she hesitated.

"I'm sorry," she said. "I managed to get permission for two people, Mina and Rory, but we're stretching a point in allowing any visitors to come in. I've had to get permission from the manager and we can't extend the invitation further. Rules have to be strict for reasons of privacy and security."

"We thought it would be a good opportunity, because Adam's doing a school project on refugees and I'm helping him," said Beatrice. "We're part of the Woodleigh delegation."

Laura looked at her with sympathy, but was firm in her response. "I'm sorry, but that's not possible. Refugees come here to be safe, and we don't admit people under eighteen unless they're in distress. This is a private zone, and we have to keep it out of the public gaze. If you want to ask me some questions about refugees, Adam, I'd be happy to see you sometime while you're staying here. I'll discuss it with Rory and tell him how you can contact me."

"Thanks, I understand," said Adam, as the door closed.

Beatrice felt humiliated. "Why did you say that?" she said to him. "You told me you were keen to go there."

"I was, but I understand the situation. They probably have people in there who won't open up in front of strangers. The staff who run the centre know that, so I suppose it could be intruding for us to go there."

"How come that Rory and Mina can go in, then?"

"Because they asked permission in the right way, and have been invited. Can't you see that, Beatrice?"

"Well, we've got some free time now, so I'm going to have a look at that castle? Are you coming with me?"

"I suppose so." Adam tagged along, but was very disappointed that he could not go into the Refugee Centre, and thought Beatrice had managed this badly. There were times when she exasperated him.

The castle rock dominated the road below it. They crossed towards it, over the busy road and gazed up at the red sandstone cliff, which was mixed in places with white limestone. "Look, there are some caves up there." Adam pointed.

"Bruce told us that people used to live in those caves thousands of years ago, before the Romans came to Britain," Beatrice recalled.

"It's all railed off. I can't see any entrance. How can we get up to the castle on top of the cliff?"

"We'll ask someone local."

Beatrice stopped a woman with a dog and a shopping basket. "Excuse me, can you tell us which way to go to get into the castle grounds?"

"You have to turn left at the traffic lights and go up the hill. You'll see the gatehouse at the top."

The road on the left, by the lights, was churning with noisy traffic, but the pavement hugged the side of the cliff, with the castle walls behind iron railings. Turning and walking up the rising pavement, they passed a timbered old pub, built against the cliffs, and continued climbing the steep hill until they came to a cobbled yard and a drum-towered guardhouse with a wooden portcullis. The stonework was worn, but it was not ancient, having been rebuilt in the old style, although it had also adopted new features such as the iron turn-style, which sat inappropriately between two old wooden gates. Presumably there were times when entrance was ticket only, but this was not one of those days.

Beyond the turn-style, a public park had been created in the castle grounds, and facing them was a statue of a strong-looking woman, with a heavy sword in her right hand. Her eyes were mild, however, and her left hand clasped a girl-child. The costumes were ancient: a flowing cloak was on her shoulders and a crown on her head. The woman looked half warrior and half gentle queen, but Beatrice knew who she was instantly.

"Who's that?" Adam was curious.

"It's the woman I came to meet," said Beatrice. "Elfleda, The Lady of Mercia."

"Oh yes. The name's here, carved in stone," he said. "Never heard of her."

"Yes, you have." Beatrice was impatient. " Bruce told us about her when we were on that hill yesterday. He explained how she defended Tamcaster from the Danes. She came from Wessex, and she was the daughter of King Alfred. Don't you remember? That's why I came to the castle. I want to write her story up for my school project. I decided that as soon as I heard about her. She's a long lost heroine, and I'm going to bring her back to life."

Beatrice's green eyes were shining. Adam looked at her in surprise. The sulks had completely disappeared. Yes, he remembered now. Bruce had said something of the sort, but why was she making such a fuss about it? There were things about Beatrice that he'd never understand.

Behind the statue and beyond a trim lawn, a tall Norman Tower reached up towards the sky; it's white stone gleaming in the morning air. *But surely, that's no old tower. It looks like a modern reconstruction.* Adam was intrigued. He left Beatrice peering at the statue and walked across the grass to read the new notice board beside the entrance: "This Norman-style tower was built by apprentice builders in 2050 as part of a national training scheme. A tower of this type was probably constructed on a site near here. The design is based on those of the period."

It was a circular tower approached by an outside stone stairway, which led to a great, iron-studded door on the first floor. Rings of arrow holes indicated three storeys. The flat roof was crenulated. *What a view there'll be from there!* Adam thought.

He turned to see that Beatrice was still gazing at the statue. "Let's go in here," he called to her, but she did not seem to hear him. He walked back and pointed. "We can go up that tower. There'll be a great view from the top."

Beatrice did not even look at it properly. "It's just a reconstruction," she said, "I'm going into the castle museum. There must be something about her in there."

"Go in the museum if you like," he said, "but I'm going to look in the tower. We can meet up again here in an hour."

"O.K. then," she said, and he watched her walk away along the path that led to the castle museum.

He climbed the steps and found that there was a man selling tickets behind the studded door. Undeterred, Adam bought one and then enjoyed exploring the three great circular rooms and the storage cellar below. Although they were unfurnished, plaques on the walls in each room gave information about how they would have looked in Norman times. Steps led up to the flat roof where, peering between the battlements, Adam got a bird's eye view of Tamcaster. With the help of an engraved map, posted between battlements, he identified some important buildings, such as the Council Hall and the University. Looking further he managed to identify the green park on the opposite hilltop from which they had surveyed the town on Monday morning.

Meanwhile, Beatrice was exploring the museum. At the entrance she enquired about Elfleda, the Lady of Mercia. The woman at reception said that the museum did not have more information about her. Beatrice was given a booklet about the displays there, which covered the more recent history of the city, with a major emphasis of the industrial development. A photograph of the statue, and a short paragraph about her was all Beatrice found, but when she spoke to the woman at the information counter, she was advised that more facts would, no doubt, be available in the City Library.

Beatrice walked fairly swiftly around the galleries, which attempted to cover everything from the Iron Age to the present. There were one or two relics from the Anglo-Saxon period, such as drinking cup and a helmet, but much more on the industrial revolution period, especially the history of the textile and car industries. Beatrice would have liked to spend longer there, but remembering the arrangement with Adam, she decided to return sometime later, after visiting the library.

* * *

Meanwhile, Mark, Elsa, Peter and Frances were following the official programme.

They were most glad to visit the Eco-House, built in local brick and stone. This building was permanently open for public viewing. Solar panels covered the roof and more were strategically placed in the attractive garden, some beside the lawn and patio and others dividing the flower and vegetable plots.

A glass panel in the comfortable living room revealed straw bales that boosted the insulation in the walls and a large south-facing window overlooked the garden. A leaflet on the windowsill explained that the eco-superior glass panes were generating electricity from the metal frames, which was stored in a canister below. Heat could be set for release on a time clock when any room temperature was low.

The kitchen featured an efficient electric stove with cooking ovens. A duct from the lounge enabled warmth to be fed through from the living room, when the temperature was low. Fresh drinking water was pumped up from a natural stream adjacent to the property.

Rainwater collected from the gutters was held in a tank for use in the showers and the toilet. The house was sited to take full advantage of the natural features: the main bedroom being over the living room, and two smaller bedrooms were placed over the north-facing kitchen.

"Gee, it's all set up, neat and smiling. They thought of everything. I could move into this home tomorrow," Elsa told them all. Her enthusiasm usually made her American tones more prominent.

When they had seen and discussed all the features of the eco house, Bruce took them to meet Stanley Daniels in the Cooperative Centre next door. Being the administrator of this community project, he welcomed his visitors graciously.

"I've always been an admirer of your cluster group concept," he told them. "In a historical, mixed-race town like Tamcaster we have to do the best we can to replicate that type of community, but it's hard going. We aim to do it through our network of area cooperatives across the city. They're voluntary organisations, run locally, with help from here. Most of them run an allotment scheme, a mend and repair facility, a community shop run by volunteers as well as some paid staff, and a complimentary health centre run by trained professionals. They also provide evening classes in topics like home cooking, household economy and leisure activities, such as music, singing, dancing and sports. There's usually a co-operative youth club and a retirement club in each area, this depends on the numbers of young and elderly living there.

"Do members have to pay a subscription?" asked Peter.

"Yes, but it's only around £50 pounds per year, and can be paid in instalments."

"How about the running of the co-operatives. Is that done by volunteers?" Peter pursued.

"Yes, it is. The membership committee decide which activities can be held in each area. Breckhill Co-op has the unusual advantage of a ring of houses surrounding the allotment. You know about that, of course, it's an ideal arrangement. We have something similar at Burnage, where houses were built on a garden village principle. Bestwood has another thriving co-op, but it's on a large corporation housing estate. You can see exactly where these co-ops are on this plan."

He pointed to a map of Tamcaster on the wall behind him.

"Every area's different. There are a lot of elderly people in Hall Green, and so they have set up a thriving social club for the elderly. It works in close contact with the community care services. They have a very good Theatre Club there as well, that's rather an unusual feature. In contrast there are some very active youth clubs in the Withington area."

"What activities do they have?" asked Frances.

"A wide range. There are sports teams and a very good youth choir. A new feature they've set up is called 'Adopt a Granny'. It links junior schools with care homes for the elderly, and children go in regularly to chat to the old people, and sometimes play games with them or go on outings."

"How about the old folk who are living on their own?" asked Elsa. "Can you do much for them?"

"There are luncheon clubs in several areas, with cars to bring people in through our automatic pool car service. Volunteer helpers are supplied whenever necessary. We also have an array of robotic services that you may care to look at in the room next door. These are automatic care machines that can be supplied to those who need special help from a personally designed robot, in their home.

Another newer initiative is credit unions. Some people have severe problems with their money. These schemes help people through financial difficulties, with modest loans being made available on manageable terms. The local committees consider what interests, talents and needs there are in each area, and try to help everyone who wants to join in the schemes."

"You mentioned evening classes and household economy," said Peter. "Do you do anything of that kind?"

"That's high on our agenda," Stanley replied. "Bruce can tell you more about that."

"Yes, the university environment department run courses and we follow through by organising local teams to support each other in sustainable living schemes," Bruce explained. "The aim's to reduce both carbon emissions and expenditure. Some people manage their affairs so well that they generate enough electricity to meet their own needs and can supply some to the local grid system too. They'll tell you all about that when you go to visit the Tamcaster Energy Support Station."

They went into another room to see the robots at work. Some were actually shaped like human beings, but others were clearly machines doing household jobs; inserting clothes and sheets into washing machines, getting them out after the work had been done, and putting them in drying machines, ironing clothes. After finishing the process, other robots could hang clothes in a wardrobe or put them in drawers.

In a completely automated kitchen, all food processing was being carried out mechanically – unpacked, chopped up, if necessary, put into ovens for cooking and baking for appropriate times.

Against an opposite wall, robots were taking the food out and preparing it for table use.

"Are these machines readily available for the elderly? "asked Frances.

"It depends on need," Bruce explained. "All requests are assessed by the Welfare Team. "They discuss preferences and possibilities with each individual. Sometimes volunteers go into the home to help, but if the elderly prefer this type of assistance, it is available. They can pay contributions to help meet the cost, or have appliances free if they can't afford that. Others choose to go to a rest home."

* * *

Meanwhile, Rory and Mina were attending an interview with a young African refugee.

Laura had explained briefly before they went in to see her that Tabula had been born in Sudan and, because of the climate changes there, desertification had caused her family to escape north. Libyan traffickers had smuggled them into Italy. Tabula had lost touch with her parents there, as they were forced to work for different gang-masters. She had no choice about the work she was made to do as a virtual slave. Tabula had later fallen into the hands of another group of traffickers who had smuggled her into Britannia. She did not know where she was but she managed to escape and was found wandering the streets in a bewildered condition. As she did not speak English, a woman interpreter was translating her answers.

"I'll have to talk to her first, because I got her confidence yesterday. That was when we first met. I'll explain who you are, and ask if she minds if you join us."

"Of course," they echoed.

"I'll slip out and tell you if Tabula's unhappy about visitors. If I don't appear after ten minutes, go back into the waiting room, and Sue will find someone else for you to join."

When Mina and Rory went into the room they saw a dark-skinned young woman dressed from head to foot in black clothing, with a headdress but no veil. She looked very nervous.

"This is Mina, who is also an African refugee, as I told you. She came to Europe with her mother. She is engaged to marry this gentleman, Rory. They are visiting us today to see the sort of work that goes on here. You told me that you would not mind them joining us. Are you sure that's still all right?"

Tabula gave a slight nod and a smile was exchanged with Mina.

"I was born in Gambia," Mina volunteered, "and escaped to Italy. I am now visiting Britannia for the first time."

This was translated to Tabula by the interpreter, who explained "So far I have just been finding out about how Tabula settled into the women's hostel last night, and whether she has had enough to eat there. One of the women workers brought her here this morning. This is Rachel, one of our African interpreters.

Laura turned back to speak slowly to Tabula.

"Now, you have been told that this town is called Tamcaster. Do you know the names of any other towns where you have been in this country?"

When this was translated, Tabula replied, "London."

"London is a very big place. Do you know what part of London you were in?"

Tabula shook her head.

"And you don't have any relatives or friends in this country?"

Tabula shook her head again.

"And you don't have any papers?"

There was another shake of the head.

"Well, you will need some. We must make up two record cards for you. I will give you one of them. Keep it with you always. It has our address on and my name and telephone number, in case you need it. I will keep the other one here in the office. You will be staying in the women's refuge for a while, so I am adding that address for you. We will give you a reference number. This is just for our own use. T.R.C. 257. That stands for Tamcaster Refugee Centre. Over two hundred and fifty refugees have now been registered with us since we opened our doors, two years ago. You are very welcome here, and I hope soon that you will find friends who you can talk to easily. Do you know how old you are?"

She gave another shake of the head.

"Suppose I were to guess. Could we say 20? Older or younger? Ah, about right. We'll say approximately 20. Do you know the month and date? Good, we have a provisional birthday. Do you know where you were born? Yes, Sudan. Do you know the district? Did you have brothers or sisters? Did you all leave the country together?"

Slowly, details were put in place, and a provisional identity card was made. Laura explained to Mina that she would arrange for Tabula to see someone from the police, who should be able to help her apply for a permit to stay in this country for four weeks whilst some further checks are made? If all went well, Tabula might be granted a refugee permit, which would allow her to stay here for at least a year, provided that she agreed to obey the laws. Someone would be appointed as her sponsor. Would she like Laura to be her sponsor, or someone else better known to her?

Laura was duly nominated and at the end of these proceedings, Tabula was taken into a women's lounge and introduced to other refugees who were in similar circumstances themselves. Rory and Mina mingled with this group, and were able to chat to them. The difficulties for all these people were only too clear. The Refugee Centre was doing all it could to help them, but they were battling against a torrent of hostile regulations and a great deal of prejudice from local residents.

At the end of the morning, Rory and Mina had coffee with Laura in the private room again and she answered a string of questions from them, before she came up with one of her own.

"And how about you, Mina? Have you got refugee status or a residency permit?"

"Not in this country. I'm just here as a tourist on a two-week permit. I have refugee status in Italy."

"But you're engaged – are you going back to Italy, Rory?"

"Not if I can help it. Mina will make an application for another visit when we fix the date of the wedding, and then a transfer of status after we're married."

"That sounds very unsatisfactory to me. She's not likely to get another permit this year. When are you planning to marry?"

"We've nothing fixed yet."

"Well you'd better get a move on, if you're really serious about this."

"We thought it would be better to let Mina acclimatise here first."

"It would be, under normal circumstances, but nothing is normal now."

"What are you worried about? Please tell us," asked Mina.

"I've seen so many disappointed people – so many hopes dashed! This country is not supportive of transfers of status within Europe. As you know we have a fixed quota of refugees in Britannia - only a thousand each year. These are divided up into the different regions and the allocation for Mercia is 250 per year. This number is very quickly reached because all the refugee centres make bids for those places. Once the quota is full, we have to send refugees back where they came from in Europe or elsewhere, unless there are very strong arguments against this. It means having a court hearing, and you could have a battle to fight, because there are so many hurried arranged marriages, especially from Africa and Pakistan. People are very suspicious of them, especially the magistrates, because they regularly find that bogus marriages have been arranged for money."

"Good heavens. We never thought..."

"You weren't to know. These cases seldom get in the newspapers."

"You mean, I might have to stay living in Italy?"

"It's possible, if Italy is your European country of entry. In Britannia, Europe is regarded as the back door to Africa and Asia, and it's been very firmly locked and bolted for permanent residence since the Freedom Party was elected to power."

Mina's lip trembled, and tears blocked her vision.

Laura reached out and took her hand.

"Are you certain that you want to marry Rory, Mina?"

"Of course I do!" The reply was vehement.

Laura turned to Rory, taking his hand. "And are you really certain that you want to marry Mina, Rory?" She looked into his eyes.

"With all my heart. I'll go and live in Italy, if need be!" His eyes were determined.

"Then, I advise you both to lose no time about it. If you want to live in this country, marry here. If you want to live in Italy, marry there. I don't know about their laws, but once you are married, Mina should be able to get British citizenship. The easiest thing is for Mina to get an extra few weeks added to her temporary visa, and then to marry. Don't apply for other extra favours before you are husband and wife."

Mina reached out for Rory on one side of her and Laura on the other. No one said anything more, and the tears were unashamed.

CHAPTER 14 - The Night Watch

On Thursday, the Woodleigh team visited the St. Mark's Allotment scheme, where Milton's elderly father, Joshua, had introduced a flavour of the Caribbean to the market gardens. At lunchtime, he cooked some of his yams, opened a bottle of rum and entertained them with tales from old Jamaica.

Rory and Mina were in a daze throughout the morning, preoccupied with thoughts about their future. The afternoon being free, they went to the registrar's office and made further enquiries. Then they drafted a letter applying for an extension of Mina's permit, posted it, and discussed how best to explain the situation to Mark and Elsa. They decided to do this after supper on Friday evening. It would give them time to consider their steps.

Laura's influence had been substantial. In addition to the vital information she had given, she had interested Rory and Mina in the Night Watch Programme. At their request, she had got permission for them to join her on one of the nights when she was on duty at the Real Coffee Bar from 10pm till 2am. When they mentioned this to Milton, he surprised her by saying "Bonnie will be there, so she can take you with her. They do good service, those young people, keeping an eye on things, and offering friendship where it's really needed."

"I go there sometimes myself," added Christine. "The bar's open on Thursday because, being pay day, it's pretty lively in town. They have teams there on Friday and Saturday nights too."

Bonnie led the way. She closed the front door and walked briskly down the street to the tram stop. The air was still warm after the scorching daytime heat and there was a slight, welcome breeze.

"I love the gloaming. It's so peaceful – the best part of such a long hot day."

"I agree," said Mina. "It's still daylight, and we can see both the sun and the moon."

The automatic tram appeared almost immediately. It stopped as soon as it reached the boarding station and the doors opened quietly. A guard, sitting by the doors, checked their tickets as they went aboard. They found seats where they could talk together easily. The guard pressed the start button and the tram moved quietly forward.

"How many people are there on the night watch?" asked Rory.

"We have about seventy volunteers altogether, but there are three teams, so we're only on duty for one of the nights - either Thursday, Friday or Saturday. There's around twelve of us each night, and we are in two shifts. I'm in the coffee bar first and on patrol later. As you're visitors, I guess you can join in as you please, but I'll introduce you to Barrie first. He's the lead person tonight."

"How long have you been doing this, Bonnie?" asked Mina.

"Two years – ever since I was eighteen. I was the youngest one there and I had to wait until my birthday. Trish hopes to start when she's old enough as well."

"And what made you want to do this?"

"I wanted to help young people who'd got no aim in life except to get drunk every time they had money to spend. There's so many like that. They throw their lives away. Some of our church youth leaders had joined the teams, and they obviously found it fulfilling. I found myself envying them, but I wasn't sure I would be up to it, so I said a prayer on a Saturday night and the very next day a young woman I didn't know came to our church, and when I talked to her over the coffee after the service, she said 'I enjoyed that service very much, but I'm quite tired actually because I've been on night watch and it was my first time.' She told me that she had wanted to join and had to wait till she was old enough, and that she really enjoyed the company and the experience. I told Mum about all this and said I thought this was a sign, but she still thought it would be best to wait a bit longer. I kept on about it and then Mum volunteered herself, and we both joined at the same time. We're on different teams though and it's something we can swap stories about."

"How about your Dad?"

"Oh yes, he got involved through Mum and me. He isn't a regular volunteer because he's so busy, and he has to be on the mark every Sunday, but he's been once or twice. He's on what they call the supplementary list. They can give him a call when they're shorthanded."

"He said he was coming tonight?"

"Yes, he's still got the pool car, so he said he'd give me a lift home. He doesn't like me using the night tram on my own. You can get drunks playing up then and sometimes it's difficult for the guard to control them all."

"Perhaps they could do with a tram team too."

"It's been discussed, but we haven't enough supporters for that."

The tram rumbled quietly through the housing estates, and then turned into a busy street, which obviously led towards the city centre. As they passed the university buildings, Bonnie indicated that they were to get off at the next stop. Several people left the tram there. The pavement was very crowded. They walked passed a cinema and turned down a passageway between tall buildings. Bonnie knocked on a green door. It opened quickly and they found themselves in the kitchen of a big coffee bar, which fronted the main street.

Bonnie had a quiet word with Barrie, who looked up from the papers he was thumbing through and smiled at the visitors.

"Good to meet you. So you're part of the delegation from Wessex. I'm Barrie Peters. We're pleased to have you with us. Make yourselves at home. We usually have a cup of coffee when we are all assembled, and follow this with a short staff meeting, where we exchange information. Before we open the doors, we have a time for communal prayer and its all go after that."

"Is this a church outfit then?"

"That's how it started, but not everyone's a church goer now, but they have to agree with the ethos. We don't try to convert people. We just help where we can. If people ask 'why are you doing this?' we explain, that the initiative came from the churches."

"How long is the coffee bar open?"

"We open at 10pm. and stay open till 2am. It's a place of refuge, where everyone's welcome. We have some trained staff available to talk privately to anyone in real difficulties. It's usually fairly quiet for the first shift. On the second one, we normally have one or two people who need to sober up. Our patrols often find them and invite them back for coffee."

"Hello, fancy seeing you here." They heard a familiar voice and looked up to see Laura, who had just arrived.

"Hi, Laura. It was you who told us about this place." Mina went over to her, and Rory waved a greeting.

"Yes, I know, but I didn't expect you to be here tonight though."

"When you're not here long, you have to take every possibility," Rory called back.

An hour later, the three of them joined one of the night patrols. They were issued with thick vests to wear over their clothes, with the words 'NIGHT WATCH' printed in bold letters. The patrol split into two groups and both did the circuit, but went round in opposite directions.

Rory and Mina were with Barrie, Laura and two others. They first walked through areas where people were dining al fresco at street bars, enjoying the cool of the evening. A paved side street round the corner was lined with noisy pubs, where people spilled out on to the streets with beer glasses in their hands. One or two loutish youths were rather scary, but there was nothing serious to concern them. At the end of this lane there were two loud nightclubs, where Barrie had some banter with one of the bouncers. The circuit then took them through theatre land, past the playhouse, a multi-complex cinema and a concert hall spilling their audiences on the street, with taxicabs being hailed from all around. Then, along a dark alley where a few women loitered who might well be plying their trade, and round to the bus station where the café had closed and a group of drunks were swaying and singing as they waited for the bus home.

"There's not usually much here to detain us at this hour," Barrie explained, "but an early walk like this helps us the get the mood of the night. Later, we find a few people who need help - like young women who can't walk straight and need to sober down. That's where some of our girls can give them a hand. Sometimes they know where they are going and a safe arm to hold is all that's needed. Others will accept the offer of a coffee, and we can guide them to our bar. Then some just quietly revive, but others will spill their hearts out, and accept an offer of a safe drive home in one of our pool cars."

They were walking back towards the coffee bar when Barrie suddenly said, "That's the observation room over there. I think we'll just have a look in." He opened a door beside a multi-storey car park, said "Follow me," and briskly stepped down a flight of steps into an underground room. Three men were watching a bank of TV monitors showing traffic junctions and stretches of pavement in the town centre. "It's only me," said Barrie. "I'm just showing some visitors round from Wessex."

"I don't suppose you have traffic like this down there," said one of the men. Staring at the congestion, the traffic and the mayhem. They agreed that they did not.

"Occasionally these boys can see trouble brewing up in a street and they give us a call on the walkie-talkie. If it's something really serious they call the police, or an ambulance," Barrie explained. "On other occasions they call us."

One of the men in the room turned round and said " There was a white BMW went dashing through the red lights earlier today. We followed it on the screens and got the registration number. That guy will get a ticket this week. We couldn't do without these screens. The city would jam up. And see those yobs over there on the other screen: they're really looking for trouble tonight. These camera shots are all recorded and will be scanned by the police for evidence, if there's trouble or disturbance tonight."

Walking back to the coffee bar they passed a scruffy looking beggar who was bedding down in a doorway for the night.

"What about people like him?" asked Rory.

"We're always on the lookout," Barrie replied. "We don't usually approach them until they speak to us. Most of them are drug addicts, and there's a separate charity that gives help to those who really want to quit. They all know where the coffee bar is, and some of them come in on winter nights. We make them welcome, have a chat and signpost them to the other charities if they are in real trouble. Our girls keep a close eye on any women who are sleeping rough, and we're very keen to see that no young refugees get caught up in that culture. They're specially vulnerable and there are always people out there waiting to exploit them."

The second patrol after midnight revealed a different story. The street cafes were all shuttered, and the pavements had been cleared of chairs and tables. The foyers of the theatres and concert halls were empty and doors were being locked. Two or three of the pubs had closed for the night, but others were alive with singers. Neon-lit clubs seething with customers also had a queue of people on the pavement. Girls in skimpy dresses were running barefoot, carrying their high-heeled shoes as they nipped along towards taxis or parked cars.

Some men were holding each other up, and others were wandering about in a glassy eyed daze. The Night Watch offered help to one or two people, who looked as if they needed it. Some flip-flops were offered to girls, and some of the others were invited to come to the coffee bar to chill out.

On one side of a busy street a group of white youths were hurling insults at some Asians across the road. Mina glanced back after she had passed the group. The shouting had stopped. Perhaps the presence of the Night Watch, dressed in their jumpers, was having a calming effect.

* * *

The telephone was ringing in the hallway. Milton left the kitchen, where he and Chris were washing up. The voice at the other end seemed agitated. "Milton. Is that you?"

"Yes, who is it?"

"Craig, I'm sorry to trouble you with this one, but I think you're the best person to contact. There's going to be some trouble tonight at the mosque in Quay Street."

"Trouble! What sort of trouble?"

"It's the J gang. They've sized the place up, and someone's got a key. There's talk of a fire bomb!"

"Fire-bomb! Are they serious?"

"If they weren't I wouldn't be ringing." The line went dead.

Milton didn't think Craig had said all he intended to. Why did the line go blank? Was it just a telephone blip, or was there some deliberate interference? Perhaps some one had attacked him. He knew it was Craig's voice. and Craig had penetrated some nasty groups in his time. He must be serious. Milton looked up Craig's home number and rang it, to see if he could continue the conversation.

A woman answered. Probably his girlfriend, "Is Craig at home tonight?"

"No, he went out to a meeting. Who are you?"

"My name's Milton. Do you know when he's likely to be back?"

"No idea. Can I take a message?"

"Tell him to ring me, if he has more to tell me." Milton spelt out the number and replaced the phone. Should he to ring the imam or the police? Remembering a friendly inspector and dialled his number.

"Harper."

"Hello, Brian. It's Milton here. Sorry to trouble you off duty but I've just had a tip-off from a reliable source: a call to say that the mosque in Quay Street needs guarding. Someone's got the key and they might try to fire it tonight."

"Who might?"

"J gang."

"Source?"

"A man I trust."

"Right. Thanks."

Next, he phoned the imam. This was more delicate and took some time.

Milton looked at his watch. He was due to go and pick up Bonnie and the others soon. He had a quick word with Chris and then went outside to switch on the pool car. On the way into town, he diverted towards Quay Street. Good, there were two police cars blocking the entrance. No one could get up there. He assumed the same thing would apply to the opposite entrance to the road. He reversed, drove on and parked by the kerb that was convenient for the Real Café Bar - which was in a blaze of light, with one of the lads standing on the doorstep.

There were about a dozen customers. Bonnie sat at a table talking to a girl with dishevelled hair and Mina and Rory were chatting to a young couple at another table. He did not want to interrupt conversations, so he ordered a coffee and sat on a barstool. He looked at his wristwatch. It was 1.50 am.

"We'll be closing to the public in ten minutes," Barrie announced. "If any of you need help getting home, or have nowhere to go, please have a word with me."

Bonnie went over to him with the young woman.

Rory called over to Milton. "We're ready when you are." They crossed towards him.

"I think the girl with Barrie needs a room for tonight," Mina said quietly.

"Barrie will fix that," said Milton.

Laura went over to clear the empty tables and wiped them down with a dishcloth.

Mina moved to help her. Barrie took the girl over to Laura. They spoke for a few minutes and then they heard Laura say to her. "Yes, no problem. I'll run you there in ten minutes."

Barrie said, "I'll ring the hostel now, and let them know."

By 2.05 a.m. they had all departed, except for Barrie, who had the responsibility for turning off the lights and locking up.

As they climbed into the pool car, Milton asked, "What's the night been like for you three?"

"I've enjoyed it," said Mina. "There was a good feeling and I'll remember it."

"I thought you would," Milton observed, as he turned the key in the ignition, looked at the windscreen and began to edge away from the pavement. "I'm glad things went better in one part of the city."

"What do you mean, Dad?" asked Bonnie.

"Keep it to yourselves, but I think there may be trouble in Quay Street tonight, so I'll do a little detour on the way home."

No one asked questions, but they saw four police cars when they passed the road in question. Making the detour required them to drive down Market Street and pass by the Phoenix Shopping Mall, where they saw an angry mob. A policeman directing traffic waved them on hurriedly. They could not see what was happening.

"Hot summer nights can be dangerous in big cities," commented Milton. He drove straight back home, but he stayed sitting at the wheel after they had got out. He had not trusted the automatic steering on this anxious night. Rory hovered as the girls left. "Aren't you coming in?" he asked.

"I'm thinking of going back to see what's up," Milton explained. Then he switched off the ignition. "No, there might be a call for me." He followed them into the house.

Christine had gone to bed, but there was a note by the telephone saying 'Ring Craig'.

He did. The woman at the other end of the line was worried. Craig had not come home. What more did Milton know? Why hadn't he telephoned her?

"I'm sorry I didn't say much to you before because I didn't want to worry you," Milton explained. "Craig phoned me just before I rang you and he give me a tip off. He said that there might be some trouble at the mosque tonight. That's all I know."

"Did you warn the mosque?"

"Yes, and I told the police."

"You might have told me."

"I'm sorry. I don't know who you are. Have we ever met? I didn't think it right to say much to someone I don't know. The police are all over town tonight. I've been out and seen them, so I don't really think there will be danger at the mosque, or for Craig. He's probably delayed because the traffic's being rerouted. Ring me in the morning if he doesn't come back." He gave her his name and number." Can I ask you your name?"

"Marie. We're partners, Craig and I."

"Thanks for telling me, Marie. God bless."

He put the phone down. Rory was still there. "Oh, dear, I'm not going to get any sleep tonight, if I don't know more. I'm going back into town. You go to bed, Rory."

"I'll come with you, if you wish." Rory was still at his elbow.

"Yes, all right. A young man may be useful tonight."

Rory turned to Mina. "I don't think we'll be long, Mina. You go to bed."

The street outside the shopping mall area was thronged with people, and a line of police, keeping them away from the entrance. Shop windows had been smashed and the displays rifled. The mood in the crowd was angry, and the police had drawn truncheons.

"What's happened?" Milton asked a young policeman.

"Four shop windows broken and damage done. We've got it all in hand, move along."

"Is Inspector Harper here? He said he might want my evidence."

"What evidence?"

"I had a tip off and I passed it on to him."

"He's over there." The policeman pointed and Milton saw him. He went over.

"Thanks for ringing me. We were able to stop that nasty little plan. We've got two youths and a petrol bomb, and we chasing looters out of the shops now. You'll have to give evidence about that phone call. Ring me tomorrow. Do you know where Craig is?"

"No idea. He hasn't gone back home, so his partner says. She's very worried."

"You nipped it in the bud anyway. This affair at the shopping mall is nasty too. It could be coincidence, but I think the two things are linked. It was probably meant to divert our attention. After the windows were smashed there was a scrimmage from folk in the street. It was a free for all. So far, we've arrested twenty people tonight, mostly for looting. It'll take a while to sift through the evidence."

"Twenty people. Members of a gang?"

"No. One or two possibly, but the rest – just ordinary folk out for the night. They lost their heads and rushed for the takings when they saw the way was clear. Then we arrived and a few of them scampered with whatever they'd seized. We've got most of them though.."

"Ordinary folk... and taking whatever they could seize! Where's common decency disappeared to!"

Milton did not get much sleep that night. Neither did Rory or Mina – their minds were in overdrive.

CHAPTER 15 - Young Initiatives

On Friday morning Milton had intended to take his visitors to the Afro-Caribbean Centre, but instead he gave them directions on how to get there by the tram. Rory realised that this was probably because he had to give a report to Inspector Harper at the police station but he kept quiet about this, as Milton had simply said he had an urgent engagement that he must keep.

When they all duly arrived, they found a ferment of activity going on. Preparations were in hand for the annual Afro-Caribbean carnival, which was to take place on the following Monday, the Summer Bank Holiday. After many years of holding this on the last Monday in August, the government had decided to revert back to the earlier custom of holding it on the first Monday. (This was partly the result of climate change, which had brought heavy rain in September. It was thought to be safer to have it in the early summer, which was now usually very hot and dry.)

Old Joshua was there to receive them when they arrived, "Good to see again, so soon."

He greeted them all with a big grin. "You chosen to come 'ere on de best day o' the year. If you go in de main 'all, you see de carnival procession bein' dressed. In the next 'all the steel band is re'earsin' an' ye won't be able to 'ear yourself speak for de din. If you go in de gardin' round de back, you'll see a sight to warm de cockles of your 'eart. De little girls are learnin' a new dance, but we must go in de classroom first. Dere's the choir waitin' to bid you welcome. Follow me."

Joshua was right about the steel band, because the noise of it from next door almost drowned out the choir, who sang lustily to try to rise above them. They were given a copy of the words of welcome, in case they had not heard them:-

Welcome to Tamcaster

(Words by Natalie Cross, aged 12,
Music by Wesley Franks, aged 13)

Welcome to Tamcaster, friends from the south,
You come at the right time - to be welcomed by mouth
of the Caribee choir, who now sing in our town,
to welcome our guests be they black, white or brown.

Welcome to Carnival, the time of the year
when we dress and parade and have nothing to fear.
It's time for the steel band - our music and dance
So let us hold hands as we sing and advance
to circle the town, then come back to the start
make everyone happy and cheer every heart.

The preparations in the hall were stunning. Some of the children were decorated like tropical birds, with great multi-coloured wings stitched on to the arms of their costumes; others wore ornate headdresses, and there was a fever of excitement everywhere.

The whole place was such a hive of activity though, that the visitors decided to decamp after a delightful hour of greetings from children in every room. They promised to see them all at the carnival, and retired with Joshua for coffee in a café nearby.

Here, he regaled them with tales about the community centre. He told them how he had complained to the council that this empty old building had been left unused after a newly built school had been opened. When told that they had not yet decided on a new use for it, he said that he had an idea.

"There's a Pakistani Community Centre, and a Indian Community Centre, but nothin' similar for de Afro-Caribbeans. Dat's not fair. I'm the Chairman of dat group, and we 'ave to 'ire premises every time we meet. Dey told me to put my proposal in writin', so I did, and it was accepted. The children were so please that dey decided to crown me. 'But you can't do that,' I said 'I'm not a king' 'No, you's better dan dat dey say.' We don't want no king. You are our chairman.' 'But dey don't crown chairmen,' I say. Then up bounces Bonnie. She was only about nine at de time. 'Es mi grandpa' she says, you can crown 'im, grandpa' o' the centre', an' dat's what dey did. I 'ad a gold cardboard crown put on mi' 'ed and' an orb and sceptre in mi' 'ands, but I don't know what to do wi' them, so I gave the orb to Bonnie and the sceptre to Trish and told 'em to keep 'em by for me. I kep' de crown though, an' I wear it every year at de Annual General Meetin'.'"

The afternoon being free, Rory and Mina said they needed to have a rest, as they had hardly slept at all after last night's escapade. Mark, Elsa and Beatrice decided to go into the town. They had not yet had a proper opportunity to explore it. Beatrice told them she wanted to go to the central library and ask for any information they could give her on Elfleda, the Lady of Mercia.

As they went into town on the auto-tram, people were talking about the rioting last night in the town centre. Going past the Phoenix Shopping Centre, they saw two large plate glass windows boarded up and people looking at the damage done overnight.

The Tamcaster Central Library was an imposing circular building standing next to the Civic Hall. Beatrice went into the main reference library and enquired at the main desk. She was advised to go upstairs to the local studies library. Here she was given a booklet about the Castle Museum, which contained a short article on Elfleda. It made reference to an original source, and Beatrice took this to the enquiry desk, asking if this material was available.

Beatrice had to wait some time, but eventually she was brought two documents, a very large county history with a bookmark in the relevant page, and an article written in an obscure historical magazine.

"This seems to be all we can find," apologised the library assistant. "Actually, there's little known about her other than the bald facts. No one ever seems to have researched her fully, which is curious, since she was King Alfred's daughter. I think this may be one of the reasons that the statue was erected in the castle park. Perhaps it was felt that people should know about her."

"That's why I'm looking into it," said Beatrice, "I'm a one of the visitors from Wessex and I think she should be better known there too, so I'm doing a school project on her. We were told we could choose any subject we liked. When I've done it, I'll send a copy to the local newspaper, and donate a copy of my paper to the library in Woodleigh."

"You do that," said the library assistant with a friendly smile, "and we'd like you to send us a copy too."

"I will," Beatrice smiled with pleasure, "and, come to think of it, I'll post one to the Devon Record Office as well." She began to feel that was doing something important, and was determined to try to discover more about this largely forgotten woman.

As Peter and Frances had gone into town that afternoon, Adam felt at a loose end. Then he remembered that Trish, who was also on holiday from her school, had said that she would like to show him some of the songs she'd written and that she would have to practice singing one of them this afternoon to be ready for the Interfaith meeting on Sunday. He could call there. If it wasn't convenient, he could go somewhere else and perhaps fix another time.

On the tram into town people were talking about the damage done overnight. It prompted him to buy the afternoon edition of the local newspaper when he got off. The front page had photographs of smashed windows in the shopping centre and he read that about twenty arrests had been made for wilful damage. *What had been happening overnight?*

When Adam rang the bell, it was Trish who came to the door. Obviously pleased to see him, she took him through to a big alcove off the living room with several musical instruments in it.

"This used to be our playroom when we were kids," she explained. "Now, it's our music room, so we do a different sort of playing. I'm glad you've come round. It's always cool to have someone when you rehearse."

Picking up her guitar, she slung the strap over her shoulder.

"This is one I wrote yesterday. I hope to use it on Sunday. Tell me what you think of it – honestly. It's based very loosely on that great speech by Martin Luther King, I guess. It just came to me. I'm trying it with an old folk tune, O Waly Waly."

She looked down and began to strum. When she was sure she had the melody, she closed her eyes, threw her head back and began to sing quietly, as if it was a prayer. Adam was spellbound.

"I have a dream that peace will dawn
and all our sorrows melt away.
I have a dream that Love will awake
and rescue every waif and stray,
that Love will open every heart
and every child will play its part.

I have a dream that we will learn
to share our food with those around
that hunger will all melt away -
become a tale of yesterday.
Then Love will open every heart
and every child will play its part.

I have a dream that we will find
our mission from the world around
from flowering plants and buzzing bees,
from rivers, pools and sheltering trees,
from fish that swim through tropic seas,
and birds that ride the flowing breeze.

And we will dance the world around
and spread the joy that we have found
to north and south and east and west.
We'll open hearts, pierce stony breasts
and peace will everywhere abound
with harmony the only sound."

The way she sang touched Adam to the core of his being.

"That was wonderful," he said.

"I'm not sure I got the rhythm right, and that repeated last line in the first two verses sounds a bit lame to me 'and every child will play its part.' It seemed to write itself, but I'm not sure."

"Have you written many songs?" he asked in awe.

"A dozen or so. I started a year ago. I love being creative. Do you?"

"I'm not very creative. I worked with Beatrice on a power-point presentation at school about climate change. She did the script and I made the slides to illustrate it. I liked that. Doing things in partnership can be cool, but I haven't written much myself."

"I started doing songs with Bonnie – adapting them to different tunes – that sort of thing, but then last year, I thought I'd write my own words. I did some gospel songs for our church. I'll show you some afterwards, but this is something different. It's not just a Christian song; it's for all the world and any faith. The tune's borrowed but the words are mine."

"I think they fit very well. What sort of event is this on Sunday?"

"I'm not clear really, either. I've only been to one Inter-faith sharing. Each faith is offering two things. Dad's doing a reading from the gospel and I'm doing this song. I wanted it to be open and acceptable to people of any faith, because there's only one God. I've no idea what sort of things other people will bring, but peace and love belong to everyone and I believe they come from God. Are you a believer, Adam?"

"I'm not sure what you mean."

Trish smiled sadly. "That means you're not."

"I'm not an atheist."

"No, you're an agnostic, like most people in this country. I suppose you don't go to a place of worship,"

"Not regularly. Neither do my parents, but I have gone to churches on special occasions. I've been to the big community church in Woodleigh a couple of times. It's a friendly place, but I'm not sure what I believe really, about life and death, I mean. There are a lot of things I can't understand. If there really is an all-loving God, why do so many terrible things happen?"

"Because so many people have shut God out of their lives. The song is saying how wonderful it would be if everyone allowed the love of God to flow through them. This is our gift, but only if we acknowledge Him and invite Him into our lives. If everyone did that the whole world would change. We would have heaven on earth."

"How do we invite God in then?"

"Through prayer. It's very simple really. Jesus came to show us the way."

"That sounds great, but I find it difficult to understand. There are so many different religions. They can't all be right."

"Something may happen one day that will change your mind. Do you want to hear any more of my songs?"

For the next hour, Adam lay back and listened and Trish took him on a tour of the world, singing songs about far away places, lost loves and newly found ones. Some were old folk songs, recast and reshaped; there were some gospel and slave songs and some which were purely her own. She was so firm in her beliefs that Adam was left feeling doubtful, but her confidence and talents bowled him over.

* * *

After dinner with the Lamb family, Rory had a quiet word with Mark.

"There's something important that Mina and I need to talk to you and Mom about. Can we have a word privately in your bedroom?"

"Yes, of course." Mark was surprised.

"I think it would be good if Beatrice is there too. I don't want her to feel left out, so I'll ask her to join us."

Rather puzzled, Elsa, Mark and Beatrice went to the bedroom next door. As there was not much space the family of three sat on the bed. Mina, who followed them in, sat on the single chair, and Rory stood, twizzling with his beard, with his back to the door.

"We learned a lot at the Refugee Centre yesterday," he began. "We had no idea that things were so difficult for refugees in this country...even for people like Mina. It appears that there is a proposal to introduce legislation in the next parliament which could make it much more difficult for her to stay here long term. It means that our marriage is threatened, so we have decided to try to have the wedding as soon as possible. Yesterday, we went to the Central Post Zone in town and Mina posted a drone letter to the Home Office requesting an extension of her visa."

"For how long?" Mark looked troubled.

"Another three weeks. If it's granted we aim to marry in Woodleigh as fast as it can be arranged."

There was pause. Mina was tense and Rory twizzled with his beard again.

"But what about your mom, Mina? Does she know about this?" Elsa enquired gently.

"Not yet. I'll tell her as soon as I can." Mina spoke quietly as she wiped her eyes.

"Oh dear, we're very sorry to hear this, but I think you'll find things very difficult," said Mark. "It takes time to organise a wedding. I'm not sure about the rules. You'll have to check."

"I have. It takes three weeks. We went to the registry office here this afternoon to find out, but the problem is that refugees need to have all the correct papers, and that will take some time. Our next job is to contact Mina's mother and get her written consent on a form supplied by the G.O.S. Refugee Commission and countersigned by the Italian authorities. It's a nightmare, but we need to know we have your support first before any of this can be started. We don't want to put pressure on you so Mina and I will go back to our room to give you time to think this through. We'll see you in the morning."

Mina stood up, preparing to go out with Rory, but Elsa stopped them for a moment.

"No," she said. "You'll get no sleep tonight if we leave it like this. Neither will we. Go downstairs and come back in fifteen minutes. It will give us enough time to collect our thoughts."

"Thanks Mom, you're a star!" Rory flashed a grateful smile and he and Mina left the room.

Mark, Elsa and Beatrice looked at each other in bewilderment.

Then Beatrice suddenly jumped up enthusiastically. "I think they're marvellous, both of them, and we must give our full support."

"But we don't want to raise false hopes. I can't see them doing all this in time, and then there are so many pitfalls. She's only been in this country for two weeks. She's a lovely girl, but will she cope with all these changes in her life? Will Rory?" Mark was troubled.

"I'm sure they will," Beatrice affirmed. "And she isn't a girl, she's a woman."

"Rory was an impulsive child. I sure hope he knows what he's doing now!" Elsa spoke quietly, but her hands were trembling.

"And Mina's in a foreign country. She hasn't found her feet here yet," Mark added.

"And Rory's not a child. He's a man. You two are living in a bygone age!" Beatrice was angry.

"Hush!" cried Mark. "They'll hear you," warned Elsa.

"Well, someone has to stick up for them."

"We aren't against them. We want to support them. But the time-scale is well nigh impossible." Mark was shaken.

Elsa looked at him and then spoke, "I agree with what you are saying, Mark, but I think we must go along with this: for their sake, for all our sakes. What's the alternative? We can't stop them, but we can help to see them through this. We can't leave them to struggle on their own. We've gotta let 'em know that we're on their side and from what I've seen of that kid, Mina, I know I'd love to have her as my daughter-in-law."

"Me to. I'm just afraid for them."

"Well don't be, Dad. I'm delighted she's my sister-in-law."

Mark looked up and studied the faces of his wife and daughter. They waited for his words.

"So, we all feel the same way really. Well, I'm glad of that."

"Let's tell them so, and not keep them waiting then," Beatrice ran to the door, opened it and called. "You needn't wait. Come back up now."

Mina and Rory ran back up the stairs. Beatrice stayed on the landing, kissed Mina and said quietly, "It's alright. We're going to support you."

Rory took Mina's hand when they came back into the bedroom, and sat on the arm of her chair.

Elsa spoke first. "You guys have got a very tough road ahead, but we want you both to know that we'll give you all the help we can." She went over to Mina and kissed her.

Mark stood up and shook Rory's hand. "This is going to be a long haul, but we're on your side."

Within moments they were all hugging each other and words were unnecessary.

CHAPTER 16 - White Peak and Dark Peak

When it had been confirmed that both teams of visitors wished to spend Saturday in the Peak District, Bruce telephoned the pool garage and booked one of their minibuses so that they could travel together and save energy.

Bruce collected the vehicle and programmed it to go to Milton's home first and then that of Councillor Simpson, who was hosting Angela Belfield, and the other team from Woodleigh, with the help of his neighbours.

Elsa chose to sit next to Angela in the auto-bus, so they could share information about how both trips was going. Detailed comparisons were impossible as the aim of Angela's group was very different. Instead of focusing on environmental and multicultural topics, they were comparing methods of rehabilitation. Angela Belfield was a social worker and she and her husband had guided two former drug addicts through a course of rehabilitation. The programme had been so successful that those who had been rehabilitated were now acting as mentors to help others. On this trip they were comparing their practice with similar groups in Tamcaster. Elsa understood that Angela had to be discreet, but was glad to learn that things were running smoothly.

Adam and Beatrice chose to sit on the back seat and were soon joined by Trish, who told them that Derbyshire was her favourite place, so she was not going to lose this opportunity.

"Bonnie and I love going for long walks in the Peak District," she told them. "We often have Saturday walks there from our church. There are wonderful, woodland valleys with rushing streams there, and rocky hills you can climb with exciting views for miles around and there are often caves underneath them that are open for the public to explore."

Bruce welcomed them all aboard, adding the information that the auto-bus was powered by lithium air batteries, which enabled it to travel cheaply and it should provide them with a quiet, smooth ride.

As they left the city behind and entered Derbyshire the changes were dramatic. They left urban Tamcaster at a big roundabout, where the bus selected a steeply rising road, with grassy hills on either side. It brought them over a high bridge from which they could look down on a wide river below.

"The River Lent below marks the county boundary," Bruce explained, as he stood up holding a microphone, "We are now entering the White Peak area. There are two different areas in Derbyshire, defined by the colour of the rocks. The land round here is limestone country, and you'll see good examples of it as we drive through the valleys. There are a few tall white stones standing in some of the fields: relics of ancient times, and there's a dramatic cliff at Matlock Bath, where the pinnacled rocks climb above the green tree tops. There's a riverside walk through the woods that some of you might like to explore. We'll stop there for an hour.

I should explain that the Dark Peak to the north, which is also spectacular, is called that because of the grit-stone rocks. The highest point of that Peak is at Kinderscout. There are several deep caves there, which can be explored, but we won't have time for that today. We're going to focus on the southern part. One of the lovely surprises for you is that today there are several village festivals taking place. We are going to visit Ashford-in-the-Water, where they have a well-dressing festival, and we aim to stop for lunch at the Magpie Inn at the head of a valley where you have a wonderful view of one of the famous Derbyshire dales."

"What's well-dressing?" Beatrice called out.

"It's a very old country custom. The villages round here were dependent on water that came from springs. In pagan times, the people used to decorate their water wells with coloured petals gathered from local wild flowers. It was a way of giving thanks to the gods. They still carry the custom on today but it's been turned into a village festival, as you'll see, with music and dancing. It's great fun and it encourages the tourist trade."

The bus stopped for half an hour at Matlock Bath, where everyone was able to stretch their legs, and admire the tall, white cliffs rising out of green woodland.

"This is beautiful. It reminds me of postcards I've seen of Switzerland," Frances said, as she took a photo. Some of the party wandered along the winding, woodland path that meandered beside the swift flowing stream that Bruce had mentioned; others explored some of the village shops.

After this break, the auto-bus carried them on through the village of Cromford, where they saw one of the original mills, designed by Richard Arkwright. Bruce explained that it had been built here at the start of the industrial revolution, because the swift running water pouring down from the hills was ideal for turning the waterwheels needed to power the mill.

"In those days they had the common sense to use renewable energy," Peter observed.

The village of Ashford-in-the-water was alive with traditional folk music and dancing. The villagers had come out to see the Morris men prancing in the streets, and to welcome the visitors who had come in cars and coaches. An accordionist was entertaining crowds outside the inn, by playing traditional tunes; the village well had been decorated with flowers, and a picture had been created from petals representing Jesus and the woman at the well.

Bruce explained that Christian illustrations had been introduced in medieval times to replace ancient pagan ones. The tradition was still carried on. Local villages held their well-dressings on different days, and competed with each other. "Each village calls a meeting to agree on a subject, and then teams work together to create a picture. The petals are fixed into a clay base frame," Trish explained.

After watching the festivities and taking photographs, the bus took them to a tavern where lunch was provided at outside tables, overlooking a fertile dale where the River Wye wound its way past rocky outcrops. A tall railway viaduct still arched the valley, long after the line had been closed.

"There was a lot of anger about that viaduct when it was built in Victorian times," Gwen told those sitting by her. "I can understand it in those days, when trains were noisy and dirty. But somehow those arches add to the beauty when there are no smoky old trains. There's a cycling and hiking path on that bridge now, with a marvellous view of the whole valley from it. "

Mina was excited by this rural area, and said that she would like to spend the afternoon exploring the river path. This idea appealed to Elsa, Frances, Angela Belfield and several others too. It provided a quiet contrast after the gaiety of the village festival.

"I'm very glad to see how quiet and peaceful this place is. I'd heard that fracking was ruining the Derbyshire countryside," Peter observed.

"It is, only a few miles away," responded Bruce. " In the Dark Peak area there used to be a wilder sort of beauty, with rugged crags and caves, but much of it has been ruined now by the fracking companies."

"That's dreadful, but I'd like to see it, though. How far away is it?" Peter asked.

"Ten miles or so. We could go over there in the bus. I think most people are opting for a stroll along the river bank." Bruce stood up and called across to those at the other tables. "Hi, everyone. Peter's interested to see something of the Dark Peak area. They're doing a lot of fracking over there, so anyone who prefers that to a walk along the dale, speak now or never."

"I'll join you. It's a little hot for walking," said Mark.

Bruce climbed into the auto-bus with Gwen, who was wearing her prosthetic leg, and did not want to be too energetic. Mark, Peter and Frances joined them, arranging to come back and meet the walkers back at the tavern in two hours time.

The bus took them north. Within twenty minutes they began to recognise a different type of scenery. Stones walls patterned gaunt bare hills, criss-crossing them and adding order to the wildness. Dark and solid stone farms sat on lonely hills or nestled by streams in the valleys below. There was something challenging about the Dark Peak, which tempted folk to climb sheer rock faces or search the lonely moors. It was a spare and empty land, with a rugged beauty of its own kind.

The scene changed when they parked the bus and clambered to the top of a high tor. The noise from the fracking resounded loader as they came nearer.

"There you are, that's fracking," said Bruce. They peered across a vast valley, which looked like hell on earth and sounded like it too. The whole base of the valley was choked with machinery: lifting gear and huge mechanical robots. Clouds of dust hovered above them forming a thick blanket; the deafening sound of drilling rang in their ears and the stench made them reach for handkerchiefs to block it out.

As they breathed through the cotton and raised their eyes to look beyond the drilling platforms, they saw an endless line of lorries, nose to tail, queuing to reach the site. One end of the line was busy with workers who appeared to be offloading tanks of water. As soon as a lorry was emptied, the men started to fill it up again with metal canisters, presumably containing the prized gas.

"They are drilling through aquifers to reach rocks below, which contain methane," Bruce yelled above the din. "When they've done that, they will drill horizontal shafts below ground, so that they can inject water and hazardous chemicals under pressure to cause hydraulic fractures that release more methane. This will be collected at the top of the shaft."

"What's methane?" Frances shouted.

"A very potent greenhouse gas. When it's released into the atmosphere, it creates CO2, hence more climate change, but the advantage of all this fearful pollution is that we get more oil to fuel long distance super flights to satisfy the super-rich."

"How much precious water do they waste?" Peter yelled.

"They have several storage lakes over there." Bruce pointed west, "and they have to keep the water pumping through or the lakes run dry."

They looked in that direction and saw that there was a tall fence, topped with barbed wire surrounding the site. The lorries were lined up against a gate, that could be opened to admit another lorry as soon as a loaded one left the site.

"No wonder there's a water shortage in many areas," shouted Frances. "They must be using gallons of it on this exercise."

"And think about all the energy that all those drills and pumps are using," Mark shouted.

"What organisation's doing this?" called Frances. Instead of answering, Bruce pointed to a big sign that read *"Moredrilla. Keep out."*

"There are ten fracking wells here and each one requires millions of gallons of water," Bruce yelled.

"Isn't there a danger of contaminating our drinking water?" asked Peter.

"There's certainly that danger. Some people are trying to prove that they've already been poisoned by it, but the companies are minting money and can afford the best lawyers in Britannia to cover their backs."

"The hazards are legion," said Peter. "Tar sands at the seaside, for one, and I'll bet that some of the men who work the machines in this environment end up with respiratory ailments later in life."

They looked down at the men operating the drilling machines, who were dwarfed by their equipment. They all wore face-masks, making them look sinister.

"I can't stand this racket." Gwen covered her left ear with her hand, but the right one was left exposed because she was holding her stick.

"And this smell is dreadful," said Mark.

"And the view," said Peter. "Let's return to sanity."

They left the hilltop and ran to the security of their electric auto-bus. Its bonnet was already shrouded in peppery dust.

"We didn't come here to admire the view," said Peter.

"No, but would you believe it? Ten years ago, people did. There was a wonderful, tranquil valley there, with sheep and cattle grazing."

"I can't bear this," Frances suddenly exclaimed. "Please turn the bus round. Let's head back to the healing wells."

As they drove away, Mark felt one of his dark moods was swirling around him again. He should not have come here, he told himself. He should have gone with Elsa, Rory and Mina on that gentle river walk through the dale. The only reason that he had come was because he was sitting at the table with Peter and Bruce. When the black shadows overcame him it was easiest to say nothing and move on with the people he was already with.

He had a headache now as well. He could still hear the noise of the drilling.

"Are you OK, Mark?" asked Peter, in his hearty way.

"I'll feel better when we're back in the White Peak area," he heard his voice saying.

He was not fully present. He felt removed from his body, unsure of the world around him and unable to make decisions. He knew the mood would lift though. It always did in around an hour or so.

Elsa understood and took his hand and the mood slowly became more bearable.

* * *

Milton had not been with them on the Derbyshire outing. Instead he had spent the day visiting people in Tamcaster who had been distressed the previous evening. His first call was on a small shopkeeper who had had his windows smashed and his shop looted. He helped him sweep up some of the broken glass, and tidy the shop up again for the morning opening.

He went on to the home of the imam from the mosque, and accompanied him on the inspection tour of the damage done to the premises, and offered to return next day with some volunteer helpers from his church to help the Muslims get things straight again.

His third call was on the family of a youth who had been injured in the scuffles. On finding that he had not come home again yet, he drove to the general hospital and found the lad in a queue waiting for an available car to take home. An exhausted emergency team had patched him up. Milton drove him back instead.

He decided to drive Christine and Bonnie into the Real Coffee Bar that evening, rather than let them catch the auto-tram.

He collected them after they had finished their shift at two in the morning. As they drove home, he switched on the local news, and picked up the information about the rioting that was now taking place in the St. Luke's District.

"I feel I should drive over there too to see what I can do," he said to Christine, as she followed Bonnie into the house.

"Don't," said Christine. "You look worn out, and you have a long day tomorrow. There are plenty of others who can go over there."

He listened to what she said and, for once, took notice, returned the pool car to the garage and walked home thoughtfully. *How do I know when I have done enough?* he asked himself. Instead, he spent several minutes in his study that evening praying for the people in St. Luke's, before he went up to join Christine in the bedroom.

CHAPTER 17 - Sunday

On Sunday morning the silence was palpable. Everyone felt it, even those who had spent a quiet night. There was a whiff of burning in the air, and even the birds did not sing. Those who switched on the Radio Tamcaster had their fears confirmed. There had been more rioting overnight, and someone had even thrown a lighted rocket through an open window in a refugee hostel. One woman had died in the explosion and several had been injured. Many people felt an urge to go to a place of worship, even some who never chose to visit one. At the Forest Full Gospel Chapel regular members of the congregation had to move along the pews to make room for welcome strangers.

Pastor Milton Lamb left his sermon in the drawer of his desk. His mind was churning as he entered the chapel, and all he knew was that he would be guided in what he said when the moment came. There had been times when he had done this before, but they were rare. His words were usually very carefully crafted.

He was surprised to catch a glimpse of the Lord Mayor in the vestibule. She had never attended one of his services before, but he knew what must have prompted it and was glad to see her there. *She's a good woman, Jenny Paynter, one who always tries to be in the right place in a time of need.*

He went into the vestry to prepare himself quietly and when it was time to go through the door into the chapel, he saw that every seat was filled and the congregation was unusually quiet and sombre. There had been no evangelical warm up. The young singers who usually gave the chapel this honour had realised that it might set the wrong tone for a day such as this.

"Welcome to you all," he began, "regular worshippers and visitors alike." After a short opening prayer he announced the first hymn, "Morning has broken". Somehow it seemed especially appropriate, possibly cleansing after the night that had passed. It was soothing to recognise the clear high tones of Bonnie and Trish, clearly audible to him, like two angels of comfort.

"As we gather this morning, we are all traumatised by what happened here in Tamcaster last night. I had prepared a sermon, which I have now discarded, instead of speaking from a script, I speak from the heart today.

Brothers and Sisters, we live in a dark world, where sinister shadows follow our steps. We live in a fallen world, which thousands of people have helped to degrade, because we are caught up in an acquisitive society, which encourages us to want more, and never be satisfied with what we have. But material possessions are not what life is all about, and there is hope, my friends. There is hope, for we know that there is a light in this darkness. We do not always see this light. There are times when the light is clouded. There are times when we turn away from it ourselves, but this we know – that the light is always there.

If we go out at night, we do not see the sun. Does this mean that the sun has been extinguished? No, of course not, it is just shining on the other half of our turning globe. It is hidden for our benefit, at what is supposed to be our sleeping time. Would we want the sun to shine all night long? No, there is a time to be awake, and there is a time to take our rest. But there are those who choose that time to do their evil deeds. They do not dare to do them in the blaze of daylight. They choose the cover of darkness instead.

There are people, even here in Tamcaster who, if they see a shop window that has been smashed by a vandal, think this is an opportunity to rob the shopkeeper. There are others who try to destroy places of worship, just because that place is not their own: just because it belongs to a faith which is different from theirs. Shame upon them, for these are cowardly people. They prey upon the poor, the refugees...the victimised. They hurt and they destroy, and take pleasure in doing so.

But this morning, I do not want to dwell on wickedness. We have had our bellyful of it. I want to speak of hope. There are good elements in

223

this town and many of you share in these activities – the community centres, the children's playgroups, the carnival processions, the welfare clubs, the community larder, the credit unions, the pensioners' lunch clubs. I could go on – you know and work in them. We have guests with us today – we have our Lord Mayor, hidden somewhere towards the back of the church, in her modest way, and then there are our visitors from Wessex. Put your hands up, so we know who and where you are. Thank you, Lord Mayor, thank you, Wessex. After this service, I'm sure you will all want to meet our guests and tell them about some of the good things we do in our community here. You are right to be proud of the contributions you make, but I felt I had to begin this service with a warning note for the dangers are clearly around us all the time."

The hymns and prayers following were all entered into with fervour by the mixed congregation, which was composed almost equally of black and white people.

When Milton mounted the pulpit and began his sermon there was rapt attention.

"Dear friends," he began. "The Good Lord gave us this wonderful home - a beautiful planet, with rich and fertile soil, watered by rainfall and smiled on by sunshine. For centuries, people have farmed here in this land of milk and honey, like the Israelites of old. There were beasts in the field and, if the people used them on the farms, they had a responsibility to care for them. If they milked their cows, they could enjoy the produce. When they sheared their sheep, they had wool for their clothing. But there were others who enclosed the fields and said that they were theirs. There were many who went hungry as a result. There were those who built factories and treated their workers like slaves. These were sad times.

But better days followed, for there were good people who fought for improved conditions. When the Factory Acts were passed the hours of toil became shorter and, instead of young children being prized for their small bodies that could crawl under machines to mend the broken threads, there were schools to educate them. Trade unions got organised and fought for fair and equal pay, for pensions and holidays, and then some of the employers looked round and said, 'We could move our manufacturing offshore, to places where workers are cheaper, and where there is less regulation, then we will make bigger profits for our shareholders,' and so it was. The rich got richer still, and the poor became poorer and society became unequal again.

Then, it reached a state where we were destroying the rich quality of the soil through overworking it. We were depleting the oceans of fish, through over harvesting them. We were poisoning the air we breathe with chemicals, and we are endangering the lives of many creatures through greed - and then the United Nations called several conferences to discuss these things, and eventually in 2015 at a conference in Paris world leaders resolved to change their ways. They resolved that they would not allow their carbon emissions to rise by more than 2%, and ideally fix them at no more than 1.5%. But tragically, they did not keep all those promises. They cut back somewhat, and today this affects the lives of thousands, particularly the young people. The unemployed get angry when foreigners come here and work for lower wages, but many of those who have come are refugees from the pollution of their homelands, which our richer lifestyle has helped to pollute. But I do not want to dwell on despair, this morning: I want to talk of hope.

So, where is the hope? The hope is in ourselves, for are we not made in the image of the Almighty? If you believe it is so, then let us shout and tell the world. Are you made in the image of Almighty God?"

Most members of the congregation shouted back with a mighty voice: "Yes, we are."

The pastor clapped his hands and shouted, "We rise above this gloom. Turn round to either side of you and shake hands with your neighbour. Exchange greetings with our visitors and give them hope." His voice changed to a quiet whisper.

" Let us pledge ourselves now to work for peace and love, and let the light of love flow through us. Leave your seats and walk around this house of God and greet our friends from Wessex. Shake hands with our Lord Mayor, Jenny Paynter. Walk round now and bless your neighbours. Shake hands and say 'May peace be with you': I do not mean the peace of silence between neighbours, but the peace past understanding: the peace that the cup cannot contain; the peace that overflows."

Pastor Lamb stepped down from the reading desk, crossed the floor and started greeting all those on the front rows, while the stewards at the back of the church embraced and shook hands with those sitting near them.

After this, the pastor called on his congregation to pray with him: for peace, love and brotherhood to flow through the town, the province, the country and across the whole world. "For are we not all brothers and sisters? Are we not all children of one loving Father/Mother God?"

Milton prayed with a sincere quiet passion, and some of the congregation prayed aloud, adding their own thoughts, and many raising their arms and eyes to the ceiling.

This type of worship was new to all the visitors from Wessex, but the sincerity of it spilled over and touched many hearts. Mina was moved to tears. Elsa put her arm round her. Rory glanced at them in some surprise, and Mark took Rory's hand. A queue of people lined up to shake hands with the Lord Mayor, who was also clearly moved by all that was going on.

Ten minutes later the pastor went back into the pulpit. "Lord," he cried, looking upwards, "Thank you for this loving community here today. We thank you for the privilege of being able to host our friends from Woodleigh in Wessex. They are here at a difficult time, when there are fractures in our society. O God, we ask that we can be used as instruments to mend these fractures, to heal these wounds. Help us to reach out to the afflicted, and also to those who create the wounds, for these people are sick in mind and need to see the light.

Help us to be agents for spreading your love far wider than this community. Let the love flow out to those who would damage us. Let it melt stony hearts. Let the love flow across this city, this province, across this whole Britannic Island. Let the love flow across the mighty oceans in danger of pollution by those who search the depths for hidden mineral wealth or to harvest vast quantities of fish. Help us to learn that this precious world is not our plaything. It a sacred place and the home of all manner of life forms. Help us to understand that we are only one of your species, but gloriously gifted, and help us to use these gifts, as you would have us do. We ask all this in the name of Jesus Christ, our friend and saviour. Amen."

Bonnie and Trish sang the hymn "Holy, Holy. Holy, Lord God Almighty" as a quiet duet, with their eyes closed. It created an awed tranquil contrast to the loud, resonant voice of their father, who became a much bigger figure in the pulpit than he was in private life.

Towards the end of the service, the pastor explained that everyone was welcome to come to the lunch being provided in the hall next door at 12.30p.m. After this, members of the inter-faith movement were going to meet at the mosque for a silent peace vigil. The Bishop of Tamcaster was joining them there. They would then walk in a silent procession to the Anglican Cathedral, where there was to a meeting of the Interfaith Council at 3pm with readings, songs and a dance on the theme "Peace in our Community." After this, there would be a half hour peace vigil in the Cathedral. What had originally been intended as a fairly small affair by the Interfaith leaders had taken on much more significance in the last few days.

Peter asked Bruce about the interfaith group during the lunch. "Our meetings don't normally involve bishops and the like," he smiled as he explained. "I've been involved with this work over the past three years. We meet monthly, often going to different places of worship and our sharing thoughts. We sometimes discuss issues such as war and peace, life after death, the possible nature of God, whatever form we see in Him, Her or it: the challenges of the day and how to deal with them from our own tradition. It's a very warm-hearted group to be in, and we've all made friends with people of different backgrounds. Our beliefs are not as wide apart as you might expect. We usually have all the eight main faiths represented at our meetings, but sometimes we have more Christians than necessary. I suppose though, we should expect that in this country."

"What about the Muslim involvement?"

"We have a strong link. We had to work a bit harder at first to get them on board, because there is a lot of suspicion in that community. Inter-faith dialogue is not part of their tradition, but when they trust you, they are happy enough to invite you to the mosque, and there are two Muslims who attend inter-faith sessions regularly. We have a rotating chairmanship, and we have a Muslim chairman at the moment. He's a university lecturer."

"Can I go along to the mosque for this peace vigil?"

"Yes, of course you can. It would be good if the whole of the Woodleigh delegation came. It would show solidarity at a difficult time. The bishop will be there. He's obviously concerned about these relationships at the moment, and his secretary telephoned me yesterday to say that he would like to join us. We'd notified him of the event, but did not expect him to have him with us, but after these riots, the whole gathering has taken on a new significance,"

"Can women come to the mosque? Even humanists like me?" asked Frances.

"Yes, provided you cover your head with a scarf. We all have to take our shoes off when we arrive there. That's the first thing we do."

After the meal there was a short discussion. Everyone from Woodleigh indicated that they would like to go to the mosque, although none of them were particularly religious. They went in the pool cars, and found a sizeable crowd was collecting. Most of the regular members of the inter-faith group were there, plus several additional partners and friends. The police were represented in the form of Inspector Harper in plain clothes with his wife. Beatrice and Adam were the youngest people present.

The mosque was quite an imposing modern building with a dome and minaret.

They gathered in the car park outside, and were soon joined by the imam and the chairman of the Interfaith Council, Farnoosh Shah, who invited them to come inside. Shoes were collected by the door, and then everyone was invited to wash their feet in an adjoining wash-rooms: one for men and one for women.

After the Bishop of Tamcaster had arrived with his wife and personal assistant, Mr. Shah opened the meeting by introducing the imam in charge of the mosque and the bishop. It was clear that the Muslims present were very glad of this opportunity to welcome the bishop, who chose to modestly stay amongst the visitors, rather than stand in a prominent place. Everyone was treated with great courtesy, especially the ladies. They were all shown the principal rooms, and then taken to the main hall, where they were invited to sit down facing Mecca, which was clearly indicated by the positioning of the imam's seat.

About fifty people arrived for the vigil, and another thirty or so Muslims joined them kneeling on the floor. Mr Shah made a short statement on behalf of the elders of the mosque, and invited the bishop to speak. The bishop had not expected this, but said that he was very glad to have this opportunity to visit the mosque, that he had been shocked to hear of the intended vandalism, and was very pleased to hear that the suspects, who had now been charged, were in custody, awaiting trial. He wished the Muslim community well in Mercia, welcomed the dialogues initiated by the Inter-faith Council, and concluded by saying "Let there be peace shared amongst us, in the name of the God we serve."

The imam then incanted a short prayer in his own language and a silent vigil began. At first Rory did not know what to do. Then he found himself visualising Tamcaster as a peaceful place: the market square, the shopping centres, the Forest Community Centre, the Refugee Centre, the Real Coffee Bar. Then he tried to expand his vision to embrace the Province of Mercia, and beyond it the whole of Britannia. He saw Wessex in particular - a peaceful land stretching from the West Country to Wiltshire, then he moved his thinking towards the thriving capital in London, This was more difficult. He thought first of some of the churches. He had been in St. Paul's, that was a good place to start and he found himself being lifted high into the dome and looking down on the cathedral, filled with worshippers. He seemed to pass through the dome and then saw St. Paul's from above. That scene dissolved, to be replaced by a view of the whole great city with the river snaking its way through the clustered rooftops.

Then he remembered that poem of Wordsworth's "On London Bridge" and he was there in the early morning watching the sunrise over a sleeping city. He looked up into the skies and he was there too. He floated for a time, seemingly lying on a bed of clouds, but then he was caught by a sudden wind that blew him south, over a sleeping land. He looked down and saw Dover Castle, then the channel and the Normandy beaches; he swept across France, lingered over Paris and then flew quickly south, across snow covered Alps to Italy. He visited known streets, glimpsing old friends getting out of bed and having breakfast. He went into the school where he had first met Mina, and the children were just arriving, joyful and happy.

He found himself flying south over Africa, so high he could see the whole shape of the continent and envisaged peace across quiet deserts and tropical rainforests. He crossed savannah, and saw lions sleeping, a zebra grazing, and elephants drinking at a pool. No one was hunting the animals and they were not troubling each other. Then he went west, across the great Atlantic Ocean. He could see a tiny ship sailing, miles below him. Suddenly he was swept into the vortex of a whirlpool wind. He was sucked higher and higher. He knew he must not resist, but go with the flow. He travelled up and up.

Above the clouds, there was darkness. He could see myriads of stars, all serene – and the sound of very distant singing. When he turned to look down, he knew why he had been brought so high. The clouds had disappeared, and from here he could see the world as a turning globe. He forced himself lower down, so that he could identify the Gambia River, winding its way through a narrow band of tropical forest. So this was Mina's homeland. He hovered there, but the world was turning. Now, all he could see was an expanse of ocean. At first all was quiet, but then from somewhere far above he heard the sound of singing.

What was this? He could not tell, but then he realised that it sounded like the voices of those two girls, Bonnie and Trish singing "Holy, Holy, Holy". Their voices came louder and clearer.

Then he heard another voice. He did not know the language, but he felt people around him were getting up and moving, and mechanically, he did the same. He was back in the mosque, surrounded by friends and everyone was at peace. People were turning to each other and shaking hands. The meditation was over. He was unsteady on his feet. He felt strangely light headed, but there was a glow in his heart. He had never before felt so peaceful.

The walk through the town seemed almost like a continuation of the meditation. Everything seemed to be at a distance, but it was a beautiful experience. He took Mina's hand and they walked together in procession. No one spoke, but then he realised that he was holding another hand on the other side of him. Cautiously, he turned to see who it was. It was an elderly man dressed in traditional Muslim costume, white pantaloons, a light blue tunic and a round cap on his head. He had a white beard, and when Rory tried to say a word to him, it was clear that the man did not understand English. Had he taken this man's hand, or had the man taken his? He had no recollection, but he was glad of this simple act of unity.

It was a short walk to the cathedral – along two streets. People watched the procession. Some clapped, many smiled and others waved to them. The atmosphere was one of happiness.

In contrast to the modern mosque they stopped before an old cathedral. It was on an ancient site, but the building was mainly Victorian gothic in character. The hall beside it was a modern round building. They went inside. Everyone gathered in a wide circle, round the inside walls. The dean moved into the centre, welcomed them all and suggested that they took a chair off the stacks and formed a big circle around the walls. It became clear that the circle would need to be in three rings, with the taller people at the back. Once this was done Mr. Shah explained that the ceremony would consist of very short presentations by each of the eight faiths present. Before this began, he suggested that everyone greeted the people on either side of them.

Rory, who had Mina on his left, found he was sitting beside a Sikh gentleman on his right, and Mina found herself next to a Hindu lady. Names and friendly smiles were exchanged, and then Mr. Shah called for a minute's silence, explaining that the presentations would be in alphabetical order. The words "Baha'i Faith" came up on television screens on opposite sides of the room.

The performance included a Baha'i reading and peace song, Buddhist gongs and chanting, a short Bible reading, followed by Trish's new song, Indian children's' dancing, a Jewish cantor, a Muslim peace prayer, and a Sikh bangla performer. The performance ended with everyone singing a beautiful tune, from words projected on to the screen:-

 "Let there be love shared amongst us,
Let there be love in our eyes.
May now Your love sweep this nation.
Cause us, o Lord to arise.

Give us a fresh understanding
of brotherly love that is real.
Let there be love shared amongst us.
Let there be love."

After this everyone was invited to sing the words once more, and almost everyone participated.

During the following buffet tea people mingled and chatted. Milton thanked the Lord Mayor for joining them for the whole day. Jenny Paynter told him, "I was proud of the people who clapped as we walked together, Christians, Muslims and city councillors. Then seeing this unity with Hindus, Sikhs and others this afternoon is what I call the true spirit of Tamcaster. It gives me confidence that we can put the events of last week behind us and move forward again together. I've been wondering whether we should cancel the Afro-Caribbean Festival tomorrow. I'll be talking to the Chief Constable about this tonight and my instinct tells me that we should carry on with it. What do you think?"

"I'm sure we should go ahead, Lord Mayor. You and the Chief Constable must decide for reasons of security, but my gut feeling is that we can't let the darkness prevail."

Rory had regained his normal composure during the interfaith presentation. He asked Mina what her experience had been during the prayer vigil.

"I remembered my old home in Gambia home," her eyes sparkled. "I saw it at peace. Then my thoughts went to Italy, my mother and the Steiner School: then here to Britannia. I saw Exeter, my aunt and Woodleigh and finally this town and I sent everyone blessings and love. It was a lovely experience. How about you? You seemed to be in a kind of trance and I did not like to disturb it."

"You're right. It was a trance. It wasn't just my own thoughts. I wasn't in control. Not all the time anyway. Something came from outside me. I've never experienced anything like it before. It wasn't frightening though. It was beautiful. I want to talk to Milton about it when I can, but he's talking to Mrs Paynter now. I'll catch him this evening."

Rory had been quite shaken by the whole experience. He did not understand it, but he felt something important had happened and he wanted to share it with people who could understand. Perhaps it had been the combination of the rousing service in the morning, the like of which he had never experienced before, followed by his first visit to a mosque, but he knew it was more than that. There was another element, which he felt had come from above. He hadn't mentioned his feelings to anyone else.

Over the evening meal that night, Rory asked Milton if he and Mina could speak to him privately. Milton suggested that instead of finishing the meal at the table, the three of them could bring their coffee into his study.

Rory tried to describe his experience in the mosque and asked Milton if this came as a surprise to him. He smiled. "Well my son, it sounds to me as if you had a real spiritual experience. That's wonderful and obviously it was something new for you. Some people have experiences of this kind regularly, others never, but worship encourages it. This is a great part of what it's all about. Lifting human beings beyond the here and now, from the physical world into the spiritual, where we really belong. We all have a spiritual dimension but most people today in the western world never know it."

"But isn't it strange that it should happen in a mosque rather than a church?"

"Not really, you had been in a church that had probably started the first feelings, but it usually requires other experiences to progress them. Mosques are holy places, as well as churches, so is a synagogue or a Hindu Temple. Such buildings seek to draw the worshippers out of the physical realm and give them a glimpse beyond. There's also another thing that probably awakened your feelings. You're in love, and I note that the travels took you in the direction of Mina's homeland, How was it for you, Mina?"

Mina described her thoughts as she had done before. "But there is a difference because I was in control of my thoughts all the time, I was not being led."

"That could be because you are more familiar with spiritual pathways. Are you a believer?"

"That depends what you mean by believer."

"You tell me what you believe."

"I believe in a loving God, but in Gambia I was taught that God had the face of a black woman — the true mother of us all. I still see it that way. Is that heresy?"

"No, it is not. That is right for you. God is beyond human understanding – so we have to create an image we can believe in. You remember this morning in the service I used a favourite term of mine "Father Mother God." God is above gender and above colour."

"You don't find it offensive for me to call God she then?"

"Not at all. God is neither one not the other, but we need to use a pronoun, and the obvious one for us Christians is 'he' because we recognise God through his son, Jesus."

"I was brought up as an African Christian and in our tradition the creator was seen as female."

"That's all right with me. How do you regard Jesus?"

"As the son of the Mother God, who came to show us a better way of living."

"Fine again. You are a believer."

"But why did I have such a deep spiritual experience in a mosque?" asked Rory. "Muslims do not see Jesus this way."

"Some Muslims recognise Jesus as a great teacher sent by God, but they do not see him as an incarnation of God. As a Christian, I think they are mistaken."

"What confuses me is that there are so many faiths all claiming that they are know the true way," said Rory, "They can't all be right."

"But we are trying to understand a great mystery that is beyond human comprehension. People of different faiths get different glimpses and create constructs they can understand. Did you ever hear the story of the three blind Indians who were walking in the jungle, and they came across an elephant? One touched its legs and said 'This creature is like a living tree.' The second touched its tusk and said 'No. You are wrong the one is like a great drinking horn.' The third one touched his trunk and said 'You are both wrong, brothers, this creature we have found is a monstrous snake.' The different faiths can all tell us something about the nature of God, but none can tell the whole story. We learn more from dialogue with each other. Who knows, God may have revealed himself on occasions to different cultures in different forms. I am not saying he did, merely that he could have done so."

Rory looked at Mina and asked her, "Is it all right with you if I ask Milton the favour we spoke about earlier?"

Mina smiled and took Rory's hand.

"Milton," said Rory "We enjoyed your service this morning, and after the lunch, Mina said to me. He's a lovely man. He's just the sort of person I would like to marry us, and I told her that I agreed, although I've never been much of a churchgoer. Would you consider it?"

Milton looked into both their eyes, smiled and said "Marriage is a very big commitment. Are you both sure it is what you want?"

They both asserted that they did, and explained the circumstances and the situation that they were caught in. Milton was very sympathetic, and was glad to know that they had support from their parents. When did they suppose it might be?

 "Well, we can't get married next week, but it's just possible that it could be next month, when you are in Woodleigh."

"If the authorities give permission then, so be it. And where would wish to have the wedding?"

"We had thought of the Woodleigh Community Church. I used to go to Sunday School there a long time ago, and I've shown Mina the building."

"Well that would require the permission of the vicar, but if the authorities give you permission to marry so soon, and if the vicar gives me permission to use his premises on a convenient day for us all, so be it."

"Thank you," Rory and Mina cried together, and hugged each other. Milton smiled, as he watched them both.

"In that case, we'd better go and tell the others," said Rory.

CHAPTER 18 - The Second Week

Undoubtedly, there was a feeling of anxiety on Monday morning. Had the right decision been made? But once the carnival procession was on its way, uncertainties began to melt. There was a strong police presence along the whole route, leading from the Afro-Caribbean Centre in St. Luke's right into the heart of the city. It continued around the inner ring road, before turning north towards the Forest Recreation Ground, where a fun-fair was due to be held, followed by a late night firework display.

It was a very hot summer day and the exuberance of the performers on parade, the lively music, the presence of so many young children, all helped the raise the spirits. Tamcaster seemed to be making a big recovery and the councillors kept their fingers crossed hoping that this mood would prevail. What had originally started out a hundred years ago as an Afro-Caribbean event had blossomed over the years into a full multi-racial carnival, with different elements being added every time.

The procession was led by the joyful group that had started the tradition in the first place, but applications to take part had been made by various Asian and eastern European communities over the years and, more recently, local teams of marching bands, singing choirs and dancing divas had joined in the spree. A magnetic surge of energy had been created: the international character of the city was reflected in the black, white, brown and almond features of the dancers.

The excitement spread quickly from those in the parade to the people watching in the streets. Many folk felt that a strong sense of community was returning after several troubled days and nights. Teams of community volunteers backed the policing, which was strengthened by the presence by a company of soldiers from the Mercian Regiment. Each ethnic group had its own supporters and the volunteers kept an eye open for troublemakers, but their own calm presence helped to keep those elements at bay. Bruce was delighted to see that the hard work he had put into preparing these teams was paying off at this crucial time.

The Afro-Caribbean communities headed the parade. A colourfully dressed girl, carrying a placard naming the team, led each group: Jamaica, Barbados, Windward Islands, Leeward Islands and Trinidad, who had brought their traditional steel band. The tuneful pans could be heard streets away, and the spectators prepared themselves by swaying to the rhythms. Many of the young dancers and musicians were second, third and even fourth generation, and their colouring expressed this, but the shining faces, and swinging floral costumes quickly won applause from the crowd.

Africans came next, with wilder music from Nigeria and Ghana. Then Indian, Pakistani and Bangladeshi teams followed, with decorated vehicles providing recorded music and songs. Then Philippinos graced the parade with flowers in their hair and looped round their necks: some throwing posies to the bystanders. The Polish dancers followed in white blouses, red neckties and floral skirts, and then the Vietnamese, led by a prancing dragon, while firecrackers exploded around them.

The entertainment continued on the recreation ground, with a travelling fair and the added fun of booths and stalls, where local talent was on show. A young Ghanaian artist displayed her exotic art, dervish dancers entertained in the arena, and Chinese cooks offered an arrange of delicacies for the crowd to sample. It was as though the troubles of last week had drifted away in the warm sunshine.

* * *

The visitors from Woodleigh found that the second week of their stay seemed to pass much more quickly.

Bruce and Milton introduced them to two of the neighbourhood carbon-reduction groups, where ten families met each month to share their ideas and experiences on heating and lighting their homes, preparing their food and sharing their transport.

Jenny Paynter showed them round the Burnage Garden Village, where the allotment sharers had been successful in persuading the council to charge a levy on the supermarkets according to their size. They were told that the money raised went into Tamcaster Allotment Fund.

As they had missed the earlier visits, Rory, Mina, Beatrice and Adam went to see the Eco-House and looked in at the Housing Association offices afterwards.

Later they joined the others at the Tamcaster Energy Storage Plant, where Helen Garfield, the supervisor, took them on a quick tour of the laboratories.

They were shown a solar concentration cell, which used lenses to focus the sun's rays with 46% efficiency, and were then introduced to a system of carbon capture and release. In another area of the building, robot machines were producing decentralised energy systems: not just solar but combined heat and power plants and various forms of micro-power.

"We are experimenting here with different types of power generation," Helen explained. "As Tamcaster is conveniently situated at the very heart of Britannia, we have connections with universities and companies interested in developing power generation from natural resources in all six provinces. Our labs are linked to the Mercian grid, so this province benefits enormously."

"Have you a link with Exeter University?" Peter enquired.

"Yes, they've done a lot of work on wave-power in the South-West, but we also have strong links with hydro power developments in Scotland. Anglia is the best area for wind-power and Sussex for sun-power. We've an agreement that allows us to store surplus energy from all these sources in underground caves. Some of them used to be coal, salt, copper or tin mines. Disused railway tunnels have been brought back into service, too."

They were taken to a big engine-house, where electricity was generated from hot water that had been used in central heating systems across the province.

"There's a piston inside this device, that drives waste hot and cold water alternatively over wires that have nickel and titanium in them. This makes them expand and contract and causes them to form a crystal lattice structure that's useful in many products," they were told.

"What sort of products?" Mark asked.

" We've a contract with hospitals around Mercia and many of them use these materials in research, and two companies making sunglasses buy our material. These sales pay for the upkeep of this machine. We also make quite a substantial profit out of the waste water which we used to throw away.

As you probably know, much of the world's solar power comes from collecting stations across Africa and India. This is fed into the GOS Global Energy Reserve. Here, we've got a minor version of that. You probably saw some solar farms when you came here on the train. Three hundred of those farms feed into this system. We also get power generated by Mercia's housing estates under the Sunroof Supply Scheme and from local wind-power too. Of course we need to control the flow coming in and going out. We discharge it here for the whole of the province, according to need, and we make a profit by selling surplus power to others. Our main customers are the London and Northumbria."

"How's the flow managed?" asked Rory.

"By robotics, but we have to set the device every day and check it every six hours. It's a delicate balance between supply and demand."

There was a similar message at the Water Storage Plant.

"There's enough water in Mercia to meet our needs," they were advised. "And we all think it's precious on a hot day like this, but the main problem is that it isn't usually in the right places at the right time,

241

so we use a network of reservoirs and aqueducts. We found that much of the water was too salty, so now we've installed a desalination plant, powered by our thermal energy. One service provides another."

They were then taken over to a Geothermal and Fusion Unit where experiments were taking place in a fusion reactor. "Modern Nuclear Fission does way with many of the old problems of radioactive activity and nuclear waste that haunted the early nuclear reactors," Helen told them. "Our geothermal heat pumps transfer heat directly from the ground below our feet to provide a heating system in the winter and a cooling system on a day like this. Our direct exchange earth loop method eliminates any danger of water leakages and any need for anti-freeze. No water is involved, instead we are linked to a solar system."

* * *

Thursday was another scorching hot day. A solar powered autobus took the visitors to the Mercian Provincial Offices, two miles outside Tamcaster. Here, they were received by the Chairman of the Provincial Council, and after a brief tour of the newly built eco-friendly building, they were introduced to the Chief Environment Officer, who showed a film about how Mercia had suffered serious air pollution in several hot summers. Anticipating a continuation of this, a training programme had been planned and leaflets had been prepared to go to all households explaining about necessary environmental defence measures.

The visitors were then taken to an underground shelter, kept permanently ready with beds, equipment and stores. Two defence officers led them through the complex, which occupied the cellars of the provincial offices, and provided emergency accommodation for up to five hundred people. Similar shelters were being built across the province, they were told.

"The weather has become increasing unpredictable over the past twenty years. We are planning for the worst. Every district now has its own supply of snow ploughs and break-down recovery vehicles, together with a warehouse filled with sand bags, water tanks and food supplies. These are under control of district emergency officers, who have support teams made up local representatives, who come here for briefings and training every month. As we can't predict these things with accuracy, our emergency officers organise enactments to pass the skills to local response teams in each neighbourhood."

"What sort of weather did you have last winter?" asked Peter.

"We had snow blizzards right across the province. The previous year, our main problem was flooding. Torrential rain began on our border with Anglia and within the next day it spread across the whole region. This brought floods to all our low-lying areas, and then ice that had to be broken up by robotic machines. Three years ago, we had forest fires. It was a sweltering summer, if you remember, and somehow a fire broke out in the National Memorial Arboretum, and spread as far north as the outskirts of Tamcaster. The River Lent brought a stop to it, but the damage was horrendous, because hurricanes spread the forest fires and completely destroyed two villages, Fenny Drayton and Clayford. The fire brigade had a hell of a time rescuing people. Thirty died in one night. One of the most inspiring things was the part played by some of our young people. There was a youth brigade at Clayford who had been trained in first aid procedures. They were alerted in good time, and helped the fire and rescue service throughout that vital week."

"What sort of youth brigade was this?" asked Adam.

"And exactly how did they help?" queried Beatrice.

"They were a eco-faith youth group, and fortunately they'd all been on a first aid course, and had badges to show they'd passed the tests. When the youth leader heard of the fire at Bowden nearby, he called them in and they helped the Red Cross and RVS workers. People were being brought into their multi-faith hall for refuge. The youngsters were helping the adult workers there, when the news broke that the wind had spread the fire to the outskirts of their own village. The police took them back home, and then they went about giving a helping hand to elderly people and mothers with young babies. Some of them stayed overnight in the shelters. This showed the councillors the useful roles that young people can play. It prompted us to form the Mercian Youth Council. All the districts and towns are represented on this now."

"What do they do?" asked Beatrice.

"They meet every month and send us information about things affecting young people in their own area. We consult them about youth issues. It's a very helpful exchange of ideas."

Beatrice noticed that Peter was taking careful notes for his official reports. That evening she discussed all this with Bonnie and Trish. They'd heard about the firestorm, but not about the youth group involvement or the Mercian Youth Council.

"I organised a first aid course for the young people at our church," Bonnie said. "We sometimes help the St. John's ambulance teams at festivals and things. We're also the church eco-warriors, clearing up the waste and making sure that everything suitable can be recycled. This helps the church to monitor our weekly carbon footprint. We offset the emissions by planting trees and shrubs."

"We've planting sessions for saplings every spring and autumn and most of the young people at church join in," Trish added, "Some of them are also involved in home economy groups."

"What are they?" asked Beatrice.

"Groups of neighbours who meet to help each other to reduce their home ecological footprints. They compare costs for heating and lighting, and sometimes they can get reductions on the tariff because they have a group arrangement. They also swap recipes and ideas about cooking. They're usually keen on locally sourced food too. That's a big thing round here. We have a farmer's market every Thursday that's very popular." Beatrice made notes of all these points, which were giving her ideas for the Cornfield Cooperative.

Rory and Mina attended all the events organised, despite worries about Mina's visa extension.

They invited Laura round one afternoon to share their fears, and she asked them what reason they had given for extending the visit.

"I just said there were personal reasons," Mina replied. "I didn't mention anything about Rory of course."

"That's just as well, but they will probably ask more questions. They're very suspicious of bogus marriages, so I wouldn't mention anything about Rory if I were in your situation."

This response worried them all the more.

Laura met Beatrice and Adam one afternoon, and answered all their questions about the refugee situation. Adam took notes, and Laura gave him a copy of the Refugee Centre Annual Report to the Tamcaster City Council. She advised him to try to get hold of the report of the Wessex Refugee Council too. He agreed to do this, and decided that his project could be a comparison of the two areas.

Meanwhile, Beatrice started writing up her project about Elfleda, Lady of Mercia. She was strangely inspired by this woman, and determined to find out as much as possible about her from the Wessex Record Office.

Rory and Mina made time for another visit to the Refugee Centre, where Mina had lunch with Tabula. Although they were unable to share a common language and their exchanges had to be done through an interpreter, they felt extremely close to each other, having shared their experiences.

They also followed Councillor Fabian's advice and visited the homeless people who lived underneath the railway arch. Annie, the senior worker in charge, explained that she had a very mixed group of people there.

"Some have been sleeping rough for years and can't settle indoors, but there are others who we can work with more substantially, especially drug and alcohol users. We introduce them to others who have improved their lives, but this only works if they really want to make the change. Refugees from other countries come here in desperation. We always check with the Refugee Centre, and make sure that they know about them. Then there are people who come because of family breakdowns. Every person's an individual and, if they will share their story, we can usually introduce them towards someone, who might help turn things around. The most difficult people to help are those with mental health problems. The medical programmes don't really do enough for those people."

"Can you help with getting them somewhere to live?" Rory asked.

"Sometimes," Annie explained. "The best quick solution is to introduce them to Fabian. He can usually find a place in one of the squats that he keeps his eyes on. If they behave themselves well enough, after six months, he adds their names to the long waiting list for assisted accommodation. If they have a disability, or if a child's involved, this can happen much more quickly."

Mina and Rory stayed long enough to be introduced to several of those who were living 'under the arch', and found one or two who they could chat to, but some were very reticent. They came away with mixed feelings. The Arch was not a place to be afraid of, but they felt that the opportunities for turning lives round there, were considerably limited.

Throughout the whole visit, Beatrice had wanted to have a private talk with Mina, but Rory had constantly been with her. The opportunity finally came on the last morning, when Rory was involved in an avid discussion with Peter, and Mina had wondered into the garden, on her own. Beatrice was surprised to see her hugging a tree at the bottom of the garden.

"What are you doing?" she called as she walked over.

"Oh, dear! You caught me. I must have looked very silly. It's a thing I have when I visit a new place. I love to smell the bark of a tree. It meant a lot to me in Gambia, and when we got to Italy I adopted a tree in the refugee camp and then in garden of the Steiner school. I used to give them a hug first thing each morning and it warmed me up for the day. I sat there in meditation for a few minutes, and once I had done that, I felt they were my trees. I suppose it was a way of saying I was at home there. I haven't managed to do this before in Britannia, so I thought I must hug one in Tamcaster. When I'm back in Wessex, I'll choose one there too."

Beatrice thought this was very odd, but assumed it had something to do with putting down roots in a new place. She went on to say what she had come for.

"I'm so glad to find you alone, because I just want to let you know how desperately upset I'll be if you and Rory have to go back to Italy. I'm still getting to know you, and I really love having an African sister. It's great that Rory's back as well, of course, after all that time on my own at home. It would be criminal if they won't let you stay…"

She broke down in tears, and Mina reached out to her, hoping that nobody saw them and then instantly not caring whether anyone did or not.

"It's a joy to know that I'm really wanted by Rory's family: all of you. I'd heard so much about you and, to be honest, despite all Rory's assurances, I was terrified of meeting you all."

The final reception for the official visitors was in the Council Hall again, where farewells and good wishes were exchanged with both the Woodleigh groups.

Jenny Paynter was gracious in her remarks. "Thank you so much for coming to visit us," she said "You have been here at a taxing time, and seen Tamcaster at its best and worst. I trust that you will take back some treasured memories. We must continue sharing experiences and learning from each other across Britannia and through overseas links too. Perilous times are closing in, but we have been encouraged by the messages of hope that you have brought from Wessex, an ancient province from which we have learnt wisdom in ages past, are doing now and may do so again. We cherish this link, knowing that it will be enhanced when our delegation goes to you next month. Now it's time to say farewell. May your journey home be comfortable, and remember always that you have friends here in Mercia. I look forward with anticipation to receiving the reports of our visits to you, next month."

As they packed their bags for the return journey there was a tinge of sadness in all their hearts. In these turbulent times, it was impossible to predict the future. They were all conscious that the human race had damaged the planet through extravagant living, and that shattering storms faced them all in future years, but they felt less alone on this planetary journey. A friendship had been born which would remain strong in their memories and they knew that this special link would help sustain them through the perils of future years.

CHAPTER 19 - Wedding Plans

Mina and Rory were now determined to stay together all the time that they were in Woodleigh. When they got off the train in Exeter, Mina and Rory left the others to call on Mina's aunt to explain the changed situation to her. Mina had always been welcome to stay over, but she was the one who had been cautious about this. Now the feelings about the relationship were clear to everyone, it was the obvious thing for Mina to move into Mark and Elsa's home.

As soon as they returned there, Mina took of her shoes, and ran barefoot to hug the bark of the birch tree that she could see from the windows. It helped to feel the soil under her feet and rooted her back to her African childhood. Rory was moved to see this and it stirred him to telephone the Rector of Woodleigh and arrange a meeting on the following day to discuss wedding possibilities.

The Reverend Stephen Spooner was an energetic, cheerful man in his mid-thirties with broad shoulders and a welcoming smile. On coming to the door, he immediately invited them both into the rectory, a newly built sustainable home, next to his modern church.

He shook his head with an amused expression as he moved some children's toys off the floor of his study.

"How many times must I tell my kids not to play in here?" he sighed. "Perhaps they think I'm challenging them to provoke me again."

They sat down in two wooden swivel chairs and he faced them from his high-backed leather computer chair.

"So how did the Tamcaster trip go?" he asked.

"Very well," Rory assured him. "We were made most welcome, and saw many aspects of city life. It's a multi-cultural place, and we were taken to several community centres belonging to different ethnic groups. We also went to their Provincial Meeting House and had a day out in the

Derbyshire countryside. We feel that we have made some lasting friendships."

"And they are paying a return visit in two weeks, I believe. I hope you'll have time to bring them to our church."

"That's on the agenda, and it's one of the things I need to talk to you about."

"Splendid. But you mentioned a personal matter. Should we deal with that first?"

"Yes, we may as well get straight to the point. Amina and I are engaged to be married and we would like to tie the knot when the exchange visit takes place. We think that your church would be ideal, but we would like our host in Tamcaster, Rev. Milton Lamb to conduct the ceremony here while he's in Woodleigh, if it's possible."

"In the next three or four weeks, you mean. That's very short notice. It may be possible, but I need to ask you a few questions first."

"Please do."

"Amina, I'll bring you in now. You haven't had a chance to speak yet, have you? Is this what you would like too?"

"It's my dearest wish."

"How long have you known Rory?"

"Eighteen months."

"That's not very long. Where were you born?"

"In Gambia, but my mother brought me to Europe when I was ten. We came to a refugee camp in Italy and were granted asylum there."

"I'm sorry to hear that you needed to seek refuge. How did you meet Rory?"

"I'd trained as a school teacher and he came to my school to give a talk about the Peace Corps. That was when we first met, over a year ago."

Rory intervened to say. "I was bowled over when I saw Mina's artwork. We started talking and suddenly I knew that this was the girl for me."

"How long have you been engaged, Amina?"

"Five weeks."

"And why this hurry to get married?"

"Rory and I have been talking to refugee workers in Tamcaster and, apparently the regulations may be tightened next year with regard to refugees marrying English people. It may become impossible for us. We want to go ahead quickly to avoid any barriers."

"It's not fair that you should be under such pressure; Marriage is a big commitment. It shouldn't be artificially hastened — especially a mixed marriage, when there are so many different things to consider. Don't get me wrong. I rejoice to see you two people keen to go ahead with this, and I can tell that you are very much in love, which is a beautiful thing. How about your parents?"

"We have their full consent. Like you, my Mom and Dad were startled with the speed of all this, but they are very supportive; so is Mina's mother. We talked the engagement through with her in Italy, didn't we, darling?"

"My mother told me she is very happy to see me with a man like Rory."

"And she is still in Italy?"

"Florence," Mina responded.

"Where do you want to live? And how will you support each other?"

"We both want to live here, and I will take a teacher training course too," Rory responded. "We can stay with my parents initially, and then we'll try to get a place of our own. I think Mina will find work as an art teacher locally. We'll have to look into all this."

"And what about residency permits for you both - as a couple?"

"I've no problems there, and we've applied for Mina to have an extension of her visitor visa. Once we're married, we should be okay"

"Are you sure about that? I'm not clear about all the regulations, but Mina will have to get a resident's permit, won't she?"

"That will be easier after we are married."

"Ah - so that's the reason for the hurry."

"Yes, it seems to make sense to us."

"I'm sorry to say, a lot of things seem to make sense which can't be allowed these days. Look, I'm not trying to put a spoke in your wheels. I'm trying to help you see this through. How much longer have you got on your visitor permit, Mina?"

"Two weeks, but I've asked for a three-week extension."

"And if you two marry during that month, what will your position be? Do you know?"

Mina looked uncertain. She turned towards Rory. He replied for her, "I've checked this out," he said. "We got advice from the Tamcaster Refugee Agency. They say that Mina's situation will have been changed, and there's a strong chance that she will be able to stay here. We only have a few weeks' grace because there is a bill waiting to go through parliament that will change the situation, and if it comes into law, in all probability she will have to return to Italy. If that happens, I will go with her."

"Amina, are you absolutely sure you want to marry Rory?"

"Absolutely."

"Rory, are you absolutely sure you want to marry Amina?"

"As sure as I'm alive myself."

"Well, you look pretty alive to me; especially at this moment. Good luck to you both. A marriage doesn't have to be in a church, of course. How about your spiritual beliefs?"

"I believe that we are all here for a purpose, and that marriage is part of it."

"That's not quite what I asked you. Do you believe in a loving God?"

It was Mina, who spoke first. "I am a Christian, like my parents. They had to leave their homeland because of their faith. We were driven out by Muslim fanatics."

"I do not understand God," said Rory "But I believe in a Loving Presence."

"We human beings will never understand the fullness of the Living God, but we can relate to his son, Jesus Christ. That's the nearest we will ever get."

"That's good enough for me," said Rory

"And me, too," said Mina.

"And why do you want to be married in a church, rather than the Town Hall?"

"To affirm my belief in a Loving Presence. I used to attend this church when I was a kid. I was in what was then called "The Venturers", a church youth group, and we attended special services here. I was in the soccer team too."

"How about you, Mina?"

"It makes our marriage Holy. I want that. My mother wants it for me, too."

"Well, those statements are satisfactory. Who is this man you would like to conduct the ceremony?"

"The Rev. Milton Lamb, our host in Tamcaster. He was Pastor of a Caribbean Full Gospel Church."

"Well, that should make for a pretty lively occasion. If you can give me his telephone number, I'll ring him, and, if all goes well, I'll be happy to attend your wedding. He has offered to marry you both here?"

"Yes, subject to your approval."

"And what date are you considering?"

"Saturday, 10th August. If possible."

Stephen looked at his church diary. "That's clear with me," he said, and wrote on the page: 'Probable Marriage. Rory and Amina.' Is it Amina or Mina?

"Mina to friends. My mother called Amina, if I was in trouble."

"We can't have trouble on your marriage day, can we?"

"Do you want to look round the church?"

"We'd love to."

"It will bring back memories," said Rory.

Stephen led them through his house, opened a door off a small passage and they stepped into a sunlit church, alive with flowering plants in tubs and boxes. "These plants here are all wildflowers that grow in the hedgerows and on the heath here. The children in our Junior Church have identified and selected them," Stephen explained.

"What a lovely touch to have all this greenery, and that wonderful area of glass roofing lets in so much sunlight. This church has changed a lot since I was a youngster," exclaimed Rory.

"We did a lot of work here soon after I arrived," said Stephen. "We are very proud of our green credentials. The church is heated by solar panels when necessary, and we aim at being carbon zero each year. That's a struggle, but we've managed it for the last three years. I'm sure that you'll be interested in this. We had a local artist in for a few days, working with our young people, and they designed and printed these two great banners that we use on special days, and at ceremonies like weddings."

Stephen stepped over and unfurled a flag, which was fastened to a pole standing against the back wall. "All the birds stitched on this design have a claim to be called local inhabitants. Some are permanent residents and others are annual migrants. See these here, flying in from afar." He indicated a procession of wild geese and pointed to others who had already settled in for the winter. Then he moved across to another banner standing firmly in a little slot in the floor. He unfurled this one too. "And all these animals and flowers are found on the heath. Some are probably our oldest inhabitants and their ancestors have been here for hundreds of years. They deserve our respect."

Rory recognised roses and thistles, red campion, orchids, foxgloves and columbine. Mina reached forward in excitement to study the details.

"This is beautiful," she said. "And was this all done by children?"

"With much help from our artist-in-residence. We employed her for a year, but she stayed on longer. She got a local job and volunteered her time, so that the second banner could be completed, and these are used on special occasions"

Rory was ecstatic. "Might our wedding count as one?"

"Of course," said the rector. "The banners can be carried down the aisle."

"Could they be carried to the church in a procession from Coppice Cluster?" asked Rory.

"If it's a fine day, by all means," said Stephen. "Our young people would be happy to do this, I'm sure. The banners are usually just carried from the church gate, and as we have a round church, the procession encircles it before entering. It's become a regular custom."

"You have many wonderful customs, like your Sunday afternoon walks and talks. My parents went on the one last July, along the coastal path."

"Did they? I was on my holiday then, so I missed it."

"It was wonderful. They said a naturalist led it. He explained about the sea birds, the different rock formations and the history of the Jurassic coast."

"Dan Bellamy, yes. He's one of my regular leaders. I see those occasions as part of our worship - acknowledging and cherishing the natural world. We are part of creation ourselves. We do not own this planet. We share it with other creatures of God. Come and see our altar. We have placed it in the centre of our church deliberately and the congregation sit around it in a circle. This is to remind us, as we worship, that we live together with God in the midst of us. When we take communion we pass the bread and the wine round the circle, taking it from a neighbour and passing it on to others. This is how we are meant to live in community, young and old, giving and receiving, helping and trusting."

"It's a great concept. Why aren't there more churches like this?"

"Good question. It has its advantages and disadvantages, of course. No one wants to be facing the back of the priest's head all the time, so we devised the idea of a rotating pulpit. It's a bit cumbersome, and it took some getting used to, but now we just accept it. You'll have to come to one of our services to see how it works."

"We'll be here next Sunday."

"Marvellous - and by then you might have more news about your application, Mina. I'll pray about it."

As they turned to leave the church, they saw other fascinating features. One was a flowing water fountain with a stone basin - presumably used for christenings - placed to the right of the main doors. On the opposite side was a growing sapling: it's roots planted in a large container. There were green paper leaves loosely tied to bare branches, which were about to bud.

"That's our prayer tree," explained Stephen. "We bring a sapling into the church each spring, and then plant it in our grounds in the autumn. Members of the congregation are invited to write prayer requests on these green paper leaves."

"That's a lovely idea," said Mina. They read some of the names and prayers that had been tied to the branches. Stephen picked a paper leaf out off a tray, and wrote on it 'Please pray for the marriage of Mina and Rory.'

"Our door is always open," he explained. "We've new requests added most days. The church secretary looks in when she locks up each evening and lists any new requests in our prayer book: we have a mid-week prayer meeting on Wednesdays."

Mina and Rory both thanked him and left the church with lighter hearts.

*   *   *

Rory's next call was on his oldest friend, Jerry Saddler. He'd been so busy since he came home that Rory had only seen him once since his return from Italy. He'd introduced Mina, of course, and they had gone for a drink in "The Holly Bush", the clusters community pub. That was four weeks ago, and now Rory had an important reason for calling at Jerry and Pam's home in Redshanks Cluster.

"Jerry. We've fixed the date - it's Saturday 10th August, 11am at Woodleigh Community Church. I've come to ask if you'll be my Best Man?"

Jerry was delighted. " 'Course I will, mate. Delighted for you both. Does that mean that everything's sorted about Mina's permit."

"Well, no. This is a provisional date. Mina's applied for an extension to her stay here. The request is still with the Home Office."

"I see. Well...We'll keep fingers crossed then. Hey, Pam, where are you?" Jerry called.

Pam appeared, wearing her kitchen apron. "What is it?" she asked. "Oh hello, Mina, Rory. Did you enjoy the trip to Tamcaster?"

"The answer to that's on hold," replied Jerry. "They've come with great news. We're invited to their wedding on 10th August."

"Oh marvellous! Congratulations to both of you!" She kissed Mina and hugged Rory with delight. "So, you've managed to sort out the Home Office."

"Don't say tactless things like that," cried Jerry. "But that's on hold too. It's a provisional date, but it still merits a drink at the Holly Tree. Is that OK with you two? We can't celebrate it without you! "

 "Of course."

"Let's go then. Take your piny off, darling. We'll do the washing up when we get back."

The Holly Tree was usually a lively place, standing half way between the clusters, it attracted many who lived there. Several people welcomed Rory as soon as he walked in. Some of them asked about the Tamcaster visit, and others were curious about Mina, but once the word was out that Rory was engaged to marry her, the couple were overwhelmed with congratulations. They had never found so many friends in ten minutes.

It was a while before they could sit down comfortably in the snug room, but eventually they did. Maurice and Sue, two other old friends, came in with them and were invited to the wedding too.

"What sort of dress will you wear, Mina?" Pam asked.

"I'll wear my African sarong. I made it to my own design, and it's got the national colours of Gambia on it, green, blue and red."

"That's spectacular for a wedding dress. You won't be in white then."

"That's not my colour." This drew a laugh.

"And what about bridesmaids?"

"There'll just be one," Rory responded. "My sister Beatrice. She's over the moon about it. And we're going to have a parade from Coppice Cluster to the church, with two church banners at the front. Have you seen them? They're terrific - made by the local kids, with substantial help from an artist. They feature the birds, wild flowers and woodland creatures of the area around."

"It's a church wedding then, and where will the reception be?"

"We haven't sorted all that out yet. It'll either be in the church hall or the community hall, I guess."

"You'll have to get a move on. You've only got three weeks. Do you have a wedding list; for presents, I mean?"

"We haven't even thought about it. I don't think that's a good idea, because it's all a bit provisional."

"What the hell do you mean? You can't have a provisional wedding." Jerry was aghast.

"It depends on the Home Office. We can only hold the wedding on that date if they extend Mina's permit to stay. She's made an application, and we haven't heard yet."

"So you're not sure about all this! What a box to be in. Let us know if there's anything we can do to help, like a great crowd of us going down and mobbing the Home Office."

"That's the last thing that would help. No, we want this wedding to be arranged quietly. If the authorities know about it, they may well not extend the permit."

"Quietly! You shouldn't have come in here then. The whole of Woodleigh will be buzzing with the news once this crowd leaves the pub."

"Don't let them spread the word." Mina was alarmed.

Rory stood up. "I'll go back into the lounge bar and explain. I'll ask the boys to keep quiet about our plans," he said.

Pam took Mina's hand. "Don't worry," she said. "I'll explain quietly to the girls. It's a secret date, but they'll all have it in their diaries, and I feel sure everything is going to be all right in the end."

Worried eyes had replaced Mina's joyous smile.

"We'll be tactful," said Jerry. "I can be, you know. It's not my nature, but I am when it's as important as this. I've had an idea about the present. If everything goes as you want it to, Mina, where do you plan to live?

"Here, in Woodleigh," she said. "That's what we want to do. Rory is applying to the university. He hopes to get a teaching qualification, and we would both like to work in local schools. I may have to do another training course here too. We've got to explore all these things."

"Good. That's what I wanted to hear. My idea's a secret, but you can tell Rory I have a plan, and I will be very discreet about it. Let him know that too."

* * *

Beatrice telephoned Brook that morning. "Hi, Brook," she said. "Good to hear your voice again. How have things been while we were away. Did you get my letter?"

"Yes, thanks," he replied. "It's been fairly quiet here. Several people have gone to Cornwall or Dorset for a summer break. I've been learning to windsurf with a guy who's an expert. It's fab when you feel the wind at your back and in your hair. Honestly, Bea. You must try it!"

"Sometime, I will. But I need to talk to you. I've got ideas for our Cornfield Co-op. There are several things I've learned in Tamcaster. How about ten tomorrow at the old beech tree?"

"Done," said Brook. "See you then."

Beatrice left home on her bike, with Max romping along by her wheels. He had not forgiven her yet for leaving him with Gramps for two weeks, and had found a good way of letting her know this. Yesterday, he rushed up to greet her: leaped to lick her face, but then turned round and ran away with his tail beneath his legs, only to repeat the exercise three times. This reduced the family to gales of laughter, but he got his message across.

Brook was waiting on the seat under the beech tree. As he stood up, Max romped across to greet him but, then when Brook suddenly reached out to kiss Beatrice, Max went wild with jealousy, leapt up and stood by, barking and bouncing until they stopped. Beatrice moved to sit next to Brook on the seat, and Max jumped up on to her lap, leaving his rump and wagging tail to face the intruder.

"I know how Max is feeling," said Brook. "He wanted to go to Tamcaster too. How did the trip go?"

"It was hilltop. We had a thrill time, and met so many people, and I learned a lot of new things. Did you know that King Alfred of Wessex had a daughter called Elfleda? There's a statue of her at the castle. Look, that's her photo, and I'm making her the subject of my school project. But more to the point, there's a youth team in Tamcaster that gets a grant from the council and it sends a regular report about youth issues and I've lots of ideas for Cornfield."

"Such as..."

261

"Well, the city council employ a young woman, called Cathy, to liaise with the youth groups. There are lots of them, and they do different things, but there's one group where they make sure that a church in the area is carbon zero. We stayed with a black family, and their two daughters are in this group, and they organise lots of things, like extra recycling, and planting trees and planning rambles around the area. They help everyone to appreciate the local wild flowers and bird life. They're coming here in three weeks time, the girls I mean, Bonnie and Trish, and they're thrill people. You'll love them. They can explain better than me. What I thought was that we could call a youth meeting, contact people from school and some of the other cluster groups whilst they're over here and kick start our next project. What do you think?"

"It'll be good meeting them and, yes we could get several of our friends together. I'm not sure what you mean about our next project, though."

"We want to expand the Cornfield Cooperative, don't we? This is a great chance to get more people involved and enthusiastic. When you meet them you'll understand better. There was one youth group over there that helped when the area was devastated by a big fire. We met the people from the Mercian Council at their offices and they told us about this. They'd all been trained in first aid: this youth group, I mean. They lived in a village called Clayford. They helped people who had to leave their homes because of the fire-storm, when it started in another village nearby, and they got special medals from the council because of what they did."

Beatrice's eyes were illuminated with excitement. Brook loved it when she was so enthusiastic. He wished he could be like Beatrice, but there was something inside which made him hesitate. At times he feared for the future, but her company helped lift the shadows.

Beatrice was disappointed by Brook's quiet responses. He was most alive when he was exploring the natural world. He sparkled best when he was on the trail of a rare bird: identifying the song and following the sound, then finding it sitting on the branch of a tree. She'd been with him when this had happened, and it was an electric experience.

"I think there's a great opportunity waiting. You remember that the mayor showed interest after our presentation, and said that the council wanted to have young people more involved. Well, now I've been to Tamcaster, I've got a clearer idea of what we could suggest. We could ask the council to invite each cluster group to include two young people of school age, one girl and one boy. Then we could convene a meeting of all those nominated and agree a programme that we'd try to follow in cluster groups. The aim would be to reduce carbon emissions. We might even have a competition and a reward for the most successful cluster."

"Yes, perhaps we could do something, but the cluster groups are already doing all they can towards carbon reduction, aren't they? And some young people do go to the meetings already. I've been to ours several times."

"I know, but the young people could agree on a co-ordinated plan to do some new things. We could meet separately to pool our own ideas and set targets. I think we'd have council support, especially if was this was listed by Peter Samphire, as one of the achievements of the visit. He asked us all to tell him about any positive outcomes they'd experienced. He's got to send a report to them as soon as possible. What we could do is have a preliminary meeting to explain all this to young people we know, so that the ground's prepared. Can we plan this, together?" Beatrice asked him anxiously.

Brook was absorbed by her enthusiasm, and began to realise possibilities. It might not work out just as she was suggesting, but he wasn't going to miss out on this opportunity to work with her.

"Of course we can. It's a great idea. We can get the cluster crowd from our class together easily before the Tamcaster people come here, and when they do, we can go birdwatching on the heath with these new friends of yours. Perhaps we can go swimming together and I can introduce them all to windsurfing."

Although this was not what she had in mind, Beatrice was elated. They kissed again, taking longer about it this time. Max watched with anxious eyes.

CHAPTER 20 - Rory and Mina

"What are we going to do about a wedding present for them?" Pam asked.

"I have that all in hand," said Jerry. "We'll provide them with a home to live in."

"You'll what? It'll cost a fortune."

"No it won't. I'll involve the co-operative and round up all Rory's old mates. He was the most popular boy in the school, you know."

"But we're not sure that they're going to be married. Mina has to get her permit extended."

"That's no problem. The house can be ready whenever they are. We'll supply one of our Type B homes from our new-build scheme."

Jerry had it all in hand. He was a key member of the Woodleigh Builders' Cooperative, able to spread the word the very next morning, when he went to their building site. Type A houses were more expensive Eco Homes and available for families to buy or rent. Type B were simple starter homes, with a living room in the centre, with a kitchenette at one side and a bedroom, with shower and toilet, at the other.

"I've got a great idea, lads," he explained to the circle as they gathered to eat their packed lunches in the lounge of their current new-build. "I'm sure that you've all heard that Rory's back, and he's brought a beautiful African fiancée with him. Well they aim to get married next month, so we must give them a welcome-home wedding present, mustn't we? Well, I have an idea. They're bound to want somewhere to live, so I suggest that we give them the deposit on one of our new-build starter homes."

"Great idea," said Sam, the bricklayer, with a touch of sarcasm. "But these places don't come cheap. How the hell do you expect us to find two thousand pounds?"

"We'll spread the word. As I said, Rory was a very popular lad at school. I'll email all the classmates and I'll ask the community shop to put a collecting box on the counter and, unless his parents have got some other ideas, they can chip in and so can all the neighbours. We can organise some sponsored activities too. It'll take time, of course, but there's no great rush. I guess they'll be staying with Mark and Elsa initially.

They'll have the choice of which type B, they would like whenever they and it are available, maybe this year, maybe next. Once they've taken possession, they can start monthly payments on our Rent to Buy scheme. What do you think? We don't need to do all the interior decoration. They can do those things themselves. Mina's an artist you know, so your skills won't be necessary this time, Mike." He nodded to Mike, the painter.

"If I'm not doing the work, I'll donate a hundred," Mike said. "Rory's done me a favour or two in the past."

"Good man, you've set the ball rolling," said Jerry "Pam and I are putting in two hundred, so that's three hundred found. I'll have a word with Mark tonight, on the quiet, and see how he and Elsa feel. There's just one more thing though, that I must tell you. We won't spread the word about this until the day of the wedding. I know that sounds odd, but it's important. Keep this to yourselves. Mina's permit to stay here runs out 3rd August. She's applied to extend it. If the application's not allowed the wedding will be postponed and rumours won't help at all. "

"How can we both spread the word and keep it quiet?" asked Sam.

"We'll mention it confidentially to a few personal friends we can trust, and if they promise to donate, we'll write it down. No money will be exchanged until after the wedding. If it's postponed, I'll only go ahead with this plan when, and if, they come back from Italy as a married couple. They want to live here together, but that might be either soon or in a year or two."

"What if the relationship breaks down?"

"It won't, I've never seen a couple so determined, but if it did the money would be returned to the sender. I'll keep track of it all."

The next time Jerry and Pam went to the community shop to collect their groceries, Jerry glanced at the voluntary counter. All the usual notices were there about local activities and a charity box was fastened to the wall for this week's good cause. *Could I post the wedding date up there, once it's really confirmed?* Jerry thought. *Everybody's welcome, and as Best Man I can announce what the present is and pass leaflets around, so anyone there on the day can let me have their contact details, if they want to join in. Then we can put the leaflet up here to replace the wedding poster.*

Behind the shop were the community workshops, where anything could be repaired for re-use, and the clothing shed where tailors beavered to make new garments and repair old ones. Together with the community hall upstairs, this building was in constant use, and Jerry quietly formed his plans for launching his wedding fund-raising spree amongst all these groups.

* * *

On Thursday, when there was still no word. Rory and Mina had been going to the drone zone every day to see if there was any reply from the Home Office and now they were beginning to feel desperate. They tried telephoning, but the line was always engaged. Asa last resort, Rory phoned a friend of his in London, and explained the situation.

"I wonder if you'd be kind enough to do me a special favour and go there to explain that there's a most important family gathering in two weeks' time. Could they possibly speed things up?"

Norman sounded doubtful about success, but he promised to go the next day and then ring back.

On Friday, they sat waiting for the sound of the telephone. There was none, so Rory dialled the number again.

"Sorry, mate. I was going to call you, but I was waiting in case they telephoned me back. The place is under siege. There's people camped outside on the pavement, trying to press their claim. I could hardly get through the door. When I eventually did, I spent all afternoon in the queue. There were people in tears all around, some getting angry and the police standing by in case of trouble. I gave the man your message and he wrote it down and said he'd pass it on to the appropriate officer, but gave no hope of this pressure speeding things up. He said, 'You can see what it's like for yourself.' I gave him my telephone number, and asked him to call me if there was any joy, but he said he didn't think they'd do anything. If they were considering dealing with the request, they would probably want to see Mina there herself. I asked him to phone me tonight if they wanted to see her. I've not heard a thing."

"Thanks for trying, mate."

Rory and Mina looked at one another in despair.

They reached for each other tearfully.

"Never mind love, I'll go back with you to Florence. I've got a passport and I'm a free man. We'll get married in Italy."

"But that's not what we wanted - and I love being here. I want to teach, here."

"You will, darling, but not for a while; after we're married you'll have every right to come back again."

"When will that be?"

"I don't know, darling. We must be patient. If we get married in Florence, your Mum will be at the wedding, and all our friends from there - yours and mine."

"Yes - thanks, darling. But it's not what you wanted. What will you do in Italy?"

"I don't know. I might go back to the Peace Corps as a volunteer."

"But you won't get paid as a volunteer."

"No, I'll need to get a part-time job as well."

"You don't speak Italian."

"I can get by. I know the basic words. You can teach me more."

"Oh, Rory, why must everything be so hard? I love that church, and the rector is a lovely man."

"I'll ring him tonight and explain."

When Rory telephoned, Stephen Spooner was obviously disappointed.

"I'm so sorry, but not very surprised, actually. I know how difficult these things are."

"Can I speak to him?" Mina was at Rory's shoulder.

"Mina would like a word." He handed the phone to her.

"I'm so disappointed. I love your church, and you were so kind. Thank you for giving us so much of your time. We'll come to your service on Sunday morning."

"Good, I look forward to seeing you both. Wait a moment...I have an idea. I'm very disappointed myself about the wedding. I was looking forward to it. Would you like me to give you both a blessing?"

"I'd love that. I'll give the phone to Rory."

"I was just asking Mina if you would like me to give you both a blessing for your engagement and forthcoming marriage, in Italy."

"That sounds fabulous. Do you mean at the service on Sunday morning?"

"That would be fine. I can invite you to come up together at the end of the service. It's just a short prayer, to send you on your way safely through life."

"Marvellous," said Rory, "But could it be more than that? How about a special blessing on Saturday week? We could invite our friends and relatives, and have the engagement party that we're already planning, afterwards in the community hall."

"I don't see why not," said the rector, "I've never done that before. Perhaps it's time I did. Come to think of it, there's an outline for just such a ceremony in a little booklet I have called "Staging Posts". I found it in my father's library when he died. I think it's by someone called Revd. Roger Grainger. It's a very old book, published in the 1980's I think. "

He found the book and planned the blessing.

* * *

At 2 pm. on the appropriate day, a group of young people came up to Coppice Close carrying two colourful banners. They stopped outside the home of Mark and Elsa, knocked on the door, and invited the whole family, including Beatrice, Gramps and Max to join Rory and Mina on the walk to the church. They were all ready and dressed for the occasion. Mina was wearing her best sari, in Gambian national colours, when Rory's sounded his great "cock-a-doodle do." Doors opened, as neighbours emerged. The whole parade walked to Sylvan Cluster, where Peter and Frances Samphire, Adam and other friends, including Adam's grandmother, Grace Forrester, strengthened the numbers.

At Redshanks Coppice the procession collected Jerry and Pam Saddler, Brook and his mother, Carrie and her father with two small children, together with other interested friends.

The final call came when they reached Skylarks Coppice. Amongst those joining the parade there were Counsellor Jill Heathershaw, Sam the joiner and his wife, together with Mike, the painter, and three other old school-friends of Rory's.

The procession continued away from the woodland area and along the high road towards the town centre. Matthew Farnfield and his wife joined the walk at this stage. The church stood on the green beside the Town Hall, where the mayor and his wife joined the walkers.

Rev. Stephen Spooner was waiting for them at the church door, with his wife and children, the church secretary and Mina's aunt. The rector led the procession to encircle the building and then gestured for everyone to go inside.

Seats had been reserved on the front row for Rory, Mina, and family members, and everyone else filed into the circular building. The young people who had carried the banners, sat down on the back row.

Stephen waited until they were settled and then moved to the centre to welcome them all, and introduced the first hymn, "All our Hope in God is founded."

Then Stephen offered this prayer: "Lord of all newness and life. Holy spirit of God, we ask you to revive whatever is stale and dead in us, and to strengthen all that is lively and good with your great purpose of love. As we share in one another's joy, may we always be learning new skills of loving, new ways of giving and receiving the life, which flows from you, O loving God, Amen."

After the congregation had said the Lord's Prayer, with the words displayed on screens, Stephen addressed them all. "Friends and neighbours, we're gathered here today for a rather unusual celebration - not that of marriage, but of engagement. I am very happy to welcome

Rory and Mina to our church to celebrate the joining together of hands for two young people who are clearly very much in love. Rory became a young member of our congregation in his school days, and was part of our youth fellowship, before I came to Woodleigh. He has happy memories of that time and is very pleased to rediscover us here, after his spell abroad working with the Britannic Peace Corps. It was while doing this that he met Mina in Italy, and we are very happy to welcome her today. Mina was born in Gambia, had to leave the area as a child and came, with her mother, to Europe as a refugee. She went to school in Italy, and met Rory when he came to give a talk about the Peace Corps."

Stephen then invited Pamela Saddler, who was a regular attender at this church, read from the Song of Songs, Chapter 2, Verses 10 to 14.

After this Mina stepped forward and gently began to sing, "Let there be love shared amongst us," which she had first heard in Tamcaster. Rory stepped up to join her, partway through. The words appeared on the screens and the congregation joined in.

Stephen spoke again, "Please greet those around you with the words 'Peace be with you.'"

After this, Rory opened a book saying, "This is one of my favourite readings. It comes from The Prophet by Kahlil Gibran: ' Love one another, but make not a bond of love: let it be a moving sea between the shore of your souls. Fill one another's cup, but drink not from one cup. Give one another your bread, but eat not of the same loaf. Sing and dance together and be joyous, but let each one of you be alone, even as the strings of the lute are alone, though they quiver to the same music. Give your hearts, but not into each other's keeping. For only the hand of Life can contain your hearts. And stand together, but not too near together; for the pillars of the temple stand apart, and the oak tree and the cypress, stand not in each other's shadow.'"

Stephen invited Rory and Mina to come forward and hold hands. "We had hoped to celebrate a wedding here in two weeks time, but this is not possible because of the bureaucracy involved. Instead we are meeting in this church to bless this young couple and wish them well in their journey of life together. They need our help in this, and they need God's grace. Mina and Rory, please turn to face each other.

Rory, please say after me, 'Mina, I love you and intend to marry you.'"

"I love you, Mina and intend to marry you."

"**Mina**, please say 'and I love you Rory, and intend to marry you.'"

"And I love you Rory, and intend to marry you."

"**Congregation**, please say the words on the screens."

"Yours Lord, is the greatness, the power and the glory. All things come of you,

Bless this couple, Lord. This is our prayer. In God's presence and before this whole congregation, Rory and Mina wish to be married. We look forward with them to the day that this will happen, wherever and whenever it takes place. May you have a long and happy life together."

The couple kissed and the congregation clapped and Jerry called out "Three cheers for them both and for the rector." The congregation responded with enthusiasm, and the service was ended with a final hymn and blessing.

Afterwards, photographs were taken on the steps of the church, before they all went a merry walk to the Clusters Community Hall for the engagement feast and party. The buffet allowed everyone to circulate. They were chatting in small groups, when Jerry rang the bell on the bar to make his announcement.

"Friends of the happy couple," he called, above the noise. "May I call you all to order? Since my old school friend, Rory, asked me to be his best man before he made sure of the date, I have decided to take it on myself to do two things. The first is to propose a toast. I call on you all to raise you glasses to Rory and Mina. May they organise their wedding better the next time round. May they have health and happiness, wherever they live, may they live long lives and grow grey hairs together. To Rory and Mina."

Everyone drank to this, and Rory was about to thank them all for coming, when Jerry silenced him again. "Hold on, Rory, I haven't finished yet. I said I was going to do two things. The toast was the first, now for the second. On occasions such as this, it's usual for the guests to bring presents to the party. Well, you've organised all this so fast that we haven't had time to buy you anything, so instead of all bringing small parcels of things we're not sure you'll want and you might not know what to do with, we've agreed to pool our resources and give you something you'll really need, sooner or later - a home. We know that you're moving away from here, so we considered giving you a caravan, but you tell us that you're coming back, so we had a better idea. We're providing you with a deposit for a home in Woodleigh. As you know, I'm a member of a building co-operative, so I've put your name down for one of our starter houses. Once you take possession, you'll be able to join our rent to buy scheme. We're building and selling them all the time, so one will be there for you whenever you need it. If you need a bigger one to house your growing family, this will give you a kick-start. "

"Thank you so much. It is most kind of you all and sounds wonderful, but we can't be certain we're coming back. We want to, but it depends on so many things," Rory explained.

"The deposit will be transferable. Our co-op is in a national federation so, if the worst happens, you could swap the deposit for one of the other sustainable new-build houses elsewhere in Britannia, or you could even sell the deposit, if necessary."

Rory and Mina were astounded and delighted.

After the party ended, they were invited to look at some of the local, new sustainable homes. Mark, Elsa, Beatrice and Mina's aunt went with them.

"This is one of our starter homes: compact and simple, suitable for a young couple," Jerry explained, as he pointed to a neat bungalow sitting in a ring of similar ones, several of which were already occupied. They faced a common plot, some of which contained allotments.

"There's a down payment of two thousand pounds (in your case, this will be taken care of), followed by an affordable monthly rent based on income and the option of ownership after several years. If you wish to transfer to our larger Type A accommodation at a future date and sign the contract and pay the extra, that's fine.

Mina and Rory followed Jerry into the bungalow, which had solar panels on the roof, and on the ground all around it. The main living room appeared quite spacious, to one side there was a kitchen, fitted with an electric cooker, washing machine, and sink. A side door led to the garden. On the opposite side of the living room was a small bedroom, with a walk-in-shower, and toilet.

"It's basic, and has all the essentials. It just needs furnishing," said Mina.
"Thanks a million, it's most generous of you and your co-op." said Rory.

But Jerry had not finished. He led them on beyond a copse of trees to show them another development.

A row of new Type A houses had been built against a small hillock. Most of the homes were still at the foundation stage, but two were completely built, and it was to one of those that Jerry led them. He opened the unpainted front door, and invited them to follow him in crying, "Welcome to No.1, Knowle Cluster. This house is already spoken for, but the original design is the same for all of them. Modifications can be made if the owner wishes it. People who begin in the Type B homes can progress to one of these."

The houses were built into the side of the hill, so that the warmth of the earth protected it. A path from the front door encircled the hillock. There was a spacious living room, with a large window overlooking a common plot, a well-fitted kitchen, and water-harvested toilets upstairs and downstairs, a bathroom and two bedrooms. The roof area that projected from the hillock was covered in solar panels. The home had a warm and friendly atmosphere and they loved it at first sight.

"Three years in Type B can lead seamlessly on to one of these. Again you have a choice of monthly rental or purchase. When fully purchased they are yours for re-sale as needed, but naturally, you pay the council rates and have the usual house expenses. What do you think of this one?"

"I think it's beautiful," said Mina, "I'd love to start painting it now but, unfortunately we won't be able to live here for ages."

"That's no problem," said Jerry. "You can't have this one, because it's sold, but it's a standard design. Whenever you are free to come, we'll have one waiting for you. We're building them all the time, both Type A and B. If you aren't able to come to Woodleigh, you can have the money we've collected to go towards a deposit elsewhere or, if there a similar scheme operating, transfer to another co-op built house somewhere in Britannia."

"But where's the money coming from? Who must we thank?"

"Thank Mark and Elsa. They were the first donors. Thank the neighbours. They're all involved, and the building co-op, and many of those who attended your blessing today, and more beside. I'm advertising this gift to the whole of Woodleigh, or rather I will be once you fix the date of the wedding."

"We must thank you, most of all, Jerry and the whole co-operative," cried Rory.

Mina turned to thank Elsa, Mark and Beatrice. Elsa embraced her. "This wasn't my idea, honey, but I think it's the perfect gift. I wonna get to know my beautiful daughter-in-law better, an' I don't want to lose my son. So, a house o' yours, here in Woodleigh, is a great idea. I hope you'll can come back to claim it, as soon as you possibly can."
"We will, I promise you. So now I have two mothers, a black one and a

white one, and I'm not going to neglect either, I promise. When I'm away, there'll be drone letters flying here, like I send to my African mom. I'll be on-line, so we all see each other on the net, and I'll off-set by planting fruit trees."

The parting took place on the following Monday at Exeter Airport, when the same group gathered.

"I don't know when the wedding will be," Rory told them. "But I want you all there. It'll probably be Florence, and that's a place to inspire us all. Tuscany's my second home now. We've many friends there, and Mina's mom, she's special. So are you, Beatrice. You'll be our bridesmaid."

"I can't wait," said Beatrice, turning to kiss Mina.

The call came for passengers to board the airbus and the last glimpse they had of Rory and Mina, was two hands waving as they entered the door of the plane.

"See you in Florence!" Elsa called to them.

They waited there until the plane had taken off, and saw it rise gently into the clouds above.

A sombre trio walked back to the pool car-park, and a line from a half remembered poem floated strangely through Beatrice's mind: "And there has gone away a glory from the earth." She could not remember where the quote came from, but she knew the lines spoke for her mood.

The following week they were back at the airport to welcome their friends from Tamcaster.

After the two successful visits had been completed, Peter made his report to the council. It contained several recommendations. One was that a youth exchange be organised in future years alongside the annual visit; another was that each cluster group should aim have two nominated young people in their party, one of each gender, and that these representatives could form a youth council, to advise and assist Woodleigh Town Council on matters relating to young people. After due consideration, these proposals were adopted.

The school commended both Beatrice and Adam for their novel home study projects. Beatrice continued to develop her account of Elfleda and later had a small book published locally called "Elfleda, King Alfred's Forgotten Daughter." Copies of it were sent to the Local Studies Department of Exeter Public Library, the Wessex and Mercian Record Offices, and Tamcaster and Woodleigh Libraries.

Rory and Mina were married quietly in Florence on Christmas Eve, 2060. Mark, Elsa and Beatrice, were all present and so, of course, was Mina's mother, and her aunt, who had travelled from Exeter with the Whiteoak family.

The following year Rory and Mina returned to Woodleigh and were able to take up residence in a small starter home, while they trained as teachers in Britannia.

When they knew that a child was coming, Mina's mother, Ahinee, was invited over to stay with the Whiteoak family for three weeks. Fortunately, the Responsible Party was now running the government again in Britannia and had relaxed some of the harsh rules about immigration. Relatives of those living in the UK were now able to visit for short stays.

Mina's mother was a remarkable African lady, who looked as if she carried the world on her shoulders, but had a calm, resigned expression in her brown eyes, which were deep-set in dark, puckered skin. Small and wizened, she wore a grey shawl over her long black gown, and walked with the help of a carved brown stick. She had a welcoming smile for all the family, and was at ease once she had done the round of introductions.

Mina had arranged to have a home birth, with the cluster midwife in attendance. As space in their new home was limited, it was agreed that only Rory and Ahinee would be at the birth. Elsa, Mark and Beatrice, being disappointed, were determined to be around, so when they got the message that the midwife had been summoned they hurried to wait in the twilight, outside the cottage.

A few minutes later they heard Mina's voice singing one of her rhythmic folk songs with loud abandon.

"Does that mean she's born?" asked Beatrice.

"No. It means she's pushing," said Elsa.

Standing by the bed and holding her hand while Mina sang was a mind-blowing experience for Rory. He jumped instinctively when she suddenly stopped and he heard a sudden shriek.

"She's coming. Keep pressing hard," called the midwife, and several seconds later a tiny, slippery, brown body was struggling in her hands. Holding the infant firmly, she carried her over to Mina, who reached out joyfully to grasp the little one.

Cradling her between her breasts, Mina, gazed lovingly at the tiny face and wondering, unfocused eyes.

"So you are Isabella. Welcome to the world!" she whispered, as she rocked to and fro.

"Hold her gently, Rory."

A sudden sense of shock went through him. Mina was handing him the baby. Never in his life had he done anything so responsible as to have his own new-born child in his hands. For a second tears blinded him.

"Isn't she marvellous!" he gasped. "However did we do this darling?" He found himself enraptured by the sight of tiny fingers and toes and the whisper of nails to come. *I'll never forget this moment,* he thought.

"You're the colour of lovely milk chocolate," he said to her, "and you've got little wisps of early, dark hair on the crown of your head."

He tried to hand the baby back to Mina, but she pointed to her mother, and Rory turned to see that she was peering over his shoulder, so he offered her the child. Ahinee received it, ever so gently, and then she took the child to the window, and lifted it up towards the white moon, whispering some African words and very gently kissing the infant's forehead.

"It is our ancient custom," Ahinee explained.

But the baby had been seen through the window, and the door opened wide enough for Elsa and Beatrice to slip in. Mark followed and hovered uncertainly in the doorway and, while the women were all cooing over the baby, he moved to embrace Rory.

"Congratulations son," he said. "A new generation has begun."

PART THREE - Voices from Yesterday

"And we are put on earth a little space

that we may learn to bear the beams of love"

William Blake

CHAPTER 21 - The Homecoming

2092

Rory:

My homecoming was rich - a time of great rejoicing. A flock of seagulls were circling above us, as we left Exeter Airport to step into the Wessex sunlight. They shrieked their welcome. This salute told us that the sea was waiting a few short miles down the road.

There is a special quality about the sunlight in Wessex. It glistened on my shirt cuffs, as I shook hands with Ivan, who was waiting for us with his retro pony trap. The light danced on the ring of red beads that Mina wore in her dark hair. It glanced on the metal rails that kept us safe in our seats; as Ivan jogged us home again along the winding Devon lane. It sparkled on the raindrops on the road and on the leaves of the hedgerows, once we had left the town behind us.

It was typical of Ivan, such a lover of the old ways, to shun the hire of a pool car in favour of his beloved horse-drawn vehicle, which had started a trend in this semi-rural area. His young children loved it and made a pet of the pony, and the jogging motion suited the country lane better than the fast motor road, which now joined the two towns. Several people in the clusters now had horse drawn vehicles, he told us. They shared stables and a grazing field, from which the fresh manure provided ready fertilizer for the vegetable plots. He said that he was reading a book about the Amish community in the United States, and was interested in some of their traditional ways of living.

Each building on the long lane to Woodleigh seemed to welcome us – the Carter's Arms, where people sat at tables outside on this warm summer evening and the gateposts on the house at the turning into Summer Lane, which brought us towards the roundhouse. After thirty years of working in the heartlands of Britannia, I was back in the place where my life had begun; home for my final working years. I was glad to escape from the ferocious weather we had endured in Mercia and prayed that the climate would be more merciful here. The portent seemed hopeful.

As soon as we drew up at Swallow's Nest, Beatrice and the grandchildren came out to meet us; great hugs for everyone. Mina was always a favourite with youngsters. The meal was all bustle and chatter, but once the three little ones had gone to bed, we had time to relax and sink quietly into cushioned chairs. I was back where I knew I really belonged, and we had peace in our hearts.

I was struck by the way Beatrice had aged. She was still nimble and eager, but I could see her mother's features in her face now. I had never noticed them before, but the strong jaw and the light wrinkles in her face when she smiled had a glimpse of Elsa in them. Her fair hair was silver now, but Beatrice kept it neat and wavy. The years had treated her well.

'Are your swallows back again this year?' Mina always asked this question when she came here in the summer. She'd been fascinated by their nest ever since Brook had told her that they flew back to it every year from West Africa. It provided her with the only direct link left with her ancestral homeland.

Brook smiled. 'They came in April as usual. No doubt you'll see them in the morning,' he re-assured her.

'You've no idea how long I've looked forward to this,' I told Beatrice. 'During all those years in Tamcaster and Mercia, we've spoken of retiring here but, I'd never imagined coming to take up a new teaching post in the school where I'd been a pupil. We enjoyed living in the heartlands, but it's taken its toll.'

Beatrice looked at me quizzically. 'Well, we're all delighted to have you back again - especially Mom. She wanted to come this evening, but she rang to say she thinks she might be going down with a cold and doesn't want to spread any germs. Peter is waiting for your help too. He says you should join the Woodleigh Town Council and give them a shake up.'

'Oh no, I've done with politics. I'll just stick to my schoolwork. Peter needn't worry. Wessex is a dream compared to Mercia. You have a tame provincial council and they've expanded the cluster housing across the whole area. All the other provinces send delegations here to see the model systems at work and to learn from them.'

'All the more reason for us to be up to the mark; we have to be ready for change whenever the time requires it, and sometimes we don't move quickly enough. You'll discover that very soon, Rory. The Provincial Council is not what it once was. Some of the old hands have dropped out and others have grown set in their ways. They need younger blood, like you two, to stir them up again.'

I groaned. 'Young Blood! I'm touching sixty, and I've not come here to take the Wessex Council by storm, and neither has Mina. We've got teaching jobs here and intend to concentrate on those. We're not going into provincial politics again, Beatrice!'

My sister gave me an enigmatic smile, and I felt rather irritated by it. So, I tried another tack. 'I'm not going to be lazy,' I told her. 'I've a book to write.'

'A book? That's not like you. What's it about?'

'Tomorrow and yesterday: it's a book about Tamcaster and Mercia and the changes that have been made during the last thirty years: what the people did and how they did it.'

'Led by Rory,' Mina said. 'I've suggested that he calls it *Yestermorrow*, because the way people need to live tomorrow is becoming more like the way they used to live yesterday. I was reminded of that the moment I saw Ivan with the horse and trap at the railway station. We need to learn from the past. In my own case I learned so much from the Gambian village life, from the Refugee camp and the Steiner School.'

'*Yestermorrow*: that's an odd title, but I like it.' Beatrice observed. 'I learnt so much about resilience from Elfleda. There's another take on that title too. A positive one, and that's really needed in a world that that's become so pessimistic. It could be read as a sign of optimism instead of dystopia . *Yes Tomorrow!* It's got a hopeful ring to it.'

'Perhaps. I hadn't thought of that, but you're right about dystopia.' I said. 'Gloom and doom about the future will get us nowhere. Who was it said that every new advancement begins with a dream. These ideas absorb me. We travelled a long way in Tamcaster, but I have to record it all, and I mean to start doing this tomorrow.'

After we retired to bed, Mina raised the subject again.

'Where are you going to start this book of yours? Will it begin with the time when we first set up home there in 2062, or will you begin when we first met in Florence?'

'I've considered that. It's not really a book about us. It's a book about Mercia and Wessex, so I can't start writing about my Peace Corps experience, although it was a very formative time for me. I won't dwell on our early days together, either. The key thing was that, having been on the visit to Mercia with the cluster party, I realised that I wanted to make my home there and fortunately, you felt the same: it would have been awful if you'd wanted to be somewhere else. No, I think I'll begin with that choice we made together, when we were both qualified teachers starting out on our professional careers.'

"Isabella was two years old then. So much has happened to us all and to the whole world since then. It's been both wonderful and horrendous."

She put out the light, and we lay there beside each other, with Mina's left foot lying over my right one, pondering the years.

'We are not the same two people, are we? We've changed each other, over the years.' I took her warm hand and gave it a squeeze.

I remembered the wild young woman I had married. I was besotted with her. Mina had been so volatile, so exciting, so full of promise, but I'd had my fears. How would she feel in quiet Woodleigh? She'd settled down amazingly well, actually, considering the turmoil of her life.

'It was the welcome I got from you all. I loved your mother immediately. She had a voice which reminded me of my best friend in the Steiner school. Lana was American too, and Beatrice was wonderful. I'll never forget that bangle exchange. Mark was so kind too. I'd always missed my father, and somehow I discovered another one here. They couldn't have been more different, except for the love that flowed from them.'

I reached out and took her hand. It was a long time before either of us got to sleep. I lay there pondering this book I wanted to write.

Yes, I had come from a very loving family, and I was delighted how easily they accepted Mina. I'd not been an easy lad to bring up. I'd always been full of pranks as a kid. I think I may have inherited much of that from Mom, but I must have been a bit of a handful for them. I was delighted by the opportunities I'd had in the Peace Corps, but I fell head over heels in love with Mina, and I didn't know how easily she would be accepted here. Then, after everything seemed to be fine, I was devastated to have to go back to Italy, but it all worked out for the best. Mina was able to have that final year with her Mom, and once we were married and wonderful little Isabella was born, I really felt we had come into our own. Tamcaster was a challenge too, but we coped well between us. I could never have pulled things off without Mina's help though. She was a wonder.

AMINA:

It was all such a gamble. I didn't know anything about Britannia. It sounded like a magical sort of place, and I wanted to come here because of Rory, but I was frightened really, although I put on a bold face. In Gambia, I'd been the daughter of a village chief. But after the terror, I was nothing. I was trembling all the time we were with those traffickers, crossing Africa and later in the boat. We had no idea where we would end up. The Refugee Camp seemed to come from heaven, and gradually I recovered there, despite the cramped conditions. My mother was valued as an interpreter and helper. I got a good education too, and met people of many races, but I was just one of hundreds of girls, living in limbo. I loved the Steiner School too: the teachers and all the children.. It was there that I developed my art and music properly, although I started this in the camp, and entertained at parties, but my future was a complete blank, until Rory burst in on the scene. I trusted him, but I didn't know what to expect. I'd heard such awful stories about girls being smuggled away. I'd heard from other girls about times when refugees were afraid to speak in their own language for fear of being victimised. I soon knew I was safe with Rory, and so I stuck with him, and dreamed of Britannia.

I was frightened at first. Would I be really wanted there? I simply didn't know, but I was made to feel so welcome after I'd arrived. Elsa reminded me of a young American teacher at the Steiner school. There were many problems in Britannia, but not with Rory's family. They were all wonderful, but perhaps it was as well that we could not rush straight into marriage. I think I needed that year back with my mother in Italy. Once we were really married I felt safe though, and I loved coming back here, to Woodleigh. I enjoyed being at Exeter University too. It was liberating, and there were students from many other countries. I loved that too.

Settling down in Tamcaster was very challenging, but I had Isabella, and it wasn't long before Rupert came along to join us. Being a young mother changed me. It gave me the confidence I needed to begin to teach English children. Then there was Brandon. He was always challenging, but I learned to handle him, and that helped me grow and become more mature. Trish became a true friend at school, and Beatrice was always there for me, whenever we met. Rory taught me patience. I always knew I was safe with him, and I taught him about women's feelings. He used to be very dull about those things. Rory and I had to fight so hard together, and as we sorted things out, we became a strong team. Yes, Rory needs to write all this down. I can understand that. We had to process the suffering, and there was a lot of suffering, but we coped with it together; personal, national and international. It wasn't just our suffering. The whole world has been suffering. Somehow, we must revive hope for the future, for the sake of the children! It's desperately important, because thoughts shape developing events, all the time. I fell asleep pondering these things. We had to make sense of it all, and we must believe in tomorrow!

I fell asleep still holding Rory's hand and resting my foot on his leg.

The next morning I woke to see that Rory was sitting up in bed beside me. He was holding a book of blank pages on his lap, and I saw that he had started to write.

CHAPTER 22 - Return to Mercia

2062

Rory:

There was something compelling about Tamcaster that drew me back again. It's difficult to define that rather special quality about the place. The city itself had little to catch the eye in those days, unless it was that castle perched on the white rock, visible from the train station and so many parts of the town. It wasn't so much the place as the people. They were so vibrant. Mina felt it too, so we both decided to apply for teaching jobs there. We had graduated from Exeter University, and got our teaching diplomas. Woodleigh was my home area and, in a sense, Mina had made it hers. She told me that her white mother was always close to her heart, so we lived in the little house prepared for us by Jerry and his workmates for two of the years when we were students at Exeter University. We moved to a larger one after Isabella birth.

We felt urged to start a new life for ourselves after graduating. Tamcaster lay at the very heart of Britannia and, being the largest city in Mercia, it played a key part in national issues. London, which had sprawled so far and eaten into so many rural areas seemed rather stifling. The countryside was never very far away from Tamcaster, with the Peak District to the north and Sherwood Forest to the east, we had good friends living there already.

The Tamcaster housing scheme operated rent-to-buy homes for new teachers, so we let our house in Woodleigh, which provided us with a small income, and made the move.

We were not alone in this decision. Adam Samphire had been constant in his love for Trish Lamb. They decided to marry, and I was invited to be best man at their wedding, conducted by Milton at his church, with Bonnie, Amina and Beatrice as bridesmaids. Adam, had done an environmental studies course and now obtained a post with Tamcaster City Council, so they qualified for housing too.

I was to join the history team at Arkwright Academy and Mina accepted a part-time post at Greenside Community College, where she was job sharing with Trish, teaching art and music. This was just as well because we soon learned that another child was on the way. I did not want to miss those early years as a father, so the following year, when Rupert was still suckling, I also switched to a similar arrangement with one of the other teachers in my school. Mina and I were then able to share duties in our home and also in the neighbourhood, which was important to both of us.

When we came back to school life, we found we were in a different world. Gone were the white holographic tables in the old classrooms. These had seemed so exciting when I was at school. Technology had moved into new realms, and Mina and I found that we learning from some of the students, who had been born in a developed cyber context. Teachers and pupils were now all supplied with holographic eye frames, and these were used in many of the lessons, particularly science, geography, history and civics. What did remain the same was the practice of alternating every fifteen minutes between exploration of the 3D cyber experience and group discussion about it with teacher and pupils. The regulation remained firmly in place limiting the amount of time any individual could spend using cyber equipment to no more than ten hours per week.

Other new developments were the disappearance of classrooms and the introduction of sliding partitions in open spaces to oblige tutorial groups and the introduction of robotic assistants, who did everything from storing information, moving the partitions, setting tests, marking them, tidying up, and cleaning the floors and tables at the end of each day.

 Mina and I deliberately chose to live in the inner city of Tamcaster, rather than the outlying suburbs, where so many of the other teachers lived. The social divide this created was not to our liking. It suited us to buy a semi-detached house, with an Asian family on one side and an Estonian on the other.

We joined the St. Luke's Cooperative, which had allotments nearby where we grew most of our food. Although we were no longer able to enjoy the closeness of a cluster group, we were part of a multi-racial community and aimed to be as self-sufficient as possible. Solar panels and a wind-turbine on old chimneystack helped to reduce our energy bills, and the organic kitchen seemed to symbolise the heart of our family. It was here that we gathered in the evening to share stories and spell out our visions for tomorrow.

Amina:

Isabella was a beautiful little child: not as dark as me, but light brown in colouring, with long black hair rippling down her back. She had Rory's eyes, a ready smile and a determined character. It was wonderful to recognise the little creature that I had carried in me for nine months; with features and behaviour patterns that she had clearly inherited from each of us.

When she was two we took her to a play centre, where there were climbing bricks reaching high up the wall above the cushions. Isabella pointed to it, ran across and started to climb. One, two, three, and she was away; reaching up with hands, and legs. Up she went, saying aloud two words to herself. "Issy can! Issy can!"

I had to call out, "that's high enough, Isabella." Eventually, when she began to pause and look down, I hauled her off the wall. Rory gasped, "Isn't she tenacious." As she turned to push herself through a snake-like tunnel, and shouted out for everyone to hear, "Issy 'natious. Issy 'natious."

One of the great delights of the house was the magnificent rear garden. Our French windows opened to a wide stretch of land, containing a tall ash tree, which I hugged on the first morning, and quickly adopted as my own. The previous owner had planted a broad lawn, that was excellent for children to play on. I walked round the edge of it, with a local wild-flower booklet identifying all those I recognised. Beyond the grass was a fruit orchard consisting of four mature apple trees, four pear trees and a plum tree standing close enough to give the impression of a substantial stretch of woodland. To the left of the orchard was a grassy hillock, covered by a wild flower rockery, with a large stone slab laid on the top, from which we could view a ring of trees in gardens surrounding us. Crazy paving led from the lawn to the back of the hillock, where a green door was revealed: a very exciting discovery for any young child, even if it only concealed a garden shed. A further air of mystery was added to this rather surprising garden by the red brick walls surrounding it. Climbing the hillock was the only way to see what lay beyond.

Beside the house there was a wooden garage. We had decided not to have a car, but to join the local car-share scheme, so we turned the garage into a play area for the children. Isabella had her own little home there at first and, on sunny days we were invited to have afternoon tea with the dolls.

Rupert also had light brown skin, and inherited his father's love for the natural world. When he was four, he squealed with delight when he found snails and slugs in the garden. He picked them up and came running into the kitchen me, crying, "Look Mom. They're wriggling!" He learned the names of the local birds very quickly, and usually went out in the evening to watch them settle on rooftops. As he grew older, Adam (his godfather) encouraged him to watch the migrating birds and keep records of the sightings.

The garage was transformed several times over the years. As Rupert grew bigger he had a share in it, and it became a racing track for his cars. He started by having his own corner but, as his interests expanded, it took over most of the floor. Isabella then decided that he could have the garage, and asked if she could have a tree house in the orchard. We built this for her eighth birthday, and fastened a rope ladder to a strong branch, which enabled her to climb up there. She told us the view was even better than the one from the hillock. She could see the wind turbines in operation on Shooter's Hill, two miles to the north.

One fine evening, during a heat wave, she took her sleeping bag there and stayed the night. In the morning, she told us how wonderful it had been to watch the sunrise as she lay there, surrounded by a dawn chorus. We were envious. and the next night, three of us slept in a tent on the lawn. Early next morning, Rupert woke us up to see the worms and snails that he had collected on his early ramble round the garden.

Rupert became very peeved when we told him that he must not climb the rope ladder. He said he wanted a share in the tree house too, but we reminded him, that he had the garage all to himself now. He argued that it was more exciting in the garden so, for his seventh birthday, Rory secretly converted the garden shed under the hillock into an underground den, complete with camp bed and old lamp, which he managed to secure by fixing a hook in the middle of the wooden roof.

Rupert was delighted with his secret hiding place and, as Uncle Adam and Auntie Trish had given him a birthday present of a Roman soldier's outfit, complete with helmet, breastplate and wooden sword, he announced that he was now St. George, and had slain the dragon in its lair. To prove the point, he took us to the cave where, he told us that the dragon had been living under the mountain that was not be approached by the path, but only through a twisty walk through the fruit forest. When we eventually found the cave, there lay the dragon with a sword thrust into his heart. (The dragon was a stuffed dinosaur, which he had become too big for.) Rupert said he was going to roast and eat him for lunch but, when the meal arrived, Rory and I were served fried sausages by the two children, assisted by Auntie Trish. We never saw the dinosaur again. He had been buried in the forest, and the sword marked his grave.

Gradually the children lost their enthusiasm for the garage, and we went back to using it again as a store for the garden tools, formerly kept under the hillock. Some time later, Isabella became interested in plays. We'd taken the children to see pantomimes and a teacher at her school involved her in a small part in a classroom production. Soon afterwards, Isabella told us that she was going to convert the garage into a theatre, and that there would be some performances to raise money for the Tamcaster Children's Hospital. She asked her schoolmates to come and do song and dance acts and tell jokes. To our amazement, next Saturday afternoon a plump, middle-aged lady knocked at the door and asked if this was where the performance was going to be held.

"Er - the children are doing something in the garage, if that's what you mean," I said.

"Good, I've got the right house then. My granddaughter, Susanne, gave me this address and we've invited the next-door neighbours to come as well, if that's all right. Is that the garage over there, where all the noise is coming from?"

"Yes, that's the garage, but I don't think there are any seats. I'll carry some chairs out, if you're staying to watch."

I asked Rupert to help and we soon had all the dining chairs, two basket ones and Gramp's old rocking chair on the driveway. The neighbours settled there, so we joined them and peered through open garage doors, while ten children cavorted around singing, dancing and then passing the Roman helmet round for contributions to the children's hospital.

This was the first of a series of shows held over the next few years. Eventually, curtains were borrowed from the French windows, and a rope was devised to open and close them. Rupert painted some scenery; Isabella wrote sketches, cast the plays and produced them and Brandon, our youngest, insisted on toddling on too. Although uninvited, there was no way of leaving him out. Isabella got several letters of thanks from the hospital, and she kept them in a bedroom drawer with some of her other trinkets and programmes from some of the later shows.

When Brandon was three, and had grown a mop of ginger hair, we took him to a safari park. He was wearing his first pair of red trousers, with two pockets, where he kept handkerchiefs. Brandy saw a monkey standing up on his legs and looking up at him. He ran over to face it. They were just about the same size. The monkey gazed back at him, gripping the low-lying branch of a tree with two small hands. Brandon looked at them, and then said to him. "Brandy got hands," displaying them to the monkey. When it did not respond, Brandon decided to go one better, and told him proudly, "Brandy got pockets!" fetching out a hanky to prove it. The monkey ran away, and Bran squealed with delight.

Rory:

Bruce Langland was never far away from our home. He and Gwen became our best friends. They knew the town very well and were able to introduce us to its many circles. Gwen had a lot of problems with her leg, and it had to be amputated. After that, she was given a modern prosthetic one, with a computer inside it giving wonderful flexibility. She had to use two sticks at first, but after a while, she found she only needed one, and eventually she was walking freely.

Bruce was still a councillor and even tried to persuade me to stand, but I told him that I didn't feel I'd been here long enough. I said that perhaps I might consider it when the children had gone through primary school. He did not forget that and, sure enough, came back to the theme some years later.

"The fact is the town needs you, Rory. The Responsible Party's struggling to find a suitable candidate in Arkwright ward, someone who knows the area well. You live there, and are based in one of the key schools, while Mina's working in the other one. It means you understand how the place ticks. We haven't got a candidate like that. To be honest, no one except me is really interested in this ward, which is a great shame. I love the place. It desperately needs a strong councillor. I've considered switching wards, but that's not a good idea because I'm heavily involved in several projects in my own ward and need to see them through."

"What projects are these?" I asked him.

"Well we are expanding our scheme to encourage people to generate their own electricity and, with some of the money earned, we're about to kick start a local scheme to provide secure investments for pensions and savings. Our aim's to work with the council on a public private partnership employing a team of workers to install green technology in local properties."

"I'll think about it," I told him. "I must discuss it with Mina before I decide, and there's the school situation too. As you know, I was part time for a while, when the children were younger. That meant that I could help Mina to do some community work. It's only two years since I returned to full time teaching and, if I were a councillor, I'd have to ask for a time-out agreement again."

Despite these reservations, I decided to go ahead, and in later years I was glad of this.

I was successful at the election, being quite well known in the area. When I took my place in the council chamber, I realised that there was fierce opposition to the grants and allowances made to the neighbourhood groups and co-operatives in Arkwright ward. The leader of the opposition Freedom Party was a paunchy giant of a man called Alderman Seagrave. He lived in a mansion on the private estate behind the castle, and lorded it over that rich housing area as if he were a knight of old.

The Responsible Party held power in the council by only two seats, so the voting was fierce and it was a sad day if one of our members fell ill and our cause was lost. This happened at the very time that a renewal of the grant for the women's hostel for the homeless came up, and the motion was defeated by a single vote. Seagrave gloated over his triumph, calling the hostel "a palace for paupers", and the opposition cheered when they won that day. I saw the grim results when the women had to be turned out. Fortunately, the Responsible Party had already used their compulsory powers to purchase some empty houses owned by second home owners, so places were found there to house the unfortunates, but the defeat meant that the community worker, who was helping them to improve lifestyles, could not have her contract renewed.

All this was difficult as money was very tight, and the town was beginning to look rather drab. Many small shops were closing down because overheads were greater than takings, and even some of the big national stores had to consider whether they could afford to continue trading.

Amina:

Rory's started telling you about town politics. Once he starts on this , there's no stopping him, but just now he's busy with school work so I'll take over here again.

 My dear mother died around the time that Rory joined the council. I had hoped that she would come to Britannia and live with us in her later years, but that wasn't to be. An Italian friend emailed me about her sudden decline and within days of this, she had gone. It made me very sad. To be honest, I don't know if she would have ever settled down in Tamcaster. It would have been a huge change in lifestyle, as she was a very active worker in the camp until her very last week. There was no clear reason for the sudden collapse. There was an autopsy, but nothing significant was found. It was recorded as 'sleeping sickness', as so many other deaths in recent years have been, particularly among displaced people in the camps.

 When I reflected on the situation, later, I was pleased about those extra years Rory and I had to spend in Florence because I was able to have some quality time with her before and immediately after the marriage. In enabled her to see us happily settled, and she took the opportunity to tell me many things about her early years with my father, and other family matters. She wanted me to have this background knowledge, and I valued it too.

I must tell you something about our schoolwork as well. The geography teacher asked me to talk to the children about life in Gambia. I did that, but told them that things would be much better there now. The civil war had been on when I was there.

I decided to contact the school I used to go to at Nkobo, and we ended up establishing a partnership between that school and Greenside. Our Parents Association helped us raise some funds, so that the children there could have holographic goggles too, and we ended up having some magical times exchanging films that the children had made. We were able to see the jungle in 3D, and we sent the children in Nkobo a film about Tamcaster and about life for children over here.

By the time Rory became a councillor, we had three amazing children in the family. That's not just a mother's boast. It's the truth.

Isabella had become a lovely girl. She was doing well at Arkright Academy and very engaged in youth athletics and also doing some stage work, both acting and singing in little school productions.

Rupert inherited my love of painting, developing both oil and water colour techniques. When he was eleven, he combined these interests in a series of paintings for an on-line collection that he called "Rupert's Birds."

As Brandon grew older he began to develop a degree of independence. He would never run barefoot over the grass as Isabella and Rupert loved to do in the summer. He always wanted the comfort of shoes and socks. He seemed to draw apart from our activities in the neighbourhood too. Instead he made friends with a group of boys who belonged to wealthier families in the gated estates.

He was introduced to a golf club and did some caddying there at weekends. Because his friends had the latest fashions in clothing and playthings, he began to spend more time with them, and started to grumble about our simpler lifestyle. This attitude disappointed us, making things a bit more difficult in the family, but we told ourselves that he'd probably grow out of this.

Beatrice:

Now that Mina's told you about her children, I feel it's time to let you know that Brook and I have one too. Even as a baby, Ivan was very fond of animals and used to play at being one. One afternoon when we had Adam and Trish staying with us, and were eating at our table, Ivan was being a lion in his cave below. Suddenly Trish yelled out loud, and looked down to see Ivan gnawing her ankle stocking. I picked him up immediately to rush him away into the kitchen. "Naughty boy!" I shouted, "Whatever did you do that for?" Ivan stared at me in astonishment and then he said solemnly "I never would have fought, I could have bit frew wool."

Ivan retained his interest in wildlife. When he was at primary school, he usually wakened with the dawn chorus, and ran into the garden to sit listening until it finished. After this, he liked to go to the community shop to watch the horse-drawn cart delivery from the organic farm. He told us that he would like to deliver "milk and things". When he was in the secondary school he got a part-time job assisting with deliveries and made a great friend of Charlie, the horse, that he kept well supplied with the carrots not considered suitable for shop display.

We wanted to have more children, but this was not to happen. Many women were finding similar problems in the 2060's. The birth rate fell dramatically worldwide and an International Medical Commission was set up to explore the cause. Although a lot of research was done, no particular reason could be proved. A group of climate scientists argued that this was a natural adjustment, caused by overpopulation of the planet by human beings. Although this idea was not welcome, I could see logic for this within the web of life.

Whatever the reason, we decided to adopt, and so, when he was five years old, David was added to our family. He was in care and came for a short holiday with us initially, but he was such a lovely child, and got on so well with Ivan, that we applied to have him permanently, and this was eventually agreed.

We loved to watch the two boys playing together. They never tired of beach ball or running races with the dog. Brook and I helped them learn to swim, and later they both earned medals in the children's swimming club.

Rory:

Sorry to break in, Bea, but as I was saying, before these pages were taken over first by my wife, Mina, and then by my sister, Bea, the Responsible Party regained control of Tamcaster Council in the year that I became a City Councillor.

During my second year on the council, there was a terrific thunderstorm. Mina and I were woken at around four in the morning by a huge explosion, which made us think that the house might collapse. Alarmed, the children all came running into our bedroom. The rain was smacking our windows furiously, and the wind that followed was the worst I'd ever experienced. Throughout it's continuous wild roaring the children sat on our bed, hugging us for comfort.

After a few minutes, I scrambled out and drew back the curtains. Another huge burst of lightning illuminated the room, and the trees in the garden were bent at alarming angles and jerking frantically. Some even looked as if they might be uprooted.

"It must be a hurricane," I shouted above the roaring. We had no more sleep that night. We tried switching on the lights, but they did not respond. I went downstairs and came back with three battery torches.

"We must get dressed before we perish with cold," I yelled..

We spent the rest of the night in the living room, huddled together on the sofa for warmth, as there was no electric power for heating.

When it was daylight, I tried to leave the house but could only open the door a few inches. The wind pressed against it so furiously that I couldn't open it further.

"I can't go to work and, anyway, the schools must obviously be closed," I shouted over the racket.

While I was still battling with the door, I saw fingers clutching it from outside. Alarmed, I struggled to see who was there. It was my next-door neighbour, Ranjit Singh. We managed to open the door enough to enable him to sidle through, and it took our combined strength to close it again.

Ranjit, who still worked at the City Hall, was exhausted. He explained that he had heard news of the storm on his radio. He had a powerful one because he was in the habit of listening to programmes from Asia.

"It's a tsunami in the Atlantic...caused by a volcano on one of the Canary Islands...Tenerife has been destroyed. They said that giant waves are heading north...in this direction. There's devastation in West Africa and Portugal, Brittany...and Wessex, where your sister lives. I thought I should let you know."

"Thanks, Ranjit. It's good of you to battle out in this storm to warn me. I'll try to telephone Beatrice, but I doubt if I can get a signal."

"You won't... not from this house...but you might from mine...I have this powerful system..."

"What have you heard about the West Country?"

"Seaside towns have been swept away, Penzance has disappeared, and the sea is advancing as never before."

I agreed to go back with him and try to telephone Beatrice. We fought with the door, bowed our heads and struggled along the path linking the two houses. Then suddenly Ranjit's big aerial came crashing down. It flew past my face, just missing us, and jammed itself against a holly bush. There it remained, quivering with the force of the hurricane.

"No hope of phoning now," I yelled at him. "I'm going back. Thanks for trying."

I banged on my door again, and Mina opened it slightly. I pushed through and we forced it back in place.

CHAPTER 23 - Tsunami

2 June 2073

Beatrice: (in retrospect) If the terrible occurrence in 2073 had happened in the winter, it might have seemed more natural. We had attuned ourselves to bleak winters and wet summers, but the tsunami hit us in May, after we had welcomed the lighter nights, magnolia blossoms and flowering cherry. Then, quite suddenly in the early evening, the sky went black with rain clouds.

We had just cleared up after the meal, and Brook had gone out to play football with the boys. As soon as the downpour started they came running back in. A huge roar of thunder clashed overhead and violent flashes tore across the room. A few seconds later, we heard the siren wailing. We'd often heard the sound, when they practised it at noon every Wednesday. It had never been sounded at any other time, so we knew this was a major emergency. Hooters had been installed on public buildings across the country two years earlier.

The instructions were clear. We all knew that the siren meant imminent danger. Everyone was to go immediately to their designated community centre. We pulled on our waterproofs, hoods and Wellington boots, left the house and trudged through the storm to the community hall.

All four clusters turned out and, when we arrived, there was a crowd in the locker -room struggling to get out of wet garments. Everyone was worried, of course.

Mom and Dad were there already, and we sat beside them in the packed hall to hear the announcements.

It was Councillor Heathershaw who mounted the platform. Her hair was greying now, instead of her blonde waves. The loud buzz of anxious voices instantly ceased. We all knew that this must be something very important.

"I'm afraid I have to tell you some terrible news," she began. "A massive tsunami is now raging in the north Atlantic. Tenerife and the Canary Islands have been devastated. Giant waves are spreading in all directions and the northern ones have destroyed coast towns in Portugal and southwest France. Our government has recorded this message and sent it to all local authorities throughout Britannia. You can hear this now." She sat down, and we heard the Prime Minister's voice relayed through the loudspeakers.

"People of Britannia: news has just been received about the worst tsunami ever recorded in the Atlantic. We believe this was possibly precipitated by a volcanic eruption on the island of La Combicsca. The tsunami is moving north. It has already hit the Portuguese coast and giant waves are now heading in the direction of South West Britannia. The areas most at risk are the counties of Cornwall and Devon. The Wessex Provincial Council are now issuing a Red Alert across both counties. The Province of Sussex, Cymru and the London Metropolitan Council are on blue alert. Everyone must remain calm and obey all the instructions issued by their Provincial Councils. With your cooperation our country will be preserved."

Councillor Heathershaw stood up to say, "There is also a recorded message from our Provincial Council. This message is being relayed to the whole Devon community via their local councils. Here in Woodleigh it's being heard simultaneously in ten different community buildings."

Another voice was heard: "People of Woodleigh: I am speaking to you as your elected mayor. It is now ten a.m. on the morning of the nineteenth of May. I have received an urgent communication from the Wessex Regional Council saying that, in the light of this tsunami, the whole region is now on alert and our civil defence procedures are being deployed. The situation is desperate. The first impact of the tidal waves has fallen on Cornwall and some time within the next twelve hours it is expected to impact the whole of the South West Peninsula. As a precautionary measure the whole population of Cornwall is being evacuated east. This evacuation has started and will continue until everyone is safely settled in other parts of the region, except for a team of specially trained military personnel, who will remain there as long as practicable. The evacuation has been well planned, and whole populations of Cornish towns and villages have been matched with host towns and villages across the eastern half of Devon, and throughout all Somerset and Wiltshire. This is a short-term evacuation. It is hoped that, after damage repair has been completed, many of the people will be able to return to their homes, but it is likely that substantial numbers of them will require alternative accommodation as near their home area as possible.

Woodleigh has been matched with St. Austell. In order to simplify the evacuation we are in the process of matching parishes there to different parts of Woodleigh. The four west cluster groups have been allocated people from the parishes of Charlestown and neighbouring areas."

Councillor Heathershaw cut the recording at that point, and explained, "The mayor goes on to talk about the matching for other parts of Woodleigh, but we do not need to hear all that. Our concern is how to house forty families. This community hall can be partitioned to accommodate some of them. I'd say four families. Then there are the anterooms, and the workshop areas, so if it's possible to house ten families in this complex using both floors, it would reduce the number of families to eight for each cluster. We do not know exactly how many families there are in the two parishes, but I suggest we aim for that target. Questions please?"

"Wait a minute," someone called out. "Aren't you doing this the wrong way round? Shouldn't we find out how many empty bedrooms there are in the cluster groups before we say we can accept that number?"

"No, we don't have the time to do that. This recording you've just heard was made this morning. Things have moved on since then. Several coaches filled with people are travelling here now. We have a moral duty to accept all these families in Woodleigh, just as Exeter has to house the whole of Truro. It is your responsibility to count the spare bedrooms, and commandeer other communal buildings, like your hall here, for people to stay in."

"How long for?" cried someone else.

"There is no way of telling. Cornwall may be saved and people might be heading back next week. On the other hand, it could be utterly destroyed. We simply don't know. Obviously, we must accommodate these people fast before the worst of the deluge hits us."

"Shouldn't they be taken further away, if we're going to be deluged?"

"There isn't any time to change things. What we need to do now is split into the four cluster groups. Discuss amongst yourselves what spare bedrooms there are in each cluster and what spaces can be turned into temporary accommodation. Councillor Jenkins and I will come round to see how you are all getting on. Can you each appoint a spokesperson to report back with your proposals in half an hour?"

I was as dismayed as everyone else. How could we possibly host an unknown number of people in so short a time? We stood in a circle muttering to each other. No one seemed keen to take the lead, so I suddenly realised that I'd better do it myself.

"Coppice Cluster," I called out. "Please make a circle of chairs over here in this corner." Everyone obeyed and then looked at me. Others followed this initiative, so Sylvan Cluster gathered at the opposite side of the room and Redshanks and Lapwing assembled at the far end.

"Well, this is a difficult task, but we're plainly in a national emergency and must play our part," I said. "These people are already on their way here. What can we do?"

"Number 14's empty," said Dad.

"But Mark, don't forget there's a family due to move in next week," said Mom.

"Well, we'll make a note of it," I responded, writing *No. 14?* in my notebook.

"She talks about seven or eight families, but we don't know how many people there'll be!" exclaimed Jane Green.

"For the purpose of this discussion, let's assume each family consists of three people. Some families will be bigger, but there'll be single people too. It might average out."

"If there are forty families and the community hall takes ten of them, the clusters will have to host thirty," said Brook. "Divide thirty by four and we have seven with two left over. So, yes, she's right. Two clusters have to house eight people and two the other two six."

"What about the new youth centre?" said Ivan. "We could put a family in there."

"Thank you, that's the sort of thinking we need," I said. "Is there any other building available?"

People looked doubtful.

"Well, what about spare bedrooms?"

"I've got one," said Mrs. Chubb.

"I've a spare room. It's not a bedroom, but it could be," said Mr. Milner, who was a bachelor. "I don't have a bed for anyone, though."

"I've got a spare single bed," said Minnie Butterfield.

"Can I have it then?" asked Len Milner. "That's a room and a bed for a single man,"

Ivan whispered something to David, who nodded.

"David can come in with me," said Ivan. "Then his room's free for someone."

I must admit that I had mixed feelings about this. It was a big responsibility, and who might it be? But my pleasure at seeing that the boys were so unselfish quickly won me over. "Three singles then. That could mean a family accommodated."

Brook smiled at Ivan and David.

Councillor Heathershaw joined us at that stage. "That's the spirit." She must have heard our conversation because she smiled at the boys too.

"Maybe we could do the same." The two Jennings sisters smiled. Mrs Jennings looked unsure, but Jenny Heathershaw ignored this, and said, "Good for you, girls."

"There's a spare room at our place," said Michael. "It's a double, so we could take a couple."

"We've got an empty house in Coppice," I told the counsellor, "But there's someone due in there next week."

"The removal can be postponed." Mrs Heathershaw spoke firmly. "It's been agreed by the emergency committee that any empty houses will be requisitioned by the council."

"But what about the new family?" asked Elsa.

"The requisition is only for four weeks. That gives time for alternative housing to be found, if the family can't go home. So how many people can you accommodate in Coppice?"

"One house, one youth club building and four rooms," I told the councillor. She jotted the information down, saying, "I'll count that as three or four families, according to numbers. That's a start." She moved on to speak to the next group.

All the time we were talking we could hear the storm raging outside. Rain was smacking the windows and drumming down on the roof above our heads.

About half an hour later, the first coach arrived from Cornwall. We saw a bedraggled group of people staggering out of the bus, and running through the downpour into the community shop below where we understood, they were given steaming mugs of tea and plates of buttered toast by the staff there.

"Let's make them welcome," Mom said. She moved towards the stairs, and the rest of our family followed her.

One of the first people that caught my eye was a small girl, about six years old, who was crying her eyes out in the midst of the great hubbub; and hemmed in by people who had their backs to her, as they crowded by the table where the drinks were being served.

"Who are you with, dear?" Mom asked her, but all the child could do was sob.

I knelt down and took her hand. "There, there, you're safe here," I told her. "What's your name?"

"Lucy," she sobbed. At that point a woman came up, exclaiming, "Oh, there you are, Lucy. I couldn't see you in the crush." She reached out towards her.

"Are you Lucy's mother?" I asked.

"No," the woman said. "The coach people put me in charge of her for the journey."

She lowered her voice. "Her mother was lost in the storm last night. The poor child was hauled out of the rubble, and we don't know if she's any relatives. She was put on the coach by a policewoman just before we left, but I've got my own children to look after." The woman looked distraught. "Oh, there they are. I see them now." She moved away.

Five minutes later, Lucy was sitting on my lap nibbling buttered toast, and sipping from a mug of tea whenever I handed it to her. I introduced her to Brook and the boys, but it was all too much for her to take in. She started to sob again. That was how I first met my adopted daughter, Lucinda.

Lucy slept in my bed that night. She clutched me closely as we heard the rain pounding on the roof above our heads, and the wind howling round the corners of the house. Brook left us to ourselves and retreated to sleep on a divan that we'd put in David's room for Lucy. David was in his own bed, which was now in Ivan's room.

The next evening, after Brook and I had showered and we were back in our bedroom, I raised the delicate subject with him. I was doing my hair and Brook was cutting his toenails.

"I think we'll have to talk to the boys about Lucy. We've no idea how long she'll be with us, but if she settles and we hear nothing more about her parents, I'd like to adopt her. Would you?"

"With all my heart," said Brook. "She's a dear little thing. Of course we haven't got to know her fully yet, but who else will take her if we don't?"

"I've no idea. We could just say to the authorities that we'd like Social Services to go through the adoption process to find new parents, but I'd hate to do that."

"So would I," said Brook. "Everyone in Devon's been asked to share the burden of the Cornish refugees. If this is our share, we're lucky. I think we should say that, if her parents aren't found. We'll accept her as one of our own. I've always fancied having a girl as well as the lads."

I was delighted that he welcomed the idea so quickly. I'd been wanting a girl in the family all along. We had accepted David gladly because he needed a home, and fitted in so well, but my preference had really been for the girl that nature seemed to deny me.

"It means that the boys will have to go on sharing a room, of course. That's possible now but it may be difficult when they grow bigger and get more things."

"They both like the idea of a little sister. I can tell by the way they talk to her."

"Yes, they've told me as much already. Ivan even said he understood that if she stayed we might not be able to afford going away for summer holidays. He said he doesn't mind because he's just getting into water sports down here and he'd prefer doing that this summer instead of going to a boarding house somewhere or Tamcaster again. Rory and Mina can always come down here if they want to see us in the summer."

"Where would they sleep?"

"Good point, I hadn't thought of that. All spare rooms are now occupied. They could have stayed with my parents, or with your mother, but it's not going to be possible now."

"Have you discussed this with Ivan?"

"No, darling. I wouldn't do that. He just came out with it. It must have been on his mind. For all I know he may have talked to David too. David said, when I was washing up and he was drying, 'It's nice having Lucy, isn't it?' I told him yes, but that there would be tears to come if we had bad news about her parents. He asked if it would that would mean she'd stay here and I told him that it was up to the authorities.' Anyway, we're all of the same mind. That's a blessing,"

"Yes, it certainly helps," I said, switching off the bedside light.

"If she stays, we'll have to explain to the boys that she's going to need a lot of love and attention."

"They'll understand. They may be pleased, dear. Boys don't like too much fuss made of them. You know how lads are."

"Yes, I do," I said, turning on my side.

No one was ever able to trace any of Lucy's relatives, so the authorities agreed she could stay with us.

There were far more people from Cornwall than we could possibly accommodate in our homes and public rooms, but the school was closed for a fortnight because of the terrifying weather, so this was made a place of temporary shelter for a large number of the families.

The weather slowly improved, but the whole town was littered with storm damage and many people had holes in their roofs. Nearly all the fences were destroyed and the telephone communication failed. The railways were all closed down for a month, and there was a section of track left hanging in the air at Dawlish where the sea broke through all the defences again, and swept right through many of the sea front buildings.

Woodleigh fared better, being high on the hill, but if the lower part of the town had been rebuilt after the big storm, it would have been swept away again as Aceton had been all those years ago.

Devon fared comparatively well, only losing the western part round Plymouth and Torrington, but Cornwall had completely disappeared beneath the waves, and our new Land's End now became the ancient town of Lydford, backed by the high tors of Dartmoor.

Rory:

The loss of Cornwall shook the nation. It wasn't only Cornwall. There was a huge incursion into North Somerset too, loss in West Wales, and also in France, where most of Brittany was swept into the sea. There were no climate change deniers now and, although Mercia was spared, these disasters became the belated wake up call that the whole world needed. Now we responded in the way we should have done a hundred years earlier.

I received an email urging me to attend an emergency meeting at the Mercian Regional Offices. They had organised a series of these meetings so that all the town councillors in the province could be fully informed about the emergency situation. We were told that the weather conditions might be violent over the next hundred years. There was no certainty, of course, but the worst scenario was that eventually Britannia could be split into several separate islands. How and when this might happen, if at all, was unknown, but the national government in London had proclaimed that each of the seven provinces must become totally self sufficient.

Similar meetings were held in London, Sussex, Wessex, Wales, Anglia and Northumbria. It was suggested that if this were to happen, there would still be a state called The Britannic Islands, but the aim now was for the main landmasses to be self-governing in domestic matters. It was up to each province to decide how they would run their affairs. There could be no guarantee of support from any other province.

In Mercia, the Provincial Council took on many new duties. We now had sole control of our own finance, legal powers, weather precautions, duty of care for all citizens, healthcare, education, policing, social care, telecommunications, agriculture, food resources and so on. There were no standards set and so no oversight was provided from London in any of these fields. The only power still held in Westminster was that of foreign affairs, which included liaison with GOS and the European Union. It was now up to each province to decide whether they wished to liaise with any other province concerning domestic affairs.

I was obviously very concerned by all this, and also worried for my parents and Beatrice in Wessex. The following summer, Amina and I took the boys to Woodleigh. We were still able to travel by rail to Exeter, although the fares had increased enormously, due to the repairs required on the railway lines. As we crossed Somerset, I saw the great sea incursions. The rail track had been diverted to skirt a huge area. I recalled how King Alfred had been able to rest on the island of Athelney after his battles with the Vikings. Was Athelney one of those islands I could see now on that great stretch of water? As I looked through the carriage window, it seemed as if historic legends were being re-enacted across that wide stretch of lonely marshland.

I enjoyed visiting my family for two weeks, but we had to camp out by the common plot, because the bedrooms were all occupied. My father,

Mark, was ageing now. His face was lined and his hair receded behind his bald patch. He had always been a worrier, and I noticed how his fingers trembled over our meals at the table. My mom, Elsa, had retained those bright sparkling eyes and still chatted enthusiastically, but she was losing her American twang at last, after so many years away from her homeland.

Beatrice had put on some weight, but was as delightful as ever. I could see something of Elsa in her now that I had not noticed before - that firm jaw-line and the way she bounced when she was excited. Brook's seriousness was now enhanced by his responsibilities. He was clearly a good father to all the children. There was a growing family. Ivan was tall, lean and lithe, like his Dad. David had a round and cheery face and now, there was the addition of little Lucy, who was shy to meet all these new family members and looked at us all wistfully through wondering, blue eyes.

It was another very hot summer and we decided to make the most of the good weather. We spent a few days camping on Dartmoor, where we erected tents and had memorable nightly feasts round our campfire.

I had a mind to see the new land's end, so Ivan and I hired horses to go riding towards Lydford. We rode up a hill half a mile beyond the castle and came to a halt beside a cliff face, near the old gorge. There, beneath a great tumble of rocks, we saw Atlantic rollers breaking against the shore. Cornwall had simply disappeared.

To the north we saw the outline of a rugged island and, looking at an old map I was carrying, I identified it as what was left of the old Hartland Point. It was uninhabited and I was told that it now carried the name of Hartland Island. I realised that it wasn't only Cornwall that had sunk beneath the waves. Clovelly, Torrington, Tavistock, some of Plymouth and most of the countryside of West Devon - all had gone.

Ivan and I felt humbled. We took off our sun-hats and sat still in our saddles for a few minutes in silence. After a last sombre look at the breaking waves, we turned the horses around, and cantered back towards our camp.

"I'm sorry I never went to Cornwall," Ivan observed. "It would have been something to remember - to have seen West Devon, and possibly Cornwall, but at least we have Lucy."

"Yes," I replied, with a lump in my throat. "At least we have Lucy."

CHAPTER 24 - Wondering?

Beatrice:

The Cornwall tragedy was a dreadful blow to my father. We had always been a close- knit family and Mark was as aware of my minor sensitivities as I was of his. He had grown up on his grandmother's farm and his love of the natural world was an inspiration to me as a child. We used to go for walks on the heath and he taught me so much about the countryside around us and the creatures who lived there that he opened my eyes and ears and helped me develop my sense of smell and hearing. I knew how deeply concerned he had always been about modern farming methods and believed that these practices were making a very big contribution to rapid climate change. He was greatly troubled by the fact that most people had not taken the warnings seriously.

As I went through my teenage years, I had some stormy rows with my mother. I loved her deeply, was a great admirer of her gentle side and her knowledge about the healing properties in the wild flowers around us, but her rather brash American accent sometimes embarrassed me when I was with my friends. Occasionally, I had the thought *Why can't you be like the other mothers around here?*

I never felt this with my Dad. He was always there for me, quiet and reassuring. Max frequently pestered us to take him out for long walks at weekends. He would keep running to his lead, hanging in the downstairs cloakroom by the front door, and then back to Dad or me once the lunch was over. His tail would be wagging and he usually had the lead in his mouth, and an expectant look in his eyes. One of us often give in to him and, if it was Dad, I immediately wanted to go out too. I could never bear to see Dad taking Max for a walk without me.

On these long walks, Dad would often start to unload his memories or talk of his fears. There was always time for this, because Max would romp ahead and disappear behind the trees to snuffle around rabbit holes and leave us to ourselves. Dad was interested in anything I had to tell him and I asked questions about the past, before I was born. Nothing was out of bounds, and if I told him a secret and said that he mustn't tell Mom, he was as good as his word.

I learned that Gramps had taken over running the farm from his mother, and Dad was the next in line, but eventually they found that they were not making enough money. They couldn't compete with the larger mechanised farms that won contracts from the supermarkets, so eventually Gramps was forced to sell up. He shared the money with Dad, who was then able to buy the new cluster house and move in it with Mom. They were then able to set up the community shop.

Dad was a quiet man in company but a deep thinking one, and he had a tendency to worry. The thing that troubled him most was climate change. He had read a lot about this and was convinced that human behaviour was speeding it up. I felt sure it was this concern that provoked his occasional dark moods. It took me some time to understand this. I became conscious of them first one day when we were walking on the heath. He was not responding to my chatter in the usual way, and I wondered if I had said anything to upset him. I expressed my concern, and remember his reply to this day.

"No, darling, it's nothing whatever to do with you. Quite the opposite... It's having a bouncy child like you for company that keeps me sane... I've been getting these gloomy bouts for a year or two now... They come on unexpectedly and last for around an hour...They lift after that. I don't know where they come from...If I believed in the devil, I'd say he sent them."

Instinctively, I took his hand and we walked on in silence. After a few minutes he continued to talk.

"Thanks for the helping hand. It's kind, darling, You are so precious to me... a promise of tomorrow perhaps...I need that reassurance, when so many things are going wrong in this world. We live in a little bubble of hope, you, your mother and I... and Rory, of course, but he's so far away now, in Italy with the Peace Corps...My family is what matters to me...Everything else is so dark."

It was a beautiful day. The sun was shining, the clouds were scudding overhead and Max was excited by the presence of such a lively world around him. Dad seemed blind to all this and it was so unlike him. I tried to wake him up.

"And Max, he's enjoying himself isn't he? Dogs seem to live in the moment. He doesn't get gloomy. Just watch him."

My father looked down at him. "Yes," he said, "I'm glad we got Max. You were always saying you wanted a dog. You're right of course. They do live in the present. We should all try to do that more. It's our thoughts about the future that can be so depressing."

We had several conversations like this. These dark visitations came about once a month and if I was aware of them, I tried to stay by him. Several times, I gave him my hand and he clutched it vigorously. I asked Mom about it all.

"Yes, dear, I know. I always try to be there for him too. He's such a worrier. He's an idealist, and he thinks we've ruined the world with all this pollution. I wish he could relax more, like his friend, Peter Samphire. Peter's aware of the problems too but, instead of getting him down, they seem to pump him up. He's always cheerful, so full of great ideas for saving the world. Dad's not an ideas sort of person. He's quiet and kind, and, gee, I love him, but I wish he had Peter's optimism. I guess it's just the way he's made. We're all stuck with who we are."

Things changed the following year, when the Responsible Party resumed control of the government again, and re-introduced incentives for farmers to improve the quality of the soil, by using organic methods and encouraging wildlife. Smallholders were actively welcomed again, and a boost was given to community supported farming.

Dad told me how relieved he was, and a spring came back in his walk.

"Thank the Lord we have a sane government again. The co-operatives can move forward at last, and there's hope for the future," he said, with a glint in his eye.

These old conversations came back to me after the Cornwall disaster. The one thing that helped was the arrival of little Lucy. She loved her new granddad, and he brightened up whenever I took her round. If she not was with me, he always said, "How's Lucy? Bring her next time you come."

Mom made Dad go to the doctor, who gave him a thorough examination, and then sent him to the hospital for a scan. He'd been having heart pains, and they put him on the list for a bypass operation. I'll always remember that Sunday afternoon when I went round to see them both. He was in the bedroom resting and seemed brighter than I had expected.

"Good of you to call," he said. "How are Lucy and the boys?"

"They're fine," I said. "Lucy's really settled in now. They've all gone down to the beach with Brook. They're kite surfing."

"Good. You should have gone with them."

"I will later, but I wanted to see how you were first."

"I feel as if I've turned a corner, now I know the situation and am waiting for the op. I feel more secure. I've been reading that book you gave me on meditation, and having a go at some of the exercises. It's steadied my thinking. I'm going to keep on with it."

Whether it was the book, or the successful operation that followed, we never really knew but he was a different man in his later years, taking life as it came rather than worrying about everything, He started listening to classical music and developed a serene presence, which surprised us all.

He and I started to have deep discussions about the mysteries of life and death, the possible nature of God, creation and human life on earth. I recall the afternoon this all started.

"I have a recurring dream," he told me. " I sometimes wonder whether the first time I had it was when I had the heart operation. There's no way of telling, of course, because I was completely out of it, but I've had it since around that time. I seem to be floating in the air, looking up at the clouds as they pass slowly over my head. It's a wonderful, peaceful dream. I'm quite still and calm, but then I think I'll turn over and look down, and I can do so easily. Below, I see the ground, and I'm high above it. There are green fields and woodland areas, the roofs of buildings, the spire of a church, and then people walking and cars on the roads. I think *I would like to see Woodleigh*, and behold, it appears. I recognise the coast: the cliffs, the round house, and then the clusters. I can even see our roof and the community plot. I feel totally at peace. I know this is where I belong, and the next moment, I wake up."

"How amazing! And did you say that you've had this dream several times?"

"Yes, I don't know how often, but I started noting it in my diary, and I've done that three times now."

"Have you told anyone else?"

"I told your Mom, of course. She said it sounded like a good omen - that it might suggest my heart's getting stronger. She probably wanted to reassure me. Since then I haven't had any of those dark moods, so I trust they're all over."

"I certainly hope so,. They've dogged you for so long."

"Of course, I don't know how much time I've got. If the heart operation has done its job, I might still have many years, but none of us knows. Another thing... I've stopped wondering about what happens next - after death, I mean. That dream...I know it sounds crazy, but it gives me a sort of assurance that everything is going to be OK —in the next world,

I mean. Sometimes I wonder if it's not really another world, but this one again, and that it's been healed, after all the damage that we've tried to do to it. Perhaps the next world is the real one, and this is a dream about it, without all the confusion, the destruction, the hatred and the wars. Perhaps this is just a warning of what could happen if we don't behave ourselves. We're like naughty children, wanting so much and denying others. The rich world people must have everything they want, and those in the poor world can just have our crumbs to live on. Next time I have the dream I want to try landing on that healed earth, and talking to people to discover what it's like there. How wonderful it could be if we didn't keep spoiling everything!"

About two weeks later, he had the dream again. Dad told me that he'd remembered to try not to wake up. He'd forced himself to carry on dreaming after he'd seen his house from on high, but he'd not been able to land, although that's what he was willing himself to do. He continued flying and found he could control the speed. He gradually increased it and discovered that he could go very fast. He flew across the channel and then thought that he wanted to see Africa - and behold, he saw an Arab town in Morocco, with dazzling white buildings and a busy market place. He looked down from a great height and saw people riding on camels across the desert, and then foothills, which became bigger. The climate up there was more temperate. He flew over the high Atlas Mountains, where there was snow on the ground. He said that it might have been Norway, but then came forests again and greenery on the lower slopes. Everything seemed peaceful. There was a lake with children bathing in it, and one of them looked up and waved excitedly to him. He tried to wave back...and that was what made him wake up again and find himself in bed beside Elsa.

"I lay awake running it through my mind for some time. It was such a marvellous experience. Everything was so much brighter, and there was a feeling of love and hope in the room."

I held his hand again, and there were tears in our eyes. "Perhaps that's the real world and this is the dream," he said.

I squeezed his hand and said, "Perhaps it is, Dad. How can we know?"

David noted the change in his granddad too.

"Granddad's always smiling now, isn't he?" he said to the other children one day when they were playing together in the house. "He wasn't like that before. I suppose it must be because he's getting older and it means he's nearer to heaven."

"Don't be silly," Ivan told him. "It's because he's had his heart sorted at the hospital."

"What did you mean by saying he's nearer to heaven?" Lucy asked David.

"Well, he can't live for ever, can he? He's an old man and old folk don't, do they? When he dies he'll go up there, and live with God and Jesus, won't he? Perhaps he's looking forward to it, like we do with the school holidays."

"When he goes to heaven, he'll meet my Mummy and Daddy there."

"I don't know," said David. "I'm not sure about all that."

"Oh yes, he will. I know that they're there because Mummy Beatrice told me it's where they must be."

I overheard these innocent exchanges because I was in the kitchen, and the door to the other room was open. *Had I said the right thing to Lucy? She had such trust in my words. Yes, I thought so, it had helped her to move on. When she was older, we could talk together about our understandings and the mysteries too.*

Next Christmas, we were all walking back home together at about ten o'clock in the evening. We had spent the afternoon with Mark and Elsa, where Rory and Mina were staying. There was a starry sky, and Brook was pointing out some of the constellations.

"Where's heaven?" asked Lucy. "Is that a star too?"

322

"No, heaven isn't a place," he said. "Those stars are thousands of miles away. Heaven is much closer. How can I describe it? It's more like a state of mind and actually I think it's all around us. We can't see it or weigh it, but we can sometimes feel it, like we can feel love for one another, so it's real all right. Sometimes, I've felt it in a lovely wood, or on a mountaintop, looking down on a lonely valley. When I was young, like you three are, I got very excited about the countryside. There was an old man who went bird watching and I went out with him sometimes to see wildfowl flying overhead in formation, or to listen for the sounds of cuckoos and wood pigeons. That was my heaven."

I was concerned for Lucy. Would Brook's ideas worry her? Would she challenge him, and say that I had told her something different? But she didn't say a word.

A week later, Lucy raised the subject with me again, when we were baking some little cakes in the oven.

"I liked what Daddy Brook said about heaven," she said. "Stars are so much further away from us than our feelings are. It means that I'm really close to my real Mummy and Daddy, doesn't it? They aren't away up there somewhere; they're inside me all the time."

"Yes, darling." I said.

CHAPTER 25 - The Great Blizzard

2075

Rory:

The next winter was the longest and darkest that we had ever known. The first snowstorm hit Tamcaster on Monday afternoon, 28th October. I was teaching a class of fourth formers when daylight failed. The electric lights did not work because there was provincial council ruling forbidding the use of lighting in daytime.

I was expecting to receive an automated message telling me to close down the lesson and send the youngsters home, but this was pre-empted by the sound of the area emergency hooter on the school roof. The classroom was very close to the alarm, so its wailing noise was deafening. I managed to shout "Everyone get their coats and assemble outside the main hall. We'll go to the shelter in an orderly procession."

A few minutes later we assembled in the corridor, alongside all the other classes. I called the register and we set off walking two abreast. When it was our turn to go outside, we walked into a blizzard so heavy that we could not see the way ahead. I ordered the students to hold hands and, walking slowly side by side, we fumbled our way forward towards the main gate.

The headmaster was standing there with a big torch, counting each class. Once we were all through, we tried to walk on the pavement, but could not see the curb that curved with the bends in the downhill road. Some pedestrians, coming out of their homes, were caught in the middle of the school line.

At the bottom of the incline, we turned right into Forest Road, which is usually busy with traffic, but there was no sound and we saw cars and a bus had been abandoned. They were parked awkwardly, presumably because the driver had been unable to see the curbs. We had to cross the road at some point to get to the public shelter, but this was difficult in the blinding snow. I told the pupils to form a single line and join hands. This seemed the only way to make sure that no one was lost.

The electric sign by the pedestrian crossing was not working. Groping my way forward I found the pole, and led the way. Somehow we stumbled forward over the road, and continued straight ahead to cross the playing fields. We were heading for the entrance to the shelter, an ancient cave at the bottom of a tree-covered bank. This was one of the old caverns, probably used for storage in historic times, but now brought back into use and equipped as the emergency shelter for this purpose.

The new wooden door that had been specially fitted was now open, and a security team were greeting people and inviting them in. I had brought the register with me so, once inside, I asked the students to gather round and began calling names out. To my relief everyone was there.

One of the welcoming group asked if we were from Arkwright Academy. I confirmed that we were, and he told us that we had been allocated to cave numbers two, three, four and five. A class from Hargreave School was waiting there in the dim light.

"Keep on walking down the tunnel, and you'll find numbers pasted to the walls. We've cut sub caverns out of the rock on both sides and we've allocated four to your school. Sorry the lights are so poor at present. We have a power emergency, and we hope to fix it soon." he said.

We asked everyone to link hands again and proceed down the walkway. It became darker as we walked on. Some yards further in, we could just see the two florescent notices. I led my class into number two, while the other teacher led his pupils into number three. Our cavern was pitch dark and we had to fumble around to discover that wooden benches lined the walls.

I called out, "Has anyone got a torch?"

Fortunately, two boys had, so I was able to issue the order "Girls sit on the right hand benches. Boys on the left."

We were all able to seat ourselves there, and once we were settled, I called out. "Is everyone O.K?"

A voice shouted out. "I think I'm going to be sick, sir."

"That's the last thing we want. Breathe deeply," I called. "Slowly in....out. in...out. Does that help?"

"I'm not sure," the voice said.

"Has anyone got a bowl?" I shouted.

No one had. "Come with me," I called. "We'll go back to the entrance. Everyone stay where you are. No fooling around, understand. I'll come back in a minute or to."

I led the boy back towards the entrance, and left him with a first-aid lady for a while, just in case he was sick. It would be awful in that confined space. We were cramped together in our cavern. I took the opportunity to borrow a torch from one of the wardens, who told me that some water and food would be available in about an hour.

"What happens if the weather doesn't improve this afternoon?" I asked him.

"We've got two hundred sleeping bags here." He said. "We're equipped for a long stay. Emergency lighting will come on soon."

"What about toilets?" I asked.

"Yes, of course we have them," he replied, "and a wash room. If we're stuck here for the night, we'll open that up. The toilets are available now. They're another hundred yards past your cave, one marked for men and one for women. They're a bit primitive, but the best we can do: chemical ones," he added. "If any of your kids have a problem, just come down and tell us. We've a team on duty here for six hours, and then another will take over."

When I went back to our cave, I found that the youngsters had started a singing game. It was a great adventure for them, but much more concerning for me. I carried the responsibility for the whole class of course.

Suddenly, the emergency lights came on. Everyone cheered.

The headmaster paid us a call half an hour later. " I'm with the older boys, in cave four, if you need me, " he said. "We have a full house there. You're lucky here in the smallest cave. The other three have two classes in each."

"Have you any idea how long we're likely to be here?" I asked him.

"I suspect we'll spend the night here," he said. "There's no let up outside."

"Can you take over here for a little while," I asked him. "I want to go over to check on my daughter, Isabella."

" Of course," he said.

I found her in cave four, with all her classmates. It was very crowded in there because the class below them was sharing the cave. Isabella was busy helping some of these children with their school work.

"It's fab," she said.

There was a general feeling of adventure among the students at first.

The headmaster caught my arm as I moved to go back.

"It looks as if we're here for the night," he said. "I'll check again in an hour and, if there's no let up, we'll reorganise the way we use these caves. If we're bedding down in sleeping bags, we'll have two caves for the girls and two others for the boys. Fortunately we have six men and seven women with us, so we can organise things without two much difficulty. Everyone can stay where they are until the evening food's been cleared out of the way, and then we'll move all the boys into caves three and four, and the girls can have one and two.

Amina:

I was not teaching on the day the siren sounded. It was one of Trish's days in our job-share, and I knew the drill, because I was one of the trained street wardens. The children were all at school, Isabella at Arkwright and the boys at the local primary school, so I was alone at home, but I had to go out and check on the residents on my side of the street.

I'd never seen heavy snow before I came to live in Tamcaster. I'd been delighted when I saw my first sprinkling of snow in Woodleigh, and thought snowballing was fun, but it never spent long on the ground in that part of Wessex.

Winter in Tamcaster was very different. We had heavy snowfalls every year, and it often lay on the ground for weeks, and was something I had to force myself to get used to.

Reluctantly, I dressed in my wellington boots, winter coat, scarf, woollen gloves and Russian fur hat and opened the front door. I couldn't see properly outside, because of the density of the snowfall. I stepped outside and closed the door. The wind was furious, but I battled my way to the garden gate. Everything was silent in the street outside and I didn't meet anyone else walking on the pavement as I padded down the hill to the corner of Forest Rd. I started my task of ringing doorbells and knocking on doors. There was no response at the first few houses. As I expected, people were at work.

Old Mrs Harker struggled to answer her door, and asked me inside. "Thank goodness you've come," she said. "That siren frightened me. What am I to do?"

"I can't stay many minutes, because I have to check on all the families on this side of the street. Are you all right? Do you need any help?" I was standing in her hallway, dripping snow on to the carpet, with the door closed carefully against the fearful wind.

"Have I got to go out to that awful shelter place?"

"No, you must stay indoors until you hear the 'All Clear Siren'. That's the long, still one. Not the wailing one they sounded half an hour ago. Have you got enough food to last you three days? You've got your instruction book handy, I hope - this one." I had brought several spare copies with me, and held one up.

"Yes, it's in the kitchen."

"Read it through again, carefully. Is any one likely to call on you in the next three days?"

"My neighbour will look in tonight, I'm sure. She usually does in the evening. That's Ethel Barlow, you know. She works at the bakery."

"Good, I'm glad to hear that. Ask her to call at my house, number fourteen, if she needs anything. Is your central heating working O.K.?"

"Yes. How long do you think this storms likely to last? Do the wardens get any long term weather information?"

"No, your guess is as good as mine. But as a street warden I have to see all the residents on this side of the road each day until the emergency ends. I'll have to go now as I have to call on all the others."

Visibility was difficult in this downfall. I had to feel my way along garden walls and hedges, and then step carefully up garden pathways. Sometimes I strayed on to snow-covered lawns, but somehow I managed to reach all the doors and ring all the bells

It took me over an hour to call at the twenty houses, and I was numb with cold and shivering when I eventually struggled back home, accompanied by old Mrs Morgan, who was beginning to suffer from dementia. I could not leave her alone in a cold house and told her that she could stay with me until the storm was over. She kept saying over and over again how grateful she was and how worried she'd been. She hadn't got much food in store, and couldn't possibly have managed to stay there on her own. She said that she doubted if anyone would call, despite the fact that she was supposed to have regular visits according to our street information records. I left a note on her doormat to tell anyone who had a key that she was staying with the street warden at number fourteen.

The snowstorm continued for three days and, as the telephones and electric lighting were not working, we had to go to bed by candlelight. Mrs Morgan stayed in Isabella's room while she was with me, and I did not see Rory or any of the children until the following Saturday morning, when it stopped snowing and they all came trooping back home, with their tales about the experience, and the boring food they were given. Those in the cave were fed essential rations and cold water, and occasionally lukewarm tea.

We struggled on as best we could for the next few weeks, stamping in our boots and blowing warmth on our chapped hands. The winds had driven the snow against the back of our house, completely covering the door, so we had to dig a tunnel through it to reach our garden. The artificial lighting in our kitchen reflected on the walls of the ice tunnel giving the impression of an Aladdin's cave reaching out to a winter wonderland. There was great beauty in this threatening world, where sound was dulled, and all water was frozen.

This was the first of several such events during that fearful winter. There were two other emergency calls to share shelters that season.

Rory:

We were there for three nights and did not emerge into the dazzling daylight until Saturday morning. The snow outside was about three feet deep, and there were Arctic conditions surrounding us. The headmaster asked the students to divide into different area groups according to where they lived, and a teacher was attached to each group, and given the responsibility of steering the children safely home.

Isabella and I plodded at the head of the Forest Road group, and children dropped out of the line as soon as they recognised their own garden gates, which were mostly just peeping above the floor of snow. I saw Isabella step over the top of our gate and reach up to ring the doorbell. I had a glimpse of Mina, who waved me, as I plodded on with sixteen more young people.

Several of them had difficulty recognising their immediate surroundings. All road names and most garden walls were buried, but we managed to recognise enough buildings to work our way round the housing estate, and across a stretch of alien, frozen world, which resembled scenes from Siberia. We staggered by some huge walls of snowdrift, shivering from the perishing cold. Tamcaster was a silent city, and by the time I groped my way home again the dark sky above looked menacing.

Over the next two years the winters got wilder, and the summers got hotter. In the near tropical heat there were times when our water disappeared altogether and we longed for the winter again, when we knew there were always banks of ice, which could be unfrozen.

CHAPTER 26 - The Return of Elfleda

2076

Rory:

The loss of Cornwall and West Devon had sent shock waves across Britannia. Then came the blizzard in Mercia. It was urgent now to persuade everyone, of the need to be self-sufficient, and this required a change of lifestyle. So many people had become dependent on public service provision that they were at a loss to know how to start. Compulsory re-education classes for adults were set up across every province. In Wessex, the cluster groups led the field. Mercia did not have this head start, but the co-operatives were called on for guidance and both Bruce and Milton became heavily involved. The same message was applied in the schools, and I was asked to join a regional preparation group, which was set up to plan educational programmes.

This group aimed to inspire young people in a positive way. There were other vital issues however:-

1. Methods of teaching had changed greatly over the years. Students studied in groups, but the cyber learning was not done through the old school eye frames, because everyone was now equipped with sets of collapsible 3D goggles. Although they studied the same programmes, the adventures they so avidly enjoyed were individual journeys and less of a shared experience, because all the students carried their own history with them, and virtual reality, with the added values of touching, smelling and tasting, gave a unique experience.

2. The dangers of radiation sickness remained of deep concern, so each encounter was limited to a maximum of fifteen minutes, with no more than two hours exposure every day. Cyber learning was balanced with sessions of group discussion, meditation, physical activity and role play.

3. There were other great problems. The sharp downturn in the economy meant that many of the shops were closing. The local authority had to cut back its services and parts of the city had a desolate air. Government cuts to local authorities meant that public transport, street cleaning and refuse collection were substantially reduced.

There were numerous needs in the local areas and the Public Safety Committee wrestled with the problem of how to inspire both young and old to become active in community affairs. My mind went back to the days when Beatrice, Brook and Adam had done so much to enthuse the youngsters in Wessex. Following our first visit to Tamcaster, they had persuaded the Woodleigh Town Council to establish a youth committee, which had two representatives from each ward, a boy and a girl. I recalled that these young people had encouraged street groups to cut down on carbon emissions and start recycling in a much bigger way. This aided messages learned in the cluster groups to be passed across the whole of Woodleigh. The messages may be somewhat different now when energy was more readily available from bio-mass and kinetic sources, but this chain of communication could still be used.

I telephoned Beatrice to ask her advice. "What was it that really fired you up?" I asked her.

"I saw how things were working in Mercia," she responded eagerly, "but a key factor was finding out about Elfleda; you remember the Lady of Mercia. She was such an inspiring example, but she'd been completely forgotten."

"Of course," I replied. "I've got a copy of that booklet you wrote. I must read it again."

"Do," she said. "The wonderful thing is that she was a local champion of self-sufficiency. In her days the enemies were Vikings. People had lost hope, but Elfleda knocked them back into shape and had new fortified towns built all over Mercia. Today, our enemy is climate change, but the message is the same. We all have to play our part and pull together to save the local community."

These words renewed my hope. I found the small book, written and published locally, when my sister was just sixteen. Mina had designed a powerful cover, a portrait of Elfleda, based on the photograph that Beatrice had taken of the statue at Tamcaster. I read the booklet through again that night, and felt that it could be a valuable tool. I must take my class to the castle, show them the statue and tell them this local story. It was a tale of how Tamcaster had been roused a thousand years ago. Could it stir them again, in this modern age?

"I challenge you," I told my class a few days later. "I want you to emulate a local heroine. How many of you have heard of Elfleda, Lady of Mercia?"

A few hands went up.

"Who was she? What do you know about her, Tamzin?"

"There's a statue of her at the castle," she replied.

"And who was she? What did she do?"

"I'm not sure. She was a ruler of Mercia, and there's a child beside her, and a sword in her hand. Perhaps she protected the children."

"She did more than that. Elfleda protected all her people from the Viking raids: she gave them courage in dark times. She was a daughter of a king. Which king?"

"Arthur."

"No, Arthur was a legendary king. Her father was a real one, the founder of Britannia. Another king whose name begins with A."

"Alfred."

"Yes, Alfred of Wessex: the man who fought to free this country from the Danes, and then aimed to unite the people of six nations into one. Elfleda married Ethelred, the ruler of Mercia, and was a builder of towns like Tamcaster, Warwick, Chester, and Worcester. She was a peacemaker. Elfleda taught people how to be resilient and support one another in times of trouble. She was the sort of leader we need today, and she has been largely forgotten. But my young sister, Beatrice, wrote a book about her when she was sixteen years old, and it's in the community hall library here. I challenge you all to find out more about Elfleda. Seek her out, and we can work together at sharing information about her. We can bring Elfleda back to life again, so that everyone in the school and people in the town know who she was and what she did."

I left it at that. It was a vague challenge, but it worked. The following week I asked them what they had found out. Tamzin told me that she had gone to the community hall, found the library and borrowed the book. She held it up so that everyone could see it. Tamzin's friend, Merry, had read too. Roger had been to the castle and photographed the statue. He produced the photo and passed it round. He'd also read about Elfleda on the Internet, and told us how she had made a pact with the Vikings, which they had abided by. They had held on to their territories in the north and east but had not troubled Mercia again for many years. Elfleda had persuaded the people of the province to build fortified towns, so that people could be safe within the walls.

The class agreed that they would like to do a project about her and the founding of Tamcaster. They would check her out on the internet, book 3D viewing sessions for their aps, create maps, write up the stories they could discover and share them with the whole school.

"I'm glad to find you so enthusiastic," I told them. "Some people might just say that all this happened a long time ago. Do you think there is any special reason why it is important today?"

"Because it's a local story which has been forgotten. It's part of our history," said Roger.

"That's true," I replied. "But does Elfleda have a special message for us now?"

"Yes, because we are facing problems with climate change, and we all need to pull together again," said Tamzin.

"Spot on. Our Regional Council is calling on us all to form local defence teams, just as Elfleda did a thousand years ago. We're not threatened by invasion today, but we're in danger from appalling storm damage if we don't combine in a big effort to help each other live differently. In addition to this, you're all aware of the shops closing and the cuts being made to public services. We need each other as never before - and we all have a part to play, young and old. There's a word for this: 'resilience'. Elfleda must have been a dynamic person, because she had to travel by horseback. The roads weren't surfaced like they are today. They were mud tracks across rough land. But she was able to inspire people here in Tamcaster, and across the entire province. She had to negotiate a pact with the Danes. That wasn't easy but she made it work. Our task is very different today, but it requires the same determination. Families need to work together to make us resilient, and you can be a part of that - especially if we're able to resurrect the spirit of Elfleda."

I telephoned Beatrice that evening and told her what we were doing. She was elated.

"They could act it out if they're so keen about her. I'd always thought it would be a good subject for a play or film. I'll have a go at writing one, if you like the idea."

"Marvellous. Better still, write a few scenes, and then I'll let them work on it. There are some creative youngsters in that class. It'll mean more to them if they devise it for themselves. I hope you understand."

"Fine, I'll do that, and if it goes to plan, I'll come down to see the performance."

Three weeks later, Beatrice emailed me and attached two scenes in typescript.

The email explained her thinking. "This is a complicated subject," she wrote. "Alfred was an amazing man, and I think Elfleda must have been a very observant young child. She was with him when the Danes attacked his palace in Chippenham and the family had to escape and hide in the woods. They were fugitives for several months, and all that time Alfred must have been making plans for the future. He managed to storm the Danish camp and defeat them, but instead of getting his revenge, he made a friend of the leader, Guthram, converted him to the Christian faith, and baptised him in the local river. It takes a big man to do that. I'm giving you this background so that you can understand some things mentioned in the two scripts I have attached."

Here they were, three attachments to the two scenes, and a postscript which read as follows:-

Five characteristics of King Alfred and Elfleda

1. **Alfred's strong leadership was possible because he loved his people, and took his Christian faith so seriously that, after beating his enemies in battle, he wanted to save their souls. Building churches in the new "burghs" was just as important to Elfleda as building castles.**

2. **Alfred laid the foundations of a lasting peace after his battles by not being vengeful towards the defeated and allowing them to hold enough land to support themselves. He also created a strong justice system throughout his country with his own book of laws, written in English.**

3. **He did not depose existing "thanes", but insisted that they must all learn to read and write English, rather than continue using their tribal languages. He required that the rulers of all the new "burghs" lived with him in his palace for a short period in order to learn his method of governance. It also helped him discover more about these people and their neighbourhood, bringing him closer to his subjects.**

4. Alfred established a network of defensible "burghs" across Wessex and, when Elfleda became the lady of Mercia, she continued this practice. Each burgh was responsible for protecting the people within a twenty-mile radius, and had to be large enough to maintain a garrison and guard all those who had flocked there during emergencies. Each royal burgh governed by an "elderman", and defended on the outer walls by groups of soldiers: four of them to every five and a half yards of wall. Alfred believed everyone should develop skills and contribute to the defence of the areas they lived in.

5. Alfred and Elfleda believed that God would protect the whole country as long as everyone played their part. Instead of bartering with immediate neighbours, farmers had to bring their produce for sale in the burgh market. Prices were controlled by weights and measures. All people were expected to be honest, obeying the laws as farmers, merchants and workers in the burgh.

Saxons had to learn new ways, because traditionally they had been self-sufficient farmers living in scattered farms and cottages. They had to labour for many months to build these new burghs. Hundreds of people had to move their families there, and learn to exchange locally minted coins for their produce. The cottage industries of weaving, basket making and pottery were transferred to the burghs too. Taxation was imposed on every hide of cultivated land to meet the cost of building the defensive burghs. A hide was around a hundred acres: enough land to support one family. A new system of controlling all this was formed by establishing the hundreds i.e. 100 hides. The local Eldermen had to collect this tax and deliver the coinage or goods to the officer in charge of each new burgh.

I had to consider all this detail and decide how I could inform the pupils in an interesting way so that it caught their imagination, and helped them appreciate the new social order that we now needed ourselves.

I understood the model because of the Wessex Clusters. Our common plot and the community shop in Woodleigh matched Alfred's design. We had, in our own time, recreated an ancient lifestyle. Now, another generation had to re-skill itself to fit the needs of today. Could the pupils grasp this? *Yes, they can. Tamzin gets it, and so can the others. They won't learn by being told but by discovering it for themselves and acting it out, first in this drama and then in the real world around them.*

I ran off several copies of the two scripts and took them with me to school the next day. I spoke to the headmaster about it first, and found that he was very interested in this project, the production, and the long-term possibilities.

"They could perform this play at the end of term," he said. "We can have one performance for the school in the afternoon and a public one that evening."

This sounded like an echo from the past. I smiled my approval, and explained all this to the pupils, making the point that the finished product had to be of high standard if we were to get our message across.

We read the two scenes in the classroom. The first one was a dialogue between King Alfred and Elfleda, who as a young girl, was learning the arts of leadership from him. Ten essential principles were spelt out, Faith and Leadership, Peace and Forgiveness, Bravery and Skills, Kindness and Responsibility, Honesty and Justice.

We discussed each of these principles in our Civics groups, shared our thoughts, and noted key values. Essays and short stories were told. Songs and role-play exercises brought these values to life.

The second scene was set in Tamcaster, when the mature Lady of Mercia was explaining what her subjects needed to do to protect themselves from the host - this was the name that they gave to the marauding gangs of Vikings who were roving, wrecking and pillaging the countryside. "Evan today, some multinational companies and some

fanatical groups weaken communities and can end up destroying them."
I added. There was some dialogue that I wanted them to fully
appreciate.

"You read those lines well, Satish," I told him. "Repeat the words at the
top of page two, so we can all discuss this situation." He obliged.

"*But why do we have to build a new town here when there's a ruined
city six miles away? The Romans built it all those years ago, and much of
their walls surround it still. You can see them from this hilltop. Yesterday,
I rode over to take a closer look. Those walls are crumbling, but, inside
them, giant hefty stones still lie there, with remnants of rounded pillars
and steep carved steps that lead to empty spaces. Wouldn't it be easier
for us to restore that ancient city, rather than drag the stones up here to
start again?*"

"You read the response, Merry," I told the child, whose bright eyes
sparkled.

"*That city sprawls too wide. Our new town must be compact, with four
strong men for each five yards of wall. When danger threatens, church
bells will ring their message and summon all those within the circuit.
They will be safe within our fortress: women, children and aged ones
close kept within the church: our men will be well trained to hold the
outer walls.*"

"So which would be best - to restore the old Roman city, or build a new
town?" I asked the class.

"If there are very heavy stones are in the old town, it would be easiest
to build there," said Jo.

"But why do they need to be building a new town at all? They could stay
in their farmsteads."

"And be murdered by the Vikings? Not likely!" said Peri.

"So the whole object of the new town is to be a place of safety. What does that mean?"

"It must be secure," said Tamzin. "The Roman city is too sprawling to hold without a great army, so they choose a rocky hill surrounded on three sides by a winding river - the strong defensive site of the castle. That was the beginning of this town."

That evening, I discussed all this with Mina, who had read the two scenes that Beatrice had sent the night before and the long email with them.

"I think this is all very exciting. It appeals to me because, as you know, when I was a child I lived in a comparatively self-sufficient African village, where my father was headman. Gangs of thugs, who said they were Muslims, although they didn't obey Muslim laws, attacked us. My father was killed, and Mother and I had to flee and fend for ourselves, and eventually we reached the safety of the refugee camp in Italy. My mother had to use all her ingenuity to survive, and she ended up helping organise activities in the camp, and I learnt to teach vulnerable children in the Steiner school. I've been through it all. You're really aiming high, but these youngsters have had no experiences like this."

"I hope I can do it, but there's a rough road to travel. How can I to get all this information across in a play. We can't have some lad in a big smock and false beard playing King Alfred and describing all his laws. The detail's important but it would bore the pants off the kids."

"That's where the music and dance comes in."

"What music? What dance?"

"Leave that to me, Rory. I've got a song in my head already." She threw her head back and sang out loudly, to a tune that I had never heard:-

The laws of King Alfred will set a new tone,
Maintaining the peace in the land that we own,
Our homes will be strong to weather each storm

And skills will be taught to each child that is born.

We'll hold weekly markets, sell geese and buy hens.
The cows and sheep will be safe in their pens.
With weights and new coins our trade will be fair.
Our girls will weave gowns for the women to wear.

Our boys will be trained in the crafts of the day,
Some will be potters and learn to mould clay.
Our swords will be sharpened by blaze of our fire.
Our songs will be shared to the tune of the lyre.

The fields will be fertile and rich with our crops,
The mill will grind wheat, our maize and our hops.
Church bells will send warnings of enemy raids
The walls will protect all our women and maids.

I could not help laughing. "How long did it take you to come up with that, darling? It's a good tune, but we need to polish the words a bit. I think it's a great idea though. Are you saying that you're willing to join me on this project?"

"Try and stop me," she said. "I've already rung Trish, and she loves the idea of our working together with your students."

"That's just what we need, darling." I was beginning to wonder if I'd been too ambitious, given the time scale. Suddenly, I could see how things could work out. "But, this is going to cut into your free time, you know. Rehearsals will have to be after 3.30 at Arkwright."

"Yes, I know that, but is there's any chance of involving Greenside in this as well? Trish and I have some talented singers and dancers now. I'm sure that they'd love to be involved."

"That's a great idea, but I'll have to check it out with the headmaster. You'd have to accept responsibility for them while they are on our premises, but I can't see a problem. This sort of thing could never have happened in the old days, when we were stuck in classrooms and working to a tight timetable for the exams. Now everything is so much freer. There's another difficulty that I'm wrestling with though: Alfred's approach. He and Elfleda were very strong Christians. It was key to their big strategy. Churches dominated these new towns, and had a big influence. Arkwright is a multi-faith school. We've got Muslims, Hindus and Jews, so that limits our scope."

" I don't see that as a problem. Update it. Trish Lamb is Chair of the Tamcaster Interfaith Council this year, so she can help you. There's a common thread running through most faiths: love God and love your neighbour. Christians find love in the example of Jesus, and other faiths discover it through their sages too."

"And what about the secular pupils who don't have a faith?"

"Teach them love the planet, darling, like we do - this wonderful world all around us - and stir them become creators,: artists, craftsmen, thinkers and doers, winning achievable success in an ordered way. Each one has to work at their own pace, and appreciate the contribution of others. This was the teaching of the Steiner School in Florence."

"You make it all sound so simple. Alfred was into conversion."

"Yes, but didn't Alfred reconcile the Celtic form of worship with some of the pagan rituals? Weren't the churches built on the same sites, and the holy days given new names?"

Mina had a wonderful way of opening things out. The Arkwright crowd were bowled over by her. We found that the boys and girls from Greenside made a very useful addition to the talent at my school. Friendships were formed between the pupils and the song and dance gave a great lift to all our rehearsals.

As I was keen that the pupils themselves should mainly devise the performance, I invited them to nominate two group leaders. Tamzin and Roger were chosen, so I gave them several copies of Beatrice's scenes and notes. The class decided to break into small working groups, and come back to me with their ideas.

Mina gave her song to the dance group, and with help, they devised a routine to fit the words, miming the movements of potters, weavers and blacksmiths.

Our own children watched some rehearsals and caught the enthusiasm. Isabella was in an exam year, so no one in her class was directly involved, but she searched for 'Anglo Saxon crafts' on the computer and introduced Rupert to a site where, using his goggles, he was able to explore a Saxon village, enter huts, and watch craftsmen at work. He did this through a computer link. Questions on screen invited him to name the tools being used by tinsmiths and woodworkers, and items of furniture, clothing and decoration. I found this site so interesting that I explored it with my civics group and they came up with more ideas.

"We could do this ourselves," said Satish. "We could create a Saxon village in our workshop lessons and demonstrate these skills to the whole school."

We followed up this idea, involving both the woodwork teacher and Satish's father, who was an engineer and a school governor. Under careful instruction, several pupils reconstructed some Saxon tools and managed to forge a helmet, breastplate and sword. A dead bull's horn was obtained from the abattoir and a metal rim added. Tamzin's friend, Merry, did a very delicate design on the polished surface, which she copied from a Saxon engraving.

A weaving shed, with upright hanging frames, was created in a disused outhouse and costumes were made there by some enthusiastic girls, who insisted on patterns of Saxon images being printed on them. Some pupils said that these clothes weren't authentic because of the print process, but I told them that this was justified because the costumes had to be finished quickly. Hand embroidery would have taken too long for our purpose.

The costumes were worn when the workshop was opened up for display, with sheepskin rugs decorating the walls. Several children from other year groups became involved in the workshop, including Isabella, who dressed herself in costume and took her turn in the weaving shed. On the day of the performance, the audience was invited to visit our Saxon village and see the weavers and metalworkers at their tasks.

The pupils had worked out a programme for the event. The performance was given in seven scenes, enacted by three teams of performers: the singers, the dancers and the actors. The singers were a mixed group of ten boys and girls drawn from the two schools. There were two principals, King Alfred and Princess Elfleda, and a choir of eight. Gentle music was provided by a quartet of harpists led by Trish. The dancers mostly came from Greenside and the actors came from Arkwright.

The Performance

1.The song of King Alfred was performed with several singers and a dancing group.

2.The marriage of Ethelred and Elfleda: represented by songs and dances. Roger, who had a strong tenor voice was the priest. Mina had coached the three singers and the choir.

3.Life in a Saxon Village was a mimed sequence, done to music. It illustrated life in a rural area, from morning to nightfall, featuring people waking, washing, making meals, drawing water from the well and tending the animals. Others were sowing and reaping, building a hut, gathering round a fire at night to tell stories of ancestors. Some of this was done in silence, but there was a work-song and a family saga was told by a grandmother. Candles inside lanterns illuminated this sequence.

4.The Viking Raid was another mimed sequence. There was a great deal of shouting and screaming, as villagers were threatened with cudgels and fled away, and Danes occupied the village.

5.Elfleda's warning. Elfleda was played by Tamzin, who looked very dashing, with a jewelled torque necklace and her golden hair flowing on to the shoulders of her blue gown. She explained that they were no longer safe in rustic homes. They needed to build a new town on the hill above the encircling river. The families would need to band together in two groups, the weavers and tinsmiths living in the new burgh and the farmers in a strengthened village. A church must be built on the hill, where they could worship and have a lookout tower. This was also their shelter in times of danger. A weekly market would be set up, where weights and measures set standards and minted coins would encourage fair exchanges. Everyone must help to build the strong walls to defend the town, and their young men would be trained as soldiers. Although a few people objected to the changes, the new plan was agreed.

6.The building of Tamcaster. Another mimed sequence, with some choral singing.

7.Life in the Saxon burgh. A lively scene to end the performance, with mime, song and dance, reaching its climax in a big feast.

The audience were offered newly cooked biscuits and mead in the adjoining room, and were told that they could go into a classroom to see the displays about the project created by the pupils and were advised to visit the Saxon workshops across the schoolyard.

The event was a big success and, next term I followed it through by asking the class what they had learned through their experiences. These were a few of the comments:-

"We enjoyed it, because we developed the ideas ourselves. It was a joint effort."

"It was good working with Greenside."

"There was something that everyone could do. I enjoyed the Saxon bake house."

"I think it's a lesson for us today. They had to make such big changes in their lives; things like leaving their farms and moving into the town. I think they were able to do that because they were all in it together, and it's a bit like that now, with these hurricanes and storms. We've all got to pull together."

When I went to the next council meeting, several people asked me where the idea had come from. Some of the councillors, like Bruce and Milton had been to the evening performance but to my surprise the lord mayor came over and asked if I thought we might be able to give the performance again in the town theatre. I told him I'd have to think about that. What had made it particularly effective were the visits to see the displays and the Saxon workshop. Could this be replicated in a theatre?

I discussed this with Mina. She was very keen to have a repeat performance.

"We've still got the display material at Greenside," she said.

"We could decorate the theatre restaurant, but I'm not sure where to house the workshop."

I telephoned the theatre manager to discuss the idea, and he told us that there was a carpentry room, where stage sets were built, that could be adapted and opened to the public.

It seemed as if this was meant to happen.

The Tamcaster Defence Committee was delighted. They agreed to support the performances financially so that there need be no charge for the seats. Good publicity was provided through the newspaper, and posters were displayed around the town, with the result that the children performed to packed houses each night.

This was all done at a time when a shift of consciousness was taking place locally and internationally. Everyone was profoundly worried by the warnings of wilder weather ahead, but there were still individualists who clung to extravagant ways of living. The idea of moving into a communal lifestyle, where cars were shared and everyone was expected to grow food and play their part in tasks was totally alien to them. Most of these were wealthy people, who lived in gated estates, but the vast majority of ordinary folk were now so worried that they were keen to cooperate.

Under the new regulations, community groups were organised in each area, and all able-bodied people were required to do some community work. Many people found the Elfleda story, with its local connection, inspiring. Her message was that we all have to discover our own inner strengths.

Britannia was only one of many countries having to take action of this sort. Portugal had been devastated by the tsunami, and great damage had been done in France and Spain. Across the Atlantic, the USA and Canada had lost several towns on their eastern seaboard. Many Caribbean islands had been overwhelmed and one or two had completely disappeared beneath the rising flood tides.

Most educated people now accepted the terrible truth that the future of humanity was at risk, and warnings from first nation tribes were frequently quoted. Governments adopted renewable energy systems and economic models began to transform. Popular opinion swung in this direction in most of the world.

CHAPTER 27 - Beyond Pain

Beatrice:

It heartened me that know that Elfleda is remembered again, and that children in Tamcaster had discovered my small book after all those years. This came at a time when I was increasingly worried about the devastation being done in our world, and the loss of African wildlife: rhinos, lions, and elephants. The sixth great extinction was clearly happening at a frightening rate. Human behaviour was damaging the web of life. Nature has its own way of handling creatures that over-dominate our eco system.

I had just read an article about the falling human birth rate, and this affected me directly because, I had been told by the doctors, after Ivan's birth, that it was most unlikely I would be able to have more children. New viruses are occurring and mutant genes are being damaged. Scientists were saying that the falling human birth rate could be a corrective part of the world lifecycle. It did not feel natural to me though. We wanted a bigger family and this was why we adopted David, and possibly Lucy so readily. I was very glad that we had done these things, but I began to wonder if I we would ever have any grandchildren?

Shortly afterwards, Mom telephoned me. Her voice was more American than usual: the sign that she was in top gear.

"Hi, Beatrice. There's something wrong with your Dad today. I can't wake him up, Seems as if he's in some sort of coma. Please come round fast. I've sent for the doctor. Must go back to him now."

I went straight round and opened the door with my own key. Mom was sitting by his bedside. He looked quite peaceful and was breathing normally, as I he was in a deep sleep.

"I've tried to rouse him several times. I shook him gently. I've kissed his cheek. I've talked to him, but he gives no response. Never seen him like this before."

"What did they say at the surgery?"

"Someone will come round as soon as possible. That was half an hour ago."

The bell rang at that moment, and I hurried to the door, and was relieved to see it was Dr. Williams, who was my own doctor too.

He tried to rouse Dad, but without any response. He checked Dad's heart with a stethoscope.

"That's a normal reading."

He felt some pulses.

"Just let him rest. We've had several cases like this recently. I can't see anything abnormal.

He'll probably wake up soon and say he's fine. You look very anxious? I don't know what's causing this, but it's escalating. Not just in this country, it seems to be all over the place. There isn't a name for it yet. We just call it sleeping sickness. He could have several of these episodes. He may never have another. If he does, I'll send him to the hospital for a body scan. The odd thing is, they usually find nothing to explain it."

Dad woke up after five hours, and said he felt normal, but it wasn't normal at all.

The next week it happened again. He was out of consciousness for twenty-four hours. The body scan showed nothing abnormal. It worried us nevertheless.

Most days when I went round to Coppice Close, I found him sitting in the sun lounge overlooking the back garden, with mother beside him, engrossed in doing one of her seascape paintings. She'd been attending an art class for two years, and had discovered a hidden talent.

"This keeps me sane," she told me. "When I get hooked into a painting, I'm in another world, and we two can enjoy it together."

Dad's eyes lit up as soon as he saw Lucy had come with me.

"Hi, Lucy," he said. "I'm watching your favourite sparrows again. Look at them all lining up there again on Mrs Snowdon's roof; each one about the same distance from the next. When one of them flies away, the others all move up the line. They're very disciplined. Last time you told me that they seem to be one big family, and spend the night in the holly bush by the stream."

"Yes, if I go by there at dusk, I can hear them all chattering," Lucy informed us," but if I go near to look, they suddenly go quiet. I think they must be brothers, sisters and cousins."

"You study all the wildlife round here, don't you? You're a real country girl," I told her.

Then I turned to Dad. "Yesterday, Lucy took me to see a hedgehog she'd found near the common plot, and the day before she told me there was a blackbird's nest in the old ash tree."

"Just like me. When I was your age, Lucy, I used to tell my granddad about all the garden creatures. I gave them names. There was Sam, the snail and Freddie, the frog, I remember those two."

"Is your granddad the old man with the straw hat in the hall photo?" asked Lucy.

"That's him: Charlie Whiteoak."

"Grandparents are important," Elsa said. "They've time to listen, haven't they, Lucy?"

"Usually, but not always," Lucy observed.

Dad continued chatting to Lucy. "My granddad always did. We had a market garden on my Dad's farm, and when Grandpa came to stay with us, I took him round and introduced him to all the little insects there and pointed out the bird's nests in the trees nearby. Grandpa had a farm too, but it was a long way off, in Derbyshire, the heart of England. That's where I learned my trade as a lad. I spent several holidays with my grandparents, when I was your age. I loved that old farm and, when I left school, I went up there to help him. My older brother was working with Mom and Dad on our farm and, with all the new mechanisation; Dad didn't need me as well. Grandpa had an old fashioned mixed farm with sheep and cattle. I learned to milk the cows and shear the sheep in Derbyshire."

"I liked to watch my mum with the cows in the milking parlour," says Lucy.

"Did you? I always enjoyed working with animals, and I liked the harvesting too, but it was hard work. I'll not forget the day I learned to handle the old tractor. It made me really proud."

"So you were a farmer too then, granddad. I didn't know that. I thought you'd always been a shopkeeper. Did you have a farm near here?"

"No, dear. I'd like to have done, but the supermarkets ruined the future for those small mixed farms. They wanted huge contracts and we'd have had to specialise far more than we wanted to. It was the death of the old way of life. In the end, Granddad had to sell his farm, and there wasn't a future there for lads like me, so I came back to my Dad's farm, but that didn't prove much better. He had the same problems down here. He'd decided to go fully organic then and my brother had got another job, so I helped my Dad and we started up a farm shop, and then I met Peter Samphire and he introduced me to the Transition Group, which had such wonderful ideas. When Granny Elsa came back from America, I knew I must stay here. I wasn't going to risk losing her and we settled down to expand the farm shop together."

"That's a bit like me, coming from the Cornish farm to Sylvan Cluster, isn't it?"

"Yes, if you see it that way. Woodleigh's a good place to be."

These little exchanges between those two voices lingered in my memory for years.

Mark made a full recovery and, as the years rolled by, he and Mom became even closer. They started having daily meditations and introduced gentle music and movement to the blend. Later, Peter and Frances asked if they could join them. As they grew older, Frances was becoming a bit more nervy and fractious, and Peter was losing some of his boundless energy. He no longer felt the need to be organising things all the time. The sessions helped them both to relax more. Word spread and others wanted to join, so they moved to the Community Hall, where the weekly group attracted more people. The Woodleigh Transition Group gave it the grand title of 'Woodleigh Heart and Soul.'

In addition to the weekly meeting, Elsa ran a series of workshops on "Health and Herbal Cures", where she shared her wealth of knowledge acquired over years. Mark later ran some classes in "Meditation and Mindfulness". Elsa's brash side had completely disappeared now. Her kindness overflowed, and when the polders in the Netherlands finally disappeared under the waves, she was one of the first people to welcome Dutch refugees to Britannia. Families were settled in many parts of Europe, and ten of them came to Woodleigh. Initially, they were housed in temporary accommodation, but they were keen to join Jerry's home-building scheme, and soon they had a cluster of their own homes, and became a welcome addition to our neighbourhood. One of those who came with them was my old school-friend, Lina, bringing three daughters with her. It was lovely to meet them all.

* * *

As he grew older, Mark replaced his bicycle with an electric scooter. The power for its batteries came from the solar panels on the roof. The scooter helped him keep in touch with friends all over Woodleigh. He tired quickly and was not able to walk very far.

On Saturdays in the summer Mom and Dad often joined us at our family picnics on the heath. Mom came in the pony trap, which Ivan loved to drive, and Dad would ride along with us on his scooter.

In the autumn, a few months after one of these outings, Mom telephoned to say that Dad had suffered a sudden stroke and I went round immediately. He went back to hospital and lingered for two months.

The last time I saw him he was lying in bed and very weak. Mom was holding his right hand, and I took his left.

He struggled to tell us something. His manner was calm, and his eyes were shining as if with an inner light. He was keen to tell us that he'd had a reassuring dream. He gripped my hand with excitement, but then he relaxed and he spoke in a whispering voice.

"I can't begin to tell you, Beatrice...it was so beautiful... the most wonderful feeling I've ever had... the voice was so musical... and I felt this gentle touch... my whole body was tingling...I never felt anything like it before... the voice rippled through me...and it said we needn't fear for tomorrow...despite all the damage we're doing to the world we see around us...the voice assured me there's a higher plane, and human beings can't harm it...that's the real world ...it can't be violated...it's waiting for us... .Elsa, Beatrice...you'll find it too ...when the time's right....tell the children, Beatrice...tell all the children...they need to know...we see an illusion created by our own brains...mad dreams...but, despite all the damage... everything we've done...the real world's still out there and we can't harm it... permanently...whatever we do. "

I gripped his hand.

"Thanks, Dad, that's beautiful," I heard myself saying.

He smiled, and then I felt his hand relax again. He did not close his shining eyes but, after a slight pause, he turned his head slightly to gaze at Elsa...and quietly slipped away from consciousness for the last time.

Those last words of Dad's were a great comfort to Elsa. She kept saying so and quoting them to others. They were consoling to me too, but Brook was rather shocked by them.

"That sounds fine on one level," he said, "but doesn't it give licence to the climate change deniers. It sounds to me like the ideas of some fanatical American far-right Christians, who say that what we do doesn't really matter, because Jesus Christ will return on the last day and sort everything out. Those who are saved will stay in paradise, and those who question the new Authority will perish in the flames of hell. There's no love found in their hearts."

This worried me a great deal, but I did not say anything to Mom, as I knew it would upset her.

We discussed the funeral arrangements, and agreed that the ideal thing for Dad would be a woodland burial. My parents were not members of any church, nor were Brook and I, but Mom said she would like Rev. Stephen Spooner to say some suitable words at the graveside.

We'd had a friendly relationship with him ever since Rory and Mina's betrothal ceremony.

Stephen had now retired from the post of rector, but still lived in the region, so Mom phoned him and he readily agreed.

He came round to discuss what we would like him to do and I took the opportunity of having a quiet word with him as we were both walking away from Mom's home, explaining my concerns.

"No, I'm sure you need not have any worries," he said in a kindly voice. "None of us can be certain about details of the afterlife. Those last chapters of Revelation have led thousands of people astray. The strange prophecies there relate to the politics of the time, and fanciful ideas about the fall of the Roman Empire, not to the world we live in today. Some of the early Christians were expecting a great revolution, but my belief is that the second coming is found when people acquire genuine love in their hearts, and pass on it to others. It's an individual experience, not a cosmic one. Your father was just such a person, and his dream expressed this beautifully."

I thanked him for those words and passed them on to Brook, who also appreciated them, and as we stood at the graveside, a few days later, we all felt reassured about Dad's passing. We remembered the growing surge of understanding about the needs of our time and found hope that our children could be spared fears for their future.

CHAPTER 28 - Building Resilience

Rory:

2076 proved to be a year of hope internationally because the Review Conference on Climate Change was successful. Cyclones, freak tempests and hurricanes had stirred world leaders into deep fear for the future, and there was virtually no opposition now to new international agreements. Furthermore, it was now announced that all carbon emissions had been eliminated and the great programme of cleaning the ocean beds was well on the way to completion. Massive resources were pledged to help the poorer countries because it was recognised that devastation anywhere in the world affected the whole eco-system, and there was real concern about food poverty. A big programme of land restoration was launched.

Another very positive sign was the election of a new Secretary-General at the Global Organisation for Sustainability (GOS) who announced that he was establishing a programme to clear terrorists from the nine failed states, and establish a ten-year stabilisation plan. In each of the countries concerned, GOS soldiers were recruited from neighbouring states, and a carefully appointed GOS Elder was put in control of each troubled country, enabling an interim government to start rebuilding it, with elections being held as soon as appropriate. Financial aid, counselling and other necessary assistance was given to the interim governments and local courts were established where perpetrators were forced to meet their victims and peace and reconciliation was established. At last, all nation states agreed that this plan was necessary for world stability, and appropriate money was provided through a special fund.

A move by faith leaders had a profound effect. Some rich potentates, including the multi-billionaire Prince Abad Rebad of Shazam were moved to assist the failed states. The Prince transformed his late father's palaces into hospitals and donated huge sums to the emergency programmes and chose to move to live with monks in a solitary retreat.

Our hearts soared when we first heard this news on television. I found myself echoing the words of William Wordsworth out load "Great is it in this time, to be alive!"

My three children were very startled and gazed at me strangely. I had to laugh when I looked at their faces. Mina embraced me, equally delighted. We had always been inspired by GOS and been bitterly disappointed by the lack of enthusiasm of so many governments and ordinary people. It was a golden moment, after so many years of worry, disappointment, and overwhelming concern for our own family and for all the schoolchildren. I remembered the depressive moods that had dogged my father, and then the hope that he'd gained at the end. At last things were coming together, but so much precious time had been wasted and there was still so much left to do in every community.

We had special problems in Tamcaster with the far right Freedom Party controlling City Hall. Their tentacles seemed stronger here than in many other places in Britannia. On the other hand, the impact of our school performance had been powerful for the majority of those who took part and for their parents. It showed that people are far more influenced by what they do themselves than what they are told about. The new Safety Committee had filmed the performance, but to create a lasting impression on all the people much more was required. What could we recommend?

Fortunately, Adam Samphire was now clerk to this committee, so I was able to discuss things with him before attending my first meeting. He had a word with the Chairman, Councillor Philip Cunningham, who had been very interested in our approach. He was a strong leader, having recently retired from being a police superintendent, and his ideas were respected.

The three of us met the week before the meeting, and I brought a paper for discussion that linked the laws of Alfred and Elfleda to a modern system of safety that we were already beginning to create.

Adam and Philip both liked the concept, and it became the genesis of the Elfleda Project.

Guidance for Sustainability Today (compared with the times of Alfred and Elfleda.)

1. We do not own this earth; we are part of its life system, the web of life, and need to cherish this. It is recognised by our scientists and great thinkers, and through seasonal rituals and also in the great faiths, such as Christianity, Islam, Hinduism, Sikhism, Judaism, etc. All have some sages and teachers who recognise these truths.

2. If we order our lives in harmony with the planet and, as far as possible, with the animal and vegetable life forms around us, the earth will be enriched. In simpler times this happened naturally but increasing industrialisation has polluted the earth, air and sea, destroying many valuable life systems. Human beings can reverse all the negative impacts they have created and assist biodiversity through sustaining green corridors, positive recycling, appropriate technology, and artistic creativity (measuring output in accordance with agreed targets.)

3. This can be planned in a self evident way based on cluster systems by grouping households in tens, twenties and hundreds, with an elected representative from each hundred households responsible to the local council. This should help all communities to feel involved in the governance.

4. Communal allotments can be provided for each group of twenty families. Surplus food can be brought to the local market for sale. It is the responsibility of the appointed Market Manager to ensure that standard approved weights and measures are used at every market.

5.An elected alderman can be responsible for overseeing and measuring the environmental impact of each local authority and reporting to the Provincial Council. The Provincial Council could nominate certain towns to take responsibility for the oversight of the rural areas within a twenty-mile radius. This area could be recognised as a district.

6. Each town and district is already responsible for the defence of people and properties from storm damage within its boundaries and an alderman supervises the defences. A Provincial Governor should be made responsible for the oversight of the whole programme of defence across Mercia. All able bodied adults should be required to undergo a training programme and undertake a role in civil defence. Appropriate shelters need be built in each locality to protect all the population in event of natural disasters.

Councillor Cunningham made several minor amendments, but he was generally satisfied with these ideas. At first reading they looked dictatorial, but when we analysed them, the humanity came through. These were family and neighbourhood groups working together for the common good. Each hundred families would be represented in the town or city council, and when important decisions were to be made, the councils were asked to listen to the representatives, and work closely with them to ease the situation.

At their next meeting Councillor Cunningham told the members how impressed he and his wife had been with the children's performance in Tamcaster, and gave out copies of my paper on similarities between Elfleda's teachings and our guidelines. He had made some additions and amendments.

"We'll make good use of the film about the school production," he added. "We could do with more initiatives of this kind. Building up the community spirit is a vital task. Activities in schools can involve parents, and this awakens consciousness in two generations. I particularly like the concept of the hundreds in your paper too. It's an ancient term that was used in a different way in Saxon times, but the grouping of a hundred families makes sound sense, and the point you make in Section Five about a Provincial Governor is most important. I will commend this idea to our Members of Parliament."

Pausing, he looked at us sternly through his light-rimmed spectacles.

"You all know how strapped for cash the City Council is now that the government grants have ceased. This means cuts to all budgets. It won't make the council popular, but somehow, we have to rally people to face the rigours of climate change. Strong public shelters are needed to protect the whole population in case of hurricanes. In most towns this will have to be done by voluntary or compulsory labour, but we're fortunate here because there are deep underground caves, beneath the city, that most people are unaware of. They were used as air-raid shelters, around a hundred and thirty years ago, during the war with Germany when we had enemy air raids. You all know about the Forest Area caves used during the Tsunami, but there's also a big network under the Eastgate Shopping Mall. I've arranged for this committee to view them next week with the City Surveyor and his team. We have to prepare plans to make them safe again for use as needed."

We looked at one another in apprehension.

"There's another network under Castle Hill," added Laura.

"They have been appropriated by the castle-gate community. They're managing their own affairs and aren't assisting in the community scheme." Councillor Cunningham's expression was blank, and he retained tight lips, while some members gave adverse looks and the name of Alderman Seagrave was mumbled quietly.

"We also need to prepare a big community larder in case people have to stay underground for a considerable length of time," Adam added. "Some could be trapped in their homes by floods or other damage. At the press of a single button in the City Hall, all our sirens can now be activated. The lord mayor, the city clerk and I are authorised to sound the warning. We intend to organise a practice event as soon as the caves have been made habitable."

"We'll have to augment the police and fire services with auxiliary teams," the chairman continued. "Every street already has two emergency wardens. They will all have to be re-trained in first aid and other necessary skills, as the numbers of paid staff fall. As people retire, many posts will disappear, so we'll need many more people trained for duties previously done by social services, community nurses, transport workers, civil servants and local government staff. No doubt, this will cause some resentment, but all essential duties have to be carried out."

"Will there be any payment for these extra duties?" I asked.

"We're going to face a desperate financial situation," the chairman replied. "Remember, no funding is coming from government. We'll have to rely on the revenue from the local rates to pay wages for professional team leaders, but not for the majority of field workers. We're moving towards a self-regulating people's democracy."

It was Milton Lamb who gave us a lead. Bruce had recommended that Milton be co-opted to the security committee. He was a white-haired old man now, with a dark wrinkled face and wise eyes, and this was his first contribution to our committee. He was heard in respectful silence.

"People need to have a movement of the heart, rather than the mind," he told us. "The heart's opened in different ways: uplifted by music, song and dance: by the power of oratory or what believers read in the scriptures. One way or another, everyone needs to discover that we're all loving creatures at heart. In times of danger, we need to share this, and help carry each other's burdens. There's a deep river of love running through the centre of the great faiths, you know. If this river gets blocked in its flow chaos can follow. People become stunted or warped. Neighbours fight each other. Whole communities can be corrupted. It's been like that through all the ages, and the worst enemies we have today are the dark forces in ourselves."

There was a long silence when he finished speaking. All eyes were on him, and others were hesitant to follow.

The chairman thanked him. "I respect your view, Milton," he said. "Your point's well-made but, whether we like it or not, we live in a secular society, and most people don't go to a place of worship or have a faith to fall back on."

"That's our problem," Milton replied. "We've become a barren land, and the people are thirsty and don't know where to find relief. There are many faiths represented in this town. I suggest that we discuss this problem with the members of the Tamcaster Interfaith Council."

At the conclusion of the meeting we formed a small group to confer with the Interfaith Council and the Tamcaster Branch of the Humanist Society to seek solutions. Milton, Bruce and I were asked to set it up. We agreed to co-opt the former mayor, Jenny Paynter, and the community worker, Laura, who was secretary of the local humanist society.

Philip asked me to come to his office to discuss the responsibilities of this new group the next day and it was when we met then he confidentially disclosed additional problems we faced.

"I need to tell you something that you must keep entirely to yourself. Don't mention it to a soul, certainly not to your wife, for her own safety. There are, among our elected councillors in this town and other places, some people whose primary allegiance doesn't belong to their electors, or to the town they serve or to the party that represent, but to a secret, undercover body. This sinister organisation is age-old. Some say it had its origins in the crusaders in medieval times. Others say it started with the Italian mafia in Sicily, or with the Klu Klux Klan in the USA, I'm sorry to say. It certainly flourishes today, and here in Britannia too.

We're trying to inspire the people to a heroic cause – to save mankind from destruction. These individuals, despite the clear evidence and the universal agreements reached by governments, are still climate change deniers. They're totally selfish and believe in manipulating everything so that they can live in comfort. They don't care a damn for the rest of humanity and have spies everywhere, and links with local thugs and troublemakers. In Tamcaster the gang goes by an odd name. I don't know whether you have any knowledge of it." He paused and looked at me steadily.

"Would this be the J gang?" I asked.

"That's one of its names. Where did you hear of it?"

"Many years ago, Councillor Langland warned me about it. Weren't they linked with the attack on the mosque, back in 2058, and possibly with the shopping centre looting the same night?"

Philip was obviously astounded by that observation. He gazed at me expressionless.

"But that was years before you came to live here. How have you heard about those events?"

Is he now beginning to distrust me? I thought. I fixed him firmly in the eye and gazed back as stolidly as he did.

"Yes. It was before I moved to Tamcaster, but I was a visitor here for two weeks that year, on a delegation from Woodleigh."

"What week was that?" he asked this sharply.

"It was on the weekend of the early August holiday."

"Who was the mayor that year?"

I felt as if I was under interrogation, but kept my cool. "Councillor Jenny Paynter."

"So she was. Of course I remember now, she had to cancel the Carnival Procession, didn't she, on security grounds."

"No, she conferred with the police and decided not to." I contradicted him.

He smiled. "Good, I can trust you then. I was beginning to wonder."

"I'll tell you more about that. Milton Lamb got a tip-off and passed it on to one of your men. I think it was an Inspector Harper. I was a guest staying with Milton's neighbour that night, so I knew all about it."

The smile disappeared. "Bad thing about Harper," he said with lowered eyes.

"Why, what happened?"

He paused and then said quietly. " He was found dead in the river the next year, and no one ever went down for it. No evidence." Philip looked at me keenly again. "I advise you not mention anything about that night in '58. There's a new generation of spies all around us. The key thing your little group need to know is to keep everything to yourselves. I'm glad you've got Jenny on it. She knows all the dangers. She's still a close friend of Harper's widow."

"A pity that the Castle Community are not co-operating with our community scheme," I observed.

"Perhaps." Cunningham was expressionless again. "They always look after themselves," he observed.

Two weeks later our new group met with the officers of the Interfaith Council, and Bruce spelt out the problem.

"The government expects every provincial council to marshal all the people to combat the effects of climate change in their areas," he explained. "This is a huge task. People do not take kindly to orders of this sort. Alongside the instructions we're sending out, we need people to collaborate with their neighbours in a way reminiscent of the 1939-45 War, a hundred and thirty years ago. We'll all have to grow food on common plots and share it out fairly with those too old or young to do this. Some people must oversee the food distribution to ensure it's fairly done."

He went on to explain how every able-bodied person would have to learn a community skill, which they would be called upon to use in time of need.

"Some will train as auxiliary nurses; others as search and rescue workers. Territorial soldiers will be needed to help defend their town or village from marauders and act as deputy police and firemen. In order to do this we need a new social commitment. The loyalty will be to our province rather than the state, which is too remote, or the village, which is too parochial. Each province must be self-sufficient. There's unlikely to be any help from beyond our borders. This means that some people will be required to leave their home town and go to other parts of Mercia, possibly as far away as Chester or Gloucester, to help whenever there are disasters. All this demands a loyalty to the province in addition to the immediate home area."

We were sitting in a circle, and Bruce asked each of us to respond in turn, explaining how these new responsibilities sounded to us and whether we had ideas for encouraging support. We all understood the need for strenuous laws. We were on our own now. Other countries and provinces would have their own problems to contend with. Clearly, there's a role for faith communities to play with regard to their own members, but is it reasonable for a committee like this one to try to shape the thinking of non-believers?

Sister Nandi of the Pure Light Trust had clear ideas to share, however: "Faith leaders have a very important role to play. There are two levels of consciousness. Most people live in the self-conscious mind, but there is a deeper mind also that we must learn to tap into. Sages live most of their time in this deep consciousness and we can all learn wisdom from their teachings. Sadly, the self-conscious mind has become the plaything of the advertising world, and it has been fouled by pride and jealousy. Our task is to cleanse this, so that these two minds can work seamlessly together. When they do, we create harmony in the soul."

"I agree with you, but to most people thoughts of this kind will sound very alien. How do you suggest we help people to achieve this?" asked Bruce.

"Through the practice of silence." Sister Nandi looked around the circle. "I suggest we all stay silent now for five minutes and consider how to proceed in the days ahead."

We were all surprised, but we complied and I found this to be a very helpful experience, however. Silence was not new to anyone in the room, but to meditate on silence as the instrument to heal our dilemma was a big step forward.

Sister Nandi gently brought us back to our task: "It is in silence that we truly learn to know ourselves. Most people never discover themselves in this life. Their deepest thoughts are drowned by the noise."

"You are right, sister," said Milton. "We're not ready to understand our neighbours until we discover ourselves. When we realise how shallow our own thinking is, we start to ask the big questions about the meaning of life. This is the true heart of spiritual growth."

"Indeed. Some begin to learn from one of the great teachers of the universe, such as Jesus Christ or the Buddha." Sister Nandi spoke very quietly. "There are just a few such visionaries alive in the world today, but we must beware of false prophets. They harden hearts. You can always distinguish between the two by seeing where the love is found - not the easy love that most young people encounter in their teenage years, but the deeper love, which includes compassion for all things, especially for the lost, the dispossessed people of the world."

The conversation moved on, but these words stayed with us and became the basis of the plan that unfolded. The recommendation we eventually agreed on was to organise a series of day conferences for all the adults in Tamcaster. A film supplied by the central government about the dangers we are now facing through climate change would be followed by practical workshops. These would include a carefully introduced silent meditation, group discussions, and a showing of the Elfleda film. The aim would be for everyone to consider the skills needed to help their local community, and identify the contribution that each person could make.

"Attendance at these day conferences will have to be compulsory." Bruce was determined on this. "It won't be popular, but I think it's necessary if we are really trying to get everyone on board. The conferences are not going to be enough, though. They will just provide the start. Afterwards, most people will have to do a part-time course of further education, providing them with life-skills and also a chosen specialist training such as building, food and nutrition, nursing and health-care etc. A few in each area will be trained in deep meditation, and Heart and Soul Groups will be established wherever possible to mediate and give help when disputes break out in a local community. Everyone will be assisted to choose an appropriate skill. Some will need to be trained in dangerous work, such as fire-fighting and, I am afraid, even riot control."

"There's a huge difference between these practical skills and the deep awareness that Sister Nandi was talking about," Laura observed.

"Of course, and both have to be explained in simple terms. Most people will have little grasp of spiritual consciousness, and will settle for the hands-on training, but everyone needs to know that the deeper training is also available," Bruce replied. "Many advisers and counsellors will be needed when times are tragic."

"And we must make it clear that there is no clash between being a Christian, Muslim, or Hindu or a humanist," added Milton. "Some people won't understand this, but that's where our Interfaith Group can help."

"Many people will have practical skills already," Jenny Paynter observed. "We need to value them and not be too dictatorial about all the arrangements. Those who have the skills will be the teachers, so we will need a register of skills in each area. How can we do this?"

"The simplest way is to ask people," suggested Laura. "If we collect a check-list of skills from every household we would know where the shortages are. This can be the responsibility of each ward committee."

"But we need to have a way of monitoring these skills. We must check certificates awarded or examinations passed." Mrs Paynter was clear headed as usual.

"I can organise some skill-share days," Laura volunteered. "Everyone has some ability and should have an opportunity to demonstrate it. We could have skill-sharing days in all the community centres. And just remember, because someone has a practical skill, they may not be good at teaching it to others, so we also need to check training abilities. Skilled observers need to attend the training sessions, and assess the ability of the teachers."

"There are real problems about healthcare," Jenny observed. "Now that every province has to be self-sufficient, we won't be able to have national centres of excellence. Those special hospitals are first-rate training centres. How are we going to fund our major hospitals?"

"A lot of money's been wasted because big drug companies keep putting up their prices," Laura observed. "For years they've been denying the value of herbs and wild-flowers. Now that every province has to provide its own healthcare system we must identify people with natural healing knowledge. We need them on our health teams."

This chimed with me. I told them of Elsa's amazing skills. "She had an alphabetic line of little bottles containing homeopathic remedies in our bathroom, when I was a child," I told them. "She had a guidebook too, telling her which one to use for every ailment, and those little pills nearly always worked for me."

We presented a full report, which was accepted by the Safety Committee, with a few minor alterations and additions. When Bruce presented this to the city policy committee, however, Alderman Seagrave scoffed it at.

"Where's the money coming from for all these frills and fancies?" he sneered. "Don't you know that we have a funding crisis, Langland? I propose that this report be noted and shelved in our archives. Is that agreed?" All the Freedom Party members stuck their hands up, and nothing more was heard of this until the following year.

The Responsible Party won the local government election in 2077, took control at City Hall, and work began to put these proposals into action.

CHAPTER 29 - Green Fingers

Amina:

A few days after those elections, in 2077 Bruce became leader of the council. He and Gwen came for dinner the next evening, and after the meal the youngsters left, and the adults moved into the lounge for coffee.

"It'll be good to have you with us in the council chamber," Rory told Gwen. "You've a fund of knowledge to pass on from all your voluntary work."

" Maybe, but I've got to find my feet first. I may be the party leader's wife, but being a councillor is a completely new experience for me. I wouldn't have stood if Bruce could carry on fighting for the Arkwright ward, but he's got a much bigger brief now and can't give much time to our local ward, so I'm glad to help out."

"We've a big task ahead," said Bruce. "The cabinet's already done the planning, and now we're in control, we can get things ratified. We must run those courses to wake the whole town to the local problems of climate change and build up resilience in every ward, like we're doing in Arkwright and St. Luke's. It's a huge challenge because comfortable wards like Castle Park and Riverside have a tendency to look down on the inner city. The idea of following a lead from these wards sounds absurd to them, and we'll face the scorn of the Freedom Party members, but we have the numbers to see things through."

"One way to start would be to establish parent-teacher links across the wards. There's so much that people can learn from one another," Rory suggested.

I had to come in there. "Like the healing garden we've got in St. Luke's. Trish and Bonnie have done some wonderful things, like helping children who are deeply disturbed. Sometimes these kids become so shy

371

that they don't want to talk to anyone, but by doing some simple garden tasks, like watering plants and looking after them regularly, Trish has found they really start to grow up. Many of these herbs have healing properties, and, believe it or not, some wounded kids can form a relationship with plants more easily than they can with people. It sounds strange, but it can be the first step to recovery."

"I can understand that," said Gwen, "It sounds a wonderful idea, but surely it has to be done locally. Disturbed youngsters would have difficulty travelling across the town."

" I wasn't thinking of them doing that. The healing garden could be replicated in other areas, like Burnage. Their garden village would be an ideal location. Bonnie and Trish could go there to explain how it works, share photographs and invite a group of parents and teachers to see for themselves. If the idea catches on, there could be another healing garden. We must teach the children about the basics of permaculture too. It can give them an essential understanding of our place in the world."

"There are many other ideas that could be spread around. The community shop perhaps, or the men's shed," said Bruce.

"What's that?" I asked. "I've heard it mentioned, but I'm not sure what goes on there."

"It's a great success. It was started because some of the retired men and unemployed ones felt there wasn't much for them to do. It's a hive of activity now. We have tools and workbenches and anyone can go there to repair things that are broken or help others do a bit of carpentry to make what they need. The idea that can be replicated anywhere. That's the sort of thing that we must encourage. There could be a men's shed in every ward in Tamcaster."

"Why call it a men's shed? Aren't women allowed in?" asked Laura.

"Good point," said Bruce. "It's just that a group of men started it up."

Rory:

The council ratified the recommendations made by the safety committee, and a series of day courses about climate change was organised covering the whole city.

Concern about how to cope with the damage caused by the storms encouraged attendance. Everyone was invited to measure their global footprint, and this was made entertaining by introducing a competitive element. Prizes were given to those who proved that they were only using renewable energy, and incentives were offered for groups of neighbours who banded together as shareholders in local carbon groups. The more who signed on, the better the offers became.

Getting everyone to sign up to the part-time training courses in permaculture was rather more difficult. It was decided to hold these on an annual basis and cover a third of the adult population each year.

Enrolment for the first year was no problem, and the parent teacher twinning groups assisted with recruitment in later years. There was a very poor response though in the three gated communities, which all had Freedom Party councillors. The Castle Park Estate held aloof in particular, but we were not too alarmed because they had a network of caves in their area, which made natural shelters. There was a similar situation in the Eastgate housing area, but we were more concerned about Riverside, where the threat from flooding was very real. We had our hands full with those who enrolled, so reluctantly we decided not to pressurise the absentees. It was their loss anyway.

Amina:

The healing garden was the first parent-teacher idea to catch on, and Burnage proved to be the ideal partner. Bonnie was a great enthusiast and was keen to give talks about it, inviting visitors to see the garden in

St. Luke's. She had made a study of herbal healing and produced a little booklet, which helped spread the idea. Enthusiastic children took the ideas back to their homes, and more families were encouraged to use their gardens for growing fruits and vegetables.

Trish and I, with some of our musical friends spread messages across the city by starting some singing groups, which proved very popular. The repertoire included some songs about the situation and this lighter touch was more effective than coercion. We had learned that spreading doom and gloom made people stop listening.

One Sunday, when we were having lunch, Rupert started asking us about some of the songs.

"I like that one called 'Resilience' but why did you call it that, Mom? I don't know the word."

"Resilience means being tough. If you're going through rough times, don't whine about it. Find a way through instead."

"It means the same as tenacious," said Isabella. She had never forgotten about her behaviour in the play-centre. It had become one of our family stories, and now she used the word whenever appropriate.

"Oh, that again," said Brandon. "Stop showing off, Izzy."

"Resilience was a key word in the Transition Movement when I was your age," Rory told them.

"Oh, here we go again," said Brandon. "Who cares about those ancient times when you were a kid, Dad, before Noah's flood?"

"It wasn't Noah's flood," I reminded them. "It was the great storm that destroyed Aceton."

"And that was before I was born," Rory said. " But I know It taught everyone a great lesson. That was when the transition movement took off in a big way. It had been tried before in the early years of the century, but it was all a struggle because the big multinational companies more or less controlled the economy in those days."

"What does 'transition' mean?" asked Brandon. "And what are multinational companies? You're talking old-time again, Dad. It's all so boring."

 "You're the one who's asking the questions, Brandon. If you will ask what these old words mean, you must listen to the answers."

"Brandon's playing you up, Dad. He isn't interested in the answers."

"How do you know he isn't interested, Isabella?" I asked.

"Because I know Brandon better than he does himself, Mom. Honestly, and I'm very interested in these things, and I think Rupert is too."

"I am, sort of," said Rupert. "As long as it doesn't take all day because I'm going out with Uncle Adam this afternoon. We're going to the new bird hide by the river."

"Transition groups help people change their lifestyles from dependency on big businesses to simple living," Rory explained. "You know how we grow most of our food on the allotment and we cycle to most places and have a share in a car pool. This reduces our use of electricity, while those people who live in the gated suburbs drive everywhere in private cars and buy their food from big stores like Monoplex. Compare that to the way your grandparents live in Woodleigh; they still live in a cluster group. You know how neighbourly everyone is there. Auntie Bea and I grew up living that way, with the community shop largely run by volunteers. You can still see simple living in action there, with the houses round a common plot. All these ideas came about through transition groups."

"I love it when we're there," said Isabella. "It's so quiet and peaceful."

"And so boring," said Brandon.

"No it's not. I'm never bored there. It's a magic place." Rupert was ecstatic. "Everyone's so friendly, and there's so many things to do, in the sea and on the heath. That cliff walk stretches for miles, with bays and estuaries, and sea birds and everything. I can't wait to go back again next summer. Uncle Brook said he'd teach me how to windsurf."

"It's alright for a week," Brandon said. "But I start to miss being in town after that. There's so much more going on down here."

"So you are saying, Dad, that it was the transition group that started up the Woodleigh cluster groups? I didn't know that." Isabella was intrigued.

"Not entirely, but it was a big influence. After Aceton was swept away, there had to be a huge rebuilding programme on the hill, and the transition group's ideas shaped the way it was done because it was realised that cluster groups were the best option in the light of climate change. The same applies today. The threat is even worse now, so we all have to pull together and play our part. That's where the resilience comes in."

"And what's that got to do with Elfleda? She was a boring old Anglo-Saxon woman. Why is she being dug up again?" Brandon was scornful.

"There's nothing boring about her. She's inspiring - that's what people are discovering. A thousand years ago she rallied the people across the whole of Mercia, and she saved the country from the Danish invaders. They couldn't depend on people from other regions coming to help them: they learned to be resilient."

"And Trish has created this amazing song about her that all the women's choirs are learning. We found that people were humming the tune all over town, after they formed a big schools' choir for the film."

"It's a haunting tune. Come on, we could be talking all day. Let's wash the dinner things, Your turn to dry, Brandon," I reminded him.

Brandon groaned, but did as he was told for once. Adam called round to collect Rupert and they rode off on their bikes. Isabella went up to her room and we heard her strumming the guitar, before she starting to sing:

> "I heard the voice of Alfred call
> from caverns deep beneath this land.
> He told of trials long ago.
> It touched my heart. I rose to stand
>
> I heard the song of Elfleda
> replying to her father-king.
> She pledged that she would lead us on
> through perils, dark and threatening.
>
> There will be storms to challenge us.
> There will be grieving in this land
> But each of us will play our part
> And we, your people, will withstand.
>
> We will build shelters to protect
> all those who need a guiding hand
> and we will live sustainably
> in Mercia's green and pleasant land.
>
> We will be powered by wind and wave,
> and blessed by gilded rays of sun.
> So we will dig and we will delve.
> Food will be shared with everyone.
>
> Yes, we will weave and we will spin.
> We shall fulfil the promise made
> to teach these arts and skills again,
> the age-old crafts that never fade.
>
> We love this land of Mercia,
> its hills and plains, its lakes and trees,

and all who share this precious home,
beasts of the field, and birds and bees.

So let us build a zone of peace,
and let the joy shine through our eyes,
and we will share the grief each time
that sorrow clouds the darkening skies."

Rory:

In the spring of the following year I was surprised to receive a letter from Bruce inviting me to become one of the Tamcaster deputy representatives on the Mercian Regional Council. I had not been a Tamcaster councillor for very long, so this new task was completely unexpected. Bruce was so busy now as leader of the Council that I did not get many opportunities to see him socially, but I caught his attention the next time I attended a council meeting. "Why me?" I asked.

"Because there's a vacancy now that Cooper has retired, and there's been real interest shown in the Elfleda productions," he said. "Several other councillors would like to introduce the same idea in their areas. Elfleda set up towns like Worcester and Warwick long before she came to Tamcaster, remember. The idea of enthusing the adults through children's school activities seems to have caught on in a big way. If you're just a deputy you will only have to attend a few meetings when the others can't attend, so it's a gentle way in. I think it's important that your face gets recognised in those sleepy quarters."

"I'll think about it," I told him.

He must have put my name forward, however, because two weeks later I received the papers for a meeting of the Regional Council in Worcester. To cut down the Council's eco-footprint, a small van took us to the meeting, which was held this time in Warwick. Inevitably, the main item on the agenda was climate change. There was a quick round up of how each of the areas had suffered during the winter storms, and how much they had already been spent on essential repairs. It was soon evident that the budget spending allocation for the whole year would be used up by Christmas. All expenditure for the remaining three months of the financial year would mean drawing heavily on our reserves. The big discussion that followed was about how best to motivate everyone to live sustainably, so that the province could reduce its carbon footprint.

Attention was given to the progress being made in Tamcaster. Bruce outlined the success of the school performances, the day workshops and the adult education courses, and over lunch several councillors from other towns wanted to talk to us.

Bruce was kept busy explaining about the global footprint sessions, and so he referred questions about Elfleda to me. It started when a councillor from Warwick said "I've heard a lot about those school productions and I'm very interested in doing something like that in my area. I'm a Head teacher and Elfleda was the founder of Warwick as well you know. Tamcaster was not at the centre of Mercia. It was border territory."

"Worcester came before Warwick." another man said.

"Yes, it was Elfleda who fired our enthusiasm. I commend her to you." Bruce was in a buoyant mood. "Rory is here for the first time, and it was he and his wife, Mina, who originated the plan that unrolled so successfully in Tamcaster."

All eyes turned on me and consequently, I did not get much lunch that day. Councillors crowded round me, as I explained about the play and the way we involved the parents

"This sounds an ideal opportunity for Judith Shakespeare," said a voice at my side.

"Who is Judith Shakespeare?" I asked.

"She is amazing - a most talented actor, and a descendent of the original Shakespeare family. She's also the most dedicated person to the climate change cause I know in Warwick, and she happens to be my niece!"

"Really. No one ever told me that you were related to Shakespeare!" another man observed, as he looked at the councillor from Warwick.

"On my mother's side, yes, I am. Judith doesn't descend directly from the playwright, but from his younger brother, Edmund, who was also an actor in the king's company of players."

"I've never heard of a younger brother who was also an actor," I said

"Most people haven't. He died young, but left a pregnant mistress. Judith will tell you the whole story, though, if you want to meet her. She's the perfect person to play Elfleda, a striking woman and one who commands the whole stage in performances."

"I'm surprised that I've not heard of her, too?"

"You would have done if you lived in Stratford. She took the whole town by storm last year when she played Titania."

"I can't wait to meet her," I told him. I did not have a long wait.

CHAPTER 30 - Judith Shakespeare

One week later

Rory:

She was tall, with dark curling hair framing her oval face and resting on broad shoulders. Her high cheekbones and dark penetrating eyes gave her a commanding appearance. She reached out to take my hand firmly and then turned to kiss Mina boldly on both cheeks. We had been invited to meet Judith over lunch at the Warwick councillor's home.

"Good to meet you both. I've heard so much about your school production of the Elfleda play. I'm impressed. All theatre is in my blood, of course."

"I'm not surprised with Will Shakespeare as an ancestor."

"Not quite but his brother Edmund was, and Will's daughter Judith was one of my ancient great aunts."

"I've heard of the daughter but I didn't even know William had a brother."

"Three actually. Gilbert, had no issue, Richard died young, but the youngest one, Edmund, was also a player and he had an illegitimate son by a wench in Deptford, and I'm of his stock. My real surname is Brown, but that is too inconsequential for an actor, so I reverted to a name I am truly descended from, which always looks good on playbills."

We all laughed.

"But what happened to Edmund?"

"It's a sad case. He died of plague and his little heir grew up in a poor house, but he overcame this and they tell me that he made a living as a maltster."

"The theatre was not in his blood then."

"No, but it came out again in Victorian times. A descendent opened a music hall in a pub in Greenwich and performed in song and dance, they tell me."

"Not quite your style!"

"Oh, I've done everything from satirical comedy to classic theatre. Elfleda intrigues me though, and I'd dearly love to play her, if you'll let me. Tell me about your school production."

"It was great fun. The children loved the idea and ran with it from the start. They did a lot of the research themselves, then wrote and acted the local story about Tamcaster."

"But not only there. She went on tour didn't she? The Lady of Mercia was behind the building of Warwick and Worcester too."

"She spread the idea right across the region, but Elfleda wasn't an actress of course. She was a politician: an inspiring one with a heart for her people. Those were dangerous times, and she built up resilient communities that were self-supporting, and equal to fighting the Danes."

"Indeed, they had to be with Viking hordes baying at the city gates. I'd truly love to play Elfleda. I'm an experienced horsewoman, you know. I used to be a jumper at gymkhanas. But I must be honest. I've lived in Warwickshire all my life, and I'd never heard of Elfleda until that Tamcaster affair went public. Then I looked her up on the web."

"You wouldn't find a lot. Historians have rejected her. Don't ask me why. Perhaps because she was a woman and most of those old writers and researchers were men. She didn't like going into battle, although she did, when there was no alternative, but her real work lay in building strong communities and fortifying towns. When dealing with the enemy, she tried negotiating before fighting, which was always her last resort and, after defeating her enemies, she followed Alfred's example, trying to convert pagans to Christianity. This was their way of creating a settlement for the future, which always included a fair trading system between the two cultures."

"Everything you tell me about her makes me more keen to follow this through. You must tell me how you managed all these ideas in a school context, and then won over the whole town."

At that point, we were summoned into another room to have dinner. This had been prepared by Blanche, the councillor's wife, and proved to be a veritable feast: soup followed by roast beef, and huge helpings of potatoes and Yorkshire puddings with onions and all the trimmings. Mina sat opposite Judith, with me on her right, and Chris, the councillor, on her left, so the conversation continued. A number of pauses were required as plates were passed around and various vegetable dishes were supplied. The table was circular, which helped.

Chris stood up carve and serve the roast, while Mina was in full flow.

"Lots of the parents got involved in the production and were keen to join our evening classes about climate change. Some made costumes or assisted with the workshops. The whole thing took months and, of course, the kids asked their mums and dads questions about the changes that had taken place in their own lives - the storm damage, the flooding, the fires. Much of it happened before they were born, but things had got steadily worse and memories remained vivid. Everyone was keen to be prepared for next time."

"What interests me most is that some of the dialogue was scripted by the children themselves. How did they cope with ancient adult speech?"

"At the start we had class discussions to decide the key themes, then we invited the children to talk the scenes through, using their own lingo. Some of these discussions were filmed, and when the youngsters saw the rushes they laughed and cheered. Then we ran scenes again slowly so that they could write the words down. They discussed the script in the classrooms and changed the dialogue to suit themselves. They tried swopping parts. Slowly we agreed the best version for each scene. It was a long process, but they weren't bored. They loved it all."

"In the actual performances, most kids stuck to the agreed script, but there were a few deviations: some scenes were mimed to music, and part of the narration was done in song." Mina added.

"It all sounds great fun," Judith enthused. "It's like a workshop that that professional actors sometimes have before they settle down to a specific script. I'm impressed that you could keep them interested for so long and end up with performances that drew all those headlines. Anyway, I'm thrilled at this new task of touring the province, and my request is that we can have the next pageant in Warwick."

"That's already agreed, and our plan is to have you playing Elfleda for as long as possible," I said. "The rest of the cast will be different with local people, children and adults, in each town. What we aim to do is have a unique pageant performed in each place. Each production will follow a series of workshops where the cast is chosen but, of course, every pageant will have to be different because it will be based on the character and history of the town and surrounding area. Most performances will be open air, moving around to different locations: a stronghold for protection, a market for trading, a school for education and training and a church or cathedral for worship - in some cases it could also be a mosque, a synagogue or a temple, according the local community."

"That's a tricky one," Mina explained. "It will need careful planning and agreement, but it's essential, because we must reflect the culture of the neighbourhood. Worship was central to Elfleda's vision. It's also a core part of local resilience. Those without any particular faith can be given the choice of joining any community group they wish to."

"I know faith was important to Elfleda," Judith affirmed. "And it is to me, too. Do you believe in the Holy Spirit?"

"Mina and I share common beliefs," I explained. "It's not exclusively a Christian one. We believe that God is part of the DNA of the planet, not a being so much as an inspiring, loving presence that breathes through creation. When we line ourselves up correctly, it can breathe through us all. If we don't believe in it, of course it doesn't work, but if we have faith, it can and does. We've seen and felt it happen."

"Particularly in dance, music and singing. My job-share partner, Trish, has taught me a lot about dance and movement, and written some of the most stirring songs. She inspires her pupils and they respond so enthusiastically. They soon catch the rhythms and are drawn into the mood of it. So are the parents, who come to watch. The vibrancy of the performance can arouse a whole community."

"Wonderful." Judith put down her knife and fork, and leant forward towards Mina, her eyes shining. "This is what I have been waiting for – to meet people who share this confidence and can put it into practice, so that we can alert the world. This is what the earth yearns for. Men and women have this capacity. It's why we're here. Every creature has a purpose, and ours is to love our neighbours as ourselves, but we have to discover it individually. I like to call myself a Progressive Christian. I believe that wonders can happen when we're truly inspired. It changes the mind-set and opens a whole new dimension."

"And I think Elfleda believed this too," cried Mina. "She encouraged the people to rebuild the church at the heart of every town, usually near to the main crossing place, where the four directions meet. She was a Christian pioneer, as was her father, Alfred."

"As long as we also remember that Mercia is a multi-faith province, and carry the other faiths with us - and the non-believers too." I added." It worked in Tamcaster because we had a strong Interfaith Council, and I'm sure it can work in other places too."

Blanche looked a little perplexed, and urged us not to forget the dinner.

2078

Mina and I were both given leave of absence from our teaching posts to work full-time on the pageant series of events. The activities ranged far and wide. We soon realised that, if we were going to engage with all the people, we needed a wide range of activities, sporting and skill-sharing particularly. The aim was to involve the whole community in doing useful things well, either in a group or individually. It was a way of discovering hidden talents that could be shared with neighbours.

"Everybody has a skill hidden somewhere inside them. We just need to help them discover it," Mina said. "I learnt that lesson when I worked in the Steiner School years ago. Children who had no confidence changed once they knew what their talent was. I remember one young boy who only spoke in whispers, and when he found that he could paint pictures of frogs and spiders, he shouted in delight as he showed them to the class."

"Everybody needs basic survival skills," I reminded Bruce, "so alongside each pageant let's also have a series of skill-sharing events. Public demonstrations of self-build homes, cooking, brewing, dressmaking, tailoring, and fun events like racing, jumping, cycling, building bikes and generating our own electricity through wind and sun power. We need a sports day and a skill-share event alongside every pageant. No one should just be a spectator. Every person, man, woman and child, needs to have a sense of their own involvement."

The first production was in Warwick, Judith's home town, and only a few miles from Stratford. She was a popular figure in the area, and it was very easy to attract others to work with us on the pageant. In reality, Warwick was one of the last of Elfleda's defensive towns, but it would have made no sense to try to follow in her footsteps. Each pageant was free standing and the obvious way to make a success of the enterprise was to start where the best opportunity lay, and involve the whole community.

Warwick is a fabled town, with its great Norman castle, where we enacted the first scenes. After this, we paraded around the town, pausing for short enactments before the great gates and on the steps of the ancient church. Here a delegation of townspeople came with a request to Elfleda. They expressed this in song:

Chorus:

"Oh, we are your people, in peril again,
We fear that our strivings have all been in vain.
But you gave us courage and showed us the way.
Now troubles have hit us and led us astray!"

Elfleda:

"O Life is a Circle and Love is a Song,
And all must be faithful and all must be strong.
Though tempests will roar at the height of the storm,
Each person has skills and a task to perform.
So some will be farmers, and some will build homes,
Create a new village and bury the bones.
And some will be weavers and others will spin.
And working together we'll bring harvest in!"

Chorus:

"If Life is a Circle and Love is our song
Whenever you stay here, things cannot go wrong.
We'll build our strong shelters to weather the storm,
And some will plant seeds, and some will grind corn.
There'll be food in our market for rich and for poor,
And we shall have justice instead of more war.
We'll learn from your wisdom; pass it on to our young.
Yes, Life is a circle and Love is our song."

Judith had a rich singing voice, and the tuneful song became popular in the neighbourhood.

People came to see the Warwick pageant from all over Mercia, and took the message back. Several towns in other districts were eager to have their own pageant, long before we were ready to help them. Each one needed very careful planning with the local people and we found that we had made a mistake in thinking we could handle two pageants each year. We needed a long time-scale for the whole project.

Mina had to start working on the Stafford pageant while I was still putting the finishing touches to the Warwick one. Both had to take place in the summer because of the out-door activities, and once they were over, the local people needed to start the essential follow-on work. Two town councillors, Chris in Warwick and Bernard in Stafford, took on these tasks. Somehow, we managed this with great difficulty in 2078, but said we would only do one pageant each year henceforward.

We held the Warwick one in June and the Stafford one in September and we invited Beatrice over to watch the last rehearsals at Stafford. She was so inspired that she volunteered to spend two weeks helping us in the following year.

We now had a template that made our task easier. First, we had to contact a range of community organisations and get several of them committed to it: councillors, women's groups, business and sporting clubs, local churches and other places of worship, youth clubs, dancing classes, choirs, schools and colleges.

All the areas selected had to commit to organising adult and youth training exercises, so that the core principles of sustainable living and resilient communities are fully understood by all participants.

Local historians were brought in to inform us about the neighbourhood. Workshops then took place on local premises where each project was discussed with representatives of interest groups. The police had to give permission for street scenes to be filmed and rehearsals to be held in public places. Gradually the script took shape, and local theatre and music groups helped with equipment and training. Then there was an intense period of rehearsal usually lasting around six weeks, culminating in a performance lasting a week, with re-enactments of certain key sequences, and the making of a film, which could be kept for future use by the various community groups. Sports days and skill-share events ran alongside the pageants.

At the end, everyone taking part was invited to pledge to live in accordance with these principles and the religious leaders undertook to assist in this. Services were held for believers in cathedrals or churches, mosques, Sikh and Hindu temples and synagogues. The promise was to live simply on this earth, so that others can simply live. Non-believers were welcome at humanist ceremonies too, but no one was forced to take the oath and no one was harassed for not doing so, because there was a quiet resolve to be a good neighbour. This theme was echoed in the songs being heard on local radio, taught in schools and community singing groups. This promise was given first by Judith, who rode her white horse through the town and by principal citizens. All the other participants were then invited to follow.

Schools inevitably played a large part in this. Busloads of children came from neighbouring parts of Mercia to see the pageant performed in their county town, and prominent people came from other areas to watch, before they were invited to hold a pageant in their own town. Children who elected to perform attended rehearsals, and teachers were recruited to help. Letters went to parents encouraging their help with costumes and items needed.

In performance areas, local building companies were invited to help erect temporary structures to conceal the frontage of some modern buildings. Credit was given to those companies in the programmes, which were often printed by courtesy of the printer's union, cutting costs and reflecting the old tradition of the medieval town guilds. Local musicians, choirs and dance groups were incorporated, so that the whole enterprise had a home-grown flavour.

The songs of reliance were created and shared by local choirs across the whole province, leaving lasting memories with the people of Mercia.

The following autumn massive hurricanes swept right across the province at a rate never seen before in this country. Two hundred people lost their lives and thousands of properties were destroyed. Snow was so deep in the winter that many people right across Mercia had to be rescued from upstairs windows. The death toll for the elderly that year was the heaviest ever recorded.

In consequence, a new provincial law was passed requiring all fit persons between the ages of eighteen and twenty-one to serve a three-year period of community service with the Mercian Provincial Council. Teams were formed to deal with all kinds of emergency, from rescuing homeless people and providing them with temporary shelters to building strong new properties in every devastated area. Qualified construction workers were required to share their skills with the young recruits.

At the heart of the new learning programmes are the 10 Principles of Modern Living were published.

1. Live lightly on the earth, only taking what you need, and restoring what you can.
2. Assist your community in matters relating to shelter, security and public duties.
3. Live peaceably with your neighbours, human and animal, offering your skills to help build a sustainable community.
4. Be respectful to the very young and the elderly, and those who are disabled or disadvantaged, assisting them when necessary.
5. Look after your health, physically, mentally and spiritually. Take regular exercise and avoid harmful drugs. Regular prayer and/or meditation can enhance life in the community.
6. Respect the laws of the land and your community including freedom of speech, whilst avoiding words that could stir up any hatred or unnecessary violence.
7. Respect equal opportunities for people of every gender and orientation and of every race and creed.

8. Recognise your talents and find ways of using them in practical community work, be it social, artistic, technological, electronic, sporting or entertaining.
9. Learn to love yourself and those around you. Recognise your weaknesses. Maintain humility.
10. Send loving thoughts to others, those around you and those in distant places. Recognise that beneath our differences, there are similarities. Beneath our outer appearance, we are all fragile souls.

(It was understood that some people may struggle to reach these standards, but all should try.)

CHAPTER 31 - The Younger Generation

Rory:

Isabella left Arkwright Academy in 2079 and, having passed her final exams with distinction was able to follow her chosen pathway. For several years she had been a key actress in school plays, demonstrating that she could tackle parts as varied as Viola in Shakespeare's Twelfth Night and Mad Maisie in the student crazy show. She was also interested in the work behind scenes and had once acted as Stage Manager. Her heart was set on a place at the Tamcaster Theatre School, which was attached to our university and reputed to be the best training ground in Mercia for work on stage or films. She applied for a three-year course in film directing and was accepted.

Mina and I had both been given leave of absence in the Spring of 2079 to allow us to work full-time on the Selly Oak Pageant. This was a challenge because, although Selly Oak was a small town, it was close to a group of industrial villages gathered so closely together that it was difficult to know where their boundaries lay. Numerous migrants had been attracted there over the last two centuries by the demand for workers in the busy industrial period. We were now having discussions with second and third generation Muslim, Hindu, Sikh and African community groups, as well as several town councils in this former industrial heartland to ensure that the right messages were spread across the whole urban area. Radical preaching and terrorism are long over now.

The invitation had come from Selly Oak Town Council, so we discussed matters with them first, identified key community groups and encouraged them to join in delivering the project.

Gradually the script took shape. Theatre and music groups from across the local small towns helped with training and equipment. Then followed a six weeks period of intense rehearsals, culminating in a series of enactments during the performance weeks. Some were held in the neighbouring towns of Aston, Hall Green and Long Bridge. Filming took place throughout.

All the local authorities selected were committed to organising adult and youth training exercises, so that the core principles of sustainable living were fully understood. The recent storms made this immediately relevant. We were agreeably surprised by the ready response when participants signed up to reducing carbon emissions. The increasingly dangerous weather was now a real incentive for adopting a different life-style.

Judith was co-opted to the Mercian Public Safety Committee and attended as many area gatherings as she could, proving she was not just an actor, but a committed volunteer.

We were having breakfast on 21st July, when the telephone rang and I heard an anxious voice at the other end of the line.

"It's Judith. I'm terribly sorry to have to tell you that I've found out that I'm pregnant and I won't be able to play Elfleda in the Selly Oak pageant next month."

I was shocked. We were half way through rehearsals, and the production was at a delicate stage.

"I'd no idea, and I'm so sorry to let you down like this. I'm sure I'll be fine for the future pageants, but not this one, I'm afraid," she was saying.

"It's Judith," I blurted out to Mina. "She's pregnant and can't perform at Selly Oak. Whatever can we do at this late stage?"

Mina reached over, taking the phone from me.

"Congratulations. How are you feeling?" I heard her enquire.

"Don't worry, Dad." Isabella was speaking. "I can do Elfleda. I'd love to."

I looked at her and saw her confidence. She was delighted. "I've sung all the songs many times. I can soon learn the dialogue. Now summer term's ended at Theatre School, I'm free for all your rehearsals."

"But you're going camping with Paul next week," I reminded her.

"I was, but I'll ring him and say it's off. We can go after the pageant's over, in September, perhaps."

"You're a bit young for Elfleda, but thanks. Yes, I'm sure you can do it." I said, recalling that Isabella had an excellent singing voice, as well as being a fine actress.

"'Course I can, and nobody knows how old Elfleda was when she first started out on this mission. I'm a mixed race person, half British and half African, and Selly Oak is a mixed race town. Whilst at Uni, I've been reading up about the history of Africa, and it's made me very angry about my British heritage. Africa is the Mother of the human race, and that's where the great migrations came from: not only that, Africa is the most fertile continent in the world, and very rich in minerals, yet it's become the poorest one. The human lifespan is short there. Thousands of children die young. Why is this? Because it's been plundered by richer nations for generations! It's an outrage, and it makes me ashamed. Yes, I'll be proud to play Elfleda in a multi-racial area. I'll get the message across, and make the people proud of their heritage, wherever their ancestors came from. They're all welcome. We'll let them share their stories and help them pull together to face the future, whatever it brings."

Isabella's eyes shone, and we were both astonished.

"You make me proud to be your mother," cried Mina. "Where did you find those books?"

"In the African section of the University library, I was there for hours, pouring over things. I found a book called "Embracing and Celebrating Africa", written by a woman called Ahinee, from Ghana. She was an artist and a poet, and had illustrated what she knew with graphic

394

paintings, and gave the sources for all the quotations. I took photographs of some of her paintings; just look at these."

Isabella drew some highly coloured photos out of her satchel and placed them on the table. One was a vivid portrait of the epic figure of an African woman, holding a baby to each breast, one coloured and one white, with an exotic landscape, rich in fertility and wildlife around her.

"That is an emblem of Mother Africa, the Empress of Humanity, and isn't that true when you put your mind to it. All the archaeologists tell us that the human race was born out of a dark skin and our ancestors came out of Africa. And look at this Christ figure: not the usual fair skinned Jesus, meek and mild, but an African prophet, with children at his feet, and multi-coloured angels by his head. This is sage who lives in two worlds, and can teach the children about the kingdom of God, because he truly belongs there. Ahinee tells of how the richest continent in the world has been plundered for minerals and precious stones. The strongest men and women were taken as slaves and most people there today are in poverty. The animals are being hunted to extinction, and the desert is growing bigger. It made me angry, but also proud of my African ancestors, when I read Ahinee's book."

"I think that's marvellous. When were these paintings done?" Mina was enchanted.

"The one of the sage was done in 1993. I can be exact because the artist was at school with Stephen Lawrence, the boy murdered at a bus stop. She says she was moved to depict the love of Jesus for young people in this one and also inspired by a recent visit to the National Gallery. This painting was hung in her school with a painting she had done of Stephen Lawrence alongside it."

"This is amazing, especially if it was done by a schoolgirl. Ahinee was my mother's name too, as you know. You remember your gran? I'm glad you found that book, Bella." Mina's eyes were moist.

"The Christ figure is African because that is how Ahinee imagined him as a child, and the imagery reflects Psalm 'The Lord is my Shepherd'. This painting was done in Stephen's memory, and shown to his mother by the head teacher.

The second painting of Mother Africa was done many years later, when Ahinee had learned a lot more about the way the continent had been raped for her riches. She describes this in detail, giving references for

her sources, and using poetry as well as painting to illustrate it all. I wonder if she's still alive today? She could be, but if so, she'll be a very old lady."

* * *

Isabella entered into everything with great enthusiasm and we found that our actors in Selly Oak, being a mixed race crowd themselves, welcomed her immediately, applauding loudly whenever she sang "The voice of Alfred." Her rendering of this song w is done that there is as an instant hit and recordings of it were played across the provinces.

There were so many different groups of singers that we came up with the idea of inviting them to create a special song called Selly Oak, which celebrated the different nationalities and cultures. So many original songs in different styles emerged that we had a problem and eventually chose to use the best three of them, accompanied by a guitar, sitar, and flute respectively. These variants were sung in the small towns they had originated in. There were four pageants in all with broadly the content much the same, but there were minor alterations. Local place names were introduced and some new scenes and songs were added at Aston, Hall Green and Long Bridge.

The pageants went so well in Selly Oak area that we had special services of dedication afterwards in the cathedral, the mosque and the Hindu temple with appropriate singing groups participating. Isabella's excellent voice caught the rhythms and the mood of the occasion beautifully. Recordings were made and sold well.

The need for resilience was soon put to the test. Flash floods hit the whole area: rivers broke their banks, many homes were flooded, villages were marooned and some people were trapped in their cars for hours. All this gave urgent meaning to the message of the pageant.

When the sunshine eventually re-appeared, the village games were reinstated. Teams were entered from most areas and a circular relay race encircled all the industrial villages on the final Saturday, starting and ending at Selly Oak. Rowing competitions were also held in decorated boats with musicians and singers going along the network of canals covering the neighbourhood, making an appropriate finale to the pageant.

* * *

The following year Judith was back again, and the pageant was at Worcester, where it was performed in a large open field beside the River Avon. There were no rowing competitions, but decorated boats floated slowly by carrying performers playing historic instruments. A town crier quoted from an ancient charter, and created amusement by reciting the old punishments for the use of unfair weights and measures in the weekly market.

A special service of dedication to duty was held afterwards in the cathedral, with town choirs participating. Short versions of this later toured neighbouring towns and villages to remind the whole county of the need to pull its weight in times of deprivation. This pattern was repeated later in most of the yearly pageants.

After the performances local teams were thanked for their service to the community in recent storms, and awards were given to individuals who had risked their lives helping people to escape disasters. There was always a fun-fare and an open sports day to round off these events.

* * *

Rupert was due to leave school in 2081, so he was considering his future at this time. His strong interests in the natural world led him to explore degrees in environmental studies and I gave him several prospectuses to look at. He disappeared into his bedroom and we saw nothing of him till lunchtime.

"I've read through those leaflets and searched the internet too," he told us. "I'd done that before anyway and I like the course at Newcastle University. Their Environment Degree looks fab. Better than what's on offer anywhere in Mercia, and I don't want to go to London. I know it'll be expensive if I live in Northumbria, but I could probably get a part-time job up there and help with the expenses. Will you look at it, Dad, and let me know what you think?"

"Of course I will, and I'll talk it over with Adam Samphire too. It's his line, so he must know a lot more about environment degrees than I do."

Rupert had always been keen on this subject, and we both wanted the best for him but, with the educational grants being tight and provincial councils being so competitive, I didn't know what his chances were of getting permission to study in Northumbria. The trend for the last twenty years had been to study locally, whenever possible. Mounting costs now meant that students needed permits to study in another province. As Adam was the Tamcaster Environment Officer, he was well placed to know the score and he proved to be very supportive.

"Professor Blane at Newcastle is the top man in environment studies, now that old Parker's retired from Oxford. Your credentials will stand in Rupert's favour," he told me. "The role that Isabella played in Selly Oak will be recalled as well. You and your family are building up a reputation in this field, Rory, so I think the chances of Rupert getting a permit are quite strong."

"You make it sound like nepotism," I said. "If Rupert needs to earn a permit to study in another province, he must surely do this in his own right, not on the basis of his family connections."

"True, but my guess is that the headmaster of Arkwright will give him a strong recommendation and that's what counts with these permits. Rupert knows his stuff. We've been out together on so many field trips, so I know his strengths in this area."

This was encouraging, but it threw up a contrast with Brandon that was painful to contemplate. Our younger son had become very moody and showed no interest in any of our family pursuits these days. I could not help wondering if it was because both Mina and I were already so absorbed in planning the Worcester pageant. Rupert had been an enthusiastic property-master for us at Selly Oak and this had meant that Brandon had been left to his own devices for a while, but he seemed to be contented. I knew he had a circle of friends at school, so we were not unduly concerned for him.

1981 was the year that Rupert left home for his new life in Northumbria. He passed his exams well in his last year at Arkwright. Several of his classmates went on to universities. Most of them went to Tamcaster, but others went to universities in Coventry, Warwick and Worcester. Rupert was the only one to win a permit to go to another province. He telephoned and sent us some brief emails giving essential details about his new surroundings, and an enthusiastic letter landed in our drone zone two weeks later. Below are a few extracts:-

"I like living in Newcastle. It's a bustling city, and it's interesting to find myself acclimatising to another province. Nearly all of the other students are from Northumbria, but as it is the largest province in Britannia, some of them come from places as far as away as Liverpool or Sheffield. They have a range of local accents, and I have to listen carefully to catch what they are saying, but they're a friendly bunch. Most come from the areas around here; places like Tyneside or Sunderland, and I'm getting used to the weird lingo, but there are one or two from other countries. There is a feisty girl on my course from Scotland who calls herself Catreena, but she spells it Catriona.

My special friend is Aidan, a local lad. We're sharing a flat together in a block of student accommodation in a converted factory overlooking a busy town square. We have our own bedrooms, but share a sitting room, bathroom, and mini-kitchen. Some people have single flats (rich chaps – have to be!), but most live in groups of two or three. There is a great communal lounge next to the refectory in our building, and it's there that we all get to know one another, play table tennis or pool, or chat over a drink - coffee or tea in the daytime, or perhaps something stronger at night - but don't worry. We can't afford much alcohol on the allowances we get!" ...

And later:-

"I'm getting stuck into Environmental Studies now. We have a massive reading list – six pages long – would you believe, but the key books are underlined, so I am starting there. The three lecturers I have are all quite good – two women and one man, who is Scottish and speaks very quickly. Sometimes I get lost in my note taking and have to appeal to Cat to help me out. She doesn't like being called Cat, but I'm still trying to

get my tongue round the "riona" bit. Talking of Iona reminds me that Aidan is very struck by the place. Apparently it's an island off the west coast of Scotland, and Aidan is always going on about it. He says that in Anglo-Saxon times, round about when Elfleda came to Tamcaster, there was this monk who was invited to come from Iona to convert all the Northumbrians to Christianity. (A big task, I should think as they were pagans at the time.) Anyway, my flat-mate is called after him, and he tells me he's a Celtic Christian, so he and I are going to spend next week-end camping on an island called Lindisfarne, somewhere further north. Aidan says it's a fab. place and it's where the other Aidan set up shop doing the conversion job. To get there you have to walk over the sands at low tide following a line of poles. I think that probably the first Aidan must have wanted to keep the numbers down. Perhaps that's why he chose such a remote refuge. They call this walk through the sands "The Pilgrim's Way." Aidan says we have to do this, not get the bus that goes over a causeway at low tide. That's cheating. You've got to do the walk quickly at the right time of day, because the tide comes in with a rush, so my next letter will tell you about our adventures on a holy island. If I manage to get back that is!"

Rupert enjoyed writing letters, although that was most unusual these days, and after the first two months they stopped coming, but he seemed to enjoy Holy Island as he went there three times. He seemed to like Catriona too, because he kept mentioning her in his random emails. Mina said he must be quite smitten with her.

We had pageants in Hereford and Shrewsbury in the following two years, which kept us very busy.

Wolverhampton was the setting for our next multi-cultural pageant. Isabella was specialising in skills for film production so she and a group of colleagues were able to make a permanent record of the Wolverhampton Pageant. This included a new character, Lady Wolfrun, a local Anglo-Saxon woman, who we featured on horseback alongside Elfleda. Brenda Collins, the town mayor, played this role. It was very appropriate, as she was one of our staunch supporters and was in a good position to oversee the essential training courses that followed.

Isabella graduated in the following summer, but she was immediately caught up in the new requirement to perform three years of community service. When she told the interviewers about her degree and the fact that she had made a film of the Wolverhampton Pageant, they decided that the best use of her talents would be in the Mercian Publicity Department. She was assigned to join a small team based in rooms alongside the Performing Arts Department of Tamcaster University. This made us very happy, as we did not lose her to another province.

She specialised in making low budget films about ordinary people who did extraordinary things. One example was in relationship between people, animals and the environment, because animals can alert us to changes in the atmosphere. Another topic was the influence of music on people's bravery and ability to cope when stressed, and yet another was the link between people and their neighbourhood, be it wide open spaces in the countryside or a dense urban environment. All these issues were relevant to the pageants we were preparing.

From this time onward the pageants were demonstrations of community involvement, and in the next one, at Gloucester, community safety groups performed in their team uniforms rather than in unusual costumes. Despite the fact that this was August, thick hailstones rained down on the assembled company, and players had to retire for an hour before the conditions allowed the performance to continue before a somewhat diminished audience.

Unlike Isabella and Rupert, Brandon had always been something of a rebel. He refused to accept our values. His attitude became more stubborn as he went through puberty.

He found his own group of friends at school and they were not ones who followed the mainstream. He attached himself to 'The Park Crowd' at Arkwright. Most of these youngsters lived in the Castle Park private estate, and earned themselves the derogatory nickname of "The Selfies".

One of the leaders of this group was Nathan Seagrave, grandson of the man who had led the opposition Freedom Party in the Council Hall for so long. A small group of admirers always surrounded Nathan. They wore clothes from a fashion house in Queen St. The unofficial uniform consisted of a pure white silk shirt, a thin black tie and school blazer above black trousers shaped tight enough to grip their legs. They also had their hair cropped, and were known by the others as "Retro Skinheads."

"I'm sorry that you've chosen Nathan as a friend," I told Brandon. "I've heard that he bullies some of the younger boys in school."

"Who told you that?" Brandon demanded.

"I've heard it from several quarters," I told him.

"Oh, Dad. You shouldn't take notice of idle gossip. You've told me that yourself."

"It's not idle gossip, Brandon. I've heard it from teachers who are very concerned about his behaviour."

"Which teachers?"

"I'm not going to give you names. Just believe me and behave sensibly."

Brandon did not appear to take any notice of my warnings.

Things came to a head one evening when he told me he had been invited to Nathan Seagrave's birthday party. He asked me for a lift there and back, so with some reluctance, I booked a pool car and arranged to collect him at 11pm.

As the councillor lived in one of the Castle Park gated residences, I had to show the invitation to the armed guard at the park gates just below the castle cliff. When I got to the right avenue the din from the party was vibrating across the whole neighbourhood.

"Is this row why the Park residents pay so much to live here?" I joked.

"What?" asked Brandon. I repeated my observation.

"This row. Is that what they pay for?" I shouted above the din.

"Are you referring to the music?" he asked.

"Is that what you call it?" I yelled.

"Of course. Nathan always hires the loudest band."

I drew up halfway up the long avenue, but within site of the mansion.

"Nip out here. I'll see you at eleven." I reversed the car and opened the door. "Have a good evening," I said. I don't know whether Brandon heard my remark above the noise, but he just disappeared into the night.

When I returned at eleven the noise was even worse. I could hear it as soon as I opened the window to show the invitation again to the night watchman at the gate.

"How do you stand this racket?" I asked him.

"Used to it," he remarked. "This place is full of young ravers."

I was surprised. I'd always thought of the Castle Park as quiet spot, and assumed that was what people paid for.

I drove on to the Seagrave mansion and up their private drive, got out and rang the doorbell, but there was such a racket going on that I never expected anyone to hear it, so I walked round the side of the house. All the lights were blazing and I caught glimpses of youngsters snogging on the sofas. A French window was open at the back of the house and people were spilling on to the lawn and disappearing in the bushes.

I could see Brandon was in the room, chatting to a girl in an of-the-shoulder gown. They both had wine glasses in their hands and were guffawing with laughter. There was no sign of any adults around, but I thought I would be tactful.

"Hi, Bran. I said I'd come back to collect you around eleven. I've got the car on the drive."

Brandon stared at me through bleary eyes. "Collect me. The party's only just getting going. It may be your bedtime, Dad, but it's not mine."

The girl laughed.

"But you asked me to come..." I started.

"That was before I joined the delectable Priscilla here."

They both roared with laughter.

"Bye bye, dad," Brandon sputtered, as he took a deep swig of wine.

"Well I kept my word...and I can't wait all night."

"No you can't," the girl said. "You weren't on the invitation list. We don't have oldies at our parties."

"How are you going to get home then?"

Brandon stared at me as if I was a stranger. My heart sank.

"Look Dad," he said. "I'm not a child. Nathan will probably lend me one of his cars tomorrow."

"You haven't passed a driving test. I think I'd better speak to Councillor Seagrave."

"My father isn't here. He and my mother are at their other house in Southfield Park.

They don't interfere with our parties," the girl said. "Tomorrow morning Brandon will be driven back by one of our chauffeurs. That's always the practice here. Good night, Mr. Whiteoak."

I was taken aback, at her insolence, and hesitated how to reply.

"Did you hear what I said, teacher?" the girl responded.

"For God's sake, take care, you two. I'm worried for you both!"

With that I turned tail and went back to the car, but I left the mansion grounds with a very heavy heart. I felt I had completely lost my youngest son, and I could not help blaming myself .*Whatever did he see in that little madam? Had I spoilt him? How had this happened? Surely, I'd treated him like Isabella and Rupert. Neither of them would ever have behaved like this. Where had I gone wrong?*

* * *

I did not sleep that night. I spent the whole time tossing and turning, much to the annoyance of Mina. When I explained things in the morning, she was as concerned as I was. Brandon did not return until 2pm next day. We were nearing the end of the Sunday roast, when he pounded through the front door and ran upstairs, shouting that he did not want any lunch and banged his door shut.

We looked at one another.

"What's bitten him?" queried Isabella.

"We had some words last night," I said.

"And I'll have a few words to say to him later," said Mina.

"How did Brandon seem to get on with his schoolmates?" I asked Rupert, who was back home for the summer break, and full of enthusiasm for Newcastle University.

"It depends what you mean by schoolmates?" he replied.

"Tell me more?" I pursued, realising that my regular periods of leave from Arkwright Academy to work on the pageants must have made me out of touch with upper school developments. I was now teaching younger students.

"Well, things were beginning to get a bit tribal, by the time I left."

"How do you mean – tribal?"

"Well, he was always two forms below me, of course, but I thought he seemed to mix in all right, but there were two sets in the upper school when I was there and I doubt if it's changed all that much. There were 'the greenies' and the 'selfies', and the between lot; the tweenies were most of the class actually. The sets seemed to be getting more fixed though by the time I left."

"Fixed - who by?"

"The main influences were the Seagraves - Nathan and Priscilla; there's no doubt about that. They chose the in-crowd, but in my day, it was really a matter of whether you lived in a gated estate or whether you were a townie with a green agenda."

"And need that make any difference?"

"It shouldn't and it didn't used to. I wasn't aware of it much anyway, not until my last year."

"What happened then?"

"I don't know. Obviously with the terrible weather we were having the greenies formed the school action groups to assist where they're needed. The 'selfies' just opted out."

"They won't be able to do that when they're eighteen, and they're enlisted for three years community service."

"That's what they're against, so they'll try to get postponement or exemption."

"That sort of thing didn't happen when I was at school," said Isabella "and I don't find any evidence of it at Theatre School either."

"At Arkwright everything was influenced by the Seagrave lot. It was Gustave in my day." Rupert was adamant about this.

"And where was Brandon in all this?"

There was no reply.

I looked hard at Rupert. He blushed slightly. "Sorry Dad, I can't answer that one. I don't think he knows himself. We used to be quite close you know. He was my little brother, but since I came home from Uni. he doesn't speak to me unless you or Mom are around. He just turns his back and walks away when I come in the room."

"How do you find him, Bella?" Mina asked anxiously.

"He's just the same with me," she said.

"Hey, we can't have this. Not in this family?" I was stunned. "Why didn't you say something before - either one of you?"

"I didn't think it was such a big deal, Dad," said Rupert.

"I think he's just moody. After all he's still going through puberty remember. Hormones and all that," Isabella affirmed.

"Perhaps he doesn't feel he belongs anywhere. We'll have to change that," said Mina.

"How?" asked Isabella.

"I'll go an' talk to him. You others leave it to me."

Amina:

I left him for an hour and then I went up to Brandon's room and tapped on the door. I heard a grunt, so I opened the door and saw Brandon fully clothed but lying on the bed.

"What's the matter, son," I said. "Why you no come down?" (I was speaking in a lingo I used when the children were small. It just occurred instinctively when I spoke to the little ones. I think it was a fond memory I had of my mother's voice, as she struggled with English, but I had not used it for many years).

"Oh Mom," he said. "I'm not a kid. Let me be."

"Then why you behave like little kid. Tell me dat.?"

"I dunno. There's so many things. Life is so difficult."

"What 'tings?"

There was no reply. He turned his head to the wall. I sat on the bed.

"What's troublin' you, Brandy."

"Everything. I don't know who I am."

"You is Brandon Whiteoak. You're mi' son and you're ye Dad's son too."

"I'm not sure of anything... Things have moved in me... I 've crossed the rubicon."

"What rubicon?"

"I can't explain."

"You'se got a bit of explainin' to do to you're Dad. You owe apology. He very upset."

"Is he?" Brandon looked up at me.

"Yes, he wants talk to you, but I said I would first."

"Why? And why are you talking in that old lingo, like you did when I was little?"

"Because you'se brought me back to my ol'e roots, an' they're deep inside me."

"Why should I apologise to Dad?"

"Because you and that girl were very rude to him. He promised to come to bring you home at eleven. He went in the car, and you and that girl sent him packing, Do you think that was a nice thing to do?"

"You don't understand. You can't. No one can. "

"Well I'll leave you now to sort yourself out. Come down and see your father. I'll be there too. We can talk things through like a sensible family. I give you one hour an' if you don't appear, we'll be back."

With that I left.

Rory:

Brandon came down an hour later but instead of come into the room where Mina and I were, he went into the lounge. When I came into the room, he was sitting with his head in his hands. I asked him if anything was wrong.

"Sorry if I was rude last night," he said slowly. "I had a lot on my mind."

"I think you'd had too much to drink," I said . "Oh Brandon, don't let things get you down. Perhaps we should talk things over."

"No." he said. "Things changed last night. You won't understand. There was so much that happened."

"You went to a party and got boozed, Brandon. That's what happened, and perhaps you went too far with that girl. You really must learn to be more responsible."

"No. I knew you'd get it all wrong. You couldn't possibly understand, Dad. You live in a different world."

"Yes, I do, and I'm glad of it. I wouldn't like to live in that Castle Park place."

"But I would Dad. That's just it. Why can't we live like that? Plenty of other people do."

"What other people?"

"My class mates. The Seagrave crew. I joined them last night at the initiation party."

"You what?" I gazed at him in astonishment. "My God, was she part of the initiation?" My heart sank into my boots.

"NO, no… of course not. That got nothing to do with it. That was afterwards."

"After what!"

"I knew you wouldn't understand. They're a closed order. It's a great honour to be invited. And they wanted me to join them and I did because I wanted to. Nobody forced me to do anything."

"And what do you think this means?" I croaked.

"It changes everything. I've chosen a different path. I'm fed up with it all, the austerity. Measuring the energy we use! Living sustainably, as you call it. You see yourself as a community leader. Well, who's following? Only the people without any real ambition to get on in the world."

"So what do you propose to do - now you've gone through this 'initiation' into the Seagrave empire?"

" I don't know yet, but I'll let you know when I do. I can tell you what I'll not be doing, though. I'll not be going to a theatre arts course like Isabella. I will not be dressing up to take part in sham parades about the Anglo-Saxons, who lived like pigs thousands of years ago. I'll probably leave Mercia altogether. There's no real future here. I'll probably go to London and train to be a merchant banker or something like that. I mean to get on in the world. I don't want to spend my life play-acting!"

"Is that what you think your mother and I are doing? I've never imposed my life-style on you. It's a free world."

"Is it? It feels free to you because you're a provincial councillor. You think you can set standards and keep people in their places, rationing the good things of life."

"What good things?"

"The alcohol for a start. The food we choose to eat, only locally sourced. Measuring the electricity we use for transport and lighting. Why don't you have a car? Why do we always have to borrow a pool car, and use candles n winter nights. I was ashamed last night to be collected at 11pm. by my Dad in a borrowed car."

"But you asked me to come."

"No I didn't. You suggested it. You said 'How are you going to get home?' I said I didn't know. You said 'I'll collect you then. What time? Ten o'clock.' I said 'Not earlier than eleven.' "

"Well perhaps that's right. I'm not sure, but you were the one who mentioned eleven."

"That was because you said. 'Mother doesn't get to sleep while you're still out.' That's how you manage to control your family, isn't it, telling us to be models of yourselves? Rupert may have fallen for it, and Isabella, but I haven't, Dad, and you'd better remember that."

"Yes, Brandon, we have standards, and we try to pass them on to our children. I'm a schoolteacher, remember, and so is your mother. We do our best to help shape the next generation, because we live in a finite world, and if all people lived in the extravagant way that some westerners do, we would need five planets to provide the resources. Mom and I would never go away and leave our children to run wild, like Councillor Seagrave did last night. I call that utterly irresponsible."

"We aren't children and we weren't alone in the house. We had a team

413

of servants at our command, and transport home was provided this morning in a stretch limo to all of last night's revellers. That's the chauffeur's job. That's what he's paid for."

Brandon suddenly jumped up and rushed to the door. "I need fresh air. I'm going for a walk on the heath. It's stifling here!"

I collapsed in the bedroom chair, profoundly shaken. Had I been blind? I had never seen anything like this coming to hit us.

Half an hour later I talked it through with Mina. She was more dismayed than I was.

"But why?" she kept saying. "I don't understand. He's never talked to me about these things. I haven't had a decent conversation with him this year. We had no problems with Isabella and Rupert, but whenever I try to talk to Brandon, he slopes off into his room saying he's a load of school work to do. But then I hear this loud music booming out. How can he concentrate on his studies through that racket?"

"It's a cyclic, generational thing," I said. "My Dad accused me of that. Youngsters imbibe background noise without letting it take over the conscious mind. The trouble is that this leaves them vulnerable to subliminal messages."

We could not help worrying.

"Brandon's a sort of throw-back," Rupert mused. "He's living in a bygone age along with so many of those people in gated communities. They're just in denial about the true state of the world. I don't know what goes on inside his head any more than you do. Of course Nathan Seagrave must be a powerful influence in his class at school, and his twin sister too."

We remained very unsure about Brandon, who continued living in a world of his own.

It was very difficult because Mina and I were deeply involved in the Shrewsbury Pageant, which meant that we had to be away from home frequently during the week. Fortunately though, Isabella was working from home now, so Brandon was not alone in the house.

We all tried our best to get through to Brandon and explore what he would like to do when he left school. He never applied himself well to studies and was clearly not interested in higher education. Maths was his best subject and his interests seemed to be in the material world. He wanted to be able to live comfortably and enjoy life. His ideas seemed to revolve around investment banking, so towards the end of his last year at school, at my suggestion, he prepared a C.V. and posted it to several banks with a short letter expressing interest in employment opportunities.

He was interviewed at two of them, and one offered him a post as a trainee. They wanted him to start work on a trial basis in August, just when we were most busy in Shrewsbury, and frequently had to stay overnight.

Mina told me that he came back home on the first day rather dejected and, over the next few days, she could get little out of him. He set out to work at the same time each morning, but the following week when we were both staying in Shrewsbury, he completely disappeared.

Isabella told us that he slipped out of the house early in the morning before she was up and about. He had left a note in his bedroom, which read as follows:-

"That bank job did not suit me, but I have a much better offer now in London. I will be working for Nathan's father and living in one of his apartments there for the next three months. Councillor Seagrave has lots of contacts and is going to arrange for me to train with a hedge-fund manager. Best wishes, Brandon."

CHAPTER 32 - The Metropolis

Rory:

In 2083 the Global Organisation for Sustainability held the most important international conference ever on world stability. The ten-year plan to assist the nine failed states had been moderately successful in seven of them. It was agreed that additional resources should be made available to assist the two countries still struggling. The others would all have democratic elections next year to elect their own governments. These elections would be supervised by GOS and it was now planned that the other two countries would be given increased support; sufficient to enable them to hold democratic elections in five years time.

Furthermore, the conference issued a statement encouraging a world vegetarian diet. There had been much discussion on this issue over the last twenty years or so. The amount of land needed for provision of fodder for cattle, pigs, goats and other such animals, no longer existed. The seas could not provide enough edible fish to meet the needs of those who liked seafood. So the conference recommended a gradual phasing out of meat and fish consumption over the next ten years. Most governments welcomed this advice. Enlightened groups held celebratory parties across the world. It was the first indication of almost total cooperation on these issues, although a few eccentrics began some artificial manufacturing of meats developed from body parts obtained from animals, but fortunately this idea did not prove popular.

Turning to our own domestic matters, Mina and I were delighted when we received an invitation to see Rupert receive his award of a Degree in Environmental Studies. We travelled by solar air-bus to Newcastle and were introduced to his special friends from the student fraternity, Catriona Murray, a delightful Scottish girl, and Aidan Crosby, with whom he shared a flat.

Catriona was a striking girl, with a Viking build, blonde hair and a quiet, determined manner. Seeing her alongside our dark-skinned son was quite a striking contrast. Aidan was a cheerful young man, with a Geordie accent and a bright sense of humour. All three received the same award, and were keen to find employment that enabled them to spread the message of a simple lifestyle. There was quite a scramble for this type of work now, because the wild weather of the last three years had forced the local authorities to make many more sustainable community appointments. Environmental safety was now the most important department in all the provincial councils. What was once called freak weather was now so common that every area had to be prepared, with trained staff and their volunteer teams ready for all disasters. Northumbria was the worst hit province in Britannia, and Scotland suffered in similar ways.

Environmental employment was one of the few categories of work that earned exemption from community service. It was rightly considered to be another form of essential public service, so these young graduates were free to find work immediately in this field, while students who had completed other courses usually had to delay their careers until the end of their three-year community service commitment.

After the awards ceremony Rupert and Catriona joined us for dinner at our hotel.

I asked Rupert if he had any employment offers yet, following his big canvassing exercise.

"No firm ones," he answered. "Obviously Catriona and are both applying for similar jobs, and we'd like to find them in the same area, but it just depends what's available and where?"

"And how about you, Catriona?" Mina asked her.

"Och, I'm in much the same position as Rupert," she said. "I'd prefer to work in Scotland if it's possible. I know my parents are of that mind too, but I'll have tae go where the work is. I like living here in Northumbria, but I've nae yet been to Mercia or any other Britannic provinces."

Rupert looked up from his study of the menu, to explain. "One possibility is that we might be able to work for an agency which operates on both sides of the border. Northumbria and Scotland have to liaise closely together because storms don't recognise boundaries, There's a joint water company and an advisory body that offers services in both areas. Catriona and I intend to live together, if at all possible, but it depends partly on the work we can get. It's great that you're here, because we both wanted you to meet Catriona before we tied everything up."

Catriona's eyes sparkled. "I've introduced Rupert to my parents, and that went well, I'm glad to say, so that's one hurdle over."

"I like them," said Rupert, "We all seem to get on fine. They live in a lovely old manse in Fife. Catriona's father's a minister in a Scottish kirk."

"Is he now, and where's the parish?" I asked.

"Och, you've probably no heard o' the place. It a wee toun called Culross on the banks of the Forth, and it's a quaint spot for a Sunday outing. They still have the old cobbled streets and pan-tiled red roofs on the cottages. It's a sleepy toun that's nae' changed in three hundred years or more. My Dad has been there now for ten years or so, and they're settled down there ye could say, but he could be moved somewhere else. Ye no' can tell with the kirk authorities."

"Culross looks like an old film set," said Rupert. "It's a historic museum of a place, preserved carefully by the Scottish National Trust as an example of seventeenth century cottage architecture."

"I don't suppose there'll be many jobs going there, then."

"No, but I fell in love with Culross, as well as Catriona," joked Rupert, "Work in Scotland would probably be with one of the agencies in Edinburgh or Glasgow. In Northumbria, there could be jobs in the capital, York. But it's a huge province and we may have to go further south like Sheffield or Liverpool to find two posts, but there's just a chance that something might develop here in Newcastle. That would suit us well, because it's not too far from the border."

We liked the look and the sound of Catriona, so Mina and I had to accept the fact that Rupert would probably be living and working far away from us.

This fact made us keener than ever to try to make contact with Brandon again.

He was still in London, and when we telephoned him he was very evasive.

He was now eighteen, the age for compulsory community service in Mercia. This could be deferred until after completion of a training or higher education course, but he was not doing this either. The Mercian authorities had not chased him. That seemed odd to me. I was rather hoping they would. It should open his eyes to the real world we lived in.

I made some discreet enquiries about him one day when I met Councillor Seagrave.

He told me that Brandon was a good worker and doing quite well for himself in London. He said had helped the boy because he was a friend of Nathan's and seemed to be at a loose end in Tamcaster. He went on to say that Brandon had requested help over finding work. He was now an adult, so it was up to him where he lived. This was no doubt true, but it left both Mina and me deeply unhappy.

The upshot was that, after few weeks, I decided to go to London, stay with an old friend, and see how Brandon was faring. When I telephoned Brandon and told him when I was coming and he said he would try to meet me at the solar-port, but could not be certain about that, and I heard nothing later. I tried phoning him again but Brandon was always out and all could only leave a message on his line with the time of the solar-bus arrival.

I knew London must be very changed since I had last been there. We now had a republic, with an elected, non-political president dividing his time between Buckingham Palace and Chequers. The Prime Minister, State Government and National Assembly were all based in Reading. Buckingham Palace gardens were open for visitors and the old houses of parliament were a museum and so was the whole of Downing St.

The journey to London was very different from the one I had made to Northumbria. Instead of flying over miles of desolate land, ruined by fracking, I found myself viewing wide, open fields and stretches of woodland, although acres of land were devoted to both wind and solar farms.

As I approached London though, I passed over miles of suburban development until I came to a massive construction site, where contractors were working on a huge engineering project to develop the Great Sliding Dome, which aims to enclose the whole metropolis from Harrow to Croydon. Lines of huge transparent arches were standing like walls guarding the capital city, waiting their turn to be installed. Alongside them were thousands of sheets of transparent roofing. I had heard on TV that the eastern boundary would be just east of Tilbury on the north of the river and Gravesend on the south. This vast structure is supposed to be rolled over the area whenever air pollution or wild weather threaten to endanger the city, but it can't be tested until the whole project is completed, in three years time. It will require an elaborate system of cooling and ventilation whenever it is applied in the summer and a warming system in the winter.

The cost and extravagant use of energy is supposed to be offset in other ways, but serious environmentalists have grave doubts about whether this scheme can really be justified. Seeing it confirmed all my worst prejudices.

Brandon did not meet me as I had requested, so I had to find my own way to the address he had given me. After making enquires, I left the airport and found a line of electric streetcars drawn up near the entrance, labelled with their destinations in alphabetical order. It did not take long to find the one heading to the Barbican. I pressed the button to open the door, and a mechanical voice said "You cannot open the door without your journey card."

I asked advice from a man near me and he pointed to a robot by the station entrance, which produced metal bus cards for each destination, whenever the right token was inserted in its mouth. I bought one from another machine alongside, and eventually entered the unmanned vehicle, which was half full. More passengers kept arriving, but once the last seat was occupied, the mechanical voice announced "Leaving Euston Station," and the streetcar started on its journey.

Looking through the windows, I was shocked to see so many beggars squatting on the pavements; some were mothers with young children, and they all had pendants with numbers on, attached to a string round the neck. In contrast, the passengers in the streetcar were well dressed and behaved, but no one aboard or outside seemed to notice the beggars.

Looking round, I saw a map of our journey was printed on the ceiling above, and observed that, when someone wished to leave the streetcar at the next stop, they pressed a buzzer on the back of the seat in front of them. The name of the stop was announced, and the car then stopped at the next appointed place. The doors opened automatically, closing after the passenger had left, and then the vehicle resumed its rumbling journey.

All this happened without assistance from any member of staff. I found it strangely impersonal. Most of the passengers were reading books or looking at the computer viewing frames that they carried on their chests, held in position by a collar and lead system. Nobody spoke throughout the entire journey, which lasted twenty-five minutes, according to my watch.

The journey ended by a huge, towering block of buildings marked BARBICAN. Being the terminus, everyone left the vehicle here, and I entered the building through great iron gates, walked passed some shops and taverns and took a lift up to the eighth floor, where the apartment was supposed to be. After walking round a seeming half-mile of corridors, I eventually found Number 410. The name Seagrave was engraved in golden letters on the door.

I pressed the button of the imposing intercom system. A mechanical voice asked me my name and business. After I had responded, the voice said "You may enter the vestibule," and the door slid quietly open. As I stepped forward, my feet sank into a thick pile carpet of a richly furnished sitting area, which stank of rich living.

The mechanical voice told me that I could sit down and wait. "Someone will attend to you as soon as possible," I was told.

After about three minutes, an inner door opened and a dejected looking young black woman appeared, dressed in a drab uniform of a grey coat and trousers. She wore a numbered pendant round her neck.

"Can I help you, sir?" she asked in a foreign accent.

"Yes, I hope you can. I have come to see my son, Brandon Whiteoak, who I believe is staying here," I told her.

"Mr Whiteoak said that you might come, and that he would be back around three o' clock. Can I bring you something to drink?"

As my watch told me it was 2.45, I said, "Yes please."

"What wine would you like? We have a big selection."

"Have you? A cup of tea would suit me better."

"Very good sir." She gave a bow and departed.

I looked round the room again. It was colourfully decorated, and the furnishings were all expensive, with rich cushions on the sofa and some paintings on the wall, each signed by the artist. They looked as if they might be originals. Two were water-colours of London streets, and one was a nondescript modern work, done by a man whose creations was reputed to fetch very high prices. I thought it looked uninspired.

I went over to the windows, and found they wee firmly locked. The outside view was of identical tower blocks.

The servant returned with a tea tray.

"Mr Brandon may wish to join you in the teas," she quaintly observed.

I thanked her and, as she turned to go, I asked her what country she came from.

"I am just A.S." she said, looking embarrassed. "May I pour your tea?"

"Don't say just A.S." I said with a smile. "Alien Status is nothing to be ashamed of. How long have you been in Britannia, and how do you like it here?"

"It is better than the camp, I think," she said shyly.

"That's good," I said. "No sugar please. Since Brandon isn't here yet, would you like to have some tea yourself?"

"Oh no. I can't. Not allowed. Cup is for Mr Brandon. I must leave you."

"What is your name?"

"I was Number 255 in the camp. Here, they call me skivvy."

"255. Oh, I see now. That's the number on that label you wear. I'm a stranger in these parts, so please forgive me if I ask any questions that you don't wish to answer, but I noticed others in the streets outside wearing labels. Do you have to wear that tally all the time?"

"It is the law for AS people. If we do not wear, the police can arrest us and send us back."

"Ah, I understand. I see you would not like that, so you feel you are better off here, do you?"

"Here, I have shelter and food. I am told I can eat as much as I like. I have never been told that before."

"That's good. I can see it in your eyes. Your label reads SP 82 - 255. May I ask what that means?"

"SP means Stateless Person. 82 is the year I was processed in Britannia."

"You had no papers when you arrived, I suppose. Is that why you are classified as stateless?" She nodded.

"Excuse me. I don't mean to pry, but what country did you come from?"

"My mother came from Somalia. I was born in camp in Italy. Excuse. I must go."

"Thank you." But she was already disappearing through the inner door. I would like to have asked her where in Italy. It was a pity that she was so shy, and I hoped my questions had not worried her.

Brandon arrived about five minutes later, looking more paunchy than I had seen him when he left home. There were bags under his eyes, and he appeared artificially jolly.

"Hello, Dad," he greeted me. "Sorry I didn't have time to meet you. I had a business engagement. I knew you'd easily find your way here. No one can miss the Barbican."

"Do you want some tea?" I asked him.

"No. Never drink the stuff," he laughed. "We've got a great wine cellar here, you know."

"So I was told by the maid. How are you keeping?"

"I'm fine, Dad. Never felt better. It's such a weight off my shoulders living here. Honestly, you should try it. It's another world."

"So I see. Who's living in this apartment, apart from you?"

"No one permanently, except the skivvy of course, but people come and go from all over the world. The apartment belongs to Nathan's granddad. He's an old man now, and he doesn't come much on weekdays."

"I remember him well. He was leader of the Freedom Party when I came to live in Tamcaster. His son, Gerald, became party leader in Tamcaster when he retired to London. He's Nathan's dad. It's quite a dynasty."

"He's the boss here now. He keeps the place, so that he can entertain businessmen and he's here every other weekend to meet someone or other. Some of these people stay for weekdays, and Nathan and Priscilla both come and go too, but I'm the resident manager, and I'm also working part time as PA to a hedge-fund manager. He's training me in the art of making money. It's amazing. It can be done with a few quick phone calls, if you know the ropes. But this apartment's fabulous. Come and have a look. I'll show you round."

Brandon's enthusiasm devastated me. It was a transformation. He seemed restored to his old vitality and friendliness, but I was shocked at so many things that he was saying and showing me.

"And how are you, Bran? You've put a bit of weight on. I suppose you're not short of food here."

"No way. We have an account with Portland Ltd. and they do regular weekly deliveries. Priscilla does the ordering and she understands what we need for all these visitors. She has cook books from around the world."

"Does she? And where does Priscilla live?"

"She's got a room here next to mine, and she's got another one in Park Lane and she's there now."

"Does she do the cooking?"

"Heavens, no. We have agency cooks chosen by Priscilla. Chinese, American, Russian. Greek. It depends who is coming to stay."

"And who does all the cleaning? This place is spotless, I must say."

"Well the skivvy's here all the time and she does the rounds, but if we have a group staying, we bring in extra help."

"I'm sure the skivvy will appreciate that. Does she have a name?"

"No, they don't, you know. It's easier to have numbers. The police can keep a check on them that way, but come and take a look round, Dad. Its quite a place, this."

He led me to a large, airy room with gold coloured furnishings, and glass doors opening onto a railed balcony on one side and a monstrously large TV wall on the other. Sofas and armchairs were scattered around.

"We call this the Amber Room," Brandon announced. "It's our drawing room, where we relax round the cocktail cabinet. Just look at the panoramic views through the window: all those skyscrapers. It blows my mind. We have some great parties in this room, and Pris and I often relax here in the evenings, when she isn't entertaining somewhere else."

"Are Priscilla and you good friends these days?" I asked tentatively.

There was a slight pause. Then he beamed his artificial smile again and said, "'Course we are, Dad. It's like Britannia and the United States. We're in a special relationship."

"And this suits you both, does it?"

"Never been happier. Next, we have the swimming pool. Just look at this. We call it the Neptune Room."

Brandon swung open a door. It was the neatest pool I had ever seen, complete with diving board, six changing cubicles along one wall and mirrors on the ceiling. On the opposite wall was a blue wall featuring a hand-painted scene of Neptune surrounded by mermaids.

"That was painted for us by Pracktoff." Brandon was very proud of this, although I confess I had never heard of the man.

"Really. How long did it take him?" I asked.

"No idea. It was before my time here, of course, but the boss loves it. I believe the great man was in residence here for a while."

There was an awkward pause. Then Brandon started speaking again at a fast pace.

"On Saturdays, I usually have a morning swim before breakfast," he told me. "I find it very refreshing. It sets me up for the week-end and the whole week in fact. We have showers in the room over there, and a sauna. And then you need to see the visitor's rooms."

He showed me a lavish apartment with a king-sized bed, tub sauna, and bathroom. "We have eight suites like this," he explained. "Just look."

He took me along a corridor, where the doors were named after the planets: Mars, Venus, Saturn, Jupiter, Mercury, Neptune, Pluto and Uranus. Then he took me through a door into another corridor. "This is the private suite. That's my bedroom door, but we'd best not go in there because it's a bit untidy. I was in a hurry this morning. The next one is Priscilla's and the double doors at the end – that's Seagrave's inner apartment. The boss keeps it locked."

As we walked round these areas, I found my mood shifting to one of depression. I scarcely uttered a word.

"Oh and you must see the kitchen and the robot room. That's a hoot." Brandon opened a door, revealing a kitchen large enough for a substantial hotel, with cookers, fridges, deep freezers, worktops, cupboards and piles of utensils, cutlery, and pots and pans stacked on shelves. In the centre of the room several mechanical robots were opening packets, weighing vegetables, stirring liquids and performing cookery tasks.

"But who's all the food for?" I asked, astonished.

"Oh it's being prepared for next weekend when we have some American and Japanese businessmen coming to stay for three nights. It'll be stored in the freezer in that corner. Over there you'll see the skivvy's place. She has to watch all the machinery, so she can turn it off if anything goes wrong and clean up any mess before she switches the robots on again."

Brandon pointed to a mattress laid on the floor in an alcove. The servant girl was squatting there watching robots at work. She glanced in our direction and I waved to her with a smile. Brandon seemed not to notice her.

"Well, I guess that's it, Dad. How long are you in London? Where are you staying?"

"With an old friend of mine who lives in Richmond," I replied. "I haven't seen him for years."

"Oh, it'll be like old times then. I'm sure you'll enjoy that."

There was a pause. "How are Mom and the others?"

"Oh, they're all fine. Isabella's coming back again for a few days next week. She's been doing some filming in Coventry for the Environment Agency, and Rupert's engaged. I expect he's told you. She's a lovely Scottish girl called Catriona. Mom and I met her when we went up for the graduation."

"So everything's fixed then."

"Rupert wanted us to meet her before any decisions were made. It was nice to know that. We're very happy for them."

I was aware that there was something unnatural about this conversation. I had the distinct feeling that, now Brandon had shown me round, he was hoping I would leave soon. We were both edgy. There was so much I wanted to say to him, but I couldn't in the kitchen with the maid sitting there, eyeing the robots.

We went back into the vestibule. I sat on the sofa, and he stayed standing.

"So, are you satisfied with the choice you've made and with your life here?" I asked him.

"Completely." He folded his arms defiantly.

"Well, I'm not," I heard myself saying. "It's your life, Brandon, and we only have one life in this world. Quite honestly, I'm not comfortable here. That girl for instance, the one you call the skivvy: the one without a name. Is she being paid a wage and does she have her own room?"

"What the hell's that got to do with you? I'm sorry Dad, but that's none of your business. She's just an asylum seeker and Mr. Seagrave is helping her by providing a roof over her head and allowing her to share our food. She has a mattress in the kitchen. That's all she's ever had and she knows nothing better. Asylum seekers aren't refugees, you know. They've no status, but we tolerate them in London and let some of them work for us. They're grateful. They grovel. They have no work permits, so they can't earn wages. Honestly Dad, you don't know anything about this city. We're going to be one of the ten domed living areas in the world. London is on the same level as New York, Singapore, Beijing and all the others: protected from climate change, the same as they are. We're part of the elite."

"Oh, Brandon, I'm speechless…You're a nineteen-year-old boy. You know nothing of life, and you're being thoroughly spoiled living in this luxury. I'm amazed at Councillor Seagrave putting you in charge of all this apartment and introducing you to hedge-fund managers. It will do you no good."

"I think you'd better go, Dad."

"I am going, but I must say one more thing. You're still my son, Brandon. I'll not reject you. You have our phone number. Ring us if and when you need help. Your mother feels exactly the same as I do, and she sends her love."

I shook his hand, felt in my pocket and gave him Mina's postcard. With that, I left, seething, but a few minutes later I calmed down and thought things through.

Brandon welcomed me well at first. He was proud to be able to show me round, but when he judged my reaction, he was hurt. Now that we've both spoken our minds, perhaps he feels as upset as I do. He was so keyed up. It was unnatural. For all I know he might be in tears now. I must give him time. Then I remembered compulsory community service. *Perhaps that will change things. Once the authorities catch up with him, his eyes may be opened.*

I spent the afternoon touring the city, and visited some of the richest living areas.

What I saw there horrified me. So many of the well-dressed people in the streets were grossly obese. Huge lumbering people who struggled to walk at all. Many had resorted to pavement scooters intended for the disabled or very elderly. These were not old people though, from their faces I would say they were mostly in the forties.

I looked in at some opulent superstores and was overwhelmed by the size of these luxury palaces. There were even moving pavements to enable the obese shoppers to be able to progress along isles without the trouble of walking. When they wanted to purchase anything they stepped off the pavement on to a steady platform beside the items they were interested in. Every isle had a team of attendant asylum seekers who ran up and down collecting the code numbers for items required and giving the customer a ticket. The item was not removed from the display, so I asked a member of staff how the system worked.

"It is very smooth. Everything bought will be delivered to the customer's home later today either by robot transport or by one of our AS workers," she told me.

"Why are so many customers wearing goggles?" I asked.

"So that they can see where the product is grown. Try on a pair."

The assistant offered me a set, which was hanging on a hook by the end of display line ten, which was labelled 'Wine'. She assisted me to put them on. Immediately a moving picture appeared of lines of native workers, wearing baskets on their waistbands, moving through a plantation gathering grapes. Beneath the brief film, 'Isle Ten' was printed.

There were rows of goggles, all marked with the name of different type of wine, coffee or tea.

In Kensington Gardens, I saw a massive old woman lying on a mobile couch with wheels. It was being propelled along the side-walk by two asylum seekers, one walking in front of her and one behind, each of them holding long poles fastened to the arms. People were admiring this contraption, but it made me depressed. I felt as if I were back in the age of the sedan chair.

I came to a road called Casino Street. Everything in there was linked to gambling, gaming or money changing. I hurried away, and took a streetcar on a long journey to Richmond-on-Thames.

I stayed that night with my old friend Norman Foster and his family. It was wonderful to meet him again, after so many years. We'd been on community service together in Italy. He seemed to have done well, being settled comfortably now, with a happy family and pleasant home. After dinner, we watched TV news, which was projected directly on his dining room wall. We watched long lines of refugees from climate change disasters marching through Europe in a desperate attempt to find a place of refuge. We saw others drowning in the Mediterranean.

"I thought these dreadful days were over," I said. It was like this in the 2020's, but GOS changed all that with their massive refugee projects. You remember those times don't you."

"We were there in the good times, Rory. Too many countries are ruled by so called Freedom Parties in Europe now and their doors have closed again, so these folk keep marching on. What courage they have, poor souls."

Norman told me that it was his usual custom to take the dog for a short walk, and I offered to accompany him, as it gave us a chance to talk quietly to each other.

He and his wife had asked me about Mina and our children and I had told them proudly about Isabella and Rupert, but said little about Brandon. On this walk round the avenues, I explained the situation in the Barbican, which seemed to sum up the conflict about the two worlds we were living in.

Norman shared my feelings. "We have a good quality of life here," he said, "but there are times when I grit my teeth and feel ashamed. You and I were idealists when we did community service. We did all we could to assist refugees. The mood's totally different now. London sees itself as an international hub, rather than as part of Britannia. The city's become a kind of island here in Sussex, with its own aerodromes just outside the dome area, at Gatwick and on the Essex flats. We have no offices of state here now that parliament's in Reading, the Sussex Provincial Assembly is at Guildford, ex King William at Sandringham, and The President mainly in Chequers. No, now that London's not a capital city it's become an international metropolis, and, of course, all the provinces govern themselves. London's not controlled by the Sussex Province, you know. Their sphere of influence is limited to the old Sussex area plus Thames Valley, Kent, Surrey and Hampshire: not with the city. Personally, I don't think that's satisfactory, but that's how it is. It means that asylum seekers have no status here and that people living in the London area don't have to do community service. That's not fair, in my opinion."

My heart sank. "I think that's terrible," I said. "Community service was an eye-opener for me."

"I can echo that, but world corporate capital rules in the metropolis, just as it does in New York, Shanghai, Tokyo, Singapore, Mumbai, Sãn Paulo and a few other international business hotspots. There are five categories of human beings living in London, it seems to me: conservationists like us, who try to live within the local capacity; sponges, who absorb everything they can for themselves; drivers, who work for the sponges, and keep forcing the pace; zippies, who opt out and have their own alternative world, and serfs, who survive if they can, or simply go under."

"Tell me about the zippies. Who are they?" I asked.

"Good question. They come from all over the world and live in a crazy sort of way, but it's inspiring to mix with some of them. A hundred years ago, they'd have been called hippies or drop-outs. I call them drop ins though, because they do some very good work. A lot of them have artistic or musical backgrounds, and they tend to live communally, and they're peace-loving people. They work on the quiet to help the refugees and a.s. folk. There's a woman called Helen Silverdale who runs her 'Happy House' in a derelict factory building. She did some good work in the Peace Corps, and when she came back to London, she just carried on with it, and folk gathered round her. There are some inspiring people and places in London too. I'm learning to take life more slowly since I've met these people. It helps when everyone is in such a rush. You could go and have a look at Helen's Happy House tomorrow if you feel like it."

"I do" I said, and he gave me the address.

It was a broken down looking building, but it had been rejuvenated in a collage of bright primary colours, with signs saying 'Welcome' and 'Come and join us' round the doorway. A chubby man, dressed like a circus clown, hailed me in the doorway.

I gave him my name and said that I was a friend of Norman Foster, and he waved me into a large area, where food was piled high on a long table, and people were collecting what they fancied and moving to sit at small tables. A young man and a middle-aged woman seemed to be assisting consumers by explaining what was in the sweets and savouries, so I went over to the woman and asked her, if people could just take what they fancied.

"That's the general idea," the woman said. "This is surplus food from the superstores, which has been discarded, but it's within the 'sell by' date. We collect it, and people who can't afford the shop prices can help themselves." I noticed that several people eating at the tables wore a.s. labels, and some looked half starved.

"Is Helen Silverdale here today?" I asked.

"She's in the office. But she's interviewing some new volunteers," I was told.

"Is it all right if I have a look round? My names Rory Whiteoak, and I'm ex-Peace Corps. I'm visiting London, and a friend of mine suggested that I came to see this place."

I was introduced to Larry, the young man, who offered to show me round.

"There's quite a lot going on today," he said, as he opened a door into a well-equipped gymnasium. "This is our keep fit suite. Most of the people here can't afford to go to the privately run ones. There's no charge for coming here, because the instructors are all volunteers and the building was given to Helen when a millionaire saw what we were trying to do in very poor premises. Are you fond of singing? If so, you could join our community choir."

He opened another door, and we crept quietly into a rehearsal for a concert. The singers were an odd assortment of people, varied nationalities, old and young, fit and disabled. One young woman was obviously blind, and an elderly man was sitting in a wheelchair. One man wore turban, and a woman looked Chinese.

"They're rehearsing for a performance tomorrow in St. James's church, Piccadilly," whispered Larry. "They raise money for our project here. We get support from several London churches, and these singers are very popular. The choirmaster is a retired professional, and he introduces a great repertoire."

We listened to a Negro spiritual, an Irish ballad, and modern song from a popular musical. The conductor was obviously enjoying himself: a great enthusiast, with a mop of white hair, which flopped over his brow as he guided the singers gently through the selection.

Larry led me to another door that brought us into a pleasant waiting area, where some instrumentalists were playing gentle music. Several people were sitting on chairs listening. Some of them looked very dejected, and I saw two with AS labels, and one woman with a small child. We did not linger here. I felt that these people should not be watched by spectators. We went through another door, which brought us back into the street.

"Those people were waiting for a counselling interview," Larry explained. We have a team of trained people, who help with hundreds of different issues. We're open seven days a week from nine till five. We've a team of volunteer counsellors, who've all been trained, and we're in touch with dozens of other agencies. No one is turned away. There's a great spirit at work here, thanks to Helen and the leaders."

 "And who were the musicians?"

"Just volunteers, members of our orchestral club. Some are professionals, others amateurs. They just love using this space. There are free concerts every day."

I remembered those words as I travelled back home on the airbus, looked round at my fellow passengers and foolishly tried to identify how aware they were of our divided world. On the one hand governments

435

were seeing the light at last: creating a stable world was now a necessity for their survival. In the great cities though, there were huge divisions between the rich and the poor, and caught in the middle were groups of philanthropists.

This is what we're here for. I told myself. *We must do everything we can to spread this spirit, and fight the selfish individuals. Moreover, human beings are part of the planet seeing itself. As far as we know we are the only part of the planet that can perceive the context, and pass the message on. This is our task. Otherwise, there's no point in living?*

I closed my eyes and fell into a sort of reverie. The voices of Brandon, Norman and Larry were ringing in my ears.

While I've been in London I've read newspapers and watched television. London's so much closer to the rich world outside and the provinces are inward looking. Perhaps this isn't healthy. I've always held on to the notion of reforming the world locally. That's the creed I followed. Is this all though? No, of course not. We need both inner and outer change, nationally and internationally. It's reassuring to learn that the governments across the world are getting the message at last and are pulling together, but seeing those beggars in London and that asylum seeker being treated like a slave in Seagrave's flat has shaken me to the roots. Perhaps we're too cut off from the outside world in Mercia: Norman's awareness of the damage being done by global corporate capital and the horrors I saw on his television last night; long lines of refugees from climate change marching north across Africa trying to escape to Europe and aerial photos of others drowning in sinking boats trying to cross the Pacific.

Most people in London seem immune to these things, sitting safe inside their growing massive dome. Is humanity already reduced to three ways of living now: a few bubbles of super-rich people: resilient zones where people live sustainably and fight the elements: and vast regions where human life's become impossible and from which everyone's desperately trying to escape.

This is outrageous. Human beings are incredibly resourceful and have developed so wonderfully over the centuries. We are gifted with minds that enable us to be creative in a thousand ways. There must be something divine buried inside us, a force that drives us on. We must kindle this ray of hope.

I found myself praying for the city of London, for Sussex, Wessex, Mercia, the whole of Britannia and for the world beyond: for the whole of humanity, for all living creatures: praying that life would continue to pulsate and a way forward would be revealed. Doing this, my heart was enlightened in a way I had not experienced before.

I knew I wasn't alone. I was surrounded by a loving life force, that could point the way ahead. This force was intangible, but it was immensely powerful.

We must connect with it, not go away into little boxes of self-contentment. If humanity is to be saved, we need to envision a better world: one where humans are not dominating, but humbly playing their proper role in the web of life. Thank Heaven that most governments are at last realising that there's no future for mankind unless they work together positively. Through the Global Organisation for Sustainability there's a road ahead, and we ordinary people need to help everyone to understand this. There are still too many Freedom Parties around, and many individuals and groups vote for them too, but thousands of others don't. Fear of the enemy outside is the real danger. But the enemy is not those who are different from us. The age-old enemy is within. We must learn how to love and heal ourselves; only if we can do this, will there be hope for the future of humanity on Planet Earth.

CHAPTER 33 - Through Fire and Flood

Amina:

Rory seemed a changed man when he came back from London. I was very concerned because he had lost his usual cheerful demeanour and was wrapped up in moods ranging from emotional excitement to depression. Of course he told me about his visit to the Seagrave apartment and his encounter with Brandon. We were both worried to think that things had come to such a pass. Fortunately, Isabella was still living with us while she was working with the community service film unit and was less uptight about Brandon. This helped to establish the family stability again.

"The best thing is to let him learn lessons from his own behaviour," she said. "I will be going to London myself in a few months. We need to film some employment community relations there and I'll make a point of visiting Brandon while I'm in the area."

Isabella was working with a team on a film to be used widely in schools and training centres across Mercia. It included shots from some of our pageants but also sequences about adult training in many programmes.

"We're going to make a film called 'Black is Beautiful,' showing lots of examples of black and brown people making great contribution to community living. We're creating mentors and role models for young people, and taking shots in familiar streets," Bella told us. "I'll show Brandon some of the things we're doing."

Adam's son, Paul Samphire, had joined the team, and they travelled to London together. Paul had been a friend of Isabella's since early school days, but now a special bond was growing between them. Paul had a practical, down-to-earth approach to most things, and knew Brandon of old, so we waited for their return with interest.

The verdict did not console us, however. "Brandon's involved in some very bad company," Isabella told us. "But I don't see how we can do anything about it. It's his own choice to move in those circles."

"What sort of circles?" I asked her.

"High living and low life mixed together." Isabella answered. "It's difficult to describe. There seems to be an endless round of parties. Hosting wealthy overseas businessmen and encouraging them to invest in the Seagrave empire."

"What empire? Where does the wealth come from?" we asked.

"Casinos, luxury hotels, night clubs, and rackets all over the place: it's not just the Seagraves. They are small fry compared with some of their cronies, who mingle with mafia gangs and protection racketeers on the one hand and stockbrokers and hedge fund managers on the other. Those people seem to act as if they can fix anything: politicians, the press, the media...whatever."

"And how is Brandon involved? Where does his money come from?" asked Rory.

"He's got two sources of income, as far as I know: from the Seagraves: for acting as their apartment manager, and another from the hedge fund man, for whom he works three days a week." said Paul.

"And what about this Priscilla girl?" I asked.

"Oh, she is something else." Isabella was scornful. "She doesn't work. She's part of the system, the family business. I've no idea how she spends her time, and don't want to explore it. We went out with Brandon one evening and tried to get him talking, but he didn't reveal much about their relationship."

"Brandon needs to watch his drinking," said Paul. "They both do. If they carry on like they are doing, there'll be some sort of bust up."

Rory:

In contrast to this sad news, we had a computer video from Rupert and Catriona a few days later. It was lovely to see them looking so happy together. Their great news was that they had both obtained employment locally. Rupert was to work for the Newcastle City Council as an Assistant Public Safety Officer, and Catriona had got a job with the Scottish Water Company, as a household adviser in their Tyneside Region. (A special trans-national agreement enabled the reservoirs in this most northerly part of Northumbria to be managed by Scottish Water).

It was very good news because it meant that they could create a home together, and would at some stage probably marry and start a family. It also meant, of course, that Mina and I would not see much of them for the next few years, which disappointed us.

We had to put some of these thoughts aside, however, because 2084 was the year of the Chester pageant, and unfortunately Judith was not able to play the lead role again, having broken her leg skiing in the Peak District. (Buxton was now a popular winter sports centre, because of the long snow covered winters, which lasted until late April in the Dark Peak area).

This was also the year that Isabella completed her community service, so she was available to play Elfleda once again. "It can be my debut appearance as a professional," she proudly told us. "It's a lovely way to start my new career."

We recalled that she was especially fond of the old town. She had been entranced by a visit to Chester when she was a small child. On that occasion we had gone on the circular walk along the walls, looking down on the rooftops, courtyards and winding roads below us. "Why aren't all towns built like this?" she had asked. "It's so much better to have the car parks outside the walls and make all the streets into wide pavements, with cycle paths. They should have done this in Tamcaster."

The pageant in Chester was of particular importance because it bordered the province of Northumbria and our local history team had discovered that Elfleda made a deal with the Danes, enabling them to have a trading base there, on condition that they accepted the civilised laws of Mercia. The result was that a mixed community settled there and the Mercian culture spread widely.

It could be said that history was repeating itself, because Chester had become a training station for sustainable living. There was an opportunity for the ideas to be shared with the adjacent provinces of Northumbria and Wales. Residential courses were now being run in Chester that could spread the skills widely, and this was to be a central theme.

The pageant began with eight sturdy men rowing a reproduction Viking ship up the River Dee to an appropriately constructed quayside. Nordic shields were fastened to the sides of the vessel. A Welsh ship, sporting a red dragon sail, followed in its wake. The public gathered on the bank side to watch as antique horns were sounded from the town walls above. High Aldermen, wearing their royal blue gowns, marched through the Watergate to greet the visitors, and lead them into the city.

The procession moved along crowded streets towards the castle, where Isabella, resplendent in the red robe of the Lady of Mercia, awaited them on a platform outside the gatehouse. She had recorded a new version of "The Song of Alfred", and this was relayed through loudspeakers as the visitors approached. Isabella's rich mezzo-soprano voice fitted the occasion. Gifts were exchanged, among Mercian, Danish and Welsh people. Folk songs followed from each tradition, before the visitors stepped into a horse-drawn carriage that would take them to the cathedral.

The procession moved on from the castle forecourt through crowded shopping streets, where spectators lined the upper walkways of the timbered Rows to watch the colourful parade. Mercian, Welsh and Danish flags were strung across the roads, and the crowds waved and cheered. A stage had been erected outside the cathedral, where the bishop and other faith leaders greeted the guests. A massed choir sang a new song set to a familiar tune, before vows were made about respect and understanding between peoples of different cultures. The finale took the form of a parade of those working in healthcare, education, skills training, building, farming, artistic expression and home making. These people were not in Saxon clothing. They wore their modern working dress, which gave a distinct link between past and present.

For the next three days a fair was held on the ancient Roodee fields, with an open-air feast of fresh food each evening, where cooks shared skills with the public. Sporting contests took place in sweltering conditions, but the atmosphere changed on the third day, when a wind suddenly swept the pitch, blowing down tents and creating havoc in the fairground.

A team of firemen was demonstrating skills on the sports field in the evening, when they received a radio-controlled message about a big firestorm blazing in Delamere Forest. The demonstration team left immediately for the site and fire- fighting volunteers set off after them to give assistance.

Isabella said that she must go too, and as our pool vehicle was in the car park nearby, Mina and I went with her, following the fire engines. The force of the prevailing wind challenged us from the left, making holding the car on the road perilous. Recycling bins were flying through the air, scattering their contents, and leaves and litter were scurrying along the road. I was relieved when we eventually drew up at a parking area facing the blazing forest.

 Several fire engines were already there. Helicopters were flying overhead, dousing the flames below. Firemen were tackling the blaze with hoses angled in different directions. A scatter of cars had brought volunteers to help distressed people, forced to leave their homes.

Isabella asked a senior fire officer how we could help.

"Do you know this area?" he asked.

"No, not really, but we're here to assist in any way we can."

"You can assist with the hoses. Some of the volunteers have been here for several hours and they need a break. We've got the professionals working on more delicate work, creating firebreaks in strategic places and communicating with the helicopters. See those three people on the hillock: they've been hosing for a long time and are pretty well done in. They're locals and have other responsibilities."

We moved towards the volunteers who were holding hoses at a distance of around twenty yards from the blaze. A middle-aged woman was relieved to let Isabella take over and showed her where to direct the stream of water. We could feel the heat of the fire as soon as we got into position.

"Thanks for coming." The woman handed her hose to Isabella. "I've been here for two hours and we don't seem to be making much difference. It's an inferno, but I've got to get back home and check that everything's all right there. Aren't you Elfleda?"

"It's a part I play," Isabella replied. "I'm telling everyone to help their neighbours, so it's time I lend a hand myself."

"Good for you. Whereabouts do you live?"

"Tamcaster, but I'm staying in Chester this week."

"You don't know this area well then. This is a huge forest, a beautiful place, and they still get nightingales here. We can't afford to lose it. It's this terrible wind that's such a problem. There are several villages nearby, and they're starting to evacuate people. I've no idea where we'll all be sent."

"You're a local then."

"Yes, but my place is two miles off. We should be safe there, but we might be deluged with refugees. I can cope though, but I'm worried about the old folk. There's a couple I know who must be at risk."

"Where are they?"

"About a mile from here, but near the edge of the woodland. Their cottage has a thatched roof. Lovely old place, but it's a hazard not worth having."

"I expect the fire crews will look out for them."

"I'm not sure. I've got a funny feeling. Do you know what I mean? I'm a bit, what you might say... psychic. I get these feelings sometimes. I know it's not safe where they are. They could come and stay with me."

I felt I should chip in here. "I've got my car over there. I'll drive over and just check they are OK, if you like."

"Will you?" the woman said. "I'd be grateful, but it's a bit difficult to find."

Mina came in. "You'd better go with him and give directions then."

"Thanks."

"I'll come too. I've got a feeling that this is important."

To my surprise Isabella handed her hose over to Mina, and the three of us ran over to my car.

The woman told us that her name was Doris. She sat beside me in the front, explaining which way we had to go and having a conversation with Isabella over her shoulder as we went along.

The wind was just as strong as before, but the forest provided a shield for us, so driving was easier as we skirted the woodland. The blaze had not yet reached this part of the forest, but the smell of charred wood was palpable.

"The cottage is just past that mound on the left hand side," Doris said.

The forest was to our right, but as we rounded the bend I saw a roaring fire straight ahead. The wind must have turned, and now trees were blazing there as well. A flaming branch flew over the car as we jerked to a halt.

"The thatch is on fire." Doris opened her door and ran towards the cottage. Isabella leapt out of a rear door and rushed after her. I turned off the engine, scrambled out and was amazed to see that they were talking to a white-haired old man, who looked distracted. He was pointing to the house and shouting, "She fell down the stairs, and I couldn't pick her up."

I suddenly realised that the car was in a perilous position. The inferno was advancing towards it. A silver-birch tree caught fire and sparks spread to those around it. I leaped back into the car and reversed to drive away. As I'd come along I'd noticed a lane leading in the opposite direction. I rushed towards it, swerved in, jammed on the brakes, turned off the ignition and ran back to the cottage. The old man was lying on his back across the pathway. There was no sign of Isabella or Doris.

"Where are they?" I yelled at him.

The old man looked terrified. "They've gone in to try and get her out. God bless 'em."

"Gone in!"

I gazed at the blazing house. The roof was on fire, and streaky smoke was billowing out of the open doorway. Suddenly Doris rushed out of the cloud of smoke, her face black and her clothes singed.

"She's broken her leg, I think, lying at the bottom of the stairs. She needs carrying, but ...I can't cope...I'm all in."

I didn't hear the rest. I plunged though the black cloud shouting "Bella!" I couldn't see anything, but I heard voices and moved towards them, nearly stumbling over the old lady. Then I heard Isabella's voice. "I've got her under the shoulders. Can you take her feet, Dad?"

"Where?" Then I felt a stocking and moved my hand down to find a heel. The other foot was underneath it. "Bend over to the left. I'm trying to take your feet," I urgently explained. "Don't worry. We'll get you out... between us."
Isabella had quickly got a sense of things, and guided me as we both managed to stand, lifting the old lady.

"Can you walk backwards through the door, Dad?"

"I don't know where the door is." The smoke had got into my throat and I started coughing.

"Turn round then, carrying her feet. I'll back out."

How we managed to get her out I'll never know. Isabella was wonderfully calm throughout, while I was panicking as I coughed and spluttered. Once outside, we found that Doris had propped the old man up against the gatepost, and within a minute the two old people were in each other's arms, sitting on the garden path.

I telephoned the emergency number and they said they'd order an ambulance. They were too busy to bother with the cottage fire just now, but they'd come when they could. I realised from the voice that this further stretch of the forest fire I'd seen was of more concern to them than the isolated thatch of an empty cottage.

We managed to get the elderly couple into the car and started to drive to the Royal Chester Hospital for an examination. As we arrived, we saw an ambulance leaving. Perhaps it was the one the fire service had ordered.

 It was not until we'd handed the old couple over to nurses at Accident and Emergency that Isabella showed me her left arm saying, " I need a check up too, Dad."

The arm was red, blistered and weeping.
"Why didn't you show me that before?" I exclaimed.

"Priorities," she said, and I could see she was in acute pain and nearly fainting.

"Oh Isabella, for God's sake! You need to look after yourself as well as others. You should have told me earlier."
I admired her grit, but had to leave her and the old couple with Doris at the Accident and Emergency Department, which was already packed with troubled people in similar conditions. I drove back urgently to collect Mina from where I had last seen her hosing the woodland fire.

It was around 2am when Mina and I left the hospital with Isabella. Her sore hand and arm had been dressed and bound and was held in a sling. She had been given medication to dull the pain, but none of us had much sleep that night in our hotel bedrooms.

* * *

It was a year before Bella's arm and hand were able to work properly again, and they were permanently scarred. She kept her usual calm. Mina and I wondered at her quiet patience. She and Paul were constant companions now. They moved into a flat together and seemed perfectly matched. There was no official engagement. Many young people don't seem to want anything formal these days, but it was very different with Rupert and Catriona, probably because her father was a minister of the kirk in Scotland.

Mina, Isabella, Paul and I went up Culross in Fife for the wedding. This was in her father's church, a lovely building, which had once been part of an ancient abbey. Catriona's father, the Revd. James Murray conducted the wedding. Aidan Crosby was best man, and Isabella and Catriona's younger sister, Fiona were bridesmaids.

The Scottish National Trust had a protection order on Culross, claiming it to be a perfect example of early cottage architecture, complete with cobbled streets and red pan-tiled roofs. It is regularly used as a setting for old Scottish films. We stayed at the neighbouring Dunimarle Castle Hotel, where a wonderful wedding reception was held. People came from many parts of Scotland, as the Murray family were well known and respected. We learned that they had ancient links with the Murrays of Atholl, and were happy to find that they were all very relaxed and friendly people.

After supper, everyone joined in Scottish country dancing, and we went to bed that night with the sound of bagpipes ringing in our ears and the rhythms of wild Scottish reels pounding in our hearts.

* * *

Beatrice:

The firestorm in Cheshire was one of several that summer, including Sherwood Forest in Nottinghamshire, the Arboretum Woods in Staffordshire, Brecon Beacons in Wales and The New Forest in Hampshire. Many of our traditional trees were destroyed, and fears spread for the future of beech, ash and oak trees in the Britannic islands.

Peter invited me to take over a role he had held for years, as the Transition International Link for Wessex. It meant that I had access to a website giving information about transition groups across the world. Soon I started emailing, and speaking to them on line. We exchanged reports of our activities, gave information about the damage that was being done to our local environment and shared thoughts on the best way to deal with it. I enjoyed this work enormously because it gave me reassurance that despite the violent storms that were now very frequent globally, there were many pockets of hope in every continent.

The news we received through the media was very frightening: rising sea levels had engulfed many of the Pacific Islands, and thousands of people, livestock and species of wildlife had been lost forever. Those who had managed to escape were being accommodated in refugee camps in Australia, New Zealand, China and Vietnam. I began to receive messages from these refugee zones also. The tragedies had been predicted long ago, but self-interest by richer nations had ruined the chances for more survivors. There was also a terrible loss of natural habitats for animal and plant species: a crime against life on earth.

Our planet itself suffered too. There had been a huge loss of water and topsoil in many areas. The Sahara desert now extended now Cancer to Capricorn in Africa, but I was in direct contact with our Transition Link Officers in Morocco and South Africa. I also had electronic contact with others in both North and South America. The rising Atlantic had destroyed much of the east coast in the USA and Canada and there were huge migrations into the central states. I was now in touch with Link Officers in Toronto, Winnipeg, Calgary, Oklahoma, Memphis and

Oakland, California. In Europe, my main contacts were with Paris, Barcelona, Hanover, Vienna and Florence.

These disasters had also affected most of the rich cities and the several of the multi-national corporations that were controlling them started to break up in consequence.

The main insurgence in Britannia had been on the east coast, where the Wash had turned into a huge bay. Most of Lincolnshire and Norfolk had disappeared. As it was no longer practicable to maintain the Anglian Province, surviving areas were absorbed into the neighbouring provinces, and a massive sea wall was built in an attempt to hold back further incursions. Mercia had to accommodate most of the refugees. Others went to Northumbria, London and Sussex.

In Wessex, the message about resilience no longer needed to be preached. Everyone understood it, and most people had learned new skills that they practised readily in times of need. Gated communities were less self-sufficient, but most people living in them were wealthy enough to pay for the services they needed. Some elderly and weak-minded people there, not rich enough to employ staff or robotic help, depended on the goodwill of neighbours or simply gave up trying and faded away. A sad feature of our times is that it has become quite common for elderly people, living alone there, to be found dead and rotting in their own spacious accommodation. Fortunately, this never happens in cluster housing, where every street has an official safety warden.

To get back to family matters, it took several years for Lucy to recover from the trauma she had suffered. The boys helped her with this. Brook trained all three of them to windsurf, and this encouraged Lucy's heart to soar also. The healthy exercise was good for them all, and Lucy developed her expertise. When the wind was blowing in the right direction, I loved to watch them surfing the waves and flying their colourful kites.

After Ivan left school he gained a college diploma in organic farming, and later was fortunate enough to be employed by Ben Norris, who had bought Woodleigh Farm from Gramps and now supplied our community shop. Eventually, Ivan became responsible for Charlie, the horse he'd learned to love since his early years. Ivan was a one-interest fanatic. He was totally absorbed in organic farming, and Brook and I recognised that he had a touch of Asperger's Syndrome.

When Ben retired, Ivan took over the running of the whole farm. After Ben died, two years later, Ivan inherited it all, and invited his long-time girlfriend, Susan, to share it with him. This was history repeating itself and a wonderful thing for them both. The old farm was now back again in our family; Ivan representing the third generation. Susan was a motherly sort of girl, who was very helpful to Ivan. We welcomed her gladly. She was a member of the Society of Friends, so they had a Quaker Wedding the following year, and then they set about developing their organic business together.

Rory:

Next Spring, we faced floods sweeping across low-lying areas right across Mercia. In Tamcaster, the north riverside area was vulnerable because the riverbank was lower than that on the southern side. There had been a plan to build a very high wall but strong opposition from the Freedom Party and those who valued the riverside walks prevented it from happening. Consequently, water came pouring across the fields, front gardens and on to the ground floors of many properties.

Adam, as the Public Safety Officer, called in the local emergency response team and, re-enforced by both the military and the local community service corps, they started the construction of the wall. Too much time had been lost, however and on a dark, wild day, a fortnight later, a continuous rainstorm came lashing down and flash floods were all over the area. A school bus was swept off the road and crashed into a nearby public house. The carnage was terrible, and the Emergency Department at Tamcaster City Hospital was overwhelmed with urgent victims.

Mina and I went there as soon as we heard about this tragedy. Ten children and the bus driver had been killed and another fourteen children and two teachers from Arkwright School were being treated for injuries. Fortunately, the pub was closed at the time, but the landlord and his wife were both wounded. Anxious parents were gathered outside, with newspaper reporters and TV crews.

We were able to speak to some of the affected children. There were several we knew with broken bones, and in a state of trauma. Some were in tears because school friends had drowned or were missing. We did what we could to console them.

While there, we unexpectedly met Trish. Seeing Mina, she came across the waiting area to explain that her father, Wesley, had been brought in suffering from a sudden heart attack.

"He was helping some of the church members whose houses had been flooded," she explained. "It was too much for him. He was trying to carry great bags full of things they wanted to save from the water, but he collapsed under the strain. He's had a stroke."

"How did he get here?" Mina asked.

"Bonnie drove him in. She was helping them too, and she managed to get him into her car. She knew that would be quicker than calling an ambulance, with so many sudden emergencies around us."

By midday we heard that everyone in the flooded streets had been collected from the upper rooms of their houses and taken to community centres, where they were being supplied with bedding and food. About two hundred families had to move into these centres urgently, and chaos was caused by electricity failures.

Mina and I had just got back from the hospital, got cups of tea and sat down exhausted when the doorbell rang frantically.

I walked towards it calling, "Who's there?".

As soon as I opened it, a wet, bedraggled man fell against me and would have collapsed on the step if I hadn't held him up. Suddenly. I realised it was Paul Samphire, drenched to the skin.

I helped him stagger into the living room, and Mina assisted him to an armchair.

"Whatever's the matter?" she cried. " Have you been hurt?"

Paul took some time to reply. "Not badly...my leg hurts...I fell out of a boat...we were rescuing people from upper rooms in the Meadows area...where the streets were all flooded. It was terrible...a whirlwind suddenly struck us...the waves were frenzied and the rowing boat was pitching and tossing... I've never seen anything like it... Thank God you're at home. I had to find you...I had to tell you first."

"We've only just got back from the hospital." Mina explained. "We were helping some of the distressed children there."

Paul did not seem to hear. He was in another world, looking dazed and confused.

"Get him a drink," I said to Mina, who offered him a glass of whisky, but Paul waved it away. "I've got to tell you," he gasped. "About Isabella!" His lips were trembling.

"What about her?" we both cried out.

Paul avoided looking at Mina and gazed at me, abstracted. "I did all I could to save her. We went in that flooded house to get a baby. She found it, but couldn't get back into the boat holding it... It was pitching and tossing. The water was frantic. I jumped overboard to help her in. I tried to lift her into the boat. She was clutching the baby, and she couldn't make it. She slipped through my fingers and the boat overturned. That threw the other man out. He grabbed the upturned boat and held on... it was bouncing in the swirling water. I saw Bella go down...I reached out and grabbed her... pulled her towards the boat...I shouted 'hang on for dear life'...She kept shouting 'I've lost the baby' and then she swallowed the water and her head went under. I dragged her up again and told her to hang on, but she wasn't even trying to. She was limp in my arms, and I looked at her face, but her eyes didn't see me. They were open and glazed. Then a lifeboat appeared from nowhere and we were hauled aboard... Bella, the other man and me. They laid Bella on the deck, and we pumped her and I tried to give her the kiss of life. Others did too...but it was no good. It was too late ...She's gone Rory. I've lost her. Love of my life. We've lost her. I did my utmost Mina, Rory. Believe me! I'm desperately sorry...I wish I was the one dead... she was life itself. I loved her more than anyone on earth...She meant more to me than everyone...even my own Mum and Dad."

Paul's chest and shoulders were heaving and the tears were pouring down his face.

Mina and I were both dumbstruck. We gazed at him in anguish.

Eventually, I heard Mina ask tremulously. "Whose baby was this?"

Paul shook his head. "I've no idea. It was just a baby. It was in a cot in one of the houses, and Bella found it...all alone and crying. She picked it up and said, 'There, there,' and held it to her breast and it stopped crying and looked up at her in wonder."

I shouted out, "Is there anyone else here? There was no reply, so I went through the upstairs rooms. They were all empty, but when I peered over the stairway, I saw two bodies, heads down, floating in the water. From their clothing, it looked like a man and a woman...must have been the parents.

I went back and told Isabella. She said, 'We must take it to the shelter', and then she said to the child, 'I'll look after you, darling, don't worry.' She carried it so gently towards the window. I climbed through and got into the swaying boat first, while the other man steadied it. Then Bella leant across and handed the baby to me, a tiny little boy, a few days old, I'd say. He started to cry again. Bella climbed through, sat down and then took him off my hands. She looked down at his face and gave a smile. Then the boat lurched suddenly... and it was chaotic again......"

He could not speak any more and looked at us wildly. Mina was too choked to speak.

I had to do something, so I went up to Paul and embraced him. "I'm sure you did everything you could, Paul. Thank you for that..." We hugged each other and cried together.

"Mina and I will never forget what you did for Isabella," I gasped, "and for all of us. I know you never married but, as far as we're concerned, you're our son-in-law, and always will be. Do Adam and Trish know about this yet?"

"No. I felt I had to tell you first. ...before my parents...I'd better go over to their place now. But I don't think Dad'll be there. He'll be out somewhere trying to help others. That's his job."

"Your mother will be home I think," Mina said. "She was at the hospital earlier this afternoon. Perhaps you don't know - Milton's had a stroke. I think he's in intensive care."

"Oh dear. I didn't know. How did that happen?"

"Milton was helping more flood victims... people from his church. It was too much for him," I stuttered.

"I must go." He stood up, and Mina got up too and kissed him.

With that, he left us... sitting on the sofa, holding each other and trembling as we wept.

PART FOUR - Moments in Time

"In dreams begins responsibility"

Robert Lowell

CHAPTER 34 - Facing the Whirlwind

Rupert:

Isabella's death shattered us all. It was so unexpected. I will never forget answering that phone call at work. Dad never rang me there, but fortunately I was not in a meeting, just sitting alone at my desk dictating a letter into my computer. I stopped to take the call, which I thought must have come from my boss, and I heard this tremulous voice, which I didn't recognise at first. It reminded me of my old granddad, Mark.

"Is that you Rupert? Are you alone?"

"Yes. Who is it?"

"It's Dad. I've got some dreadful news to tell you?"

I started. *Was it about Mom?*

"It's Isabella. You've heard about the floods. It's been terrible here. Isabella was helping victims...and a boat overturned and....and she's gone, Rupert. We've lost her."

"You mean she's missing?"

"No. I'm afraid it's worse than that. She, she drowned....trying to rescue a baby!"

He broke down in tears. I was stunned.

"Oh Dad...I can't take it in...she's so full of life. Are you certain?"

"I'm afraid there's no doubt. Paul tried to rescue her. He got her out and tried respiration, but it was too late. We have the body."

I sat there, speechless, with my cell phone in my hand, aware of a tear trickling down my cheek.

"Oh, Dad. That's terrible! How's Mom?"

"She's very low. She can't stop crying. Oh, Rupert, can you come?"

I struggled to respond. "I'll...I'll try to, Dad, but I have to speak to my boss. Is there a funeral?"

"Not yet. We'll have to organise something, but there are so many people who've been lost! It's terrible, Rupert, terrible."

"Are you and Mom safe?"

"Oh yes, we are quite safe at home. At least, I think we are, but it's still sheeting down.

They're evacuating people from so many areas now, and they don't know where to take them. We've run out of church halls and community buildings and we're having to use some empty school classrooms that are scattered around. What's it like in Newcastle? "

"It's not raining here, but we're covered in snow!"

"Snow.... But it's only October!"

"I'll speak to my boss and ring you back."

"And can you ring Brandon, please? We're not up to it. Do you have his number?"

"Yes. I'll do that."

This was all so unlike Dad and Mom. They were such strong people.

I rang my boss first, and left a message for him. Then I phoned Catriona, and she reminded me that she had a week's leave owing and said that, if I were going to Tamcaster, she'd come with me. This gave me great comfort.

Brandon was shaken too.

"Bella. I can't imagine it. She's always been there for everyone." He asked me to keep him informed. He'd come too, if he was wanted and if he could make it.

The next day, Catriona and I were on a train to Tamcaster.

Rory and Mina were grieving in different ways. Dad had plunged himself into his work at school.

"It's all that keeps me sane," he told me. He had even volunteered to do extra duties and did not come home until six most evenings, and then he usually brought homework back for marking and seemed to bury himself in this, once the meal was over. It was clearly a lifeline for him. Mom had taken compassionate leave from school, and was spending the lonely hours doing a series of portrait paintings in the room that Brandon used to have. There was no evidence of this ever having been his room. It was now transformed into a artist's studio. The first portrait she did was of Isabella, based on a photograph she had taken two years ago.

This made things rather difficult when Brandon came over for the funeral. I collected him from the railway station and told him that he would be sleeping on a camp bed in the lounge.

"It's a long time since I've done that sort of thing," he observed. He sounded a bit hurt, but said he understood.

He told us later that he had peeped into his old room, and did not recognise it.

The whole city was in turmoil. So many people had died in the floods that one big service for all the victims was held in the cathedral. Over two hundred names were read out, including those of Isabella Whiteoak and the Rev. Milton Lamb. Separate memorial services were held for them a few days later. Bruce Langland, who was an elder at Forest United Reformed Church, conducted one there for Isabella, and so many people wanted to attend that it was also relayed by audio in the packed church hall next door. Paul Samphire, in spite of his anguish, was brave enough to pay tribute to Isabella for her compassion and dedication to duties as a member of voluntary service team. Other contributions from the platform included ones from Rory, Mina, Councillor Jenny Painter on behalf of the City Council, and me. After a short silence, members of the congregation were invited to add their own thoughts and memories. I counted fifteen short tributes, including one from Beatrice. She and Brook were staying with Adam and Trish, because Mom and Dad's house was full.

I was keen to have a serious talk with Brandon, but it was not possible until the two big occasions were over. On the day before he returned to London, we went for a brisk walk in the park. Catriona would have liked to come, but realising that this would be a brotherly chat, she joined Mina in the painting studio.

"How do you like living in London?" I asked.

"It suits me much better than down here," he said rather hurriedly. "There's so much going on. I don't think I'd be able to settle back in Tamcaster again, or anywhere else. The pace of life is so much faster in the metropolis. I like to be busy."

"So what exactly is your work, these days?"

"I've still got the two jobs: running the reception centre, and working in finance. They both put me in touch with so many people, not just from London, but from all over the world: New York, Shanghai, Singapore. They're mainly business people, who have shares in properties or companies in London. Some of them live here for a while: some just come for a few days, and it's my job to show them round, and introduce them to others."

"What sort of businesses are they in?"

"A lot of it is real estate. Flats in London, which can be sold or rented out on varied contracts. There are some big hotels, casinos and clubs in the holdings and student accommodation also. That's big business now and rakes in a good return."

"And is Priscilla involved in all this too?"

"You bet she is."

"Are you two a couple now?"

"I hope so...Yes, of course we are."

"That sounds a bit uncertain."

"Why are you asking all these prying questions?"

"Sorry Bran. I didn't want it to sound like that."

"Well it does. Priscilla and I are good friends and we sometimes share an apartment. There are so many of them to choose from, apartments I mean, not girls." He laughed awkwardly. "There are plenty of both, of everything in London. Priscilla and I, well, we haven't made a life commitment to each other... not yet anyway."

That was as far as I got, but Catriona and I discussed this little conversation later.

"Perhaps we could have a holiday there sometime and look Brandon up." I suggested.

"That's a great idea." Catriona was keen. "I've never been to London, and I've heard so much aboot it. Och, just think of it...we could sail doon the Thames, and see some of the famous museums like Buckingham Palace and 10, Downing St. Then there's Hyde Park and the Palace Gardens. I'd love to go to a London theatre and to the Proms at the Royal Albert Hall. If Brandon escorts overseas visitors, he'll know the best places and the tricks o' the trade. As for his relationship with Madam Priscilla, time will tell. That's their affair. It's noo our business."

I saw Catriona's point, but I had real worries about my young brother and had little doubt that if she was to meet Priscilla, Catriona would see straight through her, and out the other side!

The opportunity occurred the following summer when we took the promised London holiday.

We discovered that the opulent world was in a state of crisis. It had been superficial and some of it heartbreaking, but now many big companies were closing down and unemployment was rampant. Brandon was elusive. He ignored our letters and phone calls, so we went on with the sightseeing. We had strawberries and cream in the Rose Garden in Buckingham Palace Gardens, and said what a pity it was that this wonderful park had been hidden from the public for so long. Another surprise was 10, Downing Street, with its stairway of portraits of past Prime Ministers and its cabinet room, set just as it had been on that fateful day in 2028, when Cornwall and the East Coast were devastated and the government required emergency powers. There was so much damage done internationally at that time that the media called it "three days that rocked the world."

In our second week, we decided to track down Brandon and called uninvited at the flat in the Barbican. We rang the bell and an electronic voice told us that it was not convenient to visit today but we could try again in three days time. We left a message and followed the instructions. On the second occasion we were luckier, but only got as far as the vestibule door, which was admitting an assortment of partygoers.

A footman, wearing white gloves, asked if we had tickets, and when I said I'd just come round to see my brother, Brandon, he told us to wait outside while he asked the hostess, Miss Priscilla.

We stood waiting in the hallway for about five minutes, and then a very haughty Priscilla appeared. She was now a platinum blonde, redder in the face and considerably stouter than I recalled, wearing a low-cut summer dress, and grasping a large wineglass in one hand.

"Mr. Whiteoak left our employment five weeks ago," she announced frostily.

"Oh, I'm surprised he didn't mention it. Do you know where I could find him? " I asked.

"Oh. I believe there's some sort of forwarding address for the bills," she said in a bored voice. Turning round she shouted to the doorman "Henry, do you know where Whiteoak's cards are kept?" Turning she said to us, "I'll have a skivvy bring one to you," and disappeared behind the closed door.

Ten minutes later a mixed-race girl in drab clothing appeared with a blue visiting card for The Wilford Clinic in Hammersmith.

"Do you know if he is working there?" I asked.

"I believe he is patient there. I was told he had breakdown," she said.

We left the Barbican and took a streetcar to Hammersmith. When we got off, we noted an area map conveniently placed in the bus shelter.

"It's not far," I said. "Second turning on the right."

"I think it might be for the best if I had a wee look round the shops here." Catriona looked at me in the cautious way she has; being ever sensitive of other's feelings. "It's a while since I saw Brandon - at Isabella's wake, no less. He might prefer to see ye alone, I'm thinking."

"Whatever you feel," I said. "We can aim to meet here in an hour's time, or in two, if need be." I saw her reasoning and went along with it. Brandon was always unpredictable, but might disclose more to me without his new sister-in-law.

I knocked on the door, and was answered by another voice on a speaking device.

"I'm Rupert Whiteoak, brother of Brandon. Is it convenient for me to see him?" I enquired.

"Press the knob and come in," said the voice.

I stepped into a quiet office, where three women were working. The nearest one looked up and smiled.

"Brandon Whiteoak is on one of our recovery courses," she said. "I'll ring his room and see if he's free just now, or later."

She keyed a number and spoke to someone who responded, and then handed the phone to me.

"Hi Brandon, it's Rupert," I said, "Catriona and I are down her for a few days, and I'd like to see you, if that's all right. I'm on my own just now."

There was a slight pause and then I heard Brandon's voice. "Yes, come up if you want. Take the lift to the third floor, I'm in the Lilac Room: fourth on the right."

Brandon had lost weight but his face looked strained, with bags under his eyes. His manner was downcast, but I got the impression that he was pleased I had called on my own. He was dressed informally in a jump suit and trainers, and sitting on a single bed.

"I've just had a session in the gym," he explained, looking downcast, "and I usually rest for a while after that. It takes a toll." He gestured me to the easy chair and I sat down.

"Good to see you again," I said. "So what are you doing in this clinic?"

"Building up my strength again, I had a breakdown you know." He gave a nervous blink.

"Oh dear. I'm sorry. We didn't know. How did that happen?"

"Oh, it was a gradual build up...I didn't see it coming...hit me like a bomb. So many things all at once, but this place is very good. They're helping me through. I got your message last week via the Barbican, but I wasn't up to seeing anyone then. I'm better today. You've called at a good time."

"What sort of course are you doing here?"

He gave an awkward jerk. "Rehab after trauma. There are ten of us and we share our stories and help each other. We have exercises each day and tasks, as well as sessions with a counsellor who gives us targets to work on. It was awful before I came here. I was trying to drown it all out, and you can't do that with alcohol or drugs. I've learned that the hard way... those things are all banned here."

"Good. How did you find this place?"

"Through my doctor. It's very expensive, but I've got the money, thank God. I don't know what I'd have done if I hadn't. I've been here six weeks... best thing I ever did."

"How long is the course?"

"Long as a piece of string. You can go on adding targets, but I'm planning on ten weeks. After that I'll go back to my apartment, and come one day a week for as long as it takes."

"Your apartment... you mean the Barbican?"

"Good God, no... I'm finished with Seagrave and his lot. I had this bust up with Priscilla. I've got my own place you know... up at Kingston. Had it for three years, but it was let out and I got the income. It was my own bit of venture capital, but the flat's empty now. I'll go back there when I leave here. That's the plan anyway."

"Oh, I thought it must be something like that. I went round to the Barbican and got this address. Sorry, it didn't work out for you with Priscilla."

Suddenly Brandon broke into tears and started thumping the pillow on his bed. "Don't mention that name! I can't bear it! Sorry Rue, but this is what I've been told to do! Pound the pillow. Get it out of my system. Anger therapy, they call it!"

I sat and watched. "It's OK Bran. It's your bed. As long as you don't harm anyone...or yourself."

"I've been through that...slashed my wrist. Oh God. Why am I telling you this?"

"You can tell me anything, Bran. It's best to get these things out."

" I thought we were a couple. I knew she was only there half the time, but I trusted her. When she told me she was pregnant, I was delighted. I believed it could be the start of a new life for both of us... all of us. We'd be a family. I thought we could live in my place in Kingston, but no! It wasn't good enough for her. She laughed at the idea, and went off for a few days. Then she came back in and said everything had been fixed. I asked what she meant, and she said 'the pregnancy'. I wanted that child, male or female, bone of my bone and flesh of my flesh; that's what I told her. It was half mine and half hers, and she had never asked my opinion. She laughed at me, and said 'That's what you think, is it? How the hell do I know who the father is? I don't want my life ruined by little brats running around!' That finished me off, Rupert. I was done in... thunderstruck. I hadn't seen it coming. I ran out of the room, because I knew if I'd stayed a moment longer I've have hit her, so I ran into my room and pounded the pillow until it burst and all the feathers were flying around."

"How awful. I'm so sorry, Brandon. It must have been terrible for you."

"I packed my bags and left that day. I went to Kingston, but it wasn't ready to be lived in. There was no heat and no food and I hadn't the energy left to go shopping. I just climbed into bed and had a sleepless night. I crawled out and got things in the next day, but I'd no strength or willpower left. I took to the bottle. I was there two weeks. Then I got worried. I was having nightmares. I thought everyone was against me. That people were after me... the Jay gang."

"What's the Jay gang?"

"Oh, it's an outfit down here... protection racket... they fix people...they're everywhere. I heard about them in Tamcaster, and thought they were just a local gang, but then I discovered that they were international...Italy...USA...everywhere...they stop at nothing...can do anything if they get the orders...I've met some of the big boys...they've been to that Barbican place...some of our parties...Seagrave family are in with the bosses....I've had dreams that they're after me."

"Why would they do that?"

"I don't think they would really but, as I said, I've had dreams about it. I've been through a nightmare and can't always think straight, but things are getting better now I'm here."

"You still have a family, Brandon. You've got me, Mom and Dad, Beatrice and Brook and their kids. They're all growing up now, and there's Grannie Elsa. They'd all understand: so would Catriona, come to that, if she was here now. You're not alone in the world, remember that. It's important."

"But I've let everyone down. Dad was mad at me when he came to London. I could see he was, although before he left he said I was still his son. I remember that, but did he really mean it?"

"Of course he meant it, Bran. Dad always means what he says, and I think he needs you around now. He and Mom are broken after what happened to Isabella. You came to the funerals and you saw how people took it."

"Yes, but Isabella was such a beautiful person, so good and caring, and I'm not like that at all. I'm a big disappointment to everyone: the black sheep of the family."

"Nonsense. You're Brandon, my only brother, with opinions of your own, and I respect that. You don't just do what the family does. You've proved that you have a mind of your own. I respect your feelings about you're baby, and so would Mom and Dad, and so would Catriona. I know they would and they'll support you now, in this crisis. Believe me."

"Will they?"

"Of course they will. Don't you remember that song that Mom had a hand in writing? It was called 'Resilience'. You said it was silly at the time because it was all about Anglo- Saxons and we lived in a modern world and had to move with the times. Well, you did! You had the guts to leave home, come to London and build your own life, and you've done well in business and got your own home in Kingston now. That shows resilience. You may not agree with all our political views, but you're one of the family and I want you to know that, and I'd like you to come and visit us in Newcastle, whenever you want."

Brandon was visibly moved and agreed to join Catriona and me on our last day in London. He took us to see his flat and later we had lunch together at Kingston, boarded a boat, and sailed down the Thames to Greenwich. We looked round that quaint old district and went aboard an ancient sailing ship called the Cutty Sark. Brandon got on well with Catriona, and accepted our invitation for him to have a week with us in Newcastle next year.

We returned home from London with mixed impressions. The metropolis was a cosmopolitan parallel world: fascinating and exciting and but self-absorbed and profligate, and there was evidence that it was crumbling. We'd enjoyed the break and we did not find London as depressing as Dad had done, but we were particularly shocked about the callous way that asylum seekers were used as cheap labour, and about the cavalier attitude towards climate change that had prevailed for so long. We looked carefully at the sea defences and realised that if the London Barrage had not been put in place around a hundred years ago, the whole area would be flooded. We were apprehensive about how long the waters could be held at bay and how the Great Dome would affect the environment and the way that the economy was going. Time would tell.

Brandon came to stay with us the following summer, and he also spent time with Mom and Dad in Tamcaster. His opinions and attitudes to things remained his own, but over the next few years, he became much more open in his behaviour, showing a humane side to his capitalist concepts, and a willingness to attempt to bridge the yawning gap between the different worlds.

CHAPTER 35 - Towards 2100

Beatrice:

We did not see anything of Brandon for some time, but we were very happy to welcome Catriona into the family. She and Rupert came to stay with us on three occasions and Brook and I visited them in Newcastle. We found that we had many interests in common: rambling, swimming, ecology, history and studying and learning from our dreams. Catriona and I had vivid ones that we could usually recall the next day, so when we were staying together the morning conversation often began with "Did you have any interesting dreams last night?"

Brook did not find this made for the best breakfast conversation, so he would often get absorbed in a crossword puzzle and leave us to it. Rupert had a passing interest and would make the occasional comment, but he did not usually recall his nocturnal adventures.

"Occasionally, I do have a very vivid dream but usually its a load of nonsense," he would say.

"Och, but hidden amid the nonsense, there can be a power o' truth," Catriona would reply. "And that nonsense is well worth exploring too. Why those particular people? What are they up to? It can all be significant if ye study the context an' note how the dream makes ye feel; cheerful or sad. A bonny dream can set me up for the dae."

I had made something of a study of my dreams, and emailed her with the titles of a few books on the subject by people who had studied it in depth. When they stayed with us next year, Catriona came armed with a pile of photocopies of notes she had made. She'd followed up all the references I'd sent and this had encouraged her to read about university experiments done in several different countries.

Rupert, clearly interested himself now, and made notes as we talked.

"Dreams are an individual's treasure hoose," Catriona assured him. "More study o' this would be a power of help in mental health an' rehabilitation, I'm certain o' that."

"And, if you start to study your dreams, you may find that you begin to have lucid ones," I told Rupert. "They are much stronger than the ordinary ones: the colours are brighter and there is a depth to them that can be explored. There are ways of steering them to areas that have resonance: subjects that are meaningful to you, and can be a helpful guide in life. This skill was known to the ancients. Just think of all the references to dream interpretations in the Bible. It's a path open to us today if we have the patience, but the world is so dominated by logic and materialism that the instinctive gifts we're born with are usually ignored and often forgotten."

"Whenever these extra bright images appear, I've trained myself to think 'is this a dream?' and then, I try pushing my finger through my hand. If I can do this, I'm dreaming, and it makes me very alert. These are the dreams I remember best," I told them.

"I think it would wake me up immediately if I knew I was dreaming," Rupert observed.

"Not if you've told yourself in advance that you want to explore them," I said.

"Sometimes I've dreamed of a fearsome beast like a lion, and by speaking kindly to it, he's become as friendly as a wee dog," Catriona told us. "Ye can alter a lucid dream as you wish. That's the joy of the thing."

We shared these ideas with Elsa, who was leading meditation classes in the community hall, and she invited me to lead a discussion on the subject. Some people were very interested, so we held a short series of workshops where members were invited to share dreams. One by one, the others were invited to say, "If this were my dream, I would feel....."

It proved quite popular, and repeat events followed.

Brook had trained all three of our youngsters to kite-surf. Ivan used to be very keen, but he was so busy on the farm that he could seldom find the time now. David fitted this in when he had days off work. Lucy had become the keenest of them all. Of course, it had taken several years for her to get over the trauma of losing her entire family. The boys had been very good about including her in their activities when they were young, but it was when Brook trained her to handle kites that her heart began to soar again. The healthy exercise helped them all, but Lucy developed her own expertise. When the wind was blowing in the right direction, it was very inspiring to watch her surfing the waves and flying the colourful kites.

Over the years, Ivan and Susan had three children, Jimmy, Sandra and Mike. They were full of energy and fun, and we often had some of them staying overnight with us, because the farm was a dedicated workplace. As he grew older Ivan became very set in his ways, and was quite strict with the children. The family usually woke up with the dawn and went to bed soon after dark, except in the winter months, when Ivan insisted that candles must be used. He joined the Britannic Organic Farmers Association and carried things to the extreme by not using any motorised transport. Instead he delivered his produce by horse and cart, and drove his family around in a specially designed pony and trap, which had a folding roof and a cubby-hole at the rear containing a bucket and shovel. This was used to retrieve any horse manure. He never left this on the roadway and on returning home he always put it to good use as rich fertiliser. This rigidity amused some of his neighbours, but Ivan never cared what others thought. He had let his hair grow long, sported a ponytail, and became a member of the Order of Druids.

Susan being much more accommodating was always ready for a chat and a laugh. To be absolutely honest I began to prefer her company to that of Ivan. That's a strange thing for a mother to say, but I never fully bonded with my own real son. I admit this, now that I am older. I would never have said it when he was young. I'm not sure where his austere approach came from, unless there's a slight touch of Brook's mother, but he is a dedicated organic farmer and a very hard worker.

David was always more sociable than Ivan. He followed Brook's career path, taking a Degree in Environmental Studies at Exeter University and got employment as an Environmental Advisor with Dorset County Council. He and his partner, Holly, had two children, Alex and Ruth. They lived about thirty-five miles away from us, near Dorchester, so unfortunately we didn't see as much of those two grandchildren, when they were growing up, as we did of Ivan's.

Lucy trained as a nurse and came to live nearby in one of the cluster houses with her boy-friend, Sam.

* * *

I was not surprised when Mina told me that she and Rory had both started looking out for teaching posts in Devon. Rory had always said that he would like to retire down here, but since the loss of Isabella the excitement of the large city had faded for them. They lost some of their vitality and began to long for the quieter lifestyle here in Woodleigh. They still owned their house in the clusters, which was let to a local family.

In 2092, there was an expansion of the Woodleigh Community College, creating several new posts. Rory and Mina both applied and were accepted. By a happy co-incidence the Partridge family, who were renting their house in Sylvan Cluster, decided to move that year, to be closer to their married daughter. They were gone by Easter. Rory and Mina arrived here in the summer holidays.

They came by airbus on the day before their removal van. Ivan met them at Exeter and brought them here in his horse trap: a curious contrast in life styles. When the van arrived the next day, Brook and I helped them convert the empty property into their home again.

They settled easily at the community college, which was familiar to them both: Rory having had his secondary schooling there. Mina had attended evening classes at the college while she was training for her teaching qualification. Rory became Head of History and Mina was became a senior teacher in the Arts and Crafts Department, with an additional assignment to teach the music to younger children. They met some old friends again in the staff room, including Matthew Farnfield, who was due to retire in twelve months time.

Rory wrote a few pages of his book "Yestermorrow" in the summer holiday, but as soon as the autumn term began, it was put aside while he focussed fully on his teaching role. In the Easter holidays he added some more. Mina and I read it with interest, and it wasn't long before we both wanted to assist him, but it was the next summer holiday before we all started in earnest.

Writing was quite a good occupation then because we had relentless rain. The weather was much the same all over Europe, and some other areas of the world were devastated by it. Manhattan Island in the United States was slowly sinking into the sea. Most of the big businesses had already moved inland. A new city was already being constructed in New Jersey to replace it. But York City, was not planned to be finished until five years after the Manhattan floods had destroyed half of the island.

Something similar was beginning to happen in London. The Thames Barrier was no longer doing its job. We heard about this from Brandon, who had now moved to Tonbridge Wells. We invited him to stay with us for a week and were astonished when, a few days later, a small electronic flying car landed by the common plot and Brandon stepped out of it.

"Is it OK for me to park here?" he called, when I came running out of the house disturbed by the noise.

"I don't see why not," I cried back. "It's common land. You're well clear of the vegetables and the drone zone, but don't be surprised if some of the local kids start climbing over your wondrous machine. I presume you've locked it securely."

He laughed and suddenly looked like the lad I used to know again. I went over and kissed him, and he brought his bag into the house.

"How long have you had the heli?" I asked him.

"Don't insult it. It's not a helicopter. It's a flying car. Didn't you see the wings fold up? I've had it just over a year," he answered. "I started flying lessons two years ago. It's great. Have you seen Woodleigh from the air? You must come up with me."

"No. I'd love to."

"Well you will, then. It's my way of thanking you for putting up with me."

"I'm not putting up with you. I'm putting you up. There's a difference, you know."

"Is there?" He carried on with the bantering. "Have you forgotten that I'm the black sheep of the family?"

"First I've heard of it. I know you've gone your own way, but it's your life."

"I hope Mom and Dad feel like that. Where do I put the my travel bag?"

"In the guest room at the top of the stairs, next to the bathroom. Lucy's in her old room again too. She had a tiff with Sam and they've split up, and she's very sore about it, so be gentle with her."

"Poor Luce. I've always been gentle with her, Beatrice. She was a sweet kid, and you did wonders for her. I respect that."

"Well, she isn't a kid any longer. She's grown up like you have, and she's got a life of her own. She's a qualified nurse now and she works at the Royal Devon Hospital."

"Good for her. What's the name of that guy she's with?

"Sam. She met him at work and they were together in Exeter. She thought she'd found the man of her life, but it didn't work out, so she's back here now. It's really upset her."

"Sorry to hear that. I know what it feels like. I've had two doses now. First Priscilla. Then Corrie."

"Yes, you told me. I'm sorry about Corrie. I liked her when we met last year. I thought you'd helped each other sort things out."

"We did, but that's history. I don't want to go through it again, explaining....."

"No, no. I didn't want you to explain it all. I was just saying I'm sorry it hadn't worked out. Period."

"Good. I'll go up and dump the bag, and can I have a shower?"

"Yes, of course. Make yourself at home."

Brandon seemed to enjoy the whole week.

He took me up in the flying car. I'd seen a few of them around but never flown in one before. It was neat and compact inside, with comfortable seats, just providing room for two. Going up was sensational: both noisy and dramatic. I could hear the spinning blades above our heads, as we shot up, vertically. When we reached the programmed height, a green light came on and Brandon pressed a button on the panel in front of him. The whirring noise stopped and the wings suddenly flapped open on both sides. It was a stunning moment. We moved quietly and horizontally forwards now and I suddenly had a beautiful view of Woodleigh from the air, nestling as it does, on the crest of the peninsula between the two yawning bays, Exe and Benbow. I had never seen Woodleigh in this way before, and suddenly felt a surge of loving warmth for the place. I could see all the housing clusters and their allotments, the roof of the community hall, with its shining solar panels, and the memory came back to me of Dad's last dream. It must have looked like this. I was deeply touched. It seemed as if he was sitting in the plane with me.

A second later, I saw the main town beyond, with the church spire, Woodleigh Town Hall and the line of wind turbines seeming to mark a boundary between the urban area and the heath. We headed in that direction, flying over a forest of treetops, and across the green corridor, which has been retained to preserve the wildlife species of flora and fauna.

For some of the flight we were on automatic pilot, and Brandon showed me the computer that controlled the flight and a screen that recorded information about other flying objects within radius and ensured that we stayed clear of them all. He also explained that there were very strict regulations now about flight paths. There were three types, he told me: "Highways" which were far above us and used by long-haul flights, "Air roads" used by airbuses and planes such as this, and "Pathways" for helicopters and recreational air-balloons. They were all radio controlled, and you knew when you joined the right flight path because of the lighted screen.

We looked down on the woods around the ancient earthwork that they call Woodleigh Castle. Then Brandon took over control again, turning left to follow the riverbank up to Exeter, where we could see the cathedral and the hospital where Lucy works. Then he took a sweep across the heath, coming back to the shoreline, with the blue sea beyond the rocky beach. We followed the line of alternating red and white cliffs until we had crossed Benbow Bay and the holiday park. We turned inland there to circle over the heath again. Now I could identify the other cluster housing on the far side of Woodleigh. Again we flew over the town centre, with its busy traffic and tiny pedestrians, saw the church and the town hall, and then suburban rooftops and traditional gardens, before coming back to our own four clusters. Down we came again, to land by our own common plot.

Lucy was working long hours at the hospital but she had two days off during Brandon's stay and during that time, she introduced him to kite surfing. On the second afternoon, I went down to the beach and marvelled to see them surfing the waves with two colourful kites dancing overhead and urging them on. At one stage, they were so elated that, first Brandon, and then Lucy tried to wave to me, and a second later, they ended up struggling in the water. They came ashore and chased one another up the beach, laughing like teenagers, each seeming to have found a new zest for life, for a few days at least.

Brandon was relaxing at last and beginning to take a wider view of the world. He told me that he had no contact whatever with the Seagrave family, but I gathered that he was still supporting himself by doing business on the stock exchange.

I invited Rory and Mina over for a meal with us all, and they came and were fairly relaxed, but Brandon completely clammed up that evening. After the meal he said he had a headache and needed to go and rest. Obviously disappointed and upset, Rory left an invitation for him to join them for a meal, but Bran told me that he'd rather not, and asked me to pass the message on. It made me feel very sad.

On his last day here, however, he said something that surprised me. "You'll probably be glad to hear that I've got a portfolio of green energy investments now. They're bringing in a very good rate of return." I was very glad to hear this.

* * *

Rupert:

After eight years of marriage, Catriona told me that she was expecting a child. We were both delighted, as we were not expecting this. The number of parents who were not able to start new families was growing around the world, and we shared Beatrice's disappointment that she was not able to conceive more children of her own.

A few months before the due time we learned that we were to have twins, and eventually two healthy baby girls joined our family. We named them Shona and Tessa. A naming ceremony was held in

Newcastle, where grandparents and several other family members joined us. Catriona was, of course, entitled to her maternity leave, so that she was able to enjoy quality time with them in the years before they started pre-school. We both felt sure that the infants benefited from the arrangement. The weather was more temperate in that year too, so we were able to make the most of the opportunity, with many outdoor activities for the twins. Having these youngsters made us all the more aware of the responsibilities we carried as part of the living planet. We, our children, and all creatures on earth are travelling on a creative journey together. We need to be aware of this, honour it and make positive contributions.

* * *

Beatrice:

In 2095 the wild weather was worse than any we had known. The North Sea invaded all the Dutch polders, and Amsterdam and Rotterdam were largely destroyed. Many Dutch families took refuge in Britannia, mainly in Northumbria and Mercia. I was delighted to meet my old school friend, Lina, again, when she brought her young family here. The Council applied to a GOS refugee fund for financial assistance when a large group of Dutch settlers came to Woodleigh, and a grant was approved which enabled our Dutch friends to build two new groups of cluster housing.

My links with overseas transition groups kept me in touch with many developments. Those in some of the poorer countries had a struggle to continue because diseases were spreading in many areas. Thousands of people in Africa and Asia were smitten with T.B. that spread rapidly because of the limited diet. Some transition towns in richer areas twinned with groups there giving support in heart-warming ways, but this gesture could not cure the problems.

As the century progressed, people began to think ahead towards 2,100, and a determination set in to ensure that things improved before that date. Diseases respect no boundaries, and plans began to formulate in the minds of progressive communities across North and South America. Similar ideas were shared across Europe and Africa. We knew we needed to establish a much better international health services across the globe and tackle both physical and mental health with a new vigour, otherwise we would face the full consequences ourselves.

Renewable energy had won the day. The powers of the few remaining multi-national corporations were waning and their hold on the international cities they had been controlling was crumbling. It was now recognised by all the main governments that the only solution possible to the multiple problems facing mankind was through international co-operation. New economic policies prevailed in both East and West: China, the U.S.A., Russia, the E.U., African and Indian governments had now all developed policies based on the principles of a circular economy. There were still many differences between these powers but they all knew that it was in their own interest to pay the GOS taxes and let the international elders handle development issues in poorer countries, rather than allow competing governments to get entangled in these issues. This approach was aided by the fact that there now was a Chinese leader with Buddhist leanings, an American President with an enlightened multi-cultural approach, and an Iranian GOS Elder who had studied Sufi teachings.

Of course, there were still many selfish individuals and organisations who hankered power and several underground organisations still created difficulties, but their strength was limited, and the age of terrorist attacks was now long over. The ownership of guns was tightly controlled by GOS regulations across the world, and the big problem now lay with those middle class people who were still addicted to the old cyber world of advertising and power games. Many of the older generation remained unresponsive to the fundamental changes required in lifestyles.

Rory and Mina invited our family over to lunch one Sunday in the spring of 1997. After the meal, the children were playing games on the lawn, while Elsa, Brook, and I sat in chairs on the patio, with Ivan, Susan,

David, Holly, and Lucy squatting on sheepskins as Rory explained his thoughts about the future.

"One reason I invited you all today was to share an idea. In three years time it will be the 2,100, effectively, the start of a new millennium. Yes I know that was said in the year 2,000 and many people celebrated the occasion with fireworks and the building of a small London dome by the River Thames, but this did not amount to anything very positive. There was no vision for the future and certainly no essential change in human behaviour patterns in the early years of this century. To our shame we carried on poisoning the environment and destroying whole species of life forms. The truth is that this whole century has been the cusp of a new age, and it's been a terrible experience. We must not carry the weight of this tragedy on into 2100. We need a better tomorrow! And it is possible.

Let's be honest. So many people now fear for the future. Optimism almost seems to have died, but the truth is that there's real reason for hope at last. Very late in the day, world governments have recognised the problems and become carbon zero. The energies of the sun, wind and water are being deployed now as never before. We have our final chance. Humankind cannot let so many dreadful mistakes continue into another century. Some forward thinkers are suggesting that we ignore what our grandparents did in 2000, and start the new millennium in 2,100 instead. It's every bit as valid to do so. We need a new beginning: this idea's catching on all over the world. For the last few months I've been following a website about it: there's a massive on-line blog. Beatrice knows this too."

I was able to confirm this, telling everyone that I was in contact with people in transition groups who were making plans of this kind in the USA, Australia, India, Germany, Sweden and Japan.

"In around a hundred towns across the world, there'll be huge public gatherings to encourage positive visioning in the face of future difficulties," Rory explained. "Mom, Mina, Beatrice and I have talked this through. Our family could make a worthwhile contribution, but we need your ideas. What do you feel we should do? Let's share our thinking!"

"Are you suggesting that we organise carnivals down here, like you did in Mercia?" Ivan asked him.

"No," Rory said. "I think we've done that to death. Something completely different."

"Rory's right. We need to do something new to really get the juices working," Elsa said.

"Such as?"

"A big work-out perhaps," said Brook, "Some exercise that will improve our muscles and help us to relax more. There's too much tension in so many people."

"There speaks the physiotherapist," said David.

"Some activity that everyone can enjoy in at their own way and at their own pace; that could make a huge difference," I suggested.

"When I was in Africa, we didn't have running water in our village. We dug wells, set up water-pumps and built toilets. I remember the day that the water first flowed in Nkobo. It was a practical project, and we could all see the benefits, so everyone took part," said Mina.

" But we've got fresh water, so we what else do we really need?" I asked.

"What did you mean by getting the juices working?" Ivan turned to Elsa.

"Some sort of ritual, that gets folk thinking about their true responsibility not just to our own homeland, but to the whole world. Not only to human beings, but to all creatures, to the land, sea and air itself. Ask yourself 'What can I contribute? How can I add value to this desecrated world and all life forms around us?' "

There was a long pause while everyone tried to think this through.

Then Rory shared his thinking.

"One thing I wondered about was trying to organise a vision quest. It's an idea that originated many years ago with native people in the Americas. A group of people meet to share food and friendship and then have a day or two of fasting and solitary exploration in some wild places. Then they re-group to share what they have learned from the rest of natural world. It can be tough, but it sometimes wakens people up to the realities about the area they live in, care about and yet are slowly harming through their way of life. This isn't my idea. There are groups planning similar vision quests now in Australia, South America, U.S.A. and Spain."

"Sounds interesting," Brook said. "But what's the real aim? The next step."

"To help re-vision our place in the order of things, so that we're in a better position, not only to live sustainably, but to give something back to the environment: Things that have been destroyed through pollution by humans. It's what a new beginning has to be about, and what we learn can be shared with people across the world, and they can share their thinking too: an international exchange of ideas, hopes and prayers for a better world."

"Why fast?" asked Holly. "What's fasting got to do with it?"

"It's a discipline that can sharpen the mind. It helps tone the body and opens sensitivity," Brook explained.

"Where would we go?" asked Ivan.

"There are still plenty of wild places in Devon. Dartmoor, Exmoor, Woodleigh Heath and several parts of our own crumbling Jurassic coast right here across the bays."

"What would we do afterwards?" asked Mina.

"Share our visions with each other and also locally to encourage a much wider participation in this area and beyond. We need more positive thinking to counteract the despair. Perhaps if we try it as a family group and it goes well, we could open the exercise up to a lot of other people in Woodleigh. The idea circulating is to have preliminary vision quests in chosen places at different times. A Great World Gathering is to be held on New Year's Eve 2100. It will begin in the Far East and spread west as the day wares on but the weather will probably be very cold in our climate, so an open-air event will have to be for hardy people. "

After some discussion that night, we decided to hold a preliminary family event at Midsummer in 2097. We agreed to gather for a family meal and then drive up to Woodleigh Heights to watch the sun go down: usually a spectacular event at that time of year. The next day would be reserved for positive meditation and/or prayer, together with observation of the natural world around us. After a simple breakfast, we would go our separate ways wandering in lonely places. It was to be a day of fasting, except for the bottles of spring water that we agreed to carry. Notebooks should be brought to record things seen or heard and significant thoughts that we had during the day. Everyone was to bring a sleeping bag to use on the next night at an open-air spot. Next day we'd all gather at Woodleigh Castle again, carrying any natural items we'd found and wished to share.

After breakfast, we would sit in a circle to share our experiences: dreams, ideas or visions. The eldest one would be first to speak and the youngest would be last. To make it more immediate, everyone should aim to use the present tense. After each person had spoken, a "talking stick" would be passed round the circle and anyone who wished could hold the stick to make a short comment or say, "If this had been my experience, I would feel…." Just a sentence would be enough, but later in the day we could have a second round of thoughts and ideas. If there was something felt inappropriate for the whole group, it could be shared with a chosen friend in our party. Positive ideas would be written up and shared with us all. A final account of it all could be shared on line with other vision groups as a preliminary step.

"If we really do this properly it can be life changing. If it was done in many groups around the world, it could be earthshaking!" said Rory.

"If the idea really catches on here, we could have a series of vision quests, involving all the clusters and then open it up in Woodleigh, for everyone interested," said Brook.

"The idea is being discussed already in many parts of Britannia. If this is done in places across the whole country, and across the world, it could be life enhancing!" said Mina.

"Spread the word round the family and with your neighbours," I told them. "Encourage them all to consider it. Put it on line: send the ideas across Britannia. I can share the plan with all our contacts around the globe. Who knows where it will end?"

Rupert:

When we heard about all this, Catriona and I were inspired by these ideas and keen to be at the gathering this year. We arranged leave accordingly. I then sent a drone letter to Brandon about it, explaining that we would be there and asking if he could join us. He replied in writing too:

"Hi Rue,

Thanks for the invitation. I enjoyed staying with Bea last summer, and would like to see you all again, but I'm not sure whether to come. It depends how I am. Things are bad just now. You remember that I told you about the girl who joined me. It went well at first. We'd met at the rehab place, and helped one another, but Corrie and I have had a second bust up. She's gone again. We were having a difficult time, and I was sticking with it, but suddenly she decided to pack her bags and go. She's off to join another guy.

I'm pretty low myself now. It's not been easy going for the last year. I thought I'd found the right woman at last, and she was so much better too. She'd got over the paranoia. I was steady also. I was off the doctor's drugs and we'd both quit the booze. It's a big blow. I nearly went back on the bottle, but I managed to hold that off. I rang the rehab place, and they've given me a buddy and he's been round here. It helps a lot.

I'll ask him what he thinks about this Vision Quest idea. It might help. On the other hand it might be too much for me: especially with the family all there. I know I'm OK with you and Catriona and with Beatrice and Luce. I'm not sure about Mom and Dad though. It might upset them. So I'll defer the decision until the actual time. I'm not saying No, it's just Maybe. Hope you two and the kids are OK.

See you soon anyway,   Brandon."

I did not show anyone that letter. I just said that Bran was not sure if he could come. Corrie wasn't able to, but Bran might be with us. He'd let us know later.

I was very disappointed because I really wanted him to come. I felt he needed this experience, and that perhaps we needed his too. It would be a valued extension of the project into a different domain.

CHAPTER 36 - The Vision Quest

Midsummer's Eve 2098

Rupert:

"We are gathering on the hilltop to watch the sun go down. There are eleven of us, representing three generations. Granny Elsa, white haired and wizened now, and looking as if she belongs to anther age, but her keen, loving eyes are as strong as ever. Because of her quiet radiance people still compete to be close to her. She was once a tall woman, but now she seems to have shrunk into herself. Her shoulders droop and she walks slowly, aided by her wooden stick. She picks her steps gently along the path.

Frances and Peter walk with her at the same slow pace. Elsa is keen to include them both in this gathering because their friendship goes back to the time when Frances was the school librarian and Elsa was a young teacher over from the USA on a year's attachment programme. It is good to see the three of them together again.

Peter is bald now, but you wouldn't know because of his wide brimmed sun hat. He holds Frances steadily on one side. Elsa takes her other hand. Frances walks with their help, because she is waiting for a cataract operation and has to be careful of her steps in the evening light.

Mom, Dad, Catriona and I were the first to arrive and we are standing near the top of the cliff, watching a wonderful sunset over the quiet heath-land, spread out below us. The only noise comes from rooks, hovering over a grove of dark trees, as they choose which branch to lodge on. The sky above them is a blaze of gold, as the sun slowly inches behind a billow of white cloud, gently tingeing it with an amber glow.

'Here they come,' Mina says. We turn and see the green e-car that Brook said he would hire. We see Beatrice, Lucy, Brook and then

Brandon scramble out and wave. I am very happy to know that Brandon is here for this family Vision Quest. Rory runs over to greet him with a great bear hug. We both knew he had arrived because we had first heard and then seen his flight-craft hovering by the common plot a few hours ago, but we did not have a chance to run out and greet him, because we were busy preparing the evening feast, now stowed in the boot of our car. So our vision quest group is complete. We are missing the children. Shona, Tessa, and their five young cousins have their own discovery day at the farm, with Susan, Ivan, David and Holly.

We sit together in total silence, as agreed, to watch the sun slowly close this warm summer day. We join hands for five minutes, and then a message is passed along the line with a squeeze. Responding to the signal, we walk over to the feast, which we can still see, in the fading light, because we have set the lantern in the centre of the tablecloth spread on the ground. Everyone is invited to join the circle. We squat down, as plates are passed from hand to hand, and nods and smiles replace words in ways that amuse us. A tender affection ripples through the whole group, as bowls are passed.

Silence has been maintained throughout the meal and as we clear up afterwards. Most people move to the cars, which are taking them home, but Catriona and I have other plans. Instead of going back to Woodleigh, we are to ride to a loved spot on Dartmoor, where we will pitch our tent by starlight, and then retire on this warm summer night.

* * *

We wake to the sounds of birdsong and the rippling water of the young River Dart. After refreshing ourselves at the stream, we shoulder our packs and set off walking in opposite directions for a solitary day and night, observing different areas of Dartmoor.

* * *

Meeting again, by the car, at dawn, we kiss and smile. A gentle understanding passed through us both that the vision quest day and night had been fruitful, but still we retain silence, as we gather our things, get in the car and drive away.

We join the others two hours later, when we all gather at Woodleigh Castle to tell our tales, but first comes our long awaited breakfast. Silence is kept until the meal is over and then all eyes turn to Elsa who, being the eldest, has been invited to speak first."

Vision Quest Stories

Elsa's Vision

"At eight thirty a.m. on Midsummer Day, we all gathered again at Woodleigh Castle. Rupert and Catriona were the last to get here. It was no surprise because we knew they were driving back from Dartmoor but we had to share a silent breakfast together, so we waited and then cheered when they arrived and, having starved for a day, everyone ate with relish.

When we had finished, Mina produced her guitar and we all joined hands, forming a ring around her for our midsummer circle dance. We all loved the old folk tune and were familiar with the steps, which were done in three rounds. I was the one to break the ring, pick up my twisted old staff, and ask everyone to sit down. They faced me in a semi-circle and I perched myself on the slope of the old embankment, and started speaking.

'Before I talk about my experiences, I'll just remind everyone that this woodland branch I'm holding is now our talking stick. Mark found it lying around when he was walking here some years ago. He brought it home he showed it to me saying, 'Just look at this stout branch, Elsa. It's so old and gnarled that I reckon that there must have been wisdom in the great oak tree it belonged to.' He shaped it appropriately and used it as a walking stick from then on, but now, it's mine. I brought it because I felt it belonged in this wood, and perhaps we'll leave it when we go, but meantime Rory told me to say that whoever holds this stick can talk for five to ten minutes about their experience and the speaker is not to be interrupted. When you've had your say, pass it to the person on your left. Oh, and some of you will have to move places, because the eldest are to tell their tales first and the youngest last.'

Once they are in the right positions, I continued, 'Now for my vision. I did not stir very far from this magical area. I was asked to spend the day observing the woodlands, and there is enough wildlife and history right here for a whole day. Vision quests can take you back in time and help you find what your heart really desires, and after I'd rooted around watching the squirrels playing and caught sight of a badger, I was led right back in my imagination to my real homeland, the countryside of South California: the land of lazy afternoons, green fertile plains and quiet lakes. I imagined that I could smell the scent of chocolate drifting strangely from the twisted boughs of manzanita trees and I could see the stony trails winding gently up hillsides, where pup raccoons play hide-and-seek in bushes. I enjoyed just sitting here and sending loving thoughts about all this to the world around me.

Sundown reminded me of another time. A summer night, when I was on another a hill by myself, watching the sun inch its way down and the red desert facing me, looking vast. I remembered that I'd been walking through rich watered land and suddenly reached the end of it. If I followed the trail down that hill I'd be entering a parched thirsty land, where little but cactus can thrive. Should I go forward to face the challenge or turn tail and go back to my comfort zone?

The choice was taken from me, because I fell asleep and dreamed about the coast at La Jolla, where huge seals basked in the sunshine, as they lay on the rocks of the bay. A mother was feeding its young, and two fat calves were chasing each other for the best position to draw most milk. Several holidaymakers were taking photographs: some from the roadway above, some from the beach below, so they were competing with each other too. I just stood watching in the quiet of a sunny day. I guess that I wasn't in the competition business.

I dreamed of these places after I'd climbed into my sleeping bag that night. Suddenly, I was in a car driving up the winding hill that led to my childhood's favourite place, the timeless village of Idyllwild. I knew that four avenues of stately trees awaited me, lined with comfortable log cabins that were always busy with visitors in the summer months and mostly left empty when the deep snow lay on the ground. It was a paradise for painters, woodcarvers, and some active retired people avoiding the busy world below the hill. This was a summer retreat for my grandparents and when I was little, I spent many happy hours 'up the hill' going for woodland walks with their dog, Prince, and playing on the swing my father had rigged up in the old back yard. Why was I here again? Surely, the good folk I used to know would have all gone away and mayhap Idyllwild would be a town o' ghosts for me now.

For some reason I am bein' drawn to places that I knew as a child. Is it just memory, or might some of this be significant in my life now? But suddenly everything is transformed. I'm no longer in the open air. This is a great dark building, perhaps an old monastery. The stone walls look as if they could withstand hurricanes and tornadoes. I hear the wind roaring outside, and am grateful for this sanctuary, old and dull as it looks. I'm walking down a corridor with others around me. Some wear gowns or cowls. Yes, I think they must be members of some religious order. I'm not wearing these things myself. I'm in a long white dress, but I know that those around me are colleagues and fellow workers in a place of peace and order.

We approach a great wooden door, just as a big clock above our heads starts to strike the hour. The sound reverberates round the whole building and, as it strikes, a man runs forward with a stepladder. He places it behind the door, and goes up it to pull back huge bolts at the top.

We have to wait while he hurries down and removes the ladder, and then I produce a large key out of a pocket and unlock the great door.

490

Others kneel down to lift bolts from the stone floor, and now I'm free to begin to open the door. The wild wind rushes in. Hail stones batter against it and sturdy men have to hold the bolts while they are locked into positions to keep them open on either side. A mob presses forward, keen for the security of the building. I shout out to them, 'You are all welcome, friends, but take care, or someone will be trampled.'

Those nearby hear and try to slow the pace, but others are pressing them from behind, and some small children fall to the ground. Several of us pick them up, trying to move them safely, but mothers scream after us, 'You have my child!'

'Come with us, mothers,' I shout, as I pick up a child and lead another to a table, laden with loaves, and soup. 'There is enough for all.'

I put the child down beside a table, where a steaming metal urn and wooden ladle are set, by a pile of empty bowls. The healthy smell of vegetable soup rises from the urn. I take off the lid, dip the ladle in, stir it round and fill the nearest bowl, handing it to the child I'd been carrying. He grips the bowl eagerly.

'Be careful. It's hot,' I warn him. He smiles and goes towards his mother, showing her the soup.

A queue quickly forms at my table and at other feeding points scattered round the room.

I glance around and see long queues of desperate people. They have clearly come from all over the world. There are native American people wearing feathered headdresses; Inuits from the north, Caribbean people and Latinos from the south, poor whites and poor blacks, Chinese, Indians, Africans, Europeans, Jews and Muslims. I cannot be sure of these definitions, but all manner of people, young and old, male and female, wait in their desperation, and the amazing thing is that the soup never runs out, and the piles of bread on the tables never diminish, as we dole out the food.

Furthermore, there is this holy silence. The people keep coming and the huge room is never filled. More and more hollow-eyed people stagger towards us, but no one is angry. There is no fighting. Everyone waits their turn, and I never tire of lifting this heavy ladle. My arm never aches. This is a sacred miracle. Surely a holy spirit is in this place. I had never been happier at any time in my life before. I want to stay here feeding the world, until those urns have run dry, but they never do.

Someone near me says, 'Thank you, Elsa. You're always there for us when we need you!'

I reply, 'Don't thank me. Thank the Holy Spirit, who's alive in this place. I am just one of the thousands of servants.'

Who spoke? I look up again as I serve the soup, and see little pygmies from Central Africa and tall thin Masai people with their shields and spears from the Kenyan plains. And I cry out, 'How did you all get here?' and they answer in one great voice, 'We walked, we sailed, we swam and we found this place of refuge, at the end of the world, at the end of time. Amen.'

I think, *how is it possible for all these people to be here, wearing their traditional costumes? Why am I here? Where is my family?*

I look around and see them at the other tables serving the soup and the bread. Mark is on a table opposite. Rory and Beatrice are to my left and right. This is as it should be, I feel. This is mythical. Localised gatherings of this sort have been held throughout the centuries, and hopefully will go on into the future. We must never give up striving to meet the need, however great it is.

But Mark has died? *How can he be here with me, and with Rory and Beatrice too?* And then I see young Isabella, bless her heart. This must be another world. That explains all these different tribes. A glow of excited wonder burns in my heart and I know that all will be well.

And I wake up and find myself resting here on the gentle turf of Woodleigh Castle, and the dream or revelation is so powerful that it is still reverberating inside me. Why am I privileged to hold the key to the door of this sanctuary? I begin to cry and I can't stop: probably because it was my vision. The tears keep flowing, *but am I weeping for sadness or for joy?* An inner voice whispers 'joy' and I start to pray that human beings will never give up on their worldwide mission: never ever. Amen.

I pass the talking stick along the line. Some are so awed that they pass it on without more than a few complementary words, but contributions include, 'If this had been my dream, I'd have felt very humbled to be the key-holder,' and, with a gentle smile. 'Only Elsa could have dreamed up this one.'

Peter's Vision

"I'm not a great dreamer. As you know, I'm a practical sort of man, so I thought about this vision quest in advance and decided I'd spend the day strolling all over the heath, and trying to work out, in my own mind, just what sort of future really lies ahead. I must confess, I didn't really study the natural world. I explored my inner self instead and had some great dialogues. I ended up writing this, and then I had a quiet dreamless night under the stars.

' I can see two men waiting for me on office chairs. They both stand up as I approach. The man on the right is large and confident. He is dressed in a smart suit and wears polished shoes. The one on the left is down at heel and mild. The well dressed man steps towards me saying, 'I've been waiting longer than that fellow, so I'll speak to you first.' He glances at the other man mumbling 'That's fair, isn't it?' The shoddy person shrugs his shoulders, and reluctantly sits down again.

'Come this way, please.' The big man opens a side door and ushers me into a plush office. There is a large desk and he moves to the swivel chair behind it, indicating a small seat that I sit on.

'So, what do you want to know?' he asks.

I see a calendar on the wall behind him and hear myself saying 'Pretty well everything. What's life like in 2120?'

'Very comfortable, where I am,' he responds.

'Where are you living?' I ask.

'London, I have a house in Hampstead facing the heath. I live there with my wife. It's secure from the wild weather, of course, being under the Great Dome. Our children are both comfortably established too. Martin's a hedge-fund manager in the city and my daughter lives in California where she runs a funeral company called Loved Companions. Wendy and I flew over to see her a few months back. She lives in stunning surroundings, at the heart of a memorial orchard. She conducts tailor-made funerals for ponies, cats, dogs, and other pets. She works mainly on line with people from all over the States. As for me, I've retired from the Real Estate Company now, so I divide my time with a few board posts and the golf club. I do a little charity work too, for my old school, Eton, and Wendy's the Chair of the Hampstead Bridge Club.'

'Does it ever get a bit claustrophobic, living under the Dome?'

'No, it took us a couple of years to get used to it, but now we couldn't live anywhere else. We're never troubled by rain, of course, and the water's piped under the whole of the heath and the surrounding gardens twice every day. It's recycled washing water, so we take care of the environment, if that's what you're thinking.'

'Are there many birds on the heath now? How do they fare?'

'Very well. It's not just the blackbirds and the thrushes now, you know. The ornithologists restock the heath every season, and we can select the birds we want. They supply the ones that get the highest number of hits. There's a questionnaire delivered once a year and we bid for whatever birds we fancy next season. We've got parakeets and golden eagles there now you know.'

'I suppose you've lost all the hedge sparrows now, and what about the migrating birds? They can't get into the Dome, can they? Surely, it must have created an unnatural balance? It can't be good for the web of life.'

'It used to be random, in the old days. Now we can have all the birds we fancy. It's the same with the animals too. We keep a few foxes, so that we can still have the traditional hunting sprees. I like rabbit pie too, so we still have bunnies digging holes to dive into, but we've no use for the hedgehogs or the badgers, so they've had their day.'

'There's no room for natural selection any longer. Do you see any dangers in that?'

'No, we decide what we want and make the most of our opportunities.'

'So one species controls the whole game.'

'The human being has come of age, that's the way I see it.'

'Do you ever wonder how long this age will last?'

'No. We only have one life, so we need to seize the moment.'

'I think I'd feel it was rather stifling to live under a dome all the time - in a sort of artificial bubble. Do you ever go beyond it to experience the wind at your back or the sunshine on your face?'

'Of course we do. My wife and I spent last winter in South Africa. Flew by jet and had a great time in the game parks. Even managed a bit of shooting myself, but I suppose that sort of thing gets up your nose. You should try it. You remember they used to say that all the lions would be dead forty years back. Didn't happen, you know. They secured the best beasts and organised it so that they bred like wildcats. All those animals they thought would become extinct...you remember the old talk....well they're safe under lock and key, and you can walk down avenues where they have 'em there in cages. If you want a days hunting, you can choose your own beast. They take you to the park, give you a rifle and release the animal you chose. You can chase it through the bush, in a specially designed metal tank, taking shots, and in the end you get the trophy - a lion's head to hang up on the wall, like that one over there.'

Suddenly, I can see it in a glass case, beside the huge TV screen. I feel sick, and look away.

'You must excuse me.' I say. 'I'm not feeling well. Can I use your toilet?'

'Course,' the man said points to a door behind me. 'I must get back to my work. I've got an appointment with my investment broker now. I'm meeting him for lunch.'

When I come out of the executive toilet, he has gone, so I walk back through the office into the waiting room outside.

The shabby man is still there waiting. He looks up and smiles.

'So what is life like for you in Britannia?' I ask him.

'I'm fairly happy with my own life, and that of my family, but I despair for the lost people in this world of ours. As for us, we do what we can to live sustainably on our little croft. There are five of us - three children, my wife and I. We share the work together. We have a pony and cart and we use it to take our produce to the weekly market and make enough to live on. What more do we need? We rise with the dawn, and one of the first tasks we share is milking the cows and the goats. They are really part of our extended family. My wife and daughter see to the hens and geese. We all share in the work of the harvest and the preparation of our meals. Our children are well educated locally, and I have hope for their future.'

'What do you fear?'

'The climate is changing so rapidly. We've had some fearfully cold winters, with deep snow on the ground from November to April, and some blazing hot summers, torrential downpours and violent winds. Everything is so uncertain. We can't bank on a good harvest any longer. In the years ahead, will there be enough to eat? There's even talk of a new ice age. I think that our children will have to leave the croft and go south, but where can they go? Europe is hostile to immigration, and warships guard the coast. All countries with tolerable climates are being threatened by desperate groups of migrants. North and Central Africa is uninhabitable. I'm told that there is good land in South Africa and Australia, but borders are guarded everywhere. Several cities have been enclosed under domes, like London, but humans were not meant to live like turtles.'

'Are you sad that you can't afford to fly to Australia or New Zealand?'

'I have no desire to fly anywhere? That was the way of the birds, but they are becoming rare in these parts now. I know my homeland, Britannia, and I don't think I could live elsewhere. When I was young I took part in one of those Elfleda plays, and afterwards we formed teams and worked together supporting our community, but now most of my old school-friends have tried to go south. Some have disappeared, others have been forced back by border police and are depressed. Some have even tried sending their children on their own, believing that unaccompanied young people might be accepted, but my wife and I would never do that.'

'Do you blame the wealthy who wouldn't change their ways, and helped speed up the climate change?'

'I blame no one, sir. It's the way of the world. There were ice ages in ancient times and for all we know they may well return. While I can rear my family under the warmth of the sun, I will. We make the most of our sun-power and wind-power with panels and turbines, which help by storing the electricity for colder times. These things are part of the Great Creation and we have our part to play in it by storing the treasures when they are available. This is our role. All creatures have a part to play. Cows and goats provide our milk, the hens provide eggs, and bees used to provide honey. I can still remember the sweet taste, but I have not found any since my boyhood years. Human beings are the harbingers, tending the earth and helping to spread its bounties across the miles.'

'I'm sure you're right about that.'

'I'm glad you agree with me. You must excuse me , sir, I must leave you now. Its nearly milking time and I don't like to keep cows waiting. They gather at the gate and watch the lane to see if I'm coming.' He touches his cap and turns to go.

'I am Peter,' I call after him. 'What's your name?'

He looks back over his shoulder. 'They call me Adam,' he says.

There was something beautiful about him. It was calming listening to his ideas. You asked me to share my feeling about the vision, Rory. I'd say it leaves me in a lovely, green valley; but one with deep shadows, so to speak. There was no hill-top experience for me."

The talking stick passes around the circle, and comments are made by most of the group.

Frances's Vision

I had a very peaceful day exploring the area. Apart from casual glimpses of people walking by, I was alone all day.

"It's my dream too, rather than my walk I want to share with you all.

In a blinding flash of light, three faces peer at me from a dark background. Two bearded men who seem to have come from the distant past and a young woman of today. The central one becomes clearer: an elderly man wearing a dinner jacket and black tie, Victorian style. The others fade slowly away.

'Why have you come to me?' I ask.

'Because you understand,' He has a gentle American twang. 'You are a librarian, Mrs. Samphire, You love books. So do I. That's why I started circulating libraries, for God's sake. Sorry, I must introduce myself,

Andrew Carnegie's the name: born in Scotland, Dunfermline, Fife, to be precise. Trained as a wee laddie on spinning machines, and might have spent my whole life in drudgery there, but I managed to break free and came here to the noo world. I'd little enough schooling, but I noo the power of books, and applied myself to study, and to business. When I was a millionaire, I did what I could to help other young folk find their way in life. My greatest pride is that I helped create a world full of circulating libraries, so that all those with a mind to, can educate themselves.'

'That dream of yours lasted a long time,' I tell him. 'It nearly ended in this country around 2015 with brutal budget cuts. Libraries were prime targets. Things got better later, under the Unity Government, I'm glad to say. Most of our libraries were refurbished again.'

I felt I owed him this information.

'A good crop usually prevails, when seeds are carefully sown,' he responds. 'These books open people's eyes to all the great achievements of mankind. Scientists read what others have done and grow on their shoulders. I guess that began with the ancient Greeks with their philosophy and myths. The arts flourished in the Renaissance, and then came Galileo with his science and look what's happened since ... Darwin, Einstein to mention only two out of hundreds of deep thinkers: consider the medical field and then the natural world with all the living creatures that have been recorded and studied. This leads to more enquiries, more research and more books spreading the knowledge way beyond the original thinkers. Where would we be without books showing light upon the human condition? Without our poets and novelists, bringing human lives into focus.....'

The voice fades into the background, as the face of the second bearded man appears instead. The ruff around his neck reveals that he belongs to earlier times, and the twinkle in his eyes shows that he is determined to have his say.

'Don't forget the playwrights: I could not have writ my plays without the books I found in rich men's houses: Plutarch's Lives, Roman histories, Greek myths, English Chronicles. I brought these dusty pages back to life again: Julius Caesar, Helen of Troy, King Harry the fifth, Hamlet, Macbeth. They strode my stage and won applause, but what astounded me was to discover that, after I had left my mortal coil, my fellow players, Hemming and Condell contrived to piece my plays together and make a book of them. The plays came to life again and were performed around the world, not least in my home town, Stratford, and then, to crown it all, my Globe Theatre was resurrected and now stands again on Southwark bank. I doff my cap to Wanamaker and to the crowd of players, male and female too, who don the motley to perform my plays in the ways of their own times.'

I want to have a conversation with Will Shakespeare. There are so many questions buzzing in my mind, but in moments a lady replaces him. She is modern, bright eyed and determined.

'These men will talk forever. They boast about their works, but now at last the women's voice is heard. It took so long for us to break the barriers. The novelists had to adopt men's names at first, but now there are more tales published by us than by the men, and women are progressing fast in science, medicine and all other fields: more of us are going to universities, pushing at the boundaries, questioning the rules and innovating. It took the suffragettes to set the ball rolling, but now there's no stopping it. Nothing can hold us back.'

"And who are you?" I ask. I like her verve but cannot place her.

'Call me Janet. I don't own my husband's name, nor yet my father's. Why should women have to be classified by either? Aren't we flesh and blood and the mothers of all humanity. The world has changed. It took too long and now it is too late. These men are so aggressive that they think they own the planet. They deny the female life force at its heart. Men fight for places in the sun. They grow more armies to compete in battle, invent new weapons and create new enemies. We mothers have learned the way to calm the children. Now is the time for us to turn the tide.'

'But you can do it in time!' I cry. 'Why ever didn't the nations abide by those climate change promises? A way ahead was found in 2015. The leaders signed a contract in Paris. If only those promises had been fulfilled, so many lives would have been saved. Our children would have had a future to look forward too, instead of morbid fears.'

'It was an unspeakable tragedy,' Janet says. 'But there's still hope, if we join hands together across the world. It's too late save the Pacific islands. There's little of value left in equatorial Africa and in Central America, but if women make a stand, the damage can be stopped. There can be no more human life without the women. Much will be saved if we are totally determined. I believe we have the strength to do this. We can't reverse what's happened, but we can stop more destruction, and we must keep those books because they tell the story of the world we lost and how much of it can be restored.'

Her voice fades and I've lost the vision in her eyes, but I her spirit has enlivened me. I waken to see a crimson dawn."

Frances's eyes brim with tears. Elsa and Peter both turn to comfort her.

The talking stick was passed from hand to hand, but most of the men are too shaken to respond.

The women support her words.

Rory's Vision

After a long walk along a deserted section of the coastal path, I spent some time gazing out to sea.

Watching the waves breaking on the shore, I started to meditate. What sort of world would I really like to see in a hundred years time? I must try to envisage it. There's so much despair in people's thinking. So many high hopes have been dashed, and there has been so much destruction by hurricanes, fires and floods that most people have lost hope. This is tragic and doesn't help the situation because, at last, there really are substantial changes for the better. Carbon energy has been rejected and there is now a steady energy flow from kinetic and geo-thermal sources. Traditional economic models have failed, and a new concept of a circular economy is being embraced and explored in multiple trials around the world.

For a hundred years there has been a mismatch between leaders of countries and the communities of enlightened people who strive to live sustainably. Now, at last, most major governments have learned the lessons and it is ordinary people who have become so deadened by despairing news that faith and hope seem to have been lost. It's essential that green activists envision and explain their ideas fully, so that a dream of the world we want can be born in every land, and every neighbourhood. Then the whole of humanity can be enlivened and work in harmony with the natural order instead of pulling against it.

The train of thought continued in the dream I had last night. I fell asleep gazing at the stars of the night sky.

Before I went to sleep I was looking up at the stars in wonderment. I enter that starry sky. Darkness is around me but a myriad of distant shining jewels are above me and on every side. There is also music. *Is it singing I hear or is it an orchestra?* I can't identify the sound. It's beautifully modulated. *Can this be the singing of the spheres or something else, timeless and inscrutable? The music is strong. It ebbs and flows and draws me towards it. How am I travelling? I am moving forwards towards shoals of stars. Am I being projected or moving at will? I'm not aware of making any movements: I am being carried on a current of air.* I move my fingers slightly. It makes no difference. I wave my arms and legs, but it has no effect on my situation. *Can I go upwards?* As soon as I ask this, I am propelled higher. *Can I go down?* I am gently carried lower. I think the word *Stop* and I am still. *Can I go faster? Yes, I can. Can I go slower? Yes. Clearly, I am in control and enjoying this effortless ride.*

Some of the stars are big and some smaller. *Is this because of distance?* The word 'Yes' came from somewhere?

Suddenly, the whole experience changes; I find myself swimming with great effort through a tidal sea. I'm swimming with the tide and it is carrying me towards land. It is daylight when I raise my head and open my eyes and to my amazement, I recognise that I am looking at the approaching cliffs of Benbow Bay. As I gaze at the layers, a shadow comes over me. I look up expecting to see a dark cloud but instead I see a monstrous flying bird, whose wings reach out over the sea on one side and the cliff face on the other. Fear grips me as the creature circles round and comes to rest on the cliff top: and its wild eyes search the beach below. The name pterodactyl comes into my mind.

Immediately I cry out, 'Let me fast forward.' A great rushing noise sounds in my ears. Everything blurs as flashing lights blind my vision. I shut my eyes. The noise continues for about a minute, while I continue swimming and then there is total silence.

Slowly, fearfully, I open my eyes. I see the same triassic cliffs, but the view is different. It is a pleasant sunny day, and a boy of about fourteen years old is waving his hands towards me. I know I must swim towards him, and I do. After several strokes, I realise that I am in shallow water. I put my feet down and feel sand. A moment later, I am striding forwards towards the rocky beach. I find that I'm wearing swimming trunks.

The boy is sunburnt, and has a open face, and wears a smock made of goatskin, with a belt round his waist, and I see a what looks like a torch thrust in it, glinting light. He plucks it out and waves it over the tide, and I realise that this instrument is catching the sun's reflection on the waters. He stands in rising tidal ripples and greets me with a pleasant smile.

'Greetings,' he says as we clasp hands. 'Forgive me for summoning you from the past. Which year are you in?'

'2098,' I say, but think *this is a dream. Immediately the voice in my head tells me. 'No, you are outside time and the teacher and the schoolboy are united through their love of these lands.'*

This makes no sense to me because the boy looks as if he belongs to another world but speaks modern English.

'Who are you?' I ask.

'Edwin, son of Samrod, the natural wisdom teacher. I am learning my father's craft."

'When and where is this?' I ask, thinking instantly that this is a stupid question, but the youth answers promptly.

'The year 2417 and this in Benbow Cove, on the Isle of Wessex.'

'The Isle of Wessex?' I query.

He smiles. 'Yes, of course. How could you know? There are now five major Britannic Isles: Wessex, Cymru, the long spine of Pennine, Scotia and Eire, and many smaller ones dotted around. My father has transcribed the old idylls of the people that explain that once there were only two large islands. That was before the great flood, when the low-lying central plains were lost. In your times, of course, there was a big city called London, but that now lies under the waves along with Anglia and Mercia. Our lays tell of the Ancient Father, King Alfred, who united the warring kingdoms, and of his daughter, Elfleda, who carried on his task. These lands and so much of Earth was lost because people of your times forgot the message of resilience that their forefathers had taught them: how to preserve the quality of life in the topsoil and the importance of protecting valuable species in the living world. Seeking power for themselves, those people were so foolish that they believed the earth had been made for them, just as the people of Noah's day did.

Today, we have learned to cherish the life of the earth and live lightly so that we can pass on this gift to our children.'

'Tell me, how have your grandparents or great-grandparents managed to cope with the storms that have divided Britannia? Did they have to evacuate to another land?'

The youth smiled. 'Some did. They became refugees, but that was not necessary really, because others hibernated in the caves. Our people had re-learned the ancient wisdom of their forefathers and regained the power of hibernation, which so many other creatures have never lost. This was how humanity survived the great ice-age, so very long ago. In your time, the instincts were dulled by the over-development of the intellectual parts of the brain, and the total neglect of other regions of human understanding. The people of your day built an economy based on material possessions, which led to competition between your tribes, They fought monstrous wars with evil weapons, quarrelling over who owned which territory, and ended up destroying vast tracks of it. No man can own any part of this sacred earth. All we can do is tend it, and share it with the other beasts. Throughout the long hibernation, we maintained a watch. We had a strong team of priests who kept a constant vigil of prayer for the safety of our planet, through all the wildest years. When the time was right, it was they who organised the great awakening.'

'You have no wars in your world then?'

'Of course not. Wars are wicked, childish play. There are no winners, and the planet itself is damaged, and all the wondrous wild life in it. Another lost gift in your time was communication between the tribes. You developed different languages, so that you could not understand each other without translators. You had to make complicated machines to show pictures about what was happening in other lands, because you neglected the age-old skill of telepathy, which enables everyone to contact family and friends wherever they are in the world. This gift is understood by numerous other creatures, by birds of the air, and creatures of the deep, like whales and dolphins -but amazingly, in your time, you were blind to all this. Your people had to create a telephone system to replace the gift of sending and receiving loving thoughts across the globe. Forgive me, I do not blame you for this folly. It was just the way you were educated. I don't mean to be rude. You needed to interpret the sacred messages left in writings on the walls by the wise men of the ancient caves, and you didn't have the capacity to do this.'

'What is that instrument you hold, and wave over the waters, as you talk?' I ask.

'It is my personal teacher,' the boy replies. 'My father makes these tools.' From a goatskin pocket he produced an iron frame with a ball of wire clipped to it. He unfolds strings and coloured ribbons, which play in the airwaves over the sea, and music ripples forth. It has the tone of an Aeolian harp and the tiny waves at our ankles seem to dance to the sweet sounds that ring out. Sea birds hover and swoop down towards us. A kittiwake settles on Edwin's jerking shoulder and dances to the tune, the shallow waters at our ankles become alive with tiny sea creatures and the red Triassic cliffs ring with unfathomable melody.

'These instruments provide the missing link.' Edwin's eyes are shining, and the whole bay echoes peace.

As I stand there, all alert, I find myself looking at the life around my feet. I am standing by a rock pool, seething with living creatures, and with seaweed providing nourishment. When he stops playing the chords, I turn to thank Edwin, but he is no longer there, although I still hear his voice reverberating with the words 'live lightly, so that we can pass this gift on to our children.'

I leave this world and suddenly discover a city of tomorrow. Its walls are of jasper. Its gates lie open for all to enter. I find am standing on one of the gatehouses. Looking down from it, I'm surprised to see that the city is full of greenery. A shining white pavement is so clean that it looks as if I could squat there to eat my lunch on it. The street is full of laughter and happiness. Children coming from school are joking, running and revelling. Older people are going about their daily business and greeting each other in a cheery way. There is a busy street market, with stalls selling healthy looking vegetables and fruits. People ride donkeys. Mothers carry infants by fastenings holding them close to the breast. This is a lively city at peace with itself in bright, morning sunshine.

Looking down on either side of the main street, I see roof gardens, where flowering plants and solar panels sit comfortably beside each other: balconies, where people sunbathe and call across to one another, and stone flagged yards, where women hang washing, children play and dogs bark. These groups of houses are closely aligned, like the cluster housing in Woodleigh

There are little towers and minarets. I hear the ring of church bells, and a Muslim call to prayer.

Beyond the lively street, I see palm trees beside a lake, set in lush greenery, where multi-coloured tropical flowers abound. In the centre of the gardens, is a bold baobab tree, displaying woody fruit and monkey bread. This is not just a city. It is a place of growth and fertility.

I can see community buildings dotted around comfortably: a bath-house, a laundry, a hospital and a school. I must explore this city. I go down a flight of stone steps to find an open archway, leading into the straight main pavement. I step out and instantly feel part of this community. People call out to wish me good day. This is a good place to be.

I turn into a side street, and find houses and flats, with windows open to the sun. I reach a stone bridge and look down to see a river flowing through the city. Here are barges, and homely boats, where families, wearing broad sun-hats, propel themselves along with water poles, and others sell vegetables from floating market stalls.

I board a waterbus, which is open to the sky, and take a seat beside a man, who wears a brightly coloured sombrero. He greets me in a friendly fashion and soon we are conversing. I say that I'm visiting the city for the first time and he responds and offers to show me interesting features as the bus progresses gently along.

'That building on the right there is a school. See the notice by the door?'

'It doesn't look like a school. It just looks like a big house that a rich person owns.'

The man laughs. 'Most of our richer people choose to live simple lives,' he says. 'Their houses aren't usually any bigger than other people's. We convert the larger houses into public amenities so that more people can enjoy them. Our schools are usually kept small. They have around a hundred pupils at the most, so every child knows all the others.'

'But don't you need sports grounds, laboratories, libraries and big assembly rooms?'

'Such buildings are all around us. Every district has all of these things, and they are open to everyone, schoolchildren and university students, just as they are to workers and homemakers. See that building with the garden roof? That's a neighbourhood community space, with a very good library and restaurant. That round building, over there, is our public entertainment area. It's really a theatre returned to its origins, with tiered seats and an open roof. We have touring players, music and dance, as well as public debates going on inside it."

The streets we are travelling along are lined with palm trees, and my friend tells me that they bear mixed fruits and coconuts. We see some people gathering fruit and others sitting on a low wall, eating bananas. Apparently, everyone is free to eat the fruit and nuts. The town council have planted the trees and they belong to the people of the city.

'I have never seen a city as comfortable as this one seems to be,' I tell him. 'Do you have no troublemakers? I don't see any policemen around.'

'No, we live in small family groups, and we find that this reduces violence and makes everyone familiar with transgender and other social issues. We don't need many police because cooperative living is a subject taught in all our schools, but, unfortunately, we do have people who break the law and spoil the situation for others. If these people are found guilty of offences in our law courts, they have to follow a re-training programme.'

'Is this done in your prisons?' I asked.

He laughs. 'No, we don't need any prisons. We used to have them many years ago, but we soon found out that they were counter productive. If you lock up some disorderly people together, they can turn the institution into an academy of crime. The situation becomes worse, not better. I am one of the re-trainers, and it so happens that I'm going to meet two offenders this afternoon. Would you like to come and see how we things organise these things here?'

I tell him I'd welcome such an opportunity, and so we spend the afternoon in a reformatory where my new friend, Pablo, involves me in dialogue with the two men in question, Marco and Zeb. They had both had tragic early experiences. Neither of them had ever enjoyed any decent home-life as a child. Marco did not know who his father was, and his mother had been a sad and dissolute woman. Zeb's parents had been killed in gun battles in a failed state, and he had been trafficked into this country by criminals, who used him to sell drugs. Neither of them had experienced school or training in a meaningful occupation, so street crime seemed the best way to survive.

They were both in their early twenties and now wanted to make the most of this opportunity, which offered them a lifeline. Marco tells me that he was caught by the police after he had mugged a man and stolen his wallet. Zeb had been arrested on a drugs charge. They met each other in a detention cell, while awaiting trial, and their cases were heard one after the other. They then travelled to the reformatory in the same van, and were grateful for the help that they had been given on arrival.

They said that custody began with a shower and a decent meal. After this, they were given adjoining bedrooms and a new set of clothing.

They joined a team of fifteen young men, who were all being offered appropriate education in small groups, and were kept busy with duties within the house and gardens. They had to do the cooking and baking under instruction from a qualified woman, keep the house cleaning and tidy, maintain of the allotments and learn to take care of the goats, hens and dogs. They had counselling sessions where they were encouraged to help each other by sharing their difficulties. All were set achievable targets, and earned privileges for good work and behaviour. There were sporting activities, including athletics, games and regular exercises each day. Marco had helped Zeb for two years as he was gradually weaned off drugs. They were now firm friends.

The education course had been completed, and after a year's assessment, they were now having training for some suitable employment. Zeb was learning to be a shoemaker. Marco was being trained in elementary nursing. The length of the sentence would depend on their progress, and the main target was to be let out on a probation order, as soon as they had reached an appropriate standard.

"But there must be others, who present a much more difficult problem. What happens to those who never change their ways," I ask Pablo.

"You are right," he says, sadly. "There are a few who never reform. Most do, under this system, but it takes a very long time to find the right trigger to wake some of them up. Those who do not respond remain labourers, doing useful work in the town under a very strict taskmaster. Eventually, they retire and die in a rest home, but we do all we can to help them become useful workers in the community."

I am taken on a tour of this incredible reformatory and see people engaged in yoga exercises and deep meditations. I sit in on a discussion group where experiences were shared and inmates were helped to support and heal each other's trauma. Achievable targets are set for future periods both in and out of their release into the community, and all this is monitored by probation officers.

Some prisoners are helping others to read and write and others are being encouraged to try their strength in athletics, in choral singing, dance and drama therapy.

"This is more like a school or hospital than a prison," I say.

"Of course," Pablo replies. "This is a place of both learning and healing."

That was the moment I wake, discover that I am lying on turf and sit up to see that dawn is breaking. I reach for my notebook, and write down the words that I have just been reading to you."

There was a long silence as the talking stick was passed from hand to hand. Most of us were too awed to speak.

"You had that vision of the stars. There's hope on other planets, you know. There's a group of scientists in London who are working on a rocket to reach outer space, beyond our galaxy. They believe it's possible that somewhere else might be habitable." Brandon is speaking.

"The worst thing we could do is stop trying here," says Elsa.

"Haven't we done enough damage to this planet? " Peter responds.

"This is our home. Surely other planets are for other creatures, beyond our ken," says Catriona.

"Rupert told me that we are all made of stardust from the birth of the universe?" respond Beatrice.

"Yes, but we we're bred in the sunlight that falls on the earth here," said Brook.

"And shaped by the tempests the earth has endured, and moulded by rhythms for thousands of years," says Lucy. "We would be making an alien invasion if we went to another planet - for which we have no preparation."

Everyone wants to come in on this discussion, but time is passing, so we invite Amina to hold the talking stick.

Amina's Vision

"I want to share my amazing dream with you all.

I awake in my birth village of Nkobo. I am still a child and my mother sends me to get water from the well. There are many streams in Gambia because the whole country has been created on the opposite banks of the great river. My country is fortunate because we have fresh water available, but of course, it has to be collected and carried home in a large pot, which becomes heavy on the head.

Several other girls are going to collect water from our nearest stream, which is about half a mile from our village. We are not permitted to collect it straight from the river because the water is polluted, so we have to go to a feeder stream where there is a fresh spring.

The path leads through a woodland area, so I have to be very careful in case there are snakes. I remember the time when I was so startled by a snake that I dropped the pot and cracked it. I had carried on, but the water dribbled out through the crack, and to my dismay, there was hardly any left in the bowl when I got back to the hut. My mother was cross and told me that I should have come straight back after the tumble. I should have realised that the water would escape. So she left me in charge of the baby and went for more water herself. I am very careful about my steps now.

Several people are gathering the fresh water emerging from underground, and so I have to wait my turn in a queue of women and girls. One of them asks me which village I come from and is envious because she has to walk much further to get to the source. At last, my turn comes. I have to scramble down the bank to dip my pot in the water, which is sparkling in the sunlight and cool to my hands. After filling the pot, it's very hard scrambling up the bank now it's full, but another girl who's waiting beside me offers to help. I hold out the pot and she takes it and puts it safely on the grass. I scramble up the bank, and then put the pot on my head.

I have to walk back very slowly and carefully, looking at my feet in case there is a tree root, which could easily trip me up. My arms are tired now, but I can see the big Banyan tree. My village is not much further. Suddenly, a big snake appears across my path. I jump. The pot falls, breaking into pieces and all the water spills out and is lost in the undergrowth.

Immediately, I am whisked away by some great force and carried off above the trees. I look down at the shattered pot and think, *this is the second time I have failed to bring the water home!* I am being carried high over the treetops. I don't know what's happening. Where am I being taken? Fear engulfs me as I looked down at the palm trees below, I realise that I am being projected towards a wide desert beyond the fertile river valley. I am now flying over miles of arid land, where there's no sign of any watercourse or human habitation. I cross over a caravan of camels, with Arab people riding them, then brown hills and more desert. Where am I being taken? Is this a punishment?

Beyond the desert, I find myself projected towards a ruined town, where people are dying and crying out for water. Then I see fighting between two groups of tribal people, on the edge of an oasis, where there's a lake and fertile land. Are they fighting for possession of that irrigated land, I wonder? Beyond this, vultures are tearing at human corpses, and then I see a game park, where rich white men are hunting elephants, and I see dead mutilated animals and a stack of ivory tusks being loaded on a lorry, while speculators squabble about the shares for their spoil. I shout out my anger, but no one hears my cry.

Beyond, there is a large city, where I see slums and poverty, but there is a team of young volunteers providing food and medical help. I rejoice to see this and linger there, and gather that they are also forming citizens groups and encouraging them to improve the area. Some teams collect rubbish and paint shabby buildings, others get alongside desperate people and help them sort out their problems.

I give thanks and pray for these people, but I know that I must fly further.

On, on I go and eventually find myself crossing an ocean. I see occasional ships but, from this height, they look like children's toys. I zoom down closer and then I come across sinking rafts filled with women and children begging to be saved, as some people fall into the water and are lost beneath the waves. 'Help them!' I cry and, just as I do, a big ship appears and lowers boats with rescue teams aboard. *Was this because I had shouted out*? I wonder. *Yes, I must be dreaming. It's not like this in real life. But if I can direct this dream, I would like to be on land again.*

A busy harbour comes in view and I am on my feet in a market place where slaves are being sold and I see the extremes of wealth and poverty etched on the faces of those around me. 'I don't want to be here!' I shout, and the scene changes into what seems to be a huge shopping mall.

I wander through avenues of rich shops and then find lanes of banks and counting houses, and another road filled with robots building computers, and another one lined with places of worship representing different faiths - temples and churches, mosques and synagogues. Buddhist monks, Catholic friars and women shrouded in black or white robes parade the streets, some in silence, and others chanting and singing. This is an Asian city, covered by a huge dome. I go up a moving staircase and find myself in a rooftop restaurant, with aerial views of minarets, spires and skyscrapers, but all beneath a huge dome to keep the natural world at bay. 'This is a man-made monstrosity,' I cry. 'Let me escape into a higher world.'

A great golden stairway replaces the rooftop restaurant, and I find myself climbing up and up. 'Where is this?' I call, mounting the steps, and a voice inside me says: 'You are going beyond - to the true roof of the world.' I realise that there are moving stairways on either side of me, one carrying people up; the other carrying people down.

'Am I still under the dome or climbing through the sky?' I wonder.

'No, you are now in the higher realms' comes a response. I continue climbing and know that I have moved beyond the great dome. It has melted into thin air, and I feel that I'm moving into a sacred realm, warmed and illuminated by the sun. I step off the stairway into a circular room, where a group of sages sit on cushions. Their clothes, features and skin colouring suggest that they come from different parts of our world.

There are nine men and nine women. I see a black man and woman in colourful robes, and I know they represent the people of Africa. They greet me with smiles, although I don't know their language. Another couple nearby look as if the belong to the Indian sub-continent. I turn round and recognise three more couples: two from America, a redskin in his traditional dress and a lady whose origin looks European, a large man in a Russian fur hat, sitting with a shawled elderly lady, and the word Baboushka comes to mind; beyond are two Orientals, in Chinese robes. All these people seem friendly and relaxed, and my inner voice tells me that they are conferring on a very difficult subject, how peace and justice can be restored to our deeply troubled world. There are beams of light emanating from the centre of their foreheads, and gentle music is heard as the lights converge. Are these angelic beings?

I wake to see the stars in the night sky and breathe the fresh air of Woodleigh heath. I am safe again, and feel consoled by that glimpse of a higher source of strength.

Was this just a dream, or an inspired vision? I don't know, but I'm very relieved that I climbed that golden staircase. After all the horrors, I now feel hope."

Ideas about angels are shared. Do they exist or are they mind concepts? Catriona says it is "way beyond our ken."

We move on to discuss the importance of dreams in our lives. Some people felt that they gave valuable instruction on the way ahead. Others were less sure.

Brook's Vision

"I spend my silent day exploring the area around the Greenstock Pools. It's a place I love: it seems lost in time, and must have looked, felt and smelt much the same two or three hundred years ago. There are no human structures: no evidence of modernity. I feel it right to choose to go there because I always find some natural features that I've never noticed on previous occasions. I learn more about the wild flowers and the little creatures depending on them with every visit. I am always at home here.

It was old Reuben who first introduced me to Greenstock when I was a schoolboy. We lay in watch for groups of wild geese to fly in from Norway. I was fascinated by their strange honking noises. They are timeless birds, and the way that they fly in formation over such vast distances thrills me.

Yesterday, I spent the whole day exploring the area around the ponds, the woodlands and heath beyond. I found an ant's nest and a fox's earth that were both new. I lay for two hours in the grass before I caught sight of the fox. Two young cubs appeared out of the hole when the mother came with a dead vole in her mouth. They were so excited that they attacked it from both sides at once.

I had an encounter with a rabbit too. It jumped out of some grass a few yards away from me, when I was sitting resting my back against an old beech tree. I kept very still and so did he. Instead of just hopping away like they normally do, he stood gazing at me with his bright eyes. We examined each other for about two minutes, and then he was gone in a flash. I love such close encounters.

Has any of you ever tried to get on the island in the big pool? I managed to reach it because I've got a big stride. There are three rocks in the water that make convenient stepping-stones. Well, to change my tenses, as we were told to; I spend my night there in my sleeping bag, and have two vivid dreams. I waken in the darkness and ponder the first of them. A neurosurgeon has asked me to assist a patient with exercises to enable him develop new pathways in the brain. Despite all my experience as a physiotherapist, I am at a loss what to say, but in the night I think of a series of arm exercises that could be tried. Then I consider a walking exercise. I fall asleep again with these ideas in my mind, and have a second dream.

I don't know if many of you have dreamed that you were other creatures. I have done occasionally. In this dream, I am a Canada goose, flying from Greenstock Pool to Norway. I am leading a young family of five, and we were riding on the current of the winds for some of the way. That's a wonderful sensation, but it becomes a battle whenever we hit a crossing wind stream. That's another thing I learned last night. My wings ached and I lost the regular rhythm, which made it hard for those who were following, and I felt guilty. When I waken up this morning I find my arms are aching.

Brook stands up and exercises himself. Some of the others follow this example and say that they feel the benefit.

 Then the talking stick does a swift circular tour, getting several appreciative words about the experience and the pools, including these contributions:-

Elsa: There are pathways everywhere including the mind, but we keep treading the familiar ones. That's a big problem today. Sound meditation helps us develop positive paths, so that we don't lose our way.

Catriona: Those wild geese know where they are going, because they are tuned into the rhythms of the universe. We have to get on that wavelength too. That's the big problem for humankind.

Rory: It's the big task for the next century and, what's more, that was the message of my dreams too.

Beatrice's Vision

"I decided to sleep under the stars on my vision quest and I found the ideal spot on soft grass, a few yards from the cliff-top at Brandy Head. I had enjoyed those commanding views when I came that way earlier in the day, and I returned in the late evening, as the light was beginning to fade.

When I closed my eyes, I could hear the gentle swish of the tide on pebbles far below. I counted each breath in and out, making them slower and deeper each time, and slumber soon overcame me.

I open my eyes and look straight into the face of Elfleda. It's not the image of her that I carry in my mind, or that carved in the statue at Tamcaster, but I know immediately that this is the true Elfleda. She gazes at me intently, and then says quietly, 'So you are Beatrice, come from the future world. I have longed to see you. Thank you for rescuing me from oblivion.'

Her voice is deep and musical. She is a queen, although she never claims the title; should I curtsy?

She laughs. 'No need for fripperies of that sort. I never asked for them in life, and do not want them now. Plain lady of Mercia was enough for me. I never stood on ceremony with my father, Alfred, and he never sought it. I was his eldest and he treated me as he would have done a son and heir - as an equal to Edward, who arrived later.' She smiled sadly 'It was little brother Edward who loved decorum and, later it was he who chose to relegate me to the shadows.'

'I have dreamed of you, Elfleda, but never thought to meet you. It puzzles me ...and for you to be able to converse so easily in modern English ...this amazes me!'

'I didn't sleep in the shadows all those years, you know. I watched this country change and my learning programme carried me through centuries. This isn't my first out-of-time encounter. I've talked to others too at times of crisis, but I feel a debt of special gratitude to you.' She smiled again.

'Are you saying you have watched events for over a thousand years?'

'My Kingdom of Mercia was but yesterday to me.'

'But there have been such momentous events in Britannia: The Norman Conquest, the Wars of the Roses, the dissolution of the monasteries, the English Civil War, the industrial revolution, parliamentary democracy, two world wars and then climate change chaos.'

'Charades...pictures on the walls of time... to prepare every one of us for the real world. There's a long time of trial before each person is fit for the world that God created.'

I stand in wonderment, and then say quietly 'There is a God then.'

'Of course...only one...although she is called by many names by different nations and tribes - and I am one of the servants.' Another smile. 'God is above gender, timeless, and I am just one of the thousands of these disciples. I learned this from my dear father, Alfred, when I was a child in Athelney. I was his first real pupil. My mother had died and we were in hiding from the Norsemen. I studied his writings and translations from the Holy Bible. I was with him when he made his laws and judgements, and later I shared this knowledge with my dear husband, Ethelred, and we passed the knowledge on to the children of Mercia. I loved those people, and was humbled to help the bishops spread the words of the Holy Gospel. We rescued many from paganism, Ethelred and I, equals under God. My husband and I walked with God, even as Alfred had walked. We were disciples to our people and gave men and women equal privileges in Mercia, as in Wessex, but over the years the women lost their rights again. We helped our people to live in peace by honest labour and defend themselves against the storms and terrors of the Norsemen. We even shared these understandings with those who fought against us: with Guthrun, King of the Vikings and others too, but those who wrote the history books lost much of this teaching, and I was forgotten because I was a woman. I thank you again, Beatrice, for retelling this story to the children of your times.'

'The pleasure's mine. I never dreamed of this encounter. It's wonderful to be able to speak to you in my own tongue.'

Elfleda gave another tinkling laugh. 'There are many things of which you never dreamed. Come with me, daughter, and I will show you much. May I call you daughter?'

'Whatever pleases you.

'I only had one daughter, poor ill-fated Elfwine. I would like another. I must introduce you to her. You are two of a kind.'

Immediately, she appears: a tall young woman, with dark hair rippling over her shoulders, reaching the sleeves of a white Saxon gown.

'My reign in Mercia was short.' Her voice was quiet, but her eyes bold. 'My uncle saw to that, although my mother had prepared me well. Britannia had to wait long years until the women won their rights again. Eventually, it was the suffragettes who won that battle. It became their task to reawaken the conscience of the nation.'

'Greet Beatrice, Elfwine, and then we shall go back together to view my kingdom once again.'

We move to embrace each other. I feel the warmth of her lithe young body.

With one hand linked to hers and the other to Elfleda, we are whisked high above Britannia, through clouds and dazzling sunrays. The air is cold and clammy, but sunbeams above reach out to warm me. We travel north across a clear blue sky. Through a gap in white clouds, I think I glimpse the mud brown waters of the Bristol Channel. We fly north over rolling hills, villages, woodlands and valleys and then swoop down again at a place where walled settlements stand on hills, encircled by waterways.

'See over there, that's Warwick, one of my townships,' Elfleda calls to us.

I see a huddle of thatched roofs held strong by stone walls within the loop of a winding river.

'A fine defensive site,' she calls again.

We fly on through the air, crossing wild heath and moorland. Small settlements are scattered along our flight-path, but no large townships. Eventually, Elfleda points out a range of hills on the skyline.

'Tamcaster lies on a hillock just short of those peaks. That is our destination, another defensive place, girdled by a wide river. We chose these sites carefully, according to Alfred's tradition: each citadel is a place of refuge for all those within radius of twenty miles, each has a weekly market and is a town of industry and worship. This is our northeast border. Beyond lies Dane-law.'

We fly towards it, descending slowly, watching the ramparts grow, as if they rise to greet us. The settlement below us bears no likeness to the bustling northern powerhouse I knew as Tamcaster. Instead, it is an old farm-town, surrounded by ditch and mudstone walls. The castle of which Elfleda is so proud is a strong, stone building with watchtowers at each corner. Outbuildings are made of wattle and daub. People scurry to and fro, emptying supplies from horse-drawn carts.

'I would never have recognised this place if you had not brought us here,' I tell Elfleda.

Foolishly, I look round to see if I can recognise the site where her statue now stands. Elfleda gives another tinkling laugh.

'My statue has not been built yet,' she jests, 'but its position will be over there.' She points in the direction of one of the outhouses, and a transparent statue appears, plainly invisible to the scurrying men, who continue with their tasks.

'Compare us,' Elfleda draws her daughter to her side and strides in the direction of the image. When she reaches it, they turn to face each other. The transparent statue is raised on a stone pillar, so the carved head of Elfleda in her helmet towers over to the new arrivals, but Elfwine, now taller than her mother, dwarfs her own child image.

'I don't think the stonemason had a photograph to work on,' I laugh. 'He probably used his wife and daughter as models.'

The images disappear.

'Can you reproduce anything, at will?' I ask Elfleda.

'Of course. There is no such thing as time. You will know this when your hour comes.'

'I find this overwhelming,' I say. 'So am I now in Saxon times?'

'Of course. You are my guest here. Come inside my hall and eat with us. Time shifting is exhausting.'

So the three of us enter the large stone building. Servants bring venison and pigeon's eggs to a large, round table. As there are no eating irons, we must use our fingers and wipe them on cloths laid out for the purpose. We wash our food down with tankards of sparkling mead, as a girl plays sweet harp music and sings in a tongue I don't understand.

When the light begins to fade, servants bring in an elaborate candelabra and stand it by the table. Lighted brands are used to fire the braziers, which then flicker, casting long shadows on the walls surrounding us.

As we finish the meal, the harpist bows and leaves, and Elfleda invites us to relax on wolf-skins, covering the floor of an alcove, near the blazing log fire.

522

'The night is coming on, so you must bed here till tomorrow, Beatrice. It will allow time for you to savour the quiet of this castle, since you have chosen to write about it so eloquently. On the morrow you can come riding with us both. We will show you the sights of the town and countryside: some of our farms and the marketplace here, where produce is sold strictly in fair measure. And before you leave we will go to the cathedral, where the father abbot will bless you for your journey home. Are there questions you wish to ask me?'

'Hundreds,' I said. 'But let me ask you what is most on my mind. You speak of walking with God. I do not understand. What does God look like?'

'I have not seen God, Beatrice, but I live with and through this presence. God is not a person; it is above gender, not a creature of this world, but a living presence to those who have experienced and accepted it. God is ever present. I sense this in every core of my being. I inherited this gift from my father, Alfred, who went to Rome when he was young. He was blessed by the Pope and came back in this knowledge. Whenever I speak of the presence, I am conscious of a guiding hand choosing the words for me. I grew up in this knowledge. It's a mystery that can't be described, but this presence guided me through life. I passed it on to my husband, Ethelred, too. We were both led in the decisions we had to make.'

'The Bible says that we are made in the image of God, but I have never understood this.'

'It's a quality of life that few people discover in what you call modern times: It's been crowded out by so many things, the noise of machinery, the constant babble of voices, sceptic concepts such as searching for evidence, pressures from the greedy material world, penetrating cyber fiction and by wars and cruelties which divide nations and cultures. Your people have forgotten how to listen to the silence. Babies know about it but, as your poet Wordsworth said, 'The shades of prison house begin to creep upon the growing child'. I grew up in a country place, with birdsong and the breaking dawn, and this magic remained with me till the night I died. It was then I discovered the real world, and recognised that my life on earth had been a dream, although I had been blessed because the Holy Spirit had been my life companion.'

'I always found you spellbinding, Elfleda. There was something that drew me to discover more about you, and there was something magical about the way your story inspired so many people.'

She looked at me with love and wonderment. 'There is nothing spellbinding about me. I am just a servant of the creator like you are but, if we are loyal servants, the inspiration can be passed on. That is what we are here for. This is our task on earth.'

I have the feeling that I must have fallen asleep soon after that, as I rested on that wolf fur, feeling the warmth of the glowing turf-fire. When I recovered consciousness I was lying on my back again gazing at a starlit sky, on the cliff-top at Brandy Head."

The group was stunned by the intimacy of that account and some wonderment was expressed by those who felt equal to the occasion.

Rupert's Vision

"Catriona and I drove to Dartmoor, as you know. We spent around thirty hours there on a silent retreat. The first night we shared a tent and set off in opposite directions in the morning. I've never been alone there for so long before. It was a humbling experience. My only companions were wild ponies and crows. I climbed three of the tors on the second day and completely wore myself out. Perhaps I should not have done this on a day when I was fasting, because I began to have hallucinations, seeing people from the past and perhaps from the future. Who knows? I started thinking strange things, like: *Yesterday, I was in my mother's womb - now I am living in this world: tomorrow - when I die, if I still have consciousness, I'll know what lies beyond the grave. What is time? Does it exist?*

I tried to start answering the questions: *Life on earth is a pilgrimage. a preparation, an exploration, a discovery and a time of wonder. Those who live life fully carry a great responsibility, before stepping beyond - into the unknown.*

When I fell in love it seemed as if it were a taste of heaven: perhaps true love, if /when it appears, is the halfway house between this world and the next. Could it be that we are born again on this planet, or perhaps on another plane of existence, and that life experience requires us to move into a different gear, according to what we have learned or failed to learn this time round? Will I have any recollection of the journey I am now on? Will I take baggage with me, or will it be a complete fresh start? Will I meet Catriona again in some other form? Will I meet my parents? If we do meet, will we know who we all are, or meet as strangers – perhaps in a totally different form? If our concept of time is illusory, could we be born in to a past age?

 These thoughts chased round in my head all day long while I was exploring the moor. I came across a stone circle. *When was this built, and for what purpose? Might those people have re-incarnated? Perhaps I lived in those times too? Did I meet my parents in some form of previous life? Have I loved Catriona before? Do we come back to perform certain tasks, or learn certain lessons?*

Do we retain our gender or can we take the other one? Is there a choice or it designed by fate?

I fell asleep pondering these questions, but I did not get any answers. When I woke up, I didn't remember any dreams. I felt sure that I'd had them, but couldn't recall anything. It was a complete blackout. I was very disappointed because I had my notebook beside me ready to jot everything down, but while coming here in the car, the dream suddenly came back to me. I wonder if there is significance in the delay.

The dream I recall is that I am watching an old woman weaving a huge wall hanging. She works at a handmade wooden loom attached to a wooden bench, using dyed wool and fur gathered from skins of sheep,

525

dogs, cats and larger animals. Some pelts hang drying in bright sunshine on an outside wall behind her. She appears to be a woman of great antiquity, but I cannot see her face because she is bent over her work. I can see the tapestry when I look over her shoulders, although it appears to have no great significance. There are threads of many colours carefully interwoven but I cannot recognise any picture or pattern. I instinctively know, however, that the tapestry is of great value, and I am very disappointed that I cannot appreciate it.

In the yard outside, there are four great vats hanging over blazing log fires. Each contains a different dye: red, yellow, blue and green. Four youths are stirring the coloured waters with large wooden ladles.

Then I turn round and see a small tapestry hanging, beside a great one. On the small one is the outline of a tree, and beside it is an etched outline of a woman figure. She is formed by four triangles one representing her head, a larger one below has stick-like arms, bent at the elbow and reaching below her hips. The two lower ones seem to represent a skirt and splayed feet. Beneath is written the name 'Eli Belinde'. It fascinates me, but I do not understand it.

The great tapestry hanging up beside it, seems to make everything crystal clear. I had been looking at the back of the tapestry, where the woman may have been correcting a fault, but now I see the right side, and I know that this is the story of creation. I cannot describe it, but it is so vibrant that it shines with radiance, and all life is there, moving and dancing before me. Birds of every kind fly against a light blue sky. The thin crust of the earth teams with fertility: plants of every variety, with animals hopping and prancing around. I can see insects, butterflies, fireflies and animals from every continent, and there at the heart of creation are a man and a woman, but not the naked and ashamed bodies of Adam and Eve. They are both clothed in shining robes, that reflect the life about them, sending shimmering, translucent beams in all directions, not only into the world but out across the waves of the oceans that embrace the whole tapestry. The seas are alive with dolphins and fish from both tropical and cold waters, leaping and swimming. Beneath them, waving in the tide, are multi-coloured marine plants, and I catch glimpses of coral, bright shells and nestling pearls."

He hands the talking stick to Catriona, who also passes it on, with the words: "I think your dream was the answer to your own questions? We are here to radiate love."

Brandon looks a little stunned as he passes the stick on.

Lucy : Perhaps you are in the world of angels. I like to think we are all fallen angels, really.

Elsa: That's a beautiful thought. Who knows? We could be. The myth of the tapestry weaver is a very ancient one. You have dipped into the deep well of creation.

Rory: I am not sure about fallen angels. Why should we feel ourselves to be so elevated? Remember we're only one of thousands of species on one of the planets.

Beatrice: But we have the gift of imagination. We know of no other creature possessing such powers.

Brook: We can't comprehend the instinct of the swallow when it flies night and day from South Africa to Britannia.

Frances: What other creatures have written books or have left great knowledge for future generations to explore?

Peter: What other creatures have done so much damage to the planet? What others have used their intelligence to create weapons of mass destruction?

Brandon: I have been through the torments of hell, and feel that I am on the cusp of discovering a way through to the other side. Don't pull me back, Peter.

Rupert: Stick with it, Brandon. We must hold fast to what we know is true.

Lucy: Blessed are the peacemakers for they shall inherit the earth.

Amina: I waited till everyone had spoken because I did not want to change the thread of dialogue, but your dream amazed me, Rupert. It's one I've had myself. Your grandmother, Ahinee told me about Eli Belinde. She was believed to be the great African godmother of us all, and those hands of hers are helping to give birth to humankind. I have seen the image on ancient pottery. The image beside it represents the tree of life.

Rupert: Did you tell me about all this, when I was a child mother? I don't recall it.

Amina: I can't remember whether I ever shared it with anyone, but it's a dream I've had several times. Perhaps you inherited it, in some mysterious way.

The stick was passed to Catriona to give us her vision.

Catriona's Vision

"My day on Dartmoor was spent studying wild flowers, ponies and streams of water. It was wonderful. I've collected a few o' the wild flowers to show you." She passed them around.

"There were so many I had nae' seen before. What a great variety is still there in a few special places like this! It hurt me to collect these samples. I felt I was taking them away from their natural home, but I wanted to show you what I found in one wee area. There was a stream trickling by, and Dartmoor ponies had come over to drink, so I joined them. I decided not to wander around, but to stay all day and watch the changes take place in a single day.

It seems to me that all these things belong together. If there had'na been a stream flowing by, those ponies would nae have gathered there, and the wild flowers would nae flourish. They need each other, and the ponies add fertility. Wee creatures hovered o'er the horse pats, and the butterflies and the bees were attracted by the wild flowers, and o'course, they spread the pollen. They all have a part to play and between them the heath is enriched.

When I fell asleep in the dell that night, my thoughts went back to another wild place I know well, in the north of Scotland, and I was minded of my maternal grandmother, Fiona McDonald. She is a dear old soul who has lived all her life in a cottage in Wester Ross, and she has known that valley and loch-side through every season for the past eighty years.

It always took my father a long time to drive along the winding roads that led there, and as a child it was a great adventure going over hills, through glens and across rough moors, where rutting stags roamed. Whenever we reached the top of a mountain, I was always keen for him to draw aside, so that I could get out, feel the fresh winds, inhale the scents and hear the calls of the birds of prey, nesting on those heather-clad hills. I loved to turn to view the path we'd followed, winding between rocky outcrops, and then see the road awaiting us in the valley ahead.

In ma' dream last night I am talking to my Gran and she is showing me a wee rabbit that she'd brought into the safety of her cottage because of a damaged leg. Gran was a bright, intelligent soul, who ran a bed and breakfast and kept a visitor book, and some of her guests had come from overseas, but when I asked her if she'd been to England, she said 'Och, no. Why should I go travellin' abroad, when the whole world comes to mae door!' She really used to say such things and I thought it canny, and loved her the more for the feelings that bode with her doon the years.

In the dream, she tells me tales of her youth and, as she does this, the wrinkles fall away from her face, and I see a lass, about my own age, talking o' wee foxes who live in the glen, and young children who try to play ball games with them. She really knew every bush in the lane, when it would flower and when it would fade, and she gave a name to every bird takin' food from her hand. She was rooted in that place, as her forbears had done and as I tell o' these things, I find mysel' talkin' in her brogue. It comes to me naturally. I canna help it.

The dream moves on and I see her as a middle-aged woman and my mother as a growing girl with two little sisters, bakin' wee cakes in the oven, because it's a birthday. When she tells them that she has seen salmon swimming in the river, out they run to stand on a old stone bridge and peer at the waters.

The focus changes, and suddenly I'm a salmon mysel' with a powerful mission. I need to reach the big river. I'm being' drawn in the direction o' the flow by a strong pull o' the mighty torrent. When I reach it, there are hundreds of big fish in the wide river. I'm feared that I might be gobbled up, for I'm grabbing wee minnows myself. The river is verra noisy and the pull is verra swift, and I know now that I must go on yet further. I've nae choice. I canna resist the force of the water, and a voice tells me that I'll end up in the sea. The sounds being made by these fish are haunting. They're calling to each other and responding with a powerful range of notes, way beyond the spectrum of human hearing.

I've nae' idea how long the dream lasts, but it's full of revelations. I become aware that I'm now just one in a great shoal of fish, and they make a powerful presence. I'm subsumed in the constant flow, but slowly I lose all fear and become proud to be part of the shoal. It makes me feel stronger. I'm part of a big clan and I get a sense o' belonging there. But after a while we feel a great surge o' water rushing towards us and we know it must be the tide. We are within reach o' the sea, because this new water tastes verra' salty. The tide is the greatest energy force on earth, and instead o' flowing, we are dragged forward. Nothing can now challenge this might and this power, but it is a glorious feeling. I am part of creation itsel'.

I wake in the night and see the stars above ma' head, and suddenly ken that it was nae' a dream, but a revelation. I'm part o' this great living universe and the energies o' the tide and the stars are wonderfully linked to every living thing in creation. Many creatures must sense this and go with the flow. All the birds that migrate, the elephants that cross the savannah in search of water, the bees and the butterflies that help pollinate the plants. I know in mi' bones that we're all part o' one living system that includes the energies o' the sun, moon and stars, and everything that moves and breathes. Moreover, as Brandon has just reminded us, all bodies are built from the stardust o' the original explosion that brought the planets into being, and our urges reflect the rhythm in it all.

I realised in way I had nae' felt before, that mankind has built an artificial wall dividing us from creation. Our arrogance makes us feel that we have a right to control the universe. We see ourselves as separate individuals with brains that divide us. That's plain wrong. We are a natural species with a great contribution to offer towards the healing o' the planet. Those thoughts kept me awake for aboot two hours, and then I slipped back into ma' dream.

I had become a fish again, but now I am battling upstream, fighting against the torrent. Every fibre urges me to move forr'ads towards my original spawning ground. Somehow, I ken that was ma home. No other pond will do. I come to a great salmon leap and find I am one of hundreds jumping up out of the water and flying through cold air, till I find myself back in water again, higher up the hillside. It's huge struggle, and I ache all over but I must keep on and up, on and up, again and again. Suddenly, I'm there, and as soon as I reach that tranquil highland pool, a great calm comes over me.

I wake to see that I'm on the same part o' the moor that I had been in yesterday and the sun's rising at the break o' the morrow. I've had many powerful dreams in my time, but none to equal this one."

Brandon: I could feel the pull of those waters in the way you described it. It reminded me of the atmosphere of a big football crowd. I don't understand that feeling of unity: where it comes from or why it grips me from time to time, but it's a very powerful feeling.

Lucy: I don't feel it in real life, but I sometimes do in dreams like this.

Elsa: It's an age-old feeling going back to primitive times when we all lived in tribes. I felt it in my dream last night too - it can be a loving sensation, and it can be a dangerous one whipping up hatred of 'the other'. You have to ask yourself - 'is this a good feeling, or a bad one?' Then you have a choice to stay with it, or move on.

Peter: Your link with your grandmother sounded tribal too, Catriona. It was a good bond, with someone rooted in her homeland. Places can be very important.

Rory: We need to develop those roots in a wholesome way. We live in a disconnected world.

Mina: When I was in the refugee camp, living with people from many nations, I felt it too, so these feelings aren't limited to race or country.

Beatrice: I felt those roots when I encountered Elfleda. They are ancient, essential elements in binding a strong community, but it's important that we extend a welcome to outsiders and bring them into the fold. If we fail to do that the tribe becomes toxic.

Catriona: My Scottish roots run deep, but the problem today is that most folk may have been transplanted so many times over generations that they do nae recognise the rhythms of their homelands."

Brandon's Vision

"As I live inland, I decide to take a coastal path in a remote area, and I'm careful to choose a part separate from Rory's and Beatrice's stretch. I choose an area where I've been warned that the cliffs are crumbling. It's a challenge, but that I find that it gives me a bad start. It's a lovely day and I am enjoying the views on a steeply rising path when I come to a sudden stop. The path's disappeared completely and I face a massive landslip. I make an attempt to climb above it, but then realise that this is too dangerous and have to go back on my tracks. I decide to try a different stretch, so I go back to where I started by a signpost, and take the other marked footpath, that carries me over a wooded headland.

It's a stiff climb up the hill. It leads me to a stile, from which I see a woodland beyond. As I climb down, a golden-haired little dog barks at me and wags its tail. I say 'hello,' and he starts to trot friskily alongside me. There is a clear path through the trees, bordered by ferns and brambles. We follow it for around ten minutes, after which we come to some open ground. In the centre of it stands a round, stone tower. I go forward to look and the little dog runs round it ahead of me.

I come to a great wooden door approached by three steps. The little dog runs up the steps, sniffs at the bottom of the door, cocks his leg, leaves his message and runs inside. I follow him and find a large, round chamber with a timbered ceiling. The room is completely bare. I wonder how old it is, and what it was used for. Some steps run down to a dark cellar and a winding stone stairway on the sidewall leads to an upper storey. I see the dog running up the steps with huge enthusiasm. With a feeling of curiosity, I follow him again.

Above is another empty room, but this one is graced with a big stone fireplace, an oak-beamed ceiling and two casement windows: one of them looks across the woodland and the other out to sea. I walk over to peer through them and find the leaded glass is still intact. The little dog has disappeared, but then I see him looking down at me from the top of yet another stairway. He gives an encouraging yap, and up I go again, to reach the roof of the building. It's guarded by battlements and features a flagpole in the centre.

The stonework is certainly not ancient. It's probably a folly built in the Georgian period and repaired later. Looking around, I have a good view of the canopy of trees behind and a wide sweep of hazy blue sea on the other sides. The white sails of three racing yachts are visible. This headland is an excellent vantage point.

The little dog runs in a circle round the battlements and, finding nothing much to sniff, runs back down the stairs again. As I'm in no hurry, I linger watching the yachts for a few minutes, and then wander slowly down. There's no sign of the dog, but suddenly I hear a howl. He bolts up from the cellar stairway and straight outside, clearly terrified.

Whatever could have been down there? I know I should try to find out. But I cowardly leave the tower as quickly as I can, and carry on my walk along the cliff path. The golden haired dog does not appear again, but I am shaken by the experience, and can't stop thinking about the tower and the dog: so much so that I dreamt of this on the open heath, before our breakfast rendezvous.

It was very vivid. I see the tower again, and the dog going through the door. I chase him, but this time, instead of running up the stairs, he goes straight down into the cellar and I follow him despite the fear. . . It's pitch black and very cold. I hear something moaning and shout, 'Who's there?' No reply, but I can hear heavy breathing. Then, to my amazement, someone calls my name 'Brandon'. I can't place the voice, but I know the tone and think it's friendly. Obviously someone who knows me must be in trouble. I hear the moan again. I go towards the voice and reach out, saying 'What's the matter? Who is it?' Another hand touches mine. It makes me jump. Then the voice says, 'I can't find the way out of here. Where are the steps?'

'Over here,' I call: and taking the hand again, I lead the person towards a shaft of light at the bottom of the stairs. We climb up together, hand in hand. On the ground floor I look to see who it is, and I'm stunned! It is a replica of me - like an identical twin brother, but he looks sick with worry, and I feel a great flood of love. Suddenly, there's a full-length mirror in the room. It wasn't there before, but we go over and look at it together: seeing two identical people, one looking sad and nervous and the other one, happy and consoling.

'Don't worry,' I hear myself saying. 'It's going to be all right in the end.' And we both smile. When I looked back at the mirror, the twin has disappeared.

I wake up. It's just getting light. Birds are singing. I feel very happy, as if a war had been won! I shout my name out loudly, jump up and wave my hands. Why? It's that smile on his face. It was joyful. I'll never forget it!"

Rupert went over to shake Brandon's hand, but Brandon kissed him and they embraced each other.

Mina, Rory, Catriona, Elsa and Lucy all exchanged kisses, and Rory shook Brandon's hand. In the excitement, the talking stick was forgotten, and a great bond of love seemed to sleep through the group.

Eventually, we sat down again, realising that there was one more dream to share.

Lucy's Vision

"My vision was wonderful. It was so clear and vivid, and I feel so comforted, although I don't know what on earth to make of it. I was a child again, about the age I was when the Tsunami came. It didn't begin like that though. I heard a great roaring wind, but I was in complete darkness and I was so frightened I didn't dare to look. Then the noise slowly faded away. Tentatively, I opened my eyes.

Two angels are standing beside me. I see them now. Their coloured wings are rippling like rainbows, and they are looking at me with such love in their eyes that I immediately ask them the question that I have not dared to ask anyone else.

'Where are my real Mummy and Daddy? Where are my brother and sisters?'

And the two angels answer in chorus, 'They are here. You have been brought to see them.'

They immediately vanish, and my real parents are standing in their place.

Mummy reaches out and kisses me. She is so real and loving, and then Daddy comes forward and hugs me ever so strongly and I know that they are really here. This is no dream. I re-live it now, as I talk to you all.

Mummy says, 'Oh, Lucy darling. We've been searching everywhere for you.'

I say, 'I've been longing to find you too.'

'Thank God, you're safe,' Daddy says.

And then they suddenly turn to look round and up rush my brother and my two sisters, and we all hug and kiss each other and cry for joy. Everyone is the age they were when I last saw them.

I say, 'I must introduce the family who have been looking after me.' I turn round but you aren't there. I call out your names, but you don't answer and then I call for Ivan and David, but they aren't there either.

Then my real mother says 'They must be in the lost world.'

'Where's that?' I ask.

'It's where you've come from,' they say. 'We were told you were being well looked after and had settled down happily, so after a while we didn't worry and stopped looking, but we thought about you every day, and they told us not to worry and promised that we would see you later. This is a wonderful place, Lucy. You must explore the real world with us.'

'Why do you call it the real world?' I ask. 'Is this heaven?'

'That's what some people say, but you will recognise it because it's like the other world without all the troubles.'

And then I see my old home, just as it used to be before the tsunami, and I see my old school friends, and they run up and dance round me and keep shouting, 'It's Lucy. Lucy's come back to see us.'

And then I stop laughing, and tell them 'I thought you'd all been washed away in that great storm.'

'That was in the lost world,' my father says. 'Let me try to explain. The world we thought we were living in wasn't real at all. It was a nightmare that we were dreaming. We thought it was real because we knew no better. Look at this globe.'

A globe appears and he spins it round, so that we can see North and South America and the Pacific with the South Sea Islands and Australia, then China.

'Here's Asia, and Africa and Europe and Britannia, complete with Cornwall. We thought we were living on that globe, but we were looking through a dark glass, and we saw all the shadows of doom and destruction. We were being prepared for the real world, because we weren't ready for it. There is enough food for everyone in the real world, and no one goes hungry. There are no wars, no armies. We don't even need a police force, and all the animals are free to roam again: even those who were becoming extinct in the lost world.'

Then my mother puts her arm round me and explains more. 'Human beings have a special responsibility to absorb and reflect true love. This is our task: our purpose on earth is to care for each other, but we have to learn this first through a dream, before we are born. We see things going terribly wrong. Some people have to go back into other bodies and dream all this again and again, until they are ready for the real world.'

'Come, Lucy, we will show you the real world.'

As he speaks, my father spins the globe around and part of it melts into rich views of the North American Rocky Mountains. We see snow on the high peaks and a deep valley in between, green with foliage. Brown bears roam through woodlands and chipmunks chase one another. This melts into a view of the wide Pacific Ocean, alive with flying fish. We dip below the surface to peer at a coral reef, with spectacular creatures darting between crevices, and a voice tells us. 'Everything wasn't destroyed down there, you know. That was in the nightmare world, not in the real one. They were trying to find more oil in the dream that you remember and all life in those coral reefs was destroyed.'

I see the globe spin round again and I look for Britannia in the north, above Europe, and it suddenly stops turning when I fix my eyes on Land's End. *Yes, it's still there. I see it for real and then I recognise*

Penzance and Falmouth, with the fishing ships sailing home to the quayside, and beyond lies St. Austell and I see my school and then our farm, and to my astonishment it's still intact. I am so excited and happy, but then I think. 'How can this be?'

I suddenly wake and ask myself: *What is real?* Although I'm very puzzled by all this, there's a deep inner comfort.

For a moment I think: *perhaps if that's true, it doesn't matter how much damage we do.* But then I immediately knew that this can't be right. Suffering's very real while we are in this world, and the more harm we do the greater the pain, for us and for others. Even if it's true that we can't damage the real world, we can damage ourselves. We disturb our thinking, twist the pathways in our brains, and then make them wider through more frequent use, and the suffering will go on for all those involved in these tragedies, and it will take so much longer before we can ever gain sight of the true world."

*

Beatrice:

The circle has now been completed, and the talking stick is passed back to Elsa.

"What have we learned from the Vision Quest?" Rory asks.

"I don't feel any clearer about what's likely to happen," says Peter, "but I think I'm more prepared."

"I still feel deep sorrow that so much wisdom is being lost." Frances keeps her head down, visibly moved by her dream and the other revelations.

"It's true that we can't read the future, but we are part of the journey and we must equip ourselves better to understand and respond to the challenges appropriately," says Rupert. "I feel more confident."

"I have gained hope," says Lucy, her eyes sparkling.

538

"I'm more at peace with myself now," Brandon observes. "I feel that I'm stepping forward towards new possibilities."

"I've glimpsed the wisdom of the ages," I add, taking Brook's hand. "It was a wonderful encounter with Elfleda; a magical dream."

"I flew with the wild geese. What more can we ask for?" says Brook.

"My journeys in that school o' fish were life-affirming." Catriona answers.

"We don't own the earth or the sun and the stars. They're all in their own elements, but we are a part of the life force. We can't dominate it. We must learn to play a loving part in it. I've always thought that, but now I know it," says Elsa.

"We struggle with the deep powers of the universe at our peril." Rory, stands up as he speaks. "We can be infused by them, but we will never master them."

"We are their children," adds Mina, standing. "The sun is like a father, energising us, and the moon is like a mother, helping birth us all."

"We can ride with our brother, the sea," says Lucy, leaping up. "We can dance with our sister, the air."

"We are warmed by our father, the sun. We must cherish our mother, the earth," said Catriona, moving to take her hand.

Everyone in the circle joins hands, and we stand together for a minute in silence. Then Mina fetches her guitar and moves to the centre: we start to dance round her, raising arms for those on the right and left to pass.

A light breeze meets us, as we emerge from the woodland.

"Just look at those lapwings," cries Brook, pointing to a couple of dancing birds. The male, with a long black feather rising from the back of his head, is doing acrobatic swoops and dives towards his mate, displaying glossy, scalloped wings: green above and white below. The female responds with a 'pee-wit' call.

"Did we set them off?" whispers Lucy in awe.

"They're enjoying the moment, like we are."

"Why not? Each precious second is all any of us ever have. So, what have we learned from this exercise? Was it worthwhile?" asks Rory.

"Yes," comes the chorus from many voices

"Why? What have we learned?" Elsa asks.

"We have bonded as a group, like never before," says Peter.

"And we've shared something of our inner selves," says Rupert. "We must continue this, and help raise spirits, here and elsewhere."

"Do I have your consent to share information from this event with transition colleagues around the globe?" I ask.

"Yes." The response comes from many voices.

"Does anyone dissent from this?"

Silence.

"Then I'll prepare a draft and share it with you all. After that I'll put it on the international website."

"And we'll send a copy of it to our local Council, asking them to publicise it, and ask the county council to encourage people to organise similar events. Any objections?" says Rory.

There are none.

"If it's accepted well in Devon, it must go forward to the Wessex Provincial Council, with a request that it's circulated around the land. This sort of thing is happening now wherever there are groups like ours and all councils are being alerted in Britannia and elsewhere." says Peter.

"Let's hope they take notice, and act responsibly," says Brook. "Nature has its own way of dealing with violators. A creature who destroys its own habitat, and that of other creatures around, suffers the consequences."

"The trouble is our whole material culture has to change," responds Frances. "That's a big call. Everyone's out for themselves."

"We need more generous communities and less selfish ones," adds Elsa," and it's quite possible. Thousands of other creatures work together in harmony - just think of the bees and the flocks of migrating birds. A lot of our selfishness is manipulated by outside forces."

"What we need is a another great Renaissance sweeping the world. It's happened before and changed hearts and minds. It can and will do this again." Rory speaks with conviction. "This one needs a new vision of our place on earth. We cannot master the universe. Our responsibility is Compassion and Cooperation".

The ceremony formally closes. Elsa gathers everyone around her, and we hold hands while she exclaims in her strong but somewhat croaky voice:

"May the sun shine on our faces,
May the wind be always at our backs,
And until we meet again,
May we carry love and blessings in our hearts
And share these gifts to all around us'.
"So be it!" we all cry, and arms are linked together.

Reluctantly, we tidy up. Bags are packed and placed in the three pool cars.

"Thank you for bringing the guitar," Peter says to Mina. "I haven't seen that one in years. It was old times again."

Frances is still weepy, and Elsa moves to comfort her. When they are ready, Peter opens the car door and, with a wave, the trio leave us.

Beatrice says that there is more loading to do, and tells everyone she would prefer to walk back home with Brook. It will give them time to think things through. Brandon offers to drive the car and Lucy jumps in eagerly, saying that the breeze is in the right direction for them to go kite surfing, and they must celebrate this way. Both give cheery waves, as they move away.

Catriona says she'd like to walk too, so Rupert agrees to take the car back to the garage and offers lifts to Rory and Mina.

Brook gets his binoculars out. "You two go on ahead," he says. "I'll catch you up, but I just want to watch those lapwings a bit longer. They're still playing courting games with each other, and this is very late for the breeding season. I can't help wondering if we influenced them."

Catriona: Brandon and Lucy look happy together. Let's hope it's a breakthrough for them both, and things don't come crashing doon again.

Beatrice: Yes, it could be so. We must think positively. They got on well with the kite surfing, yesterday, and it's good for Lucy to have someone to train. She's a good instructor. It's been a consolation since she split up with Sam. Under the surface they're both very frail.

Catriona: It's good for Brandon to be a learner again, too. What did you make of his dream?

Beatrice: Very symbolic: the storied tower with its upper room and open roof surveying the worlds beyond: that's how Brandon likes to see himself, but beneath it all, he has his doubts.

Catriona: You bet he has! The man in the dungeon below made that clear. Brandon was afraid of him at first, but then acknowledged him.

Beatrice: His secret fears. He embraces his alter ego. Yes, that can't be bad. It's real progress.

Catriona: Lucy's a sweet soul, but she must have been devastated to lose her whole family when she was a wee bairn and that shadow's dogged her whole life.

Beatrice. She settled down with us more easily than I ever thought possible, but now that she's trying to make an adult life for herself, she's feeling the pain again.

Catriona: What do you make of this tale about the afterlife?

Beatrice: She wants it to be true. It makes sense to her, so she's desperate to believe it.

Catriona: Och, don't we all want it to be true? Maybe i' is, but it's got the feel of being too good to be true for me. Rupert could'na remember his dream at first, and then it came back in a thunderclap. It was a wonderfully creative, the birth of the universe - that woman weaving!

Beatrice: And how about you: with those visions of your ageless grandma and the discovery of the glories under the water?

Catriona: Most of the earth's surface is covered that way. We beings crawled out of the sea originally, so maybe that's where it will end again, for many at least, as Rory's first dream suggested. But I don't know at all. I just hope and pray. How about you and that mother figure who haunts you – the sassenach, Elfleda?

Beatrice: Yes, you're right, she does haunt me. But I love it. I've dreamed of her before, but never so vividly as last night. I would not call her a mother figure. She's certainly not Elsa: more like the big sister I never had.

Catriona: I'm no so sure that Elsa isn't inside her too, with her folk wisdom of all the ages. When you get excited you remind me of Rory, that driving force that leads the way.

Beatrice: You're right, Rory inherits a lot of that from Elsa. Mother took the lead when we were young. Dad was the gentle partner and together they made a fine team. I couldn't have chosen better parents if I'd been given the opportunity to select them myself. I wonder what Rory will cook up for us to do when New Year's Eve comes round.

Catriona: Och, a lot will happen before then. I'm sure we'll all have plenty of opportunities to share and mull over ideas in the next two years. When the century comes to a close, nae' doot, there'll be many gatherings around the world. Some will be hedonistic celebrations but, infinitely more important, it will surely be the verra last opportunity for people on earth to make pledges aboot tomorrow - the real new millennium! Places like Woodleigh will play their part in the local scene, and many families like ours will make their contributions. Will some of these dreams come true, or are they just part of an old song blowin' in the wind?

Beatrice: We can't let that happen, Catriona, and I don't believe it will: remember the power of ten. We are in touch with forty-five sustainable living groups in the UK who think and work much as we do, and we already know of sixty groups overseas – in America, Australia, the Far East, in Africa, India and elsewhere: Mina's in touch with a group in Gambia, and Rory with one in Florence. Just think, if they can hold a positive vision of a far better world, and if they all work with another ten groups, consider how this could grow. Ten by ten by ten is a thousand. There could be fifty thousand candles shining in the night at the end of the millennium, and they should have the light of ages in them. If our contacts carry the sacred message that light is stronger than darkness, that love can prevail over hate and fear of the stranger: if we can remind them of the ten loving principles, there will be power in this new millennium. We must all seize the opportunity. We cannot allow it to slip through our fingers again, as those grandparents of ours did in that long lost year, 2000.

Catriona: Aye, you`re right, o' course. We need positive notions not negative ones, and we have sound reasons for hope, with world governments on the good side at long last, and with the Global Sustainability Organisation supporting the poorer states in all this. There's been so much negativity in the media, it's put fears into ordinary folk far beyond what's necessary. We need the world tide of thought to turn, and that's what we're aboot. We had a mix o' ideas in last night's dreams, but Elsa got us off to a very good start wi' her bowl of broth that never emptied, and Peter's shabby man had more powerful ideas than his business man did. I feel sorrow for Frances though, as she mourns the loss of that great stack of books recording the wisdom of ages.

Beatrice: So do I, but we have the Internet and, as some skills are lost others emerge. That's life. Look at Rory's dream of that inspiring young lad on the beach with his Aeolian strings, Brook's flight with wild geese and you in a shoal of salmon returning to the spawning ground. There's been too much negative thinking this century. We must tune in again to the ancestral powers, link with the vibes around us, and open up the neglected pathways in the brain. Those in despair can't believe in a world at peace, but people of vision can help to build it.

We walk on, carrying the conversation with us, until we reach a high point from which we see windsurfers cresting the waves. We recognise the distant outlines of Brandon and Lucy seemingly dancing on the waves of time, with the wind at their backs and their colourful kites leading them on. I find myself breathing the words of the song, "Let there be love shared amongst us!"

Catriona catches my arm. 'Aye. So be it,' she cries, and waves to them wildly. "They're living in the moment and so they should. It's all any of us ever really have!"

Rory shares our sustainable living vision with the Devon Councillors, who give their support and spread the word across Wessex. Bruce, Trish and old Jenny Painter do the same in Tamcaster and a lead is given around the whole of Mercia. The message is sent to Transition Towns across Britannia and to sister organisations around the globe; but these groups are not acting alone. Thousands of groups share similar

545

thoughts. The Global Organisation for Sustainability backs such local initiatives and so do hundreds of celebrities. Messages are broadcast on numerous TV channels. World Faith and Humanist leaders promote co-operation. So now do most political parties, alongside popular singers, choirs and choral groups. Massive attention is caught at the seminal moment at the end of the century. Sustainable living and the positive role that human beings have to play in the web of life is now the flagship offering for the Millennium: backing for this idea flows through the air waves, and ripples touch thousands of different organisations: humanist groups, sporting bodies, schools, universities, science seminars and arts festivals. Positive thinking is opening new pathways throughout humanity, and widening channels are turning the dreams and visions into achievable targets for a better world. Another Great Renaissance is awakening and bringing with it new ways of living and thinking, fresh artistic visions and scientific possibilities, and love for the whole living planet is at the heart of the message.

On the night of 31st December 2099, millions of groups are to gather across the globe to send loving thoughts and perform a multitude of rituals, according to their culture. Human beings are reaching out to realms beyond: and this is universal. Of course, so much more could have been saved if this had only happened a hundred years ago, but now, after such loss and suffering, there is hope and determination on a scale never known before. So be it.

The Family Tree

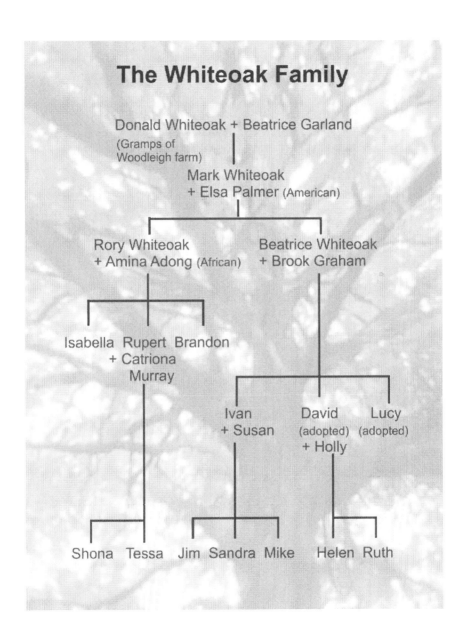

The Whiteoak Family

Donald Whiteoak + Beatrice Garland
(Gramps of
Woodleigh farm)

Mark Whiteoak
+ Elsa Palmer (American)

Rory Whiteoak
+ Amina Adong (African)

Beatrice Whiteoak
+ Brook Graham

Isabella Rupert Brandon
+ Catriona
Murray

Ivan
+ Susan

David
(adopted)
+ Holly

Lucy
(adopted)

Shona Tessa Jim Sandra Mike Helen Ruth

Author's Last Words

At last I see my thoughts in print,
my dream of cluster housing:
I count them, ten by ten;
a common plot that's shared by all,
a custom lost in time.

I know most of this cast so well;
they freely speak their lines.
each person has a mindset.
This helps to shape the tale.

They form a winding circle dance
in tune with nature's sure advance,
and each step leads to new ideas,
that may take shape in future years:
a tempting trail, with constant bends
that indicate a way beyond
this human frame, whose time will end.

Author's Note

The origins of *Yestermorrow* lie in numerous encounters throughout my life. First came childhood memories of the Manchester Blitz in 1941 and later the end of World War Two, when we felt a surge of joy at the outbreak of peace, but also horror at the knowledge that the victory had been brought about by the allies' use of the atomic bomb, on Japanese civilians.

My hopes were then placed firmly in the hands of the newly founded United Nations and its aim to end war on earth. It appeared to be the dawn of the New Age, and the Universal Declaration of Human Rights, together with the freedom then offered to millions of European refugees and later to the state of Israel as homeland for the persecuted Jewish people seemed to confirm my naive trust.

My two years of National Service in the army enabled me to face harsh new realities, and took me to the Suez Canal Zone, where I encountered a state of emergency. After these rigours I experienced the liberty of Manchester University. This introduced me to student debates, Shakespearean drama and the world of politics and protest. While studying in Kent I joined the Campaign for Nuclear Disarmament - on the night it was founded at the Central Hall Westminster. I took part in their first protest, until police removed us from a peaceful sit-down outside 10, Downing Street.

I moved on to enjoy the freedom of international youth hostels across western Europe, where young people of many nations shared values and dreamed of the awakening world their own generation could serve. (Later on I had opportunities to visit Moscow, Yugoslavia and the German Democratic Republic and made friends there with a few individuals who quietly acknowledged similar ideals, but from a different perspective.)

Over the next thirty years, I became a Careers Advisory Officer and worked for education authorities in Warwickshire and Nottinghamshire. Realising that we needed positive alternatives to war, I joined the United Nations Association and had opportunities to visit UN Offices in New York, Geneva and Vienna, and took part in a university study tour of development programmes in Africa.

I was also a keen actor in the Little Theatre world, and wrote several plays. Latterly, I was introduced to yoga meditation, the interfaith movement and the United Reformed Church. Towards the end of my working life, I fell in love and married. Many of these developments have fed into aspects of this novel. My encounters with Vietnamese refugees, involvement in the Million Minutes of Peace project and participation in an international seminar at the Brahma Kumaris World Spiritual University at Mount Abu, Rajasthan, were also seminal.

Following a Celtic pilgrimage to Lindisfarne, I became influenced by the writings of Matthew Fox, Thomas Berry and Satish Khumar. My wife, Jenny, introduced me to the worlds of poetry, circle dancing and the exploration of dreams. We joined GreenSpirit, and it was this movement that first alerted us to the urgency of combating climate change.

After we moved to Devon, I joined Glenorchy Church, volunteered at the Open Door Charity and became embroiled in the Transition Town Movement. These varied experiences, together with articles in Positive News highlighting the need for optimistic rather than dystopian visioning, assisted the birth and development of *Yestermorrow*.

I must express my gratitude to Rob Masding, Therese Bourcier Mayo and Andy Lock for their advice and encouragement, and also to my wife, Jenny, for her assistance, constant support and thoughtful guidance.

Acknowledgements

Books which influenced me were:

"The Transition Handbook" by Rob Hopkins,
"News from Nowhere" by William Morris,
"GreenSpirit", edited by Marion Van Eyke Macain,
"The Meaning of Jesus" by Marcus Borg
and Tom Wright,
"The Great Work" by Thomas Berry,
"The Lady who fought the Vikings"
by Don Stansbury,
"The Winning of the Carbon War"
by Jeremy Leggett,
and The Magazine "Positive News"

Painting of Noel by Naa Ahinee Mensah
Design and Layout by Rob Masding

About the Author

After graduating in English and History at Manchester University, he spent most of his working life in the Careers Advisory Service, initially in Warwickshire, and later in Solihull Borough and Nottingham City and County, where he helped to develop international links and exchange visits through the National Institute of Careers Guidance. He was an actor in the Little Theatre Movement and wrote several plays, one of which, *Worlds Apart,* about Vietnamese refugees, was a winner in an original playwriting competition organised at Nottingham and Derby Playhouses. His historical novel, *"Uncivil War,"* deals with real events in Nottinghamshire between 1642 and 1646, which involved the use of child soldiers.

Married to the poet, Jenny Johnson, he now lives in Devon, is a member of Glenorchy United Reformed Church, and is engaged in the Transition Town Movement.

You may contact Noel by visiting:
www.noelharrower.uk/yestermorrow.htm

33690318R00331

Printed in Poland
by Amazon Fulfillment
Poland Sp. z o.o., Wrocław